D0850127

BLOOD OF ASAHEIM

Chris Wraight

A WARHAMMER 40,000 NOVEL

BLOOD OF ASAHEIM

Chris Wraight

BLACK LIBRARY

For Hannah, with love. Also, many thanks to Nick, Lindsey and Graeme
for all their editorial hard work.

A BLACK LIBRARY PUBLICATION
First published in Great Britain in 2013 by
Black Library,
Games Workshop Ltd.,
Willow Road,
Nottingham,
NG7 2WS, UK

10 9 8 7 6 5 4 3 2

Cover by Raymond Swanland.

A CIP record for this book is available from the British Library.

UK ISBN 13: 978 1 84970 306 2
US ISBN 13: 978 1 84970 307 9

See the Black Library on the internet at
www.blacklibrary.com

Find out more about Games Workshop
and the world of Warhammer 40,000 at
www.games-workshop.com

Printed and bound by CPI Group (UK) Ltd, Croydon, CR0 4YY

It is the 41st millennium. For more than a hundred
centuries the Emperor has sat immobile on the Golden Throne of
Earth. He is the master of mankind by the will of the gods, and master
of a million worlds by the might of his inexhaustible armies. He is a
rotting carcass writhing invisibly with power from the Dark Age of
Technology. He is the Carrion Lord of the Imperium for whom a
thousand souls are sacrificed every day, so that he may never truly die.

Yet even in his deathless state, the Emperor continues his eternal
vigilance. Mighty battlefleets cross the daemon-infested miasma of
the warp, the only route between distant stars, their way lit by the
Astronomican, the psychic manifestation of the Emperor's will.
Vast armies give battle in his name on uncounted worlds. Greatest
amongst his soldiers are the Adeptus Astartes, the Space Marines,
bio-engineered super-warriors. Their comrades in arms are legion:
the Imperial Guard and countless planetary defence forces, the ever-
vigilant Inquisition and the tech-priests of the Adeptus Mechanicus
to name only a few. But for all their multitudes, they are barely
enough to hold off the ever-present threat from aliens, heretics,
mutants - and worse.

To be a man in such times is to be one amongst untold billions. It is
to live in the cruellest and most bloody regime imaginable. These are
the tales of those times. Forget the power of technology and science,
for so much has been forgotten, never to be re-learned. Forget the
promise of progress and understanding, for in the grim dark future
there is only war. There is no peace amongst the stars, only an eternity
of carnage and slaughter, and the laughter
of thirsting gods.

'You will be faster than they are, stronger, quicker to sense corruption and with full sanction to destroy it. You will be girded in the armour of gods and carry the blades of ruin. You will never age, never wither, never weary. And yet, in all of this, what remains your greatest gift?

'Only this: while you are a brotherhood, you are unbreakable. While you form the shieldwall, guarding your pack-mates as if they were your own kin-blood, you cannot be resisted. Solely by treachery can this power be undone, as we have learned. We emerge from the lesson stronger, tempered by the knowledge of how low our species can sink. We now know what waits for us should we fail, and that is well, for it is better to know your enemy's face than for it to remain hidden by shadow.

'Never forget this. When night comes again, as it surely will, only your brotherhood will protect you. Preserve it, and you will endure. Let it fracture, let it fail, and I tell you truly: our time, humanity's time, will be over.'

The primarch Leman Russ
Words recorded on Ialis III, c.170.M31
Incorporated into Liber Malan; *source-data lost*

'The Wolves of Fenris? They will tire at the end. We will all tire at the end. What else is there, once war is eternal, but fatigue?'

Attributed to the primarch Mortarion
Quoted in Liber Infestus
Date and source unknown

Prologue

Blood rose in his gorge, foaming and flecked with bone, spilling from split lips and over cracked fangs. He stumbled down the walkway, feeling metal struts flex and snap under his limping tread. Gunfire, tinny and echoing, rang down from the airways above him. The noise was an irrelevance by then – a cluttered fury that signified nothing but the slow death of the drifting Arjute-class heavy troop conveyer. The Imperium would not miss it; it could spare a million of them and never notice.

He coughed up more blood, feeling the flesh of his throat constrict. He tried to smile, and the corner of his mouth ripped where the burns latticed against softer flesh.

It would miss him. The Imperium would miss Hjortur Ageir Hvat Bloodfang, Wolf Guard of Fenris, *vaerangi* of Berek Thunderfist: blood-shedder, beast-slayer, tale-teller. Sagas would mark his passing, declaimed in the icy vaults of home by skjalds who had feared and loved him, just as all in the Rout had feared and loved him.

He started to chuckle as he limped, and blood bubbled down his chin and into his clumped and matted beard.

He'd caused hell. He'd done some damage. He'd do some more before they brought him down, too. Blood of Russ, he'd make them all bleed a little more.

He stumbled, falling to his knees and feeling the mesh of the metal floor grate against his fractured poleyn-guard. He heard his breathing scrape and wheeze within the flickering mess of his helm's interior.

Above him the roof was a jumbled mass of burned-out pipelines, hanging like vines from the darkness. Somewhere up ahead a red light rotated in rhythm with a superfluous warning klaxon. He heard crashes from further back, further down: the resounding clang of iron-edged boots against metal, the hard clunk of magazines being loaded.

Hjortur pushed himself back to his feet. The enclosed corridor ran away from him, plunging down steeply, winding into the bowels of the conveyer's enginarium. The metal around him was hot. He staggered along it, reeling from the walls, breaking off shards of steel as his armour snagged against them. He felt enclosed, hemmed in, cornered.

He sensed a movement – twenty metres behind, stealthy like the others had been.

Not stealthy enough.

Hjortur twisted at the waist and squeezed a round away, watching the projectile streak off into the dark through blood-screened eyes. He couldn't make out his victim but heard the sounds of his death: the crack of breaking armour, the wet *schlick* of flesh parting, the stifled boom of detonation.

No screams. The hunters that closed on him didn't scream. He didn't know what they were. Human, perhaps. If so, they were heavily augmented and stuffed with bionics, for they moved liked he did and hit almost as hard. That was worrying. It shouldn't have been possible.

He started to limp off again, and the bestial phlegm-growl of his broken breathing hummed in his ears. His retinal display screamed at him, detailing pedantically just how badly he'd been torn up: two lungs gone, chest cavity flooded, seventy minor fractures and six big ones. His skin was a mess of partly-clotted plasma and slowly knitting tissue, all seething with a contradictory mix of stimms and pain suppressors.

Pretty bad. He was breaking up, just like the ship around him.

He heard more footsteps clattering down the corridor, then silence as the hunters crouched down into firing positions. He broke into a sprint, wincing as lances of white-hot pain shot up his shattered shins.

A second later and the corridor filled with solid rounds, crashing and cracking from the walls and filling the narrow space with spinning clouds of metal. He felt the heavy bang of projectiles thudding into his back, tearing fresh gouges in the weakened ceramite and burrowing down towards the flesh beneath.

He reached a T-junction and threw himself around the corner into cover, clanking against the floor and panting, waiting for the hail of fire to break off.

The junction was dark. The air tasted of engine oil and ship-bilge. He could hardly see five paces into the murk. When he blinked, blood cascaded down his cheeks.

The gunfire ceased. He waited two more seconds, enough for the first of them to get up and run down the corridor after him. He could smell them coming, sense their unfamiliar odour even over the stinking melange of the lower decks.

What are you? What kind of creatures are you?

As the first one approached he burst back to his feet, powering his huge, ravaged body into motion, swinging round into the corridor he'd just run down and flexing his claw-hand to gouge.

His pursuer skidded to a halt, suddenly confronted by a vast armoured behemoth rearing up out of the oily shadows. The hunter tried to scramble backwards, but his momentum carried him into lethal range.

Hjortur lashed out with his claws. Their disruptor field had long since burned out, but the dented blades still punched through the hunter's armour, skewering him. Hjortur lashed out, churning up the hunter's ribcage and flinging him hard against the nearside wall. The hunter's torso broke open into a flailing ball of skin-scraps and sinew.

Another one was too close. The hunter scrambled back out of claw-range, his black limbs skittering on the metal like an insect's.

Hjortur pounced, slicing his claw down and dragging the hunter back. The impaled warrior tried to turn, tried to get a weapon hand into position, but it was all far too slow.

Hjortur crashed his other fist down, mashing the hunter's helm, visor and skull into a glass-flecked soup of pulp. Blood splashed up along Hjortur's forearms, adding to the riot of streaks and stains already there.

He felt solid rounds crack against his armour again – one, two, three direct hits, rocking him backwards. A shot slammed between the gaping cracks in his breastplate, punching through flesh, grinding into the bone beneath.

Hjortur growled as he swung round, searching for a target in the dark, blinking to clear his vision of blood.

The first he knew of the frag grenade was a gentle *tink-tink-tink* as it bounced down the corridor.

If his senses hadn't been crushed, he'd have spotted it sooner. If his muscles hadn't been ripped apart, he'd have been able to leap clear in time. If his armour hadn't been carved open, he'd have withstood the blast.

It exploded. The blast-wave hurled him backwards, throwing him onto his back and sending him skidding into the far wall of the junction.

Hjortur's head bounced back savagely, prompting fresh spikes of pain from his twisted neck. He felt more sharp pops from within, the hot flush of fluids sluicing across his organs. A wave of sickly dizziness swept over him, and his hands went cold. He felt his bolter drop from numb fingers.

Blinded, reeling, he tried to push himself up. He dimly made out the silhouettes of more figures standing above him. He swung his fist clumsily at the nearest. A blade shot out from over to his left, severing his arm at the wrist. Hjortur felt the metal slide under his splintered forearm-guard, slicing agonisingly through what remained of his claw-hand.

More blades flashed in the gloom, plunging into his body, pinioning him to the metal deck. His back arched as they stabbed him, and a ragged, throaty gurgle of pain escaped his mouth.

The hunters kept up the assault. They worked as a team, moving sword-edges quickly, as if panicked by the thought that he might – *still* – get up. They locked his ankles down. They ran gouges along his torso, exposing glistening viscera. They threw chains across his legs and throat, yanking his head back against the floor.

By the time they had finished, Hjortur Ageir Hvat Bloodfang, Wolf Guard of Fenris, *vaerangi* of Berek Thunderfist, lay impaled on the lower decks of the Arjute-class heavy troop conveyer like an insect pinned to a collector's card. Twelve short swords held him in place, six adamantium-link chain-lengths held him down, seven barbed gouges were lodged in his chest, each one standing at the head of the gushing fountain of thick, semi-clotted blood.

That was what it took to subdue him. Hjortur coughed up a wet, grim snort of satisfaction. He'd extracted his tally of pain.

How many hunters had he killed? Maybe a hundred. This had been a serious operation. They had come prepared.

The blurred black-clad figures withdrew. Hjortur tried to raise his head, but the chains pulled tight. His breath came in tight, short gasps. He could feel his armour systems gutter and fizz out. He could feel his body getting colder, shutting down, giving up the ghost.

Giving up the ghost. Hjortur felt delirious. *Giving up the ghost.*

A single hunter remained, hanging over his face like a vision in smoke. He could make out the fuzzy outline of a closed-face helm. He saw a cherubic device printed on the forehead – golden, spike-crowned against a sable ground. He saw plates of armour glinting, matt-black and rimmed with silver. He smelled the sooty aroma of a cooling weapon muzzle, and heard the faint whine of a power-pack winding down.

The world around him began to melt away. He concentrated, determined to look at his killer, right up to the end.

Fenrys.

The thought swam into his mind unbidden. He saw an image of the peaks of Asaheim, vast and snow-streaked, picked out in hard lines of frosty clarity. He knew then that he would never go back to them, never feel their knife-sharp air sting on his tongue. That knowledge pained him more than his hundred wounds.

The blurred figure swung closer, kneeling beside Hjortur and peering down at him. Hjortur saw his own face reflected darkly in a glassy visor, and barely recognised himself.

They will replace me, he thought. *The pack needs a leader.*

The hunter withdrew a tapered gun. It was a strange-looking thing – curved and sweeping and sculptural. Hjortur struggled to maintain focus.

I should have appointed a successor. Gyrfalkon? Gunnlaugur?

The hunter placed the muzzle's tip at Hjortur's fractured temple and pressed it through the flesh. Amid his cacophony of serried pain, Hjortur barely winced.

'Do you know who we are?'

The voice was heavily altered, filtered through a crackling vox-distorter. It might have been human; it might not.

Hjortur tried to answer, but the blood in his throat and mouth made him gag. He shook his head fractionally, making the needle in his temple tear at the flesh.

The hunter reached up with his free hand and depressed a switch at the side of his helm. His visor snapped up, revealing a gaunt face within, lit up by angry red internal illumination. Hjortur's killer leaned closer.

'Do you know who sent us?'

I could never choose between them. I should have chosen. What will Berek rule?

Hjortur tried to focus. It was difficult. The world had narrowed down to a gauze of pale mist, like ghost-frost spreading over glass.

The hunter opened his left palm. A little golden cherub's head nestled against the black synleather, surrounded by a spiked halo.

'Do you know who sent us?'

I should have chosen.

One more surge of effort, one final attempt to drag his faltering vision back into some form of clarity.

Then realisation dawned, as cold and sick as breaking fever.

'Yes,' said Hjortur, choking as he spoke.

The killer above him smiled – a thin movement of thin lips, perfunctory, frigid with wintry satisfaction.

'Good. It is good that you know.'

The hunter pressed the trigger, and the bolt slipped into Hjortur's brain. It was a theatrical gesture, an unnecessary accelerant to the death that was already overtaking him. The mercy stroke, it might have been called in another age; the assassin's courtesy.

Hjortur hung on for a few seconds more, trying to speak, his residual features rigid with shock.

Then, his body racked with starbursts of pain, his lone working heart swollen and weeping, his broken jaw lined with blood-thick drool, he died.

1
JÁRNHAMAR

Chapter One

After leaving U-6743 he took the Inquisitorial line cruiser *Obsession for Integrity* through the warp from Orelia – a long jump and a wearying journey. His dreams were bad, just as they always were when traversing the open hells of the void. He remained in his cell during that time, alone, refusing company and taking little food. The iron walls shuddered during the enforced diurnal cycle, over and over.

The cruiser dropped into real space at Nishagar, where he made his last and least formal rite of decommissioning to Inquisitor Halliafiore's transmission agent. Most of what he had still retained was surrendered then: everything, save for the Onyx skull-pendant and his stalker bolter, a weapon he had come to prefer to the Godwyn-mark issue he'd carried previously. Losing the rest of it all – the devices, the kill-tallies, the armour decoration – made little difference to him, no more than waking from a long sleep with half-remembered dreams still clinging to the edges of memory.

After that it was a mid-range stint in an Imperial Navy frigate whose name he never learned. He scared the hell out of the regular troops with his brooding and grey-eyed stare. He didn't mean to do that. The fact that they couldn't master their awe depressed him slightly.

Only at Kattyak was he able to switch to passage on a Fenrisian vessel – *Yvekk*, a clunky system-runner with a full kaerl crew and a leaking enginarium containment shell. At least the attendants were able to speak to him in Juvykka. For a while even that made him feel awkward, having been confined to Gothic for so long. The kaerls weren't in awe of him, which helped, but they knew the proper forms of address and deference for a Sky Warrior, which also helped.

Only at the end, once they broke through the veil on the fringes of the Fenris system, did he take a little pleasure from the sounds of murmured Juvykka on the decks, the same sounds that he had heard as a child beside glowing fires, that he had shouted out on the ice when hunting, that he had listened to from the mouths of Priests after ascension. Not all pleasures of life were relinquished by service; those were the things that took him back, right at the end of the long transfer: the sounds, the smells, the textures of age-dried fur, of rune-etched steel, cured hide, lacquered hair in armour-compressed plaits.

During the final approach he came up to the bridge, standing on the observer platform while mortals and servitors scurried around him and prepared for orbital clearance.

The grey-white curve of the planet slowly filled the forward viewers. He saw snarls of dirty cloud drifting across the northern hemisphere, twisted into immense storm-curls. He knew what was under the shadow of those clouds. He imagined hammering columns of angled rain beating the sea down into a leaden mass, drenching the decks of the struggling *drekkar* until they listed nearly to the foam-line.

Seeing the violence of the planet from afar, having lived with it up close for so long – that was a strange and uncomfortable sensation. He had missed it, and that was a strange thing too.

The runner's captain, Rurik, a slab-faced man in snow-grey fatigues, shuffled up to him as he stood. Rurik had been trying to find an excuse to speak ever since the last tatters of the warp had slipped away behind them. It wasn't obsequiousness, exactly; just an understandable desire to make contact, to exchange words with one of the lords. Sky Warriors did not often travel on support craft like *Yvekk*; his own presence was an unfortunate consequence of him having dropped out of command structures for too long.

'Good to be back, lord?' Rurik asked, daring a smile.

Ingvar Orm Everrson, the one who had once been called Gyrfalkon, did not know the answer to that question. As he watched the planet growing in the viewer and saw the orbital defence stations swim up out of the dark, a whole host of emotions ran through him, none of which he was able to classify or analyse.

It was the same, and not the same; you never trod in the same river twice. Callimachus had told him that, passing on a saying older than the Imperium itself, a fragment of commonplace wisdom that predated it all.

Ingvar narrowed his eyes, as if he could peer through the scars of cloud and into the storm below. Somewhere down there was the ice, the place he had come from, the savage home that had forged him.

Good to be back?

'Land the ship,' he said softly, his grey eyes never leaving the viewer.

Once down, back with the granite of the Mountain under his feet again, he noticed how different it smelled. Or maybe it smelt the same and he was different. Fifty-seven years was a long time, even for him.

Ingvar let the mix of aromas filter into him. His old human range of sensation had long been superseded by a richer, deeper, wider spectrum of awareness, and he picked up traces that even his old battle-brothers might have missed. All warriors of the Adeptus Astartes had their senses refined by the process of ascension; the *Vlka Fenryka* liked to believe that the process went further with them than any others.

Ingvar had learned to doubt such boasts. The Wolves of Fenris were a boastful breed, and his time away from the halls of the Aett had exposed their foundations.

Or perhaps not. He thought back to Onyx and its multiplicity of Chapters. Ingvar had always been sharper than Callimachus, picking up the scent of prey a fraction earlier than him. He'd been far quicker than Jocelyn too, though never really tested against Leonides. They had all laughed about it; the others had found his distended physiognomy both grotesque and impressive.

'If you can smell so much,' the Blood Angel Leonides had once asked, 'how come you wash so little?'

Ingvar remembered the laughter. He remembered joining in, playing along with his disjointed new pack of mismatched brothers, doing what every newly assigned Blood Claw had done since the days of the Crusade: finding his station, assessing hierarchy, doing what needed to be done to fit in.

If he'd been tempted to reply seriously, he might have pointed out that olfaction was an easily underestimated capability. It gave early warning of danger. It allowed a trail to be followed. It exposed corruption.

Would they have been impressed? It was difficult to impress an Ultramarine with anything: Blood Angels were nearly as bad.

Ingvar let his nostrils flare, and took a deep breath.

Old rock, damp with trace humidity. Mortal sweat, twenty metres down. Filter-engine lubricant, past replacement age. Cured leather. Embers, from

a long way away. Bronze, etched in acid. Alien matter, recently introduced.
Ingvar smiled at himself.

That is me. I am an alien here, treading spores into stone from halfway across the galaxy. The Aett knows that I no longer belong.

He looked up. The doorway before him was barred by two bronze panels, each etched in a riot of knotwork dragons, krakens and sea-wyrms. Framing the doors was bare rock, as blunt and jagged as the half-worked walls of the tunnel he'd just walked down.

Typical Fenrisian juxtaposition: artistry the equal of any in the Imperium placed next to rude hackwork.

'Open,' he said, noticing the way his trial-hardened voice echoed dully from the stone around him.

The bronze doors slid smoothly apart. On the far side was a half-lit chamber, pungent with smoking brazier pans.

A figure waited for him in the darkness.

'Welcome home, Gyrfalkon,' said Ragnar Blackmane.

'So it's true?' asked Váltyr.

Gunnlaugur grunted. 'It is.'

Váltyr shook his head. 'When did they tell you?' he asked.

'Six hours ago.'

'*Skítja*,' Váltyr swore.

'He came in on a runner. They didn't send a warship. If they had, I'd have known sooner.'

Váltyr placed his slender hands together.

'Will he return, then?'

Gunnlaugur smiled wryly, a look that said, *Why would they tell me?*

The two were alone, hunched over a firepit and surrounded by lambent shadows. Gunnlaugur's chamber was high up on the eastern flanks of the Fang, close to the edge where the biting winds of Asaheim came over the Hunter's Gap. Ironhelmsshrine was within reach; on rare clear days, it could be seen from the narrow realview portal mounted on the external wall.

Out of battle armour, there were only marginal physical difference between the two warriors. Gunnlaugur, the one they called Skullhewer, was a fraction heavier-set, a finger's width shorter. His shaven head still had residual traces of flame-red hair in the stubble, though his beard was slush-grey and stiff with age. His features were the same tight, brutal ones that had propelled him to clan chief of the Gaellings when he had been mortal, only now filled out and made heavier by aggressive muscular augmentation.

He sat on a stone slab in front of the fire, massive and stooped, his shoulders draped in furs. He ran a dagger through his hands, playing with the killing edge, flicking it between thick, dextrous fingers.

'We are wounded, brother,' Gunnlaugur said. 'Tally it up. We lost Ulf on Lossanal, Svafnir on Cthar, Tínd to the greenskins.'

As he spoke, his dark eyes reflected the warm light of the coals.

'We're under strength,' he said. 'He'll have to come back, just to make us viable. And where else can he go? Who else will take him?'

Váltyr listened intently. His narrow face was hot, and the glow exposed the many scars latticed across his cheeks.

His hands were still. Váltyr never played with blades. His longsword, *holdbítr*, was strapped across his back just as it ever was. The weapon was only drawn to be used in combat, or for veneration, or for ritual maintenance, and even then he never left its side, watching the Iron Priests intently as they invoked the sleeping spectres of murder that dwelt within.

Blademasters – *sverdhjera* – were a strange breed, guarding their weapons as if they were children.

'He chose to leave,' said Váltyr. 'He could have stayed, and we would have welcomed him then. He could have contested for the–'

'You'd have made the same choice he did,' said Gunnlaugur. 'I'd have done it too, if they'd asked.'

He hacked up a gobbet of phlegm and spat it into the fire. Trace particles of acid made it fizz angrily against the coals.

'I could protest,' Gunnlaugur said. 'Blackmane has a Blood Claw waiting in the wings as well, one he's eager to give us to knock into shape. That would make us six – enough to hunt again.'

Váltyr snorted. 'That's what we're reduced to now?'

Gunnlaugur nodded.

'Plenty of packs are running with losses,' he said. 'Every Great Year more come back diminished. Remember when Hjortur died? Remember how shocked we were? Tell me truly, would you be shocked now to hear of a *vaerangi* dying on the hunt?'

Váltyr grinned.

'If it was you, yes.'

Gunnlaugur didn't return the smile. He stared into the fire, and the blade spun and flashed absently in his fingers.

'I'll take the Blood Claw,' he said. 'We need new blood, and he'll learn quickly from Olgeir. But as for him...'

Váltyr looked steadily into Gunnlaugur's eyes.

'Blackmane will choose,' he said.

Gunnlaugur nodded slowly. 'That he will.'

He stilled the movement of the dagger.

'Our Young King,' he said, rolling his eyes. 'Barely fanged. What in Hel are we coming to, brother?'

For a moment it looked as though Váltyr had an answer. Then the blademaster shook his sleek head.

'I really am the wrong person to ask,' he said.

Ingvar stood before Blackmane. Out of habit, his eyes ran over the Jarl's armour, scanning for weaknesses, assessing strength, gauging the likely route of attack. The process was automatic with him, as unconscious an act as breathing.

The experience was sobering. When Ingvar had last served as a member of the Rout on Fenris, he had barely known the name Ragnar Blackmane – a Blood Claw in Berek's Great Company, already tipped for an illustrious future, but no more so than many of the headstrong berserks they pulled off the ice.

Now, six decades later, the whelp had grown. Ragnar's face still had the supple bloom of youth but his armour was scarred as badly as any other Jarl's, draped with age-bleached trophies of a hundred kills and carrying the clenched-fist sigils of Berek's old company amid the howling wolfshead device of his own. The blackmane pelt was slung over rune-graven shoulder guards, tight with weathering. A huge chainsword hung idle at his side, chipped and scratched from use.

Ragnar smiled, exposing short, sharp fangs. Glossy sideburns ran down each jaw, each as black as the long top knot that mingled fluidly with the pelt on his shoulders.

'I never knew you,' Blackmane said. 'I heard much, though.'

Ingvar bowed. He could feel every hair on his forearms standing up.

Why am I threatened by him?

'How does it feel to be back?' asked Ragnar, gesturing towards one of two stone benches. 'Strange?'

Ingvar sat on the nearest bench, feeling exposed without his armour. Even with *dausvjer* sheathed at his side, his grey shift and fur-lined cloak felt like flimsy protection against the Fang's permanent chill.

'Somewhat,' he replied.

Ragnar sat opposite. His movements were easy and unencumbered. The machine-grind of his suit's systems was barely audible. Something about him radiated confidence, ebullience, vigour. The Young King had none of the grizzled majesty of Grimnar, nor the raw elemental potency of Stormcaller, but now that Ingvar had witnessed him in the flesh he finally began to understand why he had been elevated so far and so quickly.

'I am curious,' Ragnar said. 'I served away from Fenris myself. What can you tell me?'

Ingvar didn't meet the Jarl's gaze.

'Little, I am afraid,' he said. 'Forgive me, lord, but...'

'...the Inquisition would have your lungs on a salver,' said Ragnar. 'And then mine. Very well, then – keep your secrets. But be aware: others will press you harder.'

'They are welcome to try,' said Ingvar. 'There's little to tell. The hunting was good. I learned the ways of others, they learned ours. After a while we worked well together. That surprised me.'

'But you were the strongest.'

Ingvar shrugged. 'I expected to be,' he said. 'Sometimes I was.'

Ragnar looked at him carefully.

'Service in the Deathwatch is considered an honour by many Chapters,' he said. 'Here it carries less weight. You broke your pack up when you accepted the summons to join them. I will be honest with you, Ingvar: if I had been Jarl when they came for you, I am not sure I would have given leave for you to go.'

Ingvar said nothing.

'Berek was indulgent,' said Ragnar. 'He had favourites, and he didn't care about appearances. Believe me, no one loved him more than I did, but we have to recognise fault when it appears. He saw something in you, Gyrfalkon, that much is certain, but you know what was on his mind at the time: Hjortur was dead, and Berek had no way of knowing what was intended for the pack.'

Ingvar listened silently, reluctant to hear old history recited again but unwilling to interrupt.

'Did it never occur to you that it looked like you were running away?' Ragnar went on. 'Gunnlaugur became Wolf Guard by default, without trial, without ever being pitted against you. You denied him that.'

Ingvar shook his head wearily. He had not expected an interrogation, and they were old allegations.

'I denied him nothing,' he said. 'The summons came and I accepted it. I would do it again. I am proud of what we did. I am proud of what my brothers did.'

'Which brothers?'

Ingvar realised that his fists had clenched tight, and relaxed them.

'All of them,' he said. 'All those who fought beside me.'

Ragnar nodded. 'Very good,' he said.

He cupped his hands. Ceramite clinked as he linked his fingers.

'Perhaps you think I'm being hard,' he said. 'I merely express sentiments that others will keep to themselves.'

'I can handle the others.'

Ragnar raised a ragged eyebrow over red-rimmed eyes. For the first time, Ingvar noticed that he looked tired.

'We have not escaped envy, up here in the realm of the gods,' Ragnar said. 'You think I am deaf to the whispers that run through this place? They say that I'm too young, that I should never have become Wolf Lord, that Berek was a fool to promote me.'

He smiled dryly.

'Berek had his weaknesses, but I do not doubt he was right. I have never doubted it. I have never listened to the whispers, but I know they are there. That was why I needed to speak to you. I needed to know that you were sure.'

'I don't understand,' said Ingvar.

'I feel certain that you do. But just in case, let me tell you what has taken place since you left us. Gunnlaugur has led Járnhamar pack with distinction. He has combined lethally well with Váltyr, but the whole group is strong. It has recovered from Hjortur's death and compensated for your absence. So now I have this dilemma: do I send you back to them? They could use another blade, but I fear for you there now. You were once a rival with Gunnlaugur for command – can you serve him?'

Ingvar looked up, directly into the tired eyes of the Jarl, meeting the gold-centred gaze.

'You shame me by asking that,' he said.

'I am not asking you anything. I am making up my mind.'

Ingvar felt his pride stir within him. It was hard to remember that Blackmane was elevated far above him in the arcane hierarchy of Fenris, that the Jarl's word was law, that if he ordered Ingvar into the maws of Hel then he was honour-bound to obey without question.

So young.

'Send me back, lord,' Ingvar said. The tone of his voice was less of a request and more of an insistence. 'Gunnlaugur was always ahead of me: he would have been *vaerangi* even if I had not left, and I would have followed him then. Nothing has changed. I belong with my pack.'

Ragnar's expression remained impassive.

'I did not know you then,' he said, 'so I cannot tell if the Deathwatch has changed you. They will know, though. If the Inquisition has turned your head then they will turn on you. Never forget what blood runs in our veins – we are wolves in temper as well as name.'

That was too much. Ingvar leapt to his feet, drawing his sword from its scabbard in a sweeping movement. He held it out, aiming the tip at Ragnar's throat.

'Do you know what this is?' he asked, his voice hard.

Ragnar regarded it coolly.

'It's a sword, Ingvar,' he said. 'I've seen plenty.'

He made no move to defend himself. Both of them knew how things stood: if Ingvar had truly been a threat to him, Ragnar would have killed him before the blade had left its sheath.

'It is *ancient*,' said Ingvar. He could feel his blood pumping in his temples. 'As old as this place. As old as the Annulus.'

Ragnar held Ingvar's gaze. 'This place is full of relics. What of it?'

'I was given this by Berek.' As Ingvar spoke, he remembered the events of decades ago with complete clarity. 'It belonged to him. Before him, it belonged to many others. It has passed through a hundred hands, each one leaving its imprint on the hilt. It has never been broken. The blood it has drunk would drown worlds. He honoured me with it, and I never used another, not even when they ordered me to take up xenos glaives that could carve Terminator plate like parchment. I carried it across the void with me, listening to its dry whispers of home, cleaving to what it reminded me of.'

The sword glinted in the semi-dark, its power-field inoperative, the outlines of runes evident in thread-thin lines of silver.

'It has borne many names,' said Ingvar. 'Berek called it *fjorsváfi*. Others call it *helsverd*, and *blodstefna*, and *doomhringir*. Long ago it was *dausvjer*, carried by Ogrim Raegr Vrafsson in the age of legend. It is part of our lifeblood. None but the elect will ever wield it.'

Ragnar's golden eyes flickered down to the point of the blade, and lingered there.

'Berek thought me worthy of it,' said Ingvar. 'The same who judged you worthy of elevation before your time. You trusted his judgement then.'

Ingvar held the sword level. The metal didn't move.

'I am a Son of Russ,' he said. 'I have nothing to prove.'

Ragnar's gaze snapped back up. For a moment, the two of them stared at one another. Blackmane's amber eyes scrutinised Ingvar's grey ones, narrowing fractionally, as if he somehow could penetrate into the soul beyond.

Ingvar felt the heavy pressure of Blackmane's countenance. Ragnar's stare was almost unbearable; it possessed an absolute conviction, a pure strain of certainty. No one, not Berek, not even Hjortur, had been able to project himself with such innate command.

The Young King.

Still the metal stayed level. Eventually, Ragnar shook his head wearily.

'Enough,' he said, gesturing for Ingvar to sheathe the sword again. 'This won't be decided by theatrics. Sit down.'

Ingvar did as he was bid. As he slid *dausvjer* into its scabbard, he suddenly realised how hard his primary heart was beating. He rested his empty hands on the cool stone of the bench.

'I like you, Gyrfalkon,' said Ragnar. 'I like your spirit.'

'Then send me back,' said Ingvar.

Ragnar smiled, but there was no warmth in it, just a wry grimace.

'Maybe,' he said. 'I'll reflect. You should do so too.'

Ingvar watched the Jarl carefully. Ragnar was a curious mix: insane levels of self-confidence coupled with a definite aura of fatigue. Perhaps command had proved harder that he'd anticipated.

'The galaxy is changing,' Blackmane said. 'Old Jarls lose their wisdom, young ones forget their strength. Stormcaller has dreams nightly that make him haggard, and he does not trouble easily. Even Grimnar laughs less than he did.'

The Wolf Lord placed his hands together again. Those deadly gauntlets, ones that had ended the lives of a thousand souls, formed a bulky pyramid.

'I would like to let Járnhamar remain here a while,' he said. 'They need to recover their strength. I would like to linger over this decision.'

Ingvar said nothing.

'But I cannot,' said Ragnar. 'We no longer have that luxury. We must keep fighting, all of us, without pause, and in such times wisdom is the first thing to fall away. I will make my decision quickly. You will know it soon.'

Ingvar bowed. 'And until then, lord? What I am to do with myself?'

'You still have your sword,' Ragnar said. 'Reacquaint yourself with the rites of your home world. Keep the edge sharp.'

Ragnar shot Ingvar a grim look. His youthful golden eyes reflected the light of fires wetly.

Confidence. Fatigue.

'Wherever I send you,' he said, 'you will have need of it.'

Chapter Two

Hafloí ran.

He churned through the snow, throwing up sprays of crystal-white behind him. His hot breath condensed in the freezing air in plumes. His hearts hammered, his lungs burned. He felt the motive systems in his armour hum and boost, operating in perfect sync with his blood-flooded muscles.

The arc of the sky swung high above him, clear and vivid. Ahead of him lay a long sweep of fresh snow running down to the black line of the river. Tight clumps of *ekka* pines clustered over to his left, getting thicker towards the steep edges of cliffs beyond. This was hard country, traversed by gorges and broken rockfields, all hidden under glistening swathes of bridge-ice and powder snow. It was treacherous, frigid, lethal, exposed to flesh-scouring winds that screamed across the plains and scythed through shivering chasms.

Hafloí grinned savagely. All of Asaheim was hard country. That was the point of it. That was why he loved it.

He pushed himself harder, sprinting down the long incline towards the hard blue shadow-edge under the encircling peaks. His armour made minute adjustments as his boots crashed against the scree, compensating for ankle-turning crevasses, absorbing the shock of the uneven terrain beneath the pristine blanket of snow.

He ran like a hunted *skriekre*, pushing his enhanced body to the limit. He leapt clean over obstacles, crashed through waist-high drifts. His limbs pumped, his arms swung, his shoulders rolled.

For a few seconds more he was alone in the valley, charging down towards the rushing water, a lone speck of movement amid the glacial indifference of Asaheim.

Then the gunship crested the sawtooth ridge behind him, growling up into the air on a column of oily smoke. It lurched up, around, swinging over the lip of the rise and out over the valley floor.

Set against the majesty of the high plateau, the gunship was an aberration. It was heavy, blunt, crude, expending staggering amounts of energy just to stay aloft. Its engines roared with a thrashing, hungry growl, and it stank of burning promethium. Its wedged nose hung low as it surged forwards on a dirty bloom of heat-haze.

Haflói heard it coming and kept grinning. He never slowed, just carried on racing. Already going at full tilt, he swerved and veered closer towards the riverbed, zigzagging wildly along the tumbling slope.

The gunship came after him, dipping its cockpit and plunging low across the snowfield. As it roared closer its heavy bolters keyed up, clanking as gigantic magazines were shunted into cavernous chambers. A second later and the linked barrels slammed into life, hurling twin lines of shells at the fleeing figure below.

The rolling barrage crashed into the ground in hissing furrows of exploding rock and vaporising snow. Haflói bucked and darted left, dancing clear of danger, jerking round suddenly and haring off towards the rapidly approaching tree line. Splatters of blackened slush streaked down his armour as he rode out the onslaught before breaking free.

The gunship roared past him. It climbed quickly, banked hard and came around for another pass, trailing its filthy curtain of smog behind it.

Too slow, thought Haflói with satisfaction, vaulting over a cracked ledge before powering down a slope of jagged rocks and ice towards the first of the pines.

He covered the ground quickly, hearing the grind of the gunship's engines grow louder with every stride he took. Just as he sensed the bolters click into firing positions he crashed into cover, shouldering through the dense, dark foliage as if plunging into water.

The trunks of the pines soared away above him like the pillars of some immense, shadowy cathedral. For the first time, Haflói had cover. He ducked down low and slowed his pace, weaving through the snowy drifts piled high at the roots. The branches above him swayed in the wind, twisting back and forth and hissing at him.

Hafloí halted briefly, catching his breath, looking up into the branches. He could still hear the thudding whine of the gunship close by, but couldn't see it through the thick cover. He concentrated, filtering out extraneous factors, letting his superlative senses do their work.

'Oh, *Hel…*' he spat, suddenly realising where it was.

The trees around him blasted apart in a hurricane of splinters. Hafloí ducked and leapt, exploding back into action as the forest destroyed itself. He heard a crack, and another, as the massive trunks were brought down. One swayed towards him, toppling directly into his path as its base was blasted away by a flurry of bolter-rounds.

He pounced out of its path, hearing the heavy whoosh of the trunk collapsing to earth behind him. More came down in a rain of severed branches and whirling needles. Gaps opened up in the canopy above, exposing the shadow of the hovering gunship and its juddering weapons.

Hafloí picked up full pace again, careering through the disintegrating forest. He vaulted over shattering stumps and ducked under collapsing beams. The air was choked with flying snow, rock shards and pulverised wood. He saw bolts impact on the earth around him and leapt out of their path.

He couldn't outrun the gunship, and with every passing second his residual shelter was being blasted away. As he ran, he swung his head frantically from right to left, searching for an alternative strategy.

'That'll do,' he muttered, spotting what he was after.

He skidded to a halt, throwing up a wave of scree and slush, then darted off to his right. The gunship adjusted course instantly, sending clattering bolt-rounds biting at his heels. Hafloí squeezed a few extra grammes of effort from his tortured limbs, sprinting hard down a steep bank as the remainder of his tree cover was ripped apart.

Then the land ended.

A dizzying precipice shot straight down, sheer and bald. Hafloí catapulted over the edge and out into the open. For a moment he was suspended in mid-air over a wide ravine, his legs and arms still pumping, wet debris showering over him from the exploding forest above.

He plummeted fast, dragged down by his heavy plate. Twenty metres below was a tangle of boulders, ice-plates and scrub. They all swept up to meet him with pitiless speed.

The gunship followed him over the edge, picking up altitude to break clear of the remaining pines before lowering its head again and resuming fire. Projectiles whistled past Hafloí's tumbling body, missing him by a hand's width.

Then he was down, crunching between two huge rocks the size of Rhino transporters. The impact was sharp, sending painful shudders up through his battered body.

He staggered, righting himself, and scrambled onwards, skidding and stumbling down narrow icy paths between the boulders, ducking into their cover as the fire from above fizzed and cracked around him.

The further he went the larger the rocks became. He'd entered a maze of overlapping stone slabs, the remnants of some massive earthquake or landslip. The boulders loomed up above him, capped with messy crowns of snow. The fissures between them were treacherous, clogged with glassy patches of ice.

Haflói barged his way further down, scraping his shoulder guards against the walls of rock that surrounded him. He was soon enclosed on either side by bulwarks of stone. The sky above him shrank to a narrow strip of white.

The gunship thundered overhead, and the fire from its gun guttered out.

Haflói allowed himself a smile. This was better cover – the granite boulders would take some shattering. He pressed on, going as quickly as he could in the labyrinth between the rocks.

The noise of the gunship faded into the distance, then grew in volume again as it came back around. Haflói paused, listening carefully. He heard the telltale whine of a hatch door lowering while in mid-air, and the dull crunch of ceramite against stone as one of its occupants leapt to earth.

Haflói drew his bolt pistol from its holster and kept moving. The icy corridors between the rocks ran like cracks across an ice-sheet – joining up, splitting apart, opening into open clearings or drying up altogether. He exchanged speed for stealth. He could hear dull footfalls running across the ravine floor: ceramite boots, crunching against gravel and frost, coming closer.

Too noisy, Hunter.

Ahead of him, Haflói saw a narrow crevasse running in from the left and joining up with the one he currently occupied. Where the two fissures met was a small opening, no more than five metres across and overlooked by towering crags on all sides. The sounds of footfalls came down the left fork, getting louder.

Haflói pressed himself into the shadow of the nearside boulder and aimed the pistol. A second later a huge grey-armoured warrior burst into view. He went helm-less, exposing a shaven pate and black-streaked beard. He seemed to sense Haflói's presence and turned to face him, lowering a boltgun.

Too late.

Haflói fired, and watched the mass-reactive round spiral towards its target. The bolt hit the warrior square in the breastplate, sending him crashing into the far boulder.

'*Hjá!*' Haflói crowed, drawing the sword at his belt and preparing to leap after him.

'Careful, now,' came a low voice at his ear.

Haflói froze.

Gingerly, he looked down. A naked blade rested against his throat, barely touching the skin. If he'd have pounced, he'd have cut his throat open.

'And that makes you dead, whelp.'

His hearts still beating hard, he slowly let his hands fall to his sides. The blade was withdrawn.

The warrior he'd downed pushed himself away from the stone, moving stiffly. His big, ugly, snub-nosed faced was creased with laughter.

The second warrior stepped away from Haflói, coming round from where he'd crept up behind him. The three of them – two Grey Hunters, one Blood Claw – faced one another. From some distance, the growl of the gunship could still be heard. The lower pitch of its engines indicated that it was coming down to land.

'*Skítja.*'

Haflói spat on the ground. He slammed his pistol back into its holster.

Olgeir, the big one he'd managed to hit with his neutered bolt-round, the one they called Heavy-hand, came over to punch him on the shoulder. The gesture was possibly intended to be affectionate; it felt like a slug from a lascannon.

'Careless, lad,' said Olgeir.

Olgeir's gnarled face was encrusted in an impossibly dense mix of scar tissue, tattoos, ironwork piercings and curls of dark, stray hair. His streaked beard was full and unruly, cascading in snarls and braided twists over his full breastplate. For the exercise he'd reluctantly left his heavy bolter, the beloved *sigrún*, behind, and he looked strangely massive without it.

Olgeir's companion shot Haflói a dry smile.

'You did well to outrun Jorundur,' he said, stowing his blade. 'He won't be happy about that.'

Baldr Fjolnir was easier to look at than his larger battle-brother. His beard was less ragged, his skin less tortured by burns and scores. He was lean, compact, with a mouth that tended to smiles and clear amber eyes. He wore his hair long, and it still bore traces of the sandy blondness it had had when he'd been in the Claws himself.

'You were waiting down here?' asked Hafloí, rubbing his neck ruefully. 'I only heard one of you land.'

Olgeir laughed again. His ugly face seemed made for it – a low, rumbling, throaty sound that rolled up from the curved barrel of his chest.

'Not too bright,' he observed.

Baldr was still smiling. There was no malice in the expression. The fair-haired warrior hardly looked capable of the extreme violence that his profession demanded, though Hafloí wasn't stupid enough to doubt that he was perfectly capable of it.

'We jumped together,' Baldr said. 'Make a note: that's something an enemy might try. They're unfair like that.'

Haloí wasn't in the mood to be baited. As his body recovered, his pride slumped further into a low, surly frustration.

'*Morkai*,' he swore, letting his head fall back and rolling it around. As the adrenaline stopped pumping, he could feel a whole cluster of aches and pains gathering to assail him. He'd pushed himself hard that time – harder than ever. 'This is a joke. *A joke*. It's not possible.'

Olgeir raised an eyebrow. 'You think?' he said. 'So little faith – I think you'll do it.'

Haloí rounded on him then. He was exhausted, driven to the edge by the endless drills, the ceaseless challenges, the days he'd already spent being tested by members of a pack he'd never even wanted to join. He hadn't done any proper fighting for weeks. He hadn't fired a proper gun, or run at a real enemy with a real blade.

'Fight me here, then,' he snapped. 'One on one – I'll break your fat neck.'

Olgeir chuckled approvingly. Baldr shook his head.

'No, you won't,' he said calmly. In the distance, Haloí heard a muffled crunch as the Thunderhawk landed. 'You'll come with us, and I'll show you what you did wrong.'

The Grey Hunter looked at Haloí, and his expression was serious. As he returned the gaze, Haloí realised, as he had done a dozen times already, that he had no choice.

'Then we'll do this again,' said Baldr. 'And again. Right until you find a way to kill us, just like we asked you to.'

The air was hot, sweltering in a haze of seamy darkness. Clangs boomed through it, rhythmic beats like the drums on an ancient slave galley. Sparks showered, bounced and died on the stone floor, hurled from the glowing, gaping jaws of a thousand foundries.

Gunnlaugur looked up, away from the magma-light of the forge floor

and up towards the distant roof. He couldn't see it. Thick columns of
smoke swam up into the heights, pooling and drifting before being filtered up through hidden vents. The cacophony of the forging went with
them – a discordant, overlapping strain of heat-softened metal being
beaten into shape by ranks of vast, tilting hammers.

Molten steel ran down gullies like river water, spitting and frothing
as it slopped over the sides. Bloated calderas tipped up, sending fresh
gushes into waiting moulds. Conveyer belts of segmented adamantium
rolled endlessly, shunting metal from bulbous cooling vats, to anvils,
back to the furnace, on and on in a round of hammering, shaping, fold-
ing, tapering and tempering until the proto-weapons emerged, carried
off reverently by dull-eyed servitors for the benediction and finishing of
tech-priests and Iron Priests.

Above it all hung the silent images of the ancient forge gods, picked out
in beaten bronze and mounted on pillars of stone. As the army of semi-
human artificers laboured, those bronze images flickered and glowed in
the sullen light of eternal fires, staring calmly and inscrutably across the
shifting gloom of the Hammerhold.

Gunnlaugur looked away from them and strode past the ranks of
machines. He had not been down into the depths for a very long time,
but it looked much the same as it had on every previous occasion. The
smell of it was oppressive – a sharp, acrid cocktail of smog, steam and
sweat that lodged in his nostrils and wouldn't budge. There was barely
room to swing an axe; none to run. It was claustrophobic, a vision of the
underworld dragged up into the realm of the living.

Few Sky Warriors came to the Hammerhold without good reason.
Gunnlaugur was no exception. It took him over an hour to find the one
he was looking for, and it led him far away from the clamour of the main
halls. Eventually retracing the routes he had taken last time, he slipped
into side vaults and down cargo ramps, dodging the heavy crawlers that
ground their way up from the deep-bore ore silos.

The booming clangs receded into a low murmur. A more modest vault
awaited him – less than twenty metres in height, less than thirty wide. No
icons of gods hung from the blackened ceiling, just bare stone worked
into gothic arches. A single anvil rested in the centre of the chamber,
black and heavy-set, shiny in the darkness. A furnace the height of two
mortal men stood beside it, lit with shimmering coals that made the narrow opening shake with heat. A few other items stood beside the furnace
– a rack hung with dozens of metalworking tools, a cauldron of water,
iron caskets full of ingots – but otherwise the space was almost bare.

No servitors droned around that place; no conveyer belts brought raw materials to the hammer's bite. Less than one weapon a year left that anvil, and many more were destroyed by their maker before they reached the Iron Priest for blessing.

Few ironworkers would have had their painstaking energies so indulged by the Jarls. Arjac, though, the one they called Rockfist, was a special case.

The man-mountain stood over the anvil like a frost giant bearing down on a prone victim. His thick armour-plate shone blood-red in the light of the furnace, picking out the battered runes that ran down the length of his arms. His bald head hung low over his work, streaked with dirty sweat.

A blade lay on the anvil-top, shining with ruddy heat. Arjac worked it skilfully, using a light hammer to hone the edge down to a bite point. The image was incongruous – Arjac's immense body, bulked out further by thick sweeps of ceramite armour, tapping delicately at the sliver of metal before him.

Gunnlaugur said nothing. He remained in the shadows, watching respectfully. Arjac never looked up. The hammer rose and fell, glistening from the firelight, chipping out sparks as the impurities in the metal were beaten out.

Eventually Arjac snatched the blade away and plunged it into the cauldron. A swollen bloom of steam hissed up around it. He withdrew it and brought it into the light of the furnace. He turned it over and over, scrutinising what he had done.

The blade was the length of his forearm, ideal for a duelling gladius. Gunnlaugur looked at it appreciatively. His was no trained eye, but he knew how to use a sword, and it looked like he could use that one.

'Fancy it, stripling?' asked Arjac, never lifting his head.

Gunnlaugur smiled. 'For me?' he said.

Arjac let the metal fall back on the anvil.

'For no one,' he sighed. 'It'll be melted down, just like the others.'

'Seems a waste.'

'A waste? Of what – metal? There's more down here than we could use in a thousand years.'

Arjac straightened out of his stoop. Fully extended, his bulk was even more intimidating. Gunnlaugur, whose own physical presence was immense, seemed almost slight in comparison.

'A waste is sending a warrior out with a defective blade,' Arjac growled, rolling his great shoulders in slow circles. 'In any case, only an idiot goes into battle with a sword.'

Arjac's huge thunder hammer, *fomadurhamar*, hung from an immense iron frame at the rear of the chamber. Even powered-down, it exuded a quiet air of implacable solidity – much like its master.

'Agreed.'

Gunnlaugur's preferred weapon was also a thunder hammer, one that shared his moniker – *skulbrotsjór* – safely stowed over the war-altar in his personal Jarlheim chamber. The two warriors shared a similar view of much in life, including which was the proper tool to break heads with.

Arjac came around from the far side of the anvil and approached Gunnlaugur. The furnace-light exposed a brawler's face, broad from tight bands of muscle, lodged deep amid stocky neck-sinew and his armour's fibre-bundles.

For a moment, Arjac looked straight at Gunnlaugur, appraising him as he would a newly-worked slab of metal. Gunnlaugur wouldn't have let many look at him like that – since being elevated to Wolf Guard, only Jarl Blackmane, the Priests and Grimnar himself had the authority to subject him to any kind of scrutiny.

Arjac, however, was different. Arjac was exceptional in every respect. His blood was that of an Iron Priest's, as was his temperament. Only his peerless skill at close range combat had kept him away from the lava forges where he longed to be. Gunnlaugur knew, just as everyone else knew, how much Arjac yearned to settle back among the true weaponsmiths, crafting artificer axe-heads and lightning claws among the silent, brooding anvil-masters.

But Arjac never complained. That generated a respect in the halls of the Fang. It had made him the first mentor Gunnlaugur had ever sought during his centuries of service in the Rout. To his surprise, Arjac had been receptive. Perhaps the Anvil of Fenris had seen something of himself in the raw Gunnlaugur. Perhaps, since he was rarely approached for serious counsel, he welcomed the chance to pass on some of his accumulated battle-lore.

Whatever the reason, the two of them always met on the rare occasions when both were present on the home world at the same time. Gunnlaugur had benefitted much from the exchanges. He hoped, perhaps optimistically, that Arjac had as well.

'You look bad,' said Arjac.

'As would you, if you'd been where we've been.'

'No doubt. How runs the pack?'

'Blooded,' Gunnlaugur said, truthfully enough. 'We're down to five. Losing Tínd caused us problems, but we did what we were sent to do, and most of us got back home.'

Arjac grunted. The big warrior seldom spoke much, and when he did
he was curt.

'Glad you did,' he said. 'Now, why are you here?'

Gunnlaugur took a deep breath. His eyes flickered over to the anvil
again, over to where the discarded blade lay cooling.

'We'll leave again soon,' he said. 'Blackmane wants us to take on a
Blood Claw. He may want us to take Ingvar Eversson back too.'

Arjac raised a charred, stubbly eyebrow.

'The Gyrfalkon? He'll come back,' he said. 'Why pretend otherwise?'

Gunnlaugur shrugged. 'Because I do not know how to handle him,'
he said. Anything less than full honesty was a waste with Arjac. 'Not
any more.'

Arjac looked at Gunnlaugur steadily. His golden eyes were unwaver-
ing, the same eyes that could detect minute flaws in steel while it lay
under the hammer.

'You really want my counsel?' asked Arjac. 'I'm not a Jarl, nor a Priest.
You could speak to Blackmane yourself.'

'I could.'

'But you won't.'

Gunnlaugur shook his head. 'I don't think so.'

'You're a fool. One day you'll see why Grimnar thinks so highly of
him.'

Gunnlaugur felt his heart sink. He didn't know what he wanted from
Arjac. He didn't even know why the issue with Ingvar was exercising
him so much. In the fifty-seven years since Hjortur had died he had
never felt the burden of command weigh heavily at all; now, suddenly,
it seemed like one of Arjac's anvils, shackled to his ankles and dragging
him down into the abyss.

'I've built the pack around me,' he said, speaking half to Arjac, half to
himself. 'Váltyr's my sword-arm – I've learned to use him, and time has
only made him deadlier. Baldr and Olgeir are as dependable as Freki.
Jorundur is a sour old hound, but he's got his uses and flies a gunship
like it's an ice-skiff. I'm proud of all this. I would not see it broken.'

Gunnlaugur shook his head.

'There's no room for him,' he said. 'Not now. He made his choice.'

Arjac's expression remained static – not judging, not scornful, not sym-
pathetic. Like the rock that gave him his moniker, he was unmoveable.

'Then you must defy Ragnar,' Arjac said. 'But tell me truly, stripling:
is that really what disturbs you?'

Gunnlaugur looked up. 'What do you mean?'

'You are Járnhamar's *vaerangi*. If your pack is your concern, then stand up to the Jarl over it – he may not bend, but he will respect you. But if *you* are the problem, if your weakness is the issue, then he will laugh in your face and cast you from his presence like a churl. I have heard the Young King likes to laugh – he will not need a good excuse for you.'

Gunnlaugur felt a flash of anger, a stab of the pride that always lurked just beneath the surface with him. Instinctively his right hand curled into a fist.

Arjac was quicker. The huge warrior shoved Gunnlaugur away from the anvil, pushing him hard in the chest. His expression flickered into something harder: contempt, spiced with the first spikes of combat-fury.

Off balance, Gunnlaugur stumbled backwards. He hit something as he staggered – a weapons-rack – and metal blades and hilt-pieces clattered to the stone around him.

'What is it, Wolf Guard?' mocked Arjac, striding after him, his enormous fists poised to strike. '*Afraid* of the Gyrfalkon? Has your blood run cold since you last sparred with him as an equal?'

Gunnlaugur kicked back, thrusting himself at Arjac. The two of them crashed together, grappling like two old bears in a cave.

'I fear *nothing*!' Gunnlaugur roared. His arms clasped around Arjac's torso, and he pushed back violently. 'You *know* this!'

Arjac took the strain, and a strange sound burst from his mouth. Half blinded by rage, Gunnlaugur nearly missed it, already pulling his fist back ready for the punch.

Then he recognised the grating chortle, the closest Arjac's forge-dried throat ever got to genuine laughter.

Gunnlaugur halted, the momentum suddenly gone from his furious assault. He broke clear of Arjac, his cheeks flushed crimson, and spun away from the embrace.

Arjac regarded him tolerantly, smiling all the while.

'Good,' he said. '*Good*. For a moment I thought you'd lost it.'

Gunnlaugur caught his breath, his anger replaced, just as quickly as it had arrived, by shame.

Why am I so quick to wrath? he thought. *Why am I so easily goaded?*

Arjac returned to the anvil, still chuckling.

'You're letting this get to you, stripling,' he said, picking up the blade and looking at it again. 'Hjortur would have named you pack-leader if he'd lived long enough to choose. Blood of Russ, *I* would have done – you can hit hard enough when you want to.'

Gunnlaugur let his arms fall to his sides. He felt strung-out. One mission after the other, year after year; it would take its toll eventually.

'So what would you do?' he asked.

'With Eversson? I'd welcome him as a brother. I'd want a blade of his pedigree in the pack. If he challenged me, I'd beat him down. If he challenged the others, I'd foster it.'

Arjac ran his gauntlet along the edge of the anvil.

'A pack is a sacred thing,' he said. 'It has a life of its own, greater than ours. You cannot control that life, you can only guide it a little. If fate brings you and Ingvar back together, the pack will shape itself around both of you, one way or another.'

Gunnlaugur listened.

'Pride makes you strong, stripling,' said Arjac. 'Let it make you stronger – you deserve to be where you are – but do not let it blind you. None of us is greater than the pack. In the final reckoning, the pack is what must survive.'

Arjac's eyes lost their focus. It was as if he were addressing himself as much as Gunnlaugur.

'Remember this,' he said. 'You, me, Ingvar, the Old Wolf himself, we are nothing in isolation. We only live for the pack: that is what makes us deadly, what makes us eternal. Nothing else matters.'

Gunnlaugur bowed. He had his answer. He had what he had come for.

'I understand,' he said.

Arjac nodded.

'Good. Then you can leave me to work.' 'I can. My thanks, lord.'

Arjac scowled. 'Do not call me that. We are the same rank.'

Gunnlaugur smiled to himself. For a moment, he had genuinely forgotten.

'Of course,' he said.

Wolf Guard. Vaerangi.

Arjac took up a hammer again. That was the cue to leave, and Gunnlaugur turned back towards the distant roar of the Hammerhold. He walked slowly, turning Arjac's words over in his mind.

We only live for the pack.

They were familiar words, but it felt strange to be reminded of them.

That is what makes us deadly, what makes us eternal.

With every step he took, he felt a little stronger.

Nothing else matters.

Chapter Three

The Thunderhawk *Vuokho* stood on the apron. Steam drifted up its ugly, chipped grey surface as the ice it had picked up on the way in evaporated in the heat of the hangar. Beyond it, further along the cavernous interior towards the entrance ramps, servitors and kaerl ground crew clattered and banged their way through a thousand menial tasks. The gunship hangars of the upper Valgard were never still; always the constant growl and whine of engines cycling up, or the tinny clunk of weapons being loaded, or the rumble of refuelling tankers crawling across the rockcrete floor.

Jorundur Erak Kaerlborn, the one they called Old Dog, looked over his pride and joy with a watchful, cynical eye. He knew every centimetre of its surface, and each fresh scratch or dent annoyed him a little more. He didn't care about the way the thing looked – given his own dark-eyed, sunken-cheeked visage, that would hardly have been reasonable – but he cared deeply about how it flew. *Vuokho* was as much a member of the pack as he was, a part of the whole, a component in the system. If it were ever lost then they would grieve for it as much as they had done for Tínd; perhaps more, for Tínd had been a difficult one, given to rages and with a fair slice of Gunnlaugur's fierce pride boiling away within him.

Jorundur didn't like taking *Vuokho* out on training missions. The machine-spirit hated the charade of it – it had been bred to hunt, just as they had been. If he had had his way he would have been left on his own with it more often, taking it out and up into the high atmosphere where the sky fell into nightshade-blue and the stars dotted the arch of the void. That was where its engines operated at the perfect pitch of efficiency, where the true power of its thrusters could be unleashed in bursts of furious velocity.

In space, a Thunderhawk was a clumsy, compromised thing, hampered by atmospheric drives it couldn't use; on land it was a bulky monstrosity, squatting against the earth like a deformed mockery of a prey-bird. Only in the inbetween spaces, the thin airs where void and matter met, only there was it unsurpassed.

'Brought it back safely, then,' came a voice at Jorundur's shoulder.

He didn't need to turn to see who was speaking. He carried on staring at the gently cooling chassis, moving his glistening, scrutinising eyes slowly over its outline.

'This time,' he replied as Váltyr drew alongside him.

Jorundur was not sociable. He had none of Baldr's easy manner nor Olgeir's generous humour. Of all of Járnhamar, Jorundur found Váltyr the easiest to rub along with; the two of them shared an appreciation of the colder side of killing.

'What did you make of him?' asked Váltyr.

'The whelp? He can run. I've seen him fight. He'll be all right.'

Váltyr nodded. 'We need new blood,' he said. 'Things have felt... tired.'

Jorundur gave a dry snort.

'That's because they are.' He drew closer to Váltyr, and lowered his voice. As he did so, lank grey-black hair fell around his face. 'Everyone is tired, blademaster. If they keep sending us out, year after year, with no chance to breathe or retrain or remember what we're doing, we will be more than tired – we'll be dead.'

Váltyr didn't pull away.

'Times are hard,' he replied evenly. 'What do you want? A soft bed and a weekly steam-bath?'

'I wouldn't turn it down.'

'No, perhaps you wouldn't.'

Jorundur was older than the next most experienced member of Járnhamar by a good hundred years. In the normal run of things he'd have shifted sideways into a heavy weapons squad a long time ago, taking his place amid the hoary old veterans with their gnarled gun-hands and *konungur*-tough hides. No one knew why he'd resisted it, staying in the ranks of the Hunters even as the chance for promotion to the Guard had passed him by. Some said it was because he lived for flying and would have missed the chance to pilot a gunship, others that he found the company of Long Fangs even more objectionable than that of anybody else.

Jorundur was happy with the speculation; he liked to keep people guessing and never explained himself. In any case he knew well enough that Gunnlaugur needed to keep him in the pack: things had long been too straitened to countenance the departure of a seasoned pair of weapon-arms, no matter how pinched-faced and snipe-tongued their owner was. As things had turned out for him, that was good enough.

'So is this thing combat-ready?' asked Váltyr, moving away from Jorundur to inspect the flanks of the Thunderhawk.

Jorundur followed him.

'What do you mean?' he asked, feeling suddenly uneasy. 'We're going back out? Already?'

Váltyr nodded, reaching the first set of wings and running his finger along the thick leading edge.

'Like you said, they will keep sending us on these missions.'

Jorundur spat on the ground, shaking his shaggy head in disgust.

'*Morkai's teeth*,' he swore. 'We're not ready. Olgeir could spend three weeks with that whelp and we still wouldn't be ready. Who'll take Tínd's place? Arse of the Allfather, this is pathetic.'

Váltyr smiled. 'I knew you'd be pleased,' he said. 'They've given us two days, and this thing needs to be fully operational. They're loading up a frigate right now. I've seen it. It's a shit-bucket, but it looks fast.'

Jorundur spat again. He could do that all day.

'Where, then?'

'Ras Shakeh.'

'Never heard of it.'

'Two months away, on the fringes of protected space. Grimnar thinks we need to be pushing out a bit, extending our reach as others withdraw theirs.'

Váltyr reached up towards a cracked picter-lens embedded halfway up *Vuokho*'s cockpit armour, but Jorundur slapped his hand away.

'*Lunacy*,' hissed Jorundur, rounding on Váltyr and prodding him in the chest, pushing him away from the sacred adamantium. 'We need to retrench, not expand. Will someone ever tell the Old Wolf that we're all taking losses? Does he think that we can pick up the slack of every half-manned Chapter in the segmentum?'

'Actually, I think he does think that.'

'Then he's as stupid as he is stubborn.'

Váltyr sighed. 'Tell him that, then,' he said. 'Gunnlaugur will brief the pack when things are settled. I came up here because I thought you'd be pleased to see some real action.'

Jorundur paused. That was a reasonable point.

He looked up at the gunship's still-hot engines, mentally running

down the list of repairs he'd intended to hand to the Iron Priest. Some
of them might be possible in two days, and a few more could be carried
out on board the frigate, but most would have to wait.

It was the incompleteness that irritated him, the constant harrying
from one job to the next, never leaving enough time to work on something properly, always patching-up, shifting-out and making-do.

Perhaps that was his age talking. Maybe that had always been the
way, and he'd just tolerated it back then. Or maybe things really were
getting worse.

'I'll get it fixed up,' he said, grudgingly. 'But tell Skullhewer it won't
be in ideal shape. One big hit, and–'

'I'll tell him,' said Váltyr, already walking away. 'Just do what you
can – I've a feeling Gunnlaugur has more pressing concerns right now.'

'Like what?' asked Jorundur.

'You'll find out,' said Váltyr, his voice as dry as ever.

Ingvar spun tightly on the ball of his right foot, thrusting out with
dausvjer, sending the blade low and hard. Then he pulled it back,
withdrawing, curling his whole body up tight, generating momentum,
feeling his muscles respond.

He repeated the movement, then again, each time adjusting the pace
a little, angling the point a fraction more, testing his stance. The repeti-
tions went on. Firelight danced around him, making his sweat-covered
skin shine. He heard the crackle and snap of fuel in the braziers, tasted
the charcoal in the air, smelled his own hot, ripe scent as his body
worked.

The physical exertion helped his mind relax. It purged the residual
sickness of the long void-journey, purifying him, restoring his animal
vitality.

He would have preferred to have sparred with a drone, something
that would have fought back, something he could have smashed apart
and left in a pile of sparking debris across the floor of the training
chamber.

But the Wolves didn't use training drones, so he was alone, going
through the motions on his own, rehearsing sword-thrusts with imagi-
nary opponents in the dark.

'Why don't you use them?' Callimachus had asked him.

Ingvar remembered the Ultramarine's studiously polite expression.
Callimachus had been trying hard to be diplomatic, but it had been
clear enough what he had thought.

'A drone doesn't attack you like a minded creature,' Ingvar had said.

Back then he had been fresh out of Hjortur's old pack, contemptuous of the skills of those he'd been thrown together with. 'It has no soul, and a warrior needs a soul. We fight each other. We fight the enemy. That's the way to learn.'

The rest of the squad had remained quiet. Back then, Ingvar had assumed they were cowed by his confidence, his ebullient manner, the proud heritage of Russ that he wore nakedly over his dull black battle-plate. Now he couldn't be quite so sure.

Callimachus had shaken his head.

'Forgive me, but it makes no sense,' he'd said. 'Why not send your neophytes into war with the skills they need?'

'They learn the skills in real combat, or they die.'

'Indeed. Which is a tragic waste.'

'Conflict tests the warrior.'

'Quite so – but the drone-drills prepare him. They are more flexible, perhaps, than you realise.'

Ingvar hadn't believed him. He hadn't believed him even after two more weeks at Halliafiore's training facility on Djeherrod when the punishing regime had driven him into a level of exhaustion he had never known before, not even on the Long Hunt back to the Aett. He hadn't believed him during the sparring sessions with the other members of Onyx Squad, when he'd been taken to the limit by all of them.

He'd only believed it truly when he'd finally come up against a Deathwatch-conditioned drone – a titanium-clad monster of spikes and flamers and needle-guns that had swooped around the cage like a trapped wasp, anticipating every move he made, reacting with astonishing speed, nearly taking his arm off and breaking several fused-ribs before he'd finally managed to put it out of action.

After that he'd been a bit more circumspect. Callimachus, true to form, had been painfully generous about it.

'I entirely respect your way of war, Eversson,' the Ultramarine had said afterwards, picking his words carefully. 'Truly, I respect it. But is it possible that there might be some virtue in learning from precedent?'

'You mean the *Codex*,' Ingvar had said, back then barely knowing of what he spoke.

'It does have some uses.'

Ingvar pulled out of the manoeuvre, letting *dausvjer* drop. He had been practising for several hours; even his body had its limits.

The exertion had done him some good. The burn in his biceps and quadriceps had a welcome familiarity about it. It felt good to be back on the home world, surrounded by the totems and sigils of the past, steeped in the harsh grandeur of the Halls of Asaheim. He was adjusting. He was remembering.

He would have preferred to have sparred with a drone.

'My lord.'

The kaerl's voice came from outside the locked and barred door to the training room. Ingvar pushed his shoulders back, letting his muscles unwind, before giving the order to unlock.

'My apologies for disturbing you,' said the man, bowing deeply as the door slid back.

'What is it?' asked Ingvar, reaching for a cloth and wiping the sweat from his face and neck.

'Jarl Blackmane wishes to inform you that he has reached a decision. He thought you should know as soon as possible, since time is always short.'

Ingvar felt a sudden pang in his stomach, an unwelcome reminder of how tenuous his fate had been since returning to the Fang.

'Fine,' he said, barely looking at the man before him. 'I'll report to the Jarl.'

The man stared at the floor, as if embarrassed.

'That will not be necessary, lord,' he said.

Ingvar looked at him sharply. 'What do you mean?'

The kaerl hesitated, aware of the awkwardness of the tidings he'd been asked to convey.

'I am commanded to inform you that you are to report to *vaerangi* Gunnlaugur. He will brief you prior to deployment to the Ras Shakeh system. Questions, supplementary orders and equipment requisitions are to go through him. The Priesthood has been informed and records amended. All has been done that was required to be done.'

The kaerl swallowed.

'Congratulations, lord,' he said. 'You are once again a member of Járnhamar.'

Chapter Four

When the pack convened it was in their old staging chamber, the one they always used before leaving Fenris. The place was in the Jarlheim, tucked away behind a shaft that ran clear down into the Hould, linked to the rest of the Aett only by a single-span bridge of cold stone.

Gunnlaugur had found it, years ago. No one knew who had carved it out, nor what uses it had been put to over the thousands of years since the fortress had been delved. That wasn't unusual. Millennia of constant war meant that the Fang was usually under-populated, and whole sections of it had collapsed, or were flooded, or were simply unexplored. Every so often, squads of kaerls would undertake expeditions into far-flung sections, hoping to open them up to habitation. Sometimes they would succeed and new chambers would be cleaned out and put to use. Sometimes they would return bearing artefacts from the forgotten past that none but the Wolf Priests knew what to make of. Sometimes they never came back. That too was not unusual; the Fang was not, and never had been, a safe place.

Gunnlaugur had never disclosed how he'd found the chamber. It was a long way from where he had his lodgings, and a long way from where the majority of Blackmane's Great Company made their base. The room was old, that was clear. Stone carvings on the walls had been worn smooth by the whining wind and cracked by frost. Runes of a strange design were still visible near the arched ceiling, hacked into the granite by long-dead hands. More than fifty warriors could have been housed there comfortably, though why such a hall had been delved so far from the major transit shafts of the Jarlheim was a mystery.

A carcass lay along one wall: the skeletal remains of a sea-going *drekkar*. The longship's planks had ossified generations ago, leaving a crusted, stony shell behind like the ribcage of a slain seawyrm. The metal *drakk*'s-head prow had survived somehow. It reared up into the roof of the chamber atop a sweep of smooth hull planks, gazing with empty eyes into the gloom.

It must have been a daunting task to have carried such a ship so high, right up into the heart of the old mountain, bracing it against the frost-sear wind and powdery dunes of snow. Perhaps the *drekkar* had been dismantled at sea level and reassembled inside the chamber, though Gunnlaugur preferred to believe that it hadn't. He liked to imagine a torchlit procession of Sky Warriors hauling the ship up from the turbulent, iron-grey seas, dragging it into the high places and towing it on rollers into the heart of the Fang. There were tunnels big enough to accommodate it and hands strong enough to lift it.

That still left the question of why they had done it, and for that he had no answer. Perhaps it had been the whim of a timeworn Jarl, sentimental for his old life out on the open sea. Perhaps it had been brought there by the Priests as part of some obscure rite to placate the soul of the mountain. Perhaps it had lain there, slowly crumbling, since Russ had walked among them.

Whatever the truth of its origins, the *drekkar* and its strange tomb had fallen out of memory in the centuries since its entombment. Like so much else on Fenris, the place had become a relic, a half-lost fragment of a rapidly disappearing past. The Allfather alone knew how long it had been there, slowly mouldering and freezing and wasting away.

Now the ship's tomb was Járnhamar's place, the chamber they came to before embarking out into the sea of stars. It had come to seem appropriate, to make their final vows to one another under the shadow of the *drakk*'s head.

Hjortur had always enjoyed the conceit. He'd liked to leap up onto the fragile decking, crushing it beneath his boots, roaring out old sea-commands in a tribal dialect none of the others could understand. They'd laughed at that, watching him flail around amid snapping spars and planks and roaring impenetrable orders.

Gunnlaugur smiled at the memory. Hjortur had been good for a laugh. He'd led the pack with blood on his claws and a grin on his scarred face.

He'd been a proper Son of Russ, that one, a bloody-minded hound, a reckless, startling monster of unrestraint.

'Come on, then,' said Váltyr, impatiently. 'Let's hear it.'

Gunnlaugur didn't reply at once. He took a moment to study the pack before him, the remnants of one that had once been larger, the broken heart of what had fallen to his command.

He saw Váltyr looking back at him, with his pale, querulous face and penetrating gaze. He saw the pent-up energy in the blademaster's limbs, the locked-in power that could explode without warning into a nerve-blinding whirl of steel. He saw the calculation, the coolly competent analytical mind, the strategeo's sharpness. He saw the edge of insecurity, too, and saw the neediness.

His eyes moved to Olgeir. The big warrior stood at ease, his unruly beard spilling over his armour, his scarred cheeks creased in readiness for a toothy smile or saliva-flecked bellow. Gunnlaugur saw the wholeheart-edness in that one, the generosity, the commitment. Olgeir was the rock, the foundation; he could never lead, but he could guide, and he could encourage. The Heavy-handed wanted for nothing more than he had. That was a weakness, a lack of ambition, but it made him invaluable.

Next was Jorundur, the Old Dog. He was sidelong, sideways, twisted and warped by age. Gunnlaugur saw the marrow-deep weariness in him, the pride, the cynic's lip-curl. But he could fly. By Russ, he could fly. And for all his sourness, the Old Dog had seen plenty and done plenty. He knew where many bodies were buried, and what paths had been trod-den to take them there, and where the shovels had been hidden and in what forges they had been made. When Morkai came for him at last, a thousand secrets would sink into the soil forever.

In Jorundur's shadow was Baldr. That one was an enigma. So pleasant, so easy, so amenable. His voice was soft when he read the sagas, recount-ing old songs with perfect, plangent clarity. No one hated Baldr Fjolnir. He went through life like a sleek fish gliding through reeds, effortlessly, slipping into the path of least resistance. And yet, when he killed, there was something else there, something guarded, something clenched, something buried. Yes, Baldr was an enigma.

And then there was the new blood, the whelp, the stripling: Hafloí, standing apart, still strung between nervy bravado and sullen withdrawal. His red hair caught the firelight, stained vivid. He looked painfully young, as raw as a gash, lodged awkwardly out of his element. Gunnlaugur liked what he saw. Hafloí would learn. His fangs would grow, his pelt would grey, his spikiness would soften. Until then he would be good for them all. They would remember what it had been like when they had been the same way, stuffed smart with puerile bellicosity, vigour, petulance, enchantment – and with the galaxy laid supine before them, begging for glorious conquest.

'So?' pressed Váltyr.

Gunnlaugur looked back at the blademaster.

'Not yet, *sverdhjera*,' he said. 'We are not all here.'

'What?' blurted Hafloí, speaking out of turn, not yet knowing his place in the order. 'There's more of you?'

Gunnlaugur looked up, over the heads of the assembled pack, back towards the low, arched entrance to the chamber. As his eyes fell on the armoured figure standing beneath it a brief tremor ran through him.

Fifty-seven years. Still, I would recognise that outline anywhere.

'Just one more,' Gunnlaugur said, his voice soft.

Baldr was the next to sense it. He whirled round, his eyes alive with joy.

'Gyrfalkon!' he cried, rushing over to greet the man under the arch.

Olgeir was next, shoving Baldr aside to envelop Ingvar in a crushing, armour-denting hug, dragging him into the chamber like a hunter hauling his prize.

Ingvar staggered out of Olgeir's rib-cracking embrace, laughing, emerging into the firelight only for the crowd of bodies to obscure him again. Váltyr approached and gave him an awkward handclasp. Baldr clapped him on the back. Hafloí hung back.

Amid all of that Gunnlaugur caught a clear glimpse of Ingvar's eye, just for an instant. It looked a little harder, a little greyer. Otherwise it was the same, the face he had spent mortal lifetimes in the company of.

'Enough,' he said eventually, stilling the noise and movement. Despite himself, a broad smile creased across his face.

Now that I see you, despite everything, it feels good to have you back.

Gunnlaugur walked up to Ingvar. For a moment, the two of them stared at one another, caught in the awkwardness of the moment. Gunnlaugur was the bigger, the broader, his armour more decorated with hunt-trophies and his pelts richer and more numerous. For all that, there was little to choose between them. There never had been.

'Brother,' said Gunnlaugur.

Ingvar inclined his head cautiously. '*Vaerangi*,' he replied.

No one else spoke. Baldr stopped smiling and looked warily between the two of them. Váltyr watched carefully. The air in the chamber seemed to thicken, like the humid precursor to a fire-summer storm.

Then Gunnlaugur moved. He flung his arms wide, grabbing Ingvar and pulling him into a rough embrace.

'We have not been whole without you,' he said, low enough so that only Ingvar heard him.

Ingvar returned the embrace, and the ceramite of his armour grated against that of Gunnlaugur. His gesture spoke of relief, of appreciation.

'That is good, brother,' he said. 'I yearned to hear it.'

Then he freed himself, stood back and regarded the pack before him. The hard lines of his face softened a little.

'But who is this?' he asked, smiling. 'We take on children now?'

Gunnlaugur gestured for Hafloí to approach.

'Careful,' he warned. 'The whelp has claws. Hafloí, this is the Gyrfalkon. He once served with us. Now he's back.'

Hafloí bowed stiffly. 'I know the name,' he said. 'You bear *dausvjer*.'

Ingvar inclined his head. 'So I do.'

'There is a wyrd on that blade.'

'That's what they say.'

'Then it should not have left the Aett.'

Olgeir took a step fowards, ready to cuff Hafloí. Jorundur chuckled darkly as Ingvar raised his hand, halting Olgeir.

'Perhaps,' Ingvar said, fixing Hafloí with dead eyes. 'But the sword goes where I go. If you have an issue with that, you may take it up with us both.'

Gunnlaugur rolled his eyes. 'Blood of Russ,' he said. 'Just introduced and already spoiling for a fight.' He shoved Hafloí away from Ingvar, sending the Blood Claw staggering. 'You'll fit in fine.'

Then he turned to the rest of the pack. Seven-strong, back to something like combat strength. They looked to him expectantly.

'We are complete,' said Gunnlaugur. 'Just as we should be. Now listen: here's what we're going to do.'

Ingvar tried to concentrate on what Gunnlaugur was saying. He felt his palms grow slick under the lining of his gauntlets. Hearing the old voices again, the old smells, it had hit him harder than he'd expected.

They hadn't judged him. None of them had the reproach in their eyes that he'd feared. Well, Váltyr perhaps, but he had always been a cold one.

It was hard not to watch them sidelong, to observe the way they related to one another, to examine them like he'd seen biologis adepts examine xenos corpses on dissection tables. They were relaxed in one another's presence, just as he had been once. Onyx Squad, for all its combined killing power, had always felt like an artificial creation. Járnhamar had once been home; for those who had remained, it still was.

Ingvar's wandering gaze flickered up to the head of the *drekkar*. That eyeless stare was as familiar to him as everything else. He remembered it watching over them before each mission, gazing coldly into empty space as objectives were outlined and timescales plotted. The *drakk's* face had never been anything other than impassive to him then. Now, on his return, it seemed almost benevolent.

In the past it had been Hjortur's voice that had rung around the chamber. Hearing Gunnlaugur's growly tones in its place was odd. For a while, it felt like a violation. Only later, as Ingvar watched the others take it in their stride, did it come to seem natural.

Gunnlaugur spoke with a coarse, blunt authority. He had always been confident, but now it was different. A warrior spoke one way when his own life was at stake; when he had the whole pack to think about, his tone changed.

It suits you, brother, thought Ingvar. *You have grown.*

'Ras Shakeh,' said Gunnlaugur, flicking the switch on a palm-held device and sending a flame-red hololith spinning up into the air before him. 'Shrineworld of the Ras subsector. It is under the Ecclesiarchy with distant support from the Adulators Chapter, though our brothers have declared themselves no longer able to contribute to its defence. They are stretched, I am told, to breaking point.'

Jorundur snorted, shook his head, but said nothing.

'Before the Ras worlds were taken under the control of the Imperial Cult,' continued Gunnlaugur, 'it is said that an arrangement once existed between them and Fenris.'

'By who?' said Váltyr.

'By Blackmane,' replied Gunnlaugur, tersely. 'And by Ulrik, and by Grimnar, and whoever else remembers what in Hel we were doing five thousand years ago.'

Gunnlaugur's tone gave away what he thought of what he was being asked to convey. Ingvar felt his spirits sag. After the euphoria of his return, it looked like the task ahead of them would not be glory-filled. It sounded perilously close to routine garrison work.

'This is not garrison work,' said Gunnlaugur. 'It is the beginning of an offensive, a multi-front assault into abandoned space covering three subsectors. We are to be part of it.'

Olgeir nodded in approval. 'Good,' he grunted.

Baldr looked thoughtful. 'Under whose command?' he asked.

'A warmaster will be appointed,' said Gunnlaugur. 'Don't get carried away: this will be years in the making. We are the advance wave, sent to secure worlds prior to major troop movements. For a while it'll be just us.'

Jorundur chuckled. 'That's not garrison work?'

'We won't be sitting on our arses,' Gunnlaugur insisted. 'There's enemy activity on the fringes, more coordinated then normal, more frequent. We'll have hunting to do.'

Baldr's expression hadn't changed. He looked pensive.

Ingvar could sense the wariness in the room from the others. They weren't stupid. They could tell when they were being shunted off to a nothing-mission.

'Who governs this world?' asked Baldr.

'The Adepta Sororitas,' said Gunnlaugur. 'The Order of the Wounded Heart.'

The silence of the chamber was broken by a collection of low growls, noisy expectorations and bitter-edged laughs.

'Enough,' snapped Gunnlaugur. 'They're servants of the Allfather.'

'They're servants of the Inquisition,' said Jorundur.

'They're crazy,' grumbled Olgeir. 'With no love for us.'

Baldr smiled softly.

'When did you last care about being loved, great one?'

Olgeir grinned, and patted the battered casing of *sigrún*.

'When I was given this,' he said. 'Not since.'

'The Sisters,' said Váltyr, acidly. 'They know it's us that's coming? They asked for us?'

Gunnlaugur sighed. 'They'd take anyone. They're hard-pressed, just like everyone else. But, yes, they know it's us. Grimnar's sent word to the canoness. Get used to it, brothers. This is who we'll be fighting with.'

Jorundur shook his shaggy head. 'I can cope with Sisters,' he said. 'I can't cope with garrison work.'

'Hel's *teeth*,' hissed Gunnlaugur. 'How many times? This is a combat mission.'

'Against what?'

'As yet unidentified. Possible cult incursions. We're waiting for more detail.'

Jorundur spat on the ground.

'Sounds terrifying,' he said.

Gunnlaugur looked distastefully down at the pool of spittle on the stone.

'We leave in less than thirty-six hours,' he said. 'Use the time well. Ensure your armour has been sanctified by the Priests and look to your weapons. Take the transit-time to reach combat fitness. That is all.'

An awkward silence followed. Ingvar remembered how it had been in the past, when Hjortur's exhortations would have filled the chamber with echoing roars, and they would have raised their weapons as one, slavering for the coming blood-terror.

It was muted this time. Olgeir did his best, with a low, rattling snarl, but no one else took it up.

Gunnlaugur didn't try to summon up more enthusiasm. His customary belligerence had a darker edge to it, something that Ingvar didn't remember seeing in him before. As he turned to leave the chamber, his eye caught Ingvar's.

'Not what you're used to,' he said. 'Work like this.'

It wasn't.

I have seen hive-fleets block out the light of nebulae. I have seen the spawning fields where orks are born. I have seen metal legions rise silently from millennial tombs. I have seen living starships orbit the hearts of forgotten empires.

Ingvar shrugged.

'There'll be hunting,' he said. 'I'm used to that.'

Before leaving, each one of the pack came up to Ingvar. They were curious, asking about what he'd done while on duty with *the others* – they never called the Deathwatch by its name – how many kills he'd made, what sagas he'd recorded for inclusion in the annals of the Mountain. Váltyr asked him little, Olgeir a lot.

Jorundur enquired about the Onyx skull pendant he wore around his neck.

'A record of service,' said Ingvar, clasping it self-consciously. 'That and the bolter – it's all I kept.'

They seemed to understand that he couldn't say much. They seemed pleased that he was back. As they spoke to him, probing for information, laughing at his stilted responses, some of the awkwardness between them faded.

'You'll have picked up bad habits,' said Olgeir, his eyes sparkling. 'We'll have to beat them out of you.'

'Try it,' Ingvar replied.

Gunnlaugur left the chamber first, accompanied by Váltyr. Before he left, he clasped Ingvar firmly by the arm.

'We'll speak properly, brother,' he said. 'When time is less pressing, we'll talk.'

Ingvar nodded. 'We should,' he said.

Jorundur was next, curtailing his questions to go and work on *Vuokho*, muttering as he left about the stupidity of taking it out so soon. He didn't smile exactly, but his bitter face lifted and the bruise-coloured lines under his deep eyes smoothed out just a little.

'He's not looked this happy in a while,' observed Olgeir.

'It's all relative,' said Ingvar.

'He'll never admit it, but he missed you. Hel, *I* missed you.'

'It's good to see you too, great one.'

Then Olgeir departed as well, taking the Blood Claw with him for yet more intensive training. Hafloí didn't say a word to Ingvar, but shot him a sullen look of challenge from over his shoulder.

That left Ingvar alone with Baldr. The heavy footfalls of the others faded into the darkness, and the chamber fell quiet.

Baldr smiled. It was a plain, easy smile.

'You've made an enemy there,' he said.

Ingvar spread his hands in a gesture of resignation.

'A fearsome one,' he agreed.

'So, then. Tell me what you see.'

Ingvar hesitated. 'What do you mean?'

'Járnhamar,' said Baldr. 'Tell me how we've changed.'

'Tínd is gone. Ulf and Svafnir are gone. I'll be honest, I never liked Tínd, but I'm sorry for the others.'

Baldr raised a sceptical eyebrow. 'Is that all?'

Ingvar sighed. 'Fjolnir, do not do this. Not now.'

Baldr smiled. 'Forgive me,' he said. 'You are newly returned. There will be time for questions later. But you do not deceive me: you see what I see.'

'And what is that?'

Baldr looked serious again.

'You see Váltyr hanging in Gunnlaugur's shadow, unwilling to stay in it and unable to leave it. You see Jorundur turning in on himself, bitter at missed chances for glory. You see Heavy-hand's laughter becoming thinner since he no longer has Ulf to spar with.'

Ingvar sighed. He had no appetite for hearing how the pack had been ravaged in his absence.

'And what of you, Baldr?' he asked. 'I suppose nothing troubles you.'

For a moment, something flickered across Baldr's face – a faint play of unease, whispering around his golden eyes.

'There's trouble for all of us,' he said. Then he smiled again. 'I knew you were coming back. Something told me you were. Why is that? It's been decades, and I knew you were coming back.'

'Lucky guess.'

'There's no luck. There's fate, and there's will. If the will is mightier, then you carve out a life for yourself. If fate is mightier, then you're carried along, twisting like a spar on the flood.'

Baldr stopped talking, suddenly tense, as if he'd said more than he'd planned to.

'I knew you were coming back,' he said again. 'Why is that?'

Ingvar tried to shrug off the question, though Baldr's manner unnerved him. There was an intensity to him that he didn't recognise.

'You sound like a Priest,' he said. 'Stop it.'

Baldr reached for a pendant hanging around his belt then. He held it up: a bleached avian skull suspended on links of metal. Iron bearings had been hammered into the eye sockets, and a rough rune – *sforja* – scratched on the bone.

'Do you remember this?' Baldr asked, letting the hanging pendant turn slowly.

As Ingvar's eyes rested on it, he felt a sudden pang of memory. He reached out for it, letting the fragile skull clink against the palm of his gauntlet.

'I had forgotten,' he said softly. 'By Russ, I am sorry, brother. I had forgotten.'

Baldr lowered the pendant into Ingvar's hand, letting the iron links coil around one another.

'Don't be sorry. Take it back. You were right – it has a wyrd on it. It has protected me, and a part of me lives in it. For all that, it knows you are the owner.'

Ingvar took it and held it up against the red light of the braziers. He remembered giving it to Baldr as a token of their friendship on the night he'd left Fenris. Back then he'd had no expectation of seeing it again. It had been a piece of his life in the Rout that he'd left behind, a splinter of his being that wouldn't follow him into his new life.

A *sálskjoldur*; a soul-ward, a fragment, a remnant, something to cling on to against the coming of Morkai.

'I had not felt myself,' Ingvar said, gazing at the bone as it spun before him. 'Not until now. This is the final piece of me, the presence that I left.' He looked back at Baldr. 'It was given freely. I have no right to take it back.'

Baldr nodded. 'I know,' he said. 'But what are rights between brothers? It has been calling to you. It is yours.'

Ingvar regarded Baldr carefully.

'You asked me what has changed,' he said. 'You have. You are more solemn, more serious.'

He collected the coiled pendant in his fist and placed it around his neck. It hung down across his breastplate, nestling next to the Onyx skull amid the crevasses of his embossed armour.

The two symbols occupied the same space uneasily: one a totem of Fenris's strange and ancient magic, the other a symbol of clandestine Inquisitorial power.

'But I thank you for this,' Ingvar said, taking Baldr's hand and clasping it firmly. 'We have always been shield-brothers, you and I. We shall be again. Of all of them, I suffered your absence the most.'

Baldr returned the grip firmly, almost hungrily.

'We have suffered without you, Gyrfalkon,' he said. 'We need you back. You will make us whole again.'

Ingvar released his grip. Talk like that made him uneasy; Gunnlaugur had used the same words.

'We shall see,' was all he said.

Chapter Five

The storm howled up from the Hunter's Pass, bringing snow-swollen clouds boiling over the sheer passes. The mountain's shoulders were lost in a haze of churning ice-white, piling up drifts against the old causeways and choking the ravines below.

Only at the summit of the Fang, high above the surrounding peaks of the Asaheim range, was the air clear. Thunderheads circled below the Valgard landing stages, angry and majestic, buffeting and snagging against the granite cliffs like breaking black-foamed waves.

Gunnlaugur studied the maelstrom remotely from the shelter of *Vuokho*'s cockpit, still waiting on the hangar apron.

'A big one,' he observed, watching the sweeps of brume and blizzard rotate on the auspex.

Jorundur, strapped in beside him, flicked the final launch controls on the console.

'Fenris always gives a send-off,' he said, frowning as he concentrated on the pre-launch sequence. 'She never likes to see her children leave.'

Gunnlaugur grunted, and sat back in his seat. Valgard hangar 34-7 stretched away from them, perched right at the pinnacle of the mountain and open to the elements at the eastern end. A maze of red lights blinked on and off, half hidden behind the veils of gusting sleet that spilled in from the entrance. He could hear the grind of refuelling tankers running clear, and the shouts of kaerls as blast-hatches were slammed and locked.

'Try not to kill us on exit, eh?' came Olgeir's cheerful voice over the comm. 'Nice and smooth now, Old Dog, nice and smooth.'

The rest of the pack were in the aft crew hold, below the cockpit. Gunnlaugur could hear coarse laughter in the background. That improved his mood. For all their complaints about the mission, the pack were glad to be under way and doing something, and that was reassuring.

'You want to fly, *hálfvit*?' replied Jorundur, his voice sour. He activated the main drive system, and a throaty, sclerotic roar broke out from below.

Olgeir's bellow of laughter made the comm-link crackle with feedback.

'Any signal from the frigate?' asked Gunnlaugur, shutting off the feed and watching the last of the ground crew scuttle out of view. The whole structure of the gunship shuddered as the engines gunned into their hammering rhythm. A messy tide of oil-speckled, fire-dotted smoke poured across the apron from the exhausts.

'Not a thing,' said Jorundur, easing power to the atmospheric retros. With a jerk, *Vuokho* lurched up from the rockcrete floor, buoyed by a raging cushion of flame and smog. 'But it'll be there. Believe me, no one else will have taken it.'

The lumen-bank mounted over the hangar entrance clicked off, and a whole series of indicators on the gunship's control console went green. The cockpit's head-up display flickered into life, overlaying a jumble of runes and vectors across the grimy plexiglass viewers. The whine from the main drives intensified, ready for the explosion of energy that would hurl them clear of the mountain.

'It's a decent ship,' said Gunnlaugur, bracing for detonation. 'Blackwing-class.'

'That what they told you?' Jorundur laughed. 'I've seen it. It's a heap of shit.'

Before Gunnlaugur could reply, Jorundur switched power to the main thrusters. *Vuokho* pounced forwards, blazing down the short hangar length before thundering clear of the mountainside. They cleared the cliff-face in a bloom of evaporating snow and engine backwash. Jorundur took the gunship out wide before banking hard, bringing the prow up and feeding more power to the main thrusters.

Gunnlaugur glanced down out of the port viewer. Below, already receding fast, was the pinnacle of the mountain, crusted with a dirty layer of sensoria towers, pockmarked hangar gates and defence batteries. The summit speared up through the moving layers of bruise-dark cloud, a lone bastion of rock and ice amid a continent's-worth of seething squalls.

It looked besieged. It looked as if the rage of the planet had closed in on it, throttling it, sweeping up to grab it by the neck and snuff the life from it.

Gunnlaugur knew the history of the mountain, at least as it was related by the overlapping and semi-legendary saga-tellings of the fire halls. He knew that the Fang had been besieged more than once: by the forces of the great enemy, by armadas sent by the Ecclesiarchy in the civil wars of the past, by the Inquisition itself.

Sky Warriors still boasted of those battles, chanting them in ritual war-rites or hearing them declaimed by the hot light of burning torches. Gunnlaugur loved them. He'd learned the Bjornssaga from the skjalds, word by word. He knew other legends by heart, other songs, some of them older than the Fang itself, their origins lost in the violent years of humanity's first stumbling amongst the stars.

He smiled as he remembered the stanzas. Even as the landscape dropped far below him, dwindling into a white haze, his mouth moved silently, speaking the eternal words soundlessly.

> *The sun turns black, earth sinks in the sea,*
> *The hot stars down from heaven are whirled;*
> *Fierce grows the steam and the life-feeding flame,*
> *Till fire leaps high about heaven itself.*

Seeing the proud spike of the mountain below made his hearts swell. That place was eternal, founded by gods and guarded by savage angels, an inviolable citadel amid a darkening galaxy. It had stood for millennia before his birth and would do for millennia after. Other worlds might fall into corruption or ruin, but the Fang would remain unsullied forever.

That was what he had always believed. That was what he still believed. *So it ever has been,* he breathed, watching the sweep of the planet's atmosphere drop into a glistening curve. *So it ever shall be.*

Gunnlaugur knew that he could never have done what Ingvar had done. He was body and soul of the *Fenryka*: the most deadly, the most faithful, the most potent of the Allfather's many servants. No others compared with the Wolves of Fenris. No life compared to that of the Sky Warriors, lived without compromise or quarter, thrust into the white-hot core of combat, gifted the mightiest weapons of humanity, charged with its ultimate defence where all others faltered.

Gunnlaugur respected his brothers in other Chapters. He had fought alongside many of them, and recognised their skill and devotion. He had

fought with mortal men too, many of whom had fallen with honour.
But they were not *Fenryka*. They were not Russ's sons.

Much do I know, and more can see.
The fetters will burst, and the wolf run free.

Gunnlaugur smiled. War was coming again. He was leaving the Fang, taking murder out across the sea of stars. Whatever else had transpired, that was good. It was the proper state of things.

'Clearing the grid, *vaerangi*,' said Jorundur, his voice barely audible over the roar of the engines. 'We'll get visual in a moment.'

Gunnlaugur looked out ahead. The milky grey of the sky had faded to black as the atmosphere thinned to nothing. Familiar constellations emerged into pure clarity, obstructed only by dozens of gunmetal-grey defence platforms in orbit above the planet. The closest of them was less than a kilometre away and hung massively in the void, the marker lights on its gun turrets blinking in the dark.

'I don't see the ship,' said Gunnlaugur, scrutinising the view forwards as the platform slipped by beneath them.

'I've got a fix,' said Jorundur. 'We're not at full tilt yet. You know this thing shouldn't even be flying?'

Gunnlaugur ignored the snipe. For as long as he'd known Jorundur he'd been complaining about the readiness of the ships he flew. He'd have found something to complain about if Russ himself had given him *Hrafnkel* to pilot.

'There it is,' announced Jorundur, gesturing to a glowing rune on the viewer display. 'Take a look at the realview. How sharp are your eyes?'

Gunnlaugur narrowed them, scanning the velvet darkness. For a long time, he saw nothing. Hundreds of vessels, from tiny system runners to gigantic capital ships, occupied the Fenris system at any one time, but few lingered for long in the planet's shadow.

Then he saw something glinting in the empty gloom like a sliver of alabaster. As Jorundur steered the Thunderhawk closer, details emerged.

It was small for a frigate, of an old design. The engine-level on it looked big; its weapons array looked small. Its shell was black, with old Rout images painted on the flanks in chipped yellow and grey. Its bridge was set lower than usual, surrounded by charred bulkheads. Faint plumes of gas vented from something jagged and reflective under its hull.

A single word, *Undrider*, had been etched along its side.

Gunnlaugur pursed his lips. 'That's the one?'

Jorundur nodded, bringing *Vuokho* to approach speed. As he did so, hangar doors on the receiving ship slid slowly open, spilling warm yellow light into the void.

'I'm told it's fast,' Jorundur said.

Gunnlaugur felt deflated. 'Right,' he said.

Jorundur smiled in vindication.

Heap of shit.

'Welcome aboard, lord,' said the *Undrider*'s master.

Gunnlaugur grunted acknowledgement, barely looking at him.

The master, an experienced kaerl rivenmaster named Torek Bjargborn, used to the perfunctory ways of Sky Warriors, didn't miss a beat.

'We're ready to go, on your order.'

Gunnlaugur's eyes roved around the command chamber. The pack stood alongside him. None of them looked impressed.

It was a small, cramped place by the standards of interstellar craft. The captain's throne was surrounded by concentric banks of cogitator stations. A dais had been raised behind it on which the pack had congregated. The floor was polished black marble. Cracks in it had been repaired with a dull grey aggregate.

Beyond and above the throne was a dome of bronze-lined crystal viewers, thick with tarnishing. As on all such ships, a low murmur of machine-clicks and human muttering provided a constant accompaniment to the grind of the sub-warp engines. An aroma of sacred oils rose from the deck, spiced with an undertone of human sweat and engine lubricant. Servitors, many hard-wired into consoles, clattered away at menial functions. There were more of them than usual, and fewer human crew.

'What's your complement status, master?' asked Jorundur.

Bjargborn didn't hesitate.

'Twelve per cent down, lord. But we do have extra servitor provision. Demands on the fleet are heavy, I'm told.'

The look on Jorundur's face said all that needed to be said.

Gunnlaugur turned to Váltyr. He gave a half-shrug.

'It only has to get us there,' he said.

'Can it even do that?' replied Váltyr.

Bjargborn had the stomach to look affronted.

'It will, lords,' he said. 'And back again. It may not look much, but it's voidworthy, and it's fast.'

'Yes, I'd heard that,' said Gunnlaugur. 'Very well, master, you have the order. Take us out to the jump-point. We'll cross the veil as soon as we can.'

Bjargborn thumped his chest, bowed, and resumed his seat in the throne.

Around him the machine chatter picked up in volume.

Jorundur's nostrils flared. 'This ship stinks.'

'All ships stink,' said Baldr.

'Not like this one.'

'I've known worse.'

Gunnlaugur ignored the conversation. He walked slowly away from the throne, under the observation dome, looking out and up at the stars. The constellation of the Hewer was visible, framed by bronze.

In a few hours that view would be gone, replaced by heavy lead shutters to blank out the madness of the empyrean. On arrival at Ras Shakeh it would be replaced by an alien set of constellations, each with its own name in another language.

The underpowered ship irritated him. It pricked at his pride, wearing at it like acid on metal.

We cannot be that short-handed. It is an insult.

He flexed his fingers, trying to let his annoyance flow out of him. It would be some time before he could exorcise the emotion through combat.

Hjortur would have railed against this. He would have howled the Fang down until he got what he wanted.

He closed his fists, squeezing hard against the inner membrane of his gauntlets.

He could be a poor judge. There will be a time to howl; this is not it.

Gunnlaugur felt the floor beneath him vibrate as the frigate began to power up. That did something to ease his mood, and he felt his clenched hands relax a little.

At last.

For what it was worth, for what little it meant to him, the mission was underway.

Ingvar didn't sleep.

Warp travel always had the same effect. He felt nauseous, unquiet, unable to meditate, unable to think, unable to do much beyond prowl back and forth in his cell, his fangs bared.

A long time ago, back when he'd been a Blood Claw, he'd asked Hrald, the Wolf Priest, why passage through the empyrean affected him so badly, whether it spoke of some taint or flaw within him. The old hook-nosed warrior had looked deep into his eyes for some time before clapping him roughly on the shoulder.

'Who knows?' he'd said. 'The warp – it's Hel. You should hate it. Only worry if you come to like it.'

Ever since then he'd suffered in isolation, keeping himself locked away, breaking off contact with his brothers until the cramps and the dizziness faded.

Jocelyn had been scornful of that. The Dark Angel had been the one he'd had most trouble with in Onyx. The others had all rubbed along together well enough, but the pale-skinned son of Caliban had been difficult: proud, high-strung, close.

'Why does it make you sick, Space Wolf?' Jocelyn had asked him during a jump, his deep eyes suggestive of mockery as much as curiosity.

Distracted by his sickness, Ingvar had growled at him involuntarily. That alone had been a minor humiliation. His squad-brothers needed no extra inclination to think of him as bestial.

'Why does it *not* make you sick, Dark Angel?' he'd replied. 'Unless your kin feel at home here. I've heard that said.'

Jocelyn had laughed that off, not deigning to show anger. Later, Ingvar regretted the exchange. Matters never came to head between them after that; equally, they never succeeded in breaking down that fog of early suspicion.

They became stereotypes of their Chapters with one another: the snarling Wolf, the haughty Angel. They should have done better, perhaps. It would have been nice to transcend expectations.

Ingvar reflected on that, alone in the practice cages of the *Undrider*, blade in hand, his stomach churning. He moved the sword back and forth, turning it under the harsh light of the lumens, finding some solace in the familiar rituals.

He wondered where Jocelyn was now. Perhaps he still served with the Deathwatch. Perhaps he was back on the Rock, rediscovering the ways of his old Chapter, just as he had done. Perhaps he was dead.

Ingvar would never know. He had no special access to information, no back-channel route to the Inquisition. They had severed things completely, rendering him as ignorant of future operations as he had been before they'd first come to Fenris to take him.

For all that, Ingvar found it hard to conceive of the universe without Jocelyn's sardonic presence in it. The Angel would be fighting somewhere, just like the others. All of Onyx Squad would be, scattered to the six corners of the galaxy, alone again, trying to relearn old lives, trying to forget what they'd seen together.

'Still don't like it?'

Ingvar didn't turn around. He'd not heard Váltyr enter the cage-room. That had been sloppy.

He completed the manoeuvre. His blade flickered in the semi-dark.

'Nothing changes,' he said, watching sidelong as Váltyr moved into his field of vision.

The blademaster wore his armour but went helmless, just as Ingvar did. *Holdbítr* was sheathed at his side.

'I couldn't sleep either,' said Váltyr. 'This ship creaks and moans like a skiff in a gale.'

Ingvar said nothing. He moved into another manoeuvre, one taught him by Leonides. It was a complicated, difficult switch, something that would seldom be used in real combat, mainly a means of training the mind to work with the blade. The Blood Angels had an interesting philosophy on close combat. As in all things, they valued the aesthetics of a gesture as much as its effect.

Váltyr watched him as he worked, peering through the wire of the training cage.

'You've learned new tricks,' he said. 'That was not taught on Fenris.'

Ingvar let *dausvjer* fall away.

'Too artful for the likes of us.'

Váltyr smiled. 'Don't let Gunnlaugur hear you say that,' he said, reaching for the door to the cage. 'May I?'

Ingvar nodded, though he had no appetite for it.

Why are you here? To prove you can still best me? Or worried I've moved beyond you?

Váltyr closed the metal door behind him and drew *holdbítr*. The blade was longer than Ingvar's – straight, double-edged, rune-etched, spell-wound and with its edge honed down to a vanishing point that would hew a Rhino's hide.

It was a fine weapon. It wasn't *dausvjer*.

'I was bored, in your absence,' said Váltyr, swinging the blade around him lazily and taking up position. 'Baldr can handle himself, but it's all hammers and bolters with the others. I missed our sparring.'

Ingvar pulled his sword into guard. He hadn't missed their sparring. He'd always been able to appreciate the skill of the blademaster, but had never loved going up against him. Váltyr's fetish for the weapon was something that disturbed him. A blade was for use, not for worship.

'Nothing too strenuous,' Ingvar said, watching the tip of *holdbítr* warily. 'Just loosening the arms.'

Váltyr nodded, and started to circle him. His lean face caught the shadows, and the pinned black in his golden eyes seemed to shrink into nothing.

'Your stance has changed,' he said.

'Has it?'

When Váltyr moved, it was characteristically quick. He seemed to have the facility to leap from total immobility into action with nothing in between. It was a fearsome talent, made all the more lethal by his habitual coolness. Ingvar had seen Váltyr eviscerate opponents before they'd even known he was planning to move.

Holdbítr swooped, and *dausvjer* flickered up to meet it. The two lengths of metal clashed, sparking from one another.

Váltyr didn't press the attack. He pulled away instantly, dancing back, resuming guard.

'Who fought best?' he asked. 'Can you tell me names? Chapters?'

Ingvar kept his eyes fixed on Váltyr's hands. Watching the blade was an error; the hands were where the attacks came from.

'I learned that such things are meaningless,' he said, shadowing carefully. 'We all had our gifts.'

Váltyr looked disappointed. 'Diplomatic,' he said, before bursting into a flurry of attacks.

Ingvar met them all, and the swords spun around one another.

There was a kind of raw perfection there. They were alone. No one witnessed their skill, their neatly matched violence. In the past, Ingvar would have found that a waste; boastful Fenrisian souls liked the open display of prowess. After long years fighting in the shadows, locked in a quiet world of enforced secrecy, that urge had abated.

He wondered if Váltyr felt the same way. The blademaster had always celebrated purity. That might have been the key to him. Or perhaps it was something more. Perhaps Váltyr needed the reassurance of it all, the gentle, repeated reminders of his uniqueness.

Holdbítr jabbed down, held double-handed. Ingvar darted away from it, letting the accumulated power in the strike dissipate. Then he pressed in close, swinging *dausvjer* hard.

It didn't trouble Váltyr. Nothing seemed to.

'I don't think you're any faster,' Váltyr observed, his voice as calm as ever as he worked.

'Speed is not the only thing,' said Ingvar.

Those words were Callimachus's.

'But it *is*, Gyrfalkon. Move fast enough, and the gods themselves will bleed.'

Váltyr demonstrated the point. He came back at Ingvar in a spinning, dazzling series of rotations and cuts.

For the first time, Ingvar struggled. He let the blows jar against his parries, attempting nothing more than defence, retreating back across the cage step by step, riding out the storm.

'Blood of Russ,' hissed Ingvar. 'Does this have to–'

Váltyr silenced him with a vicious left-right swipe that nearly hurled *dausjver* from Ingvar's grasp. Then he piled in again, mixing up standard thrusts with the chaotic, freeform bladework he loved.

'Just keep up,' he said. 'If you can.'

Ingvar crashed against the wall of the cage, scraping along it as he fended off the incoming storm.

So that's what this is, he thought. *You are here to remind me of the order of the pack.*

Ingvar shoved clear of the cage edge and moved back towards the centre. Keeping *holdbítr* at bay took up every last dram of his physical skill. Facing Váltyr's expertise again was a chilling experience.

'Show me something new, then,' said Váltyr. '*Unnerve* me.'

That was when it happened. The moment was over in less than a heartbeat, less than a thought, but the clarity of it was breathtaking.

Ingvar saw the gap, opened by Váltyr's enthusiasm. Leonides would have called it a half-breach or *sotano*, the sudden thrust upwards at a three-quarter angle, jutting past the guard and beneath the breastplate.

The twist to get there was excruciating, too narrow and confined for all but the sharpest hands. But he knew, in that instant, that he could do it. He knew he could stab the blade through, blooding him, throwing him off, ending the fight.

Ingvar had never beaten Váltyr before, not truly, not when he was concentrating.

So when he pulled back, the fact that he hadn't made the move was a choice, not an omission. It was not a mistake. He had not erred. Another decision had been made.

Váltyr hammered away at him, his sword-edge smearing into a silver gauze of movement. Two, three more strikes, and Ingvar was rammed against the cage-edge again, his room for movement closed down.

Ingvar looked down. *Holdbítr* was pressed against his throat, lodged up to the skin.

Váltyr smiled. 'Close, this time,' he said. 'You still know how to move.'

He let his blade fall away, leaving a thin line of blood against Ingvar's flesh. Ingvar reached up to feel it, wincing.

Váltyr strolled away from him, swishing his sword idly through the air. Ingvar watched him go.

'You missed something, Eversson,' said Váltyr. 'I made a mistake, right there at the end.'

Ingvar sheathed *dausvjer*.

'Didn't catch it,' he said. 'You were too fast. Again.'

Váltyr laughed. 'We should do this more often. Perhaps you could teach me some of those Blood Angels tricks.'

Ingvar nodded. 'Surely. When this is healed.'

Váltyr bowed, with a victor's gratitude. 'Perhaps I'll sleep now,' he said, opening the door to the cage and stepping through it. 'You should do likewise.'

'I'll try.'

Ingvar watched Váltyr go. There was a slight spring in the *sverdhjera's* step – barely perceptible, but definitely there.

Alone again, Ingvar drew his blade and looked at it for a moment. Then he stepped into guard and executed the *sotano*. Perfectly.

I could have done it. I could have halted him.

Callimachus came to mind again, soft-spoken, courteous, reserved.

'Why didn't you strike him?' Ingvar had demanded, back when Jocelyn had initiated yet another challenge to the squad leader's authority.

Callimachus had looked at him with a tolerant, cautious eye, as if weighing up whether a Wolf of Fenris could really be expected to understand such things.

'I was taught this,' he'd said. 'Do not win every battle that you can, only those that you must. I did not wish to shame him.'

'He'll think you're weak.'

'What does that matter? I am not.'

Ingvar looked up, out towards the door that Váltyr had taken.

The decision had been the right one. Váltyr did not need another reason to resent his return; the inevitable tension between them would be eased by his victory.

For all that, frustration burned away within him. He was too much of a Fenrisian not to chafe against defeat, real or imagined. Before Onyx, he would never have willingly lost a fight.

Before Onyx, he would not have had the skill to avoid it.

These contradictions will grow, he thought. *I will become a contradiction.*

He knew he wouldn't sleep. The hours would pass in wakefulness, made sharper by the knowledge of his concession to another's pride.

He started to move again, forcing his aching muscles back into practice strikes, making them move faster than before, more savagely.

I could have done it.

The sword danced in the dark, tracing tighter arcs than ever, propelled by his sullen anger.

He imagined Váltyr's face before him, not bright with triumph, but open-eyed with surprise.

I could have done it.

* * *

Baldr woke suddenly. His eyes snapped open, staring into perfect dark.

He lay on his back, breathing heavily. He could feel the layers of sweat on his skin, chilling rapidly. Both his hearts were working hard, beating out a tremulous pattern that he could hear as well as feel.

'Lumen,' he whispered.

A single globe flickered into life, casting a bleached glow over the narrow cell. It showed up pressed metal walls pocked with bands of rivets; a mesh floor; a low ceiling; a single bunk, worked out of a solid slab of stone.

Baldr didn't move. He watched, he breathed, waiting for his body to recover.

He could still hear the echoes. The voices were very faint, hovering just on the edge of hearing, but they were still there. He hadn't been able to understand them even in his dreams. Now they ran through his waking mind, cycling in an incessant babble of half-sensical syllables and phonemes.

He reached up for the warding pendant at his chest, only then remembering that he'd given it to Ingvar. His fingers closed over emptiness.

That may have been rash.

The grind of the engines hammered away far below, thrumming up the walls of the cell and making them shiver. The hum of it was maddening after a while unless you could tune it out, which he couldn't.

That is surely the problem. I cannot tune them out. I must learn to ignore them.

Baldr knew he should have sought out Stormcaller while on Fenris. The problem had become too intrusive, too frequent, and he'd long since passed the point where guidance had become necessary.

He wasn't even sure why he'd resisted it. Not fear, not of a straightforward kind. Perhaps caution, or maybe an unwillingness to trouble the great ones on account of half-remembered nightmares and unidentifiable inklings.

It was worse when in the warp. Many minds had strange dreams while in the warp. Baldr knew that Ingvar suffered, and he had considered confiding in him. Years ago he would have done so without hesitation, but now, after so much time and space had come between them, things were not so easy.

He opened his mouth, taking a slow draught of cold air. His second heart stopped beating. His first returned to its normal rate.

He could hear the activity of the ship on the decks around, above and below him. Kaerls trudged down corridors, filtration units wheezed as they pushed recycled air around, slaved stabiliser systems ticked over gently, emitting occasional chittering bursts as the *Undrider*'s machine core instructed them to adjust some parameter or other.

It felt like being in the belly of a single giant organism.

He pulled himself up onto his elbows. No more sleep would come to him that night. His clammy hair fell in lank strands around his face. He lifted a hand up to his eyes, and saw sweat glistening on the flesh. He watched a line of moisture run down the curved surface of his palm, leaving a thin trail like rain on glass.

Things would be easier once out of the empyrean. Perhaps a stint of garrison work, leavened with manageable combat missions, would be beneficial. Dull, perhaps, but restorative.

Baldr let his hand fall back to the bunk. The sweat on his skin evaporated fast, chilling him. He didn't reach for a cloth to wipe it clear – his body was more than capable of adjusting. In any case, the cold would do him good. It would introduce some clarity.

He lowered himself back down, resting his head again. His open eyes stared, defocused, up at the ceiling.

Dull, but restorative.

I should not hope for such things.

It would be easier once out of the empyrean.

Chapter Six

'We are coming through now, lord.'

Bjargborn's voice betrayed some of measure of relief. Gunnlaugur guessed it hadn't been easy for him sharing a cramped, poorly-equipped frigate with a pack of prowling, unsatisfied Sky Warriors. He'd done well, all things considered.

'Very good, master,' said Gunnlaugur, slicking his beard down with lacquer ready to receive his helm. 'Bring us in close.'

Gunnlaugur liked mortals. He liked their simplicity and prized their bravery. Kaerls were a tough breed even without genetic manipulation – they stood their ground, they followed orders, they knew how to hold an axe when the situation demanded it. Bjargborn was a good example of the type.

The master swung round in the throne to direct the break back into real space. Ahead of him the lead panels on the observation dome creaked and snapped, ready to withdraw when the bolts were pulled.

The seven members of Járnhamar stood on the dais behind the throne, just as they had done at the start of the warp-transit. All of them wore their armour. Gunnlaugur could sense their eagerness to have earth under their feet again. It was most palpable in Baldr, for some reason. He'd lost his habitual air of unconcern, and looked drained by the warp passage.

'The veil is breaking,' reported Bjargborn. 'Navigator reports that your desire to come in close will be satisfied.'

The *Undrider*'s hull creaked, as if braced against crosswinds. The low grumble of the warp engines cycled down, ready to be replaced by the imminent roar of real space drives.

'Let's get a look at this place, then,' breathed Gunnlaugur, his eyes fixed on the observation dome, ready for the withdrawal of the shields.

A crack echoed up from the frigate's bowels, and the deck trembled. A sound like an elongated scream shuddered across the command chamber, followed by a rushing hiss.

The void drives thundered into life. The ether-screens slammed back into place. For a second, the viewer panes were smeary with snags of false colour. Then they clarified into the deep velvet of the void, punctuated by a pinprick-sharp starfield. In the centre of the display, dead ahead, was a rust-red world scarred by iron-black birthmarks.

The cogitators around the throne burst into life as screeds of data suddenly flooded into the sensoria. Servitors started up their swollen-tongued chattering, and banks of bronze-ringed lights flickered. The *Undrider* was once again in the world of physics and matter.

'Bring her up to approach speed,' ordered Gunnlaugur calmly, walking forwards to Bjargborn's side to get a better look at the view ahead. 'Anything on the auspexes?'

Bjargborn worked smoothly, his fingers running over levers and dials set into the arms of his throne.

'Nothing yet, lord. Translation has been affected with ninety-two per– Ah. We're getting something. Are we getting something? Yes, I've got ship signatures.'

Gunnlaugur felt the hairs on his neck stiffen.

'Show me,' he said.

Behind him, he heard Olgeir's low growl. The sweet tang of kill-urge suddenly pricked in his glands.

'Unencrypted traffic picked up,' reported Bjargborn, flicking a switch to send the feed to bridge-wide audio. 'No location yet.'

Speakers set on either side of the command throne crackled into a fizz of white noise.

Ingvar drew up alongside Gunnlaugur. His grey eyes fixed steadily on the blood-red orb suspended in front of them. His expression was taut.

'Do not broadcast that signal,' he said.

Bjargborn's hands moved to comply, but it was too late. For a few seconds, the fizz dissolved into recognisable word shapes, thick with phlegmy distortion.

'–sccrxxscrt… sfccgh… skeerrs… talemon mon mon morrdar ek'skadderjjul… nergal alech frarrjar… ach h'jar nergal–'

The feed broke off.

'How many ships?' Gunnlaugur demanded.

'One, lord,' said Bjargborn. His face was white. He didn't understand the words, but he knew what kind of mouth uttered them. 'I think.'

Gunnlaugur turned round to face the pack. He felt his blood already beginning to pump.

'Ensure full power to the weapons.' He seized his helm from his belt and lowered it over his head. 'Maintain full speed.'

Járnhamar were moving too. Jorundur took position by the throne, his eyes sparkling with sudden excitement. The others donned helms, twisting them into place with a series of tight hisses.

Gunnlaugur glanced up at the observation dome, scouring the starfield. His animal spirits were active already, priming his muscles, making him alert, speeding his thoughts.

'Find it,' he snarled. 'Then kill it.'

Void battles were strange and varied things. Most were settled over unimaginably vast distances and conducted via the statistical feeds of locator machines, neither captain ever setting eyes on his opponent. Some lasted for months, with ships dropping in and out of the warp in a drawn-out attempt to gain positional advantage. Some were brutally simple – a rammed hull cracking apart in a destructive orgy of engine detonation, an overloaded shield generator causing a cascade of ruinous chain reactions. The variables to consider were immense, the variety inexhaustible.

Which was why Jorundur enjoyed it. No motive cogitator had the imagination, the *flair*, to take on void war. It was left to flesh-and-blood captains, men and women who knew the tolerances of their ships like they knew the limits of their own bodies, souls who could eke out the last gramme of power and aggression while the universe exploded in fire and blood around them.

This situation, of course, was different. Jorundur had no more understanding of the *Undrider*'s finer-edged capabilities than a newly-inducted ensign. It would have been prudent to leave matters in Bjargborn's hands, trusting in the mortal's experience of his vessel's powers.

But that would have been no fun. And, despite what many believed about Jorundur, his capacity to find enjoyment in his work had not been entirely lost over the centuries.

'There it is,' he said, pointing at a fast-moving blob on the forward auspex picter. 'Give me hololithic local space. What are the shields doing? Speed to maximum – we need to close it down.'

Bjargborn complied without hesitation. A three-dimensional matrix flickered into life above them, glowing in lines of red and gold, dominated by the globe of Ras Shakeh. It showed the position of the *Undrider* closing fast on the planet. Another signal emerged from the far side of the world, moving directly towards them to intercept.

Jorundur had no idea what the ship was doing there. He could hear Gunnlaugur trying to establish comms with the world below and failing. All he knew was that it was there, that it was commanded by something unholy, and that it needed to die. The circumstances of its presence could wait until its carcass was burning up on re-entry.

'What are we facing?' he demanded, watching the signal race into range. 'Give me something to work with.'

'On screen,' said Bjargborn, switching long-range scanner readings onto a picter mounted next to the command throne. A three-dimensional schematic sheered into life on the hololith, spinning around its axis.

'Arch-enemy,' said Gunnlaugur immediately.

'A destroyer,' confirmed Bjargborn, watching fresh columns of data running down the hololith boundaries. 'Its weapons are powering up.'

Jorundur scrutinised the flickering image rotating before him. The bridge around him ran with shouts and orders as weapon systems were brought online and the void shields raised. The lumens overhead dimmed, replaced by the dull red glow of combat lighting.

'Can we kill it?' demanded Gunnlaugur. 'Decide now.'

Jorundur growled. He needed more time. The outline of the destroyer was… odd. Its guns looked misshapen. It might have been Idolater-class, but if so then something bizarre had happened to its hull. The *Undrider* was probably faster, but his hunch was that it was weaker and packed less of a punch.

'Ashamed you even asked,' he growled, fixing his eyes on the hololith and gauging distances. 'Maintain speed and course. Prepare for drop to nadir on my mark, ten thousand kilometres.'

Bjargborn scurried to comply. Warning lights strobed across the picter array, warning of energy spikes out in the void.

'Lance strike!' shouted a kaerl from the sensoria station.

'Too far away,' breathed Jorundur. 'They're too–'

Space ahead of them exploded into a blaze of harsh, caustic light. The *Undrider* slammed to port-zenith, sending unsecured crew members tumbling across the marble floor. Klaxons blared out, and the combat lumens flickered twice before resuming.

'Evasive action!' ordered Bjargborn.

'Do not *dare*,' threatened Jorundur. 'In closer.'

Gunnlaugur, still on his feet, looked at him sharply. 'Closer?'

'We can't hit it back at this range,' snapped Jorundur. 'All we've got is speed.'

'Hits to forward voids,' reported a servitor. The voice was dry and empty of concern. 'Damage on dorsal plates. Repair crews dispatched.'

Ingvar approached the throne and stared hard at the hololith image of the enemy ship. Jorundur ignored him.

'Down now, *hard*,' he ordered. 'Scrape the planet's edge, find us some more speed.'

The *Undrider* plunged towards the world below, and the huge orb began to fill the real space viewers. As it did so another energy beam scythed past, missing the crenelated spine of the frigate by less than a kilometre. The growl of the engines swelled to a howling whine and the deck trembled beneath their feet.

'This is hurting,' warned Bjargborn, as more warning lights blinked on across a dozen consoles.

The structure of the bridge started to rattle. The sound of something shattering echoed up from a lower deck, followed by a diminishing run of sharp cracks.

Jorundur ignored all of it. Proximity indicators rattled down in front of him, tracking the shrinking gap between the two ships. They were still too far out, and the enemy had the range on them.

'Open fire, master,' he ordered.

'We don't have–'

'Open fire or lose your teeth.'

The *Undrider*'s forward lance sent a shard of sun-white light arcing into the void. Banks of lascannons opened up all along the prow, briefly flaring up against the dark before disappearing in a hail of scattered beams.

The barrage caused no damage, but the enemy adjusted trajectory, just by a fraction, enough to postpone the next volley. By then the *Undrider*'s course across the fringes of Ras Shakeh's atmosphere was hurling it onwards even faster. Continents blurred by underneath them in smudges of red and black.

A *few seconds more…*

The enemy barrage hammered in again. The destroyer opened up with ship-to-ship las-fire and the *Undrider* took hits all along its exposed starboard flanks, making the shielding buck, flex and crackle.

'Losing voids!' shouted a kaerl from the cogitator banks, seconds before a hard bang made the chamber shake. The *Undrider* swung keenly down and to port, lurching off course just as a baroque cluster of cabling exploded overhead, showering the floor in bouncing, tumbling sparks.

'And that's enough running,' said Jorundur, standing defiant and unconcerned against the ship's yawing tilt. 'Now we return the favour.'

He caught sight of the enemy in the realview portals then – a bruise-black, bulbous destroyer, swinging in closer for another pass. Its forward lance was already blazing white, ready for the next spike. The telltale glitter of void shields shimmered across its outline, still intact.

A fresh salvo scythed out from the *Undrider*'s cannons. The crews had a good aim – as the glare faded Jorundur saw a swathe of hits across the enemy underside. Something blew up under the dagger-sharp prow, knocking the lance up out of position and sending a splash-pattern of static across the ship's shields.

'Closer now,' hissed Jorundur, his fists clenching. '*Rake* them.'

The *Undrider* shot upwards, sheering a little and trailing debris, still fast enough to evade most of the hail of las-fire aimed at it. The engines laboured, sending stuttering impacts vibrating through the bulkheads and gantries. Biting detonations along the hull tipped it over several degrees but didn't slow it.

For less than a second it passed right beside the enemy, close enough to see its glistening, tumorous hide through the crystal of the realviewers. Banks of lascannons snapped out in unison, hurling a thicket of deadly neon-bright spears across the gap. The return barrage was just as vicious – two walls of heat and light slamming through and past one another, cracking into the swimming energy of the void shields, bursting through and boring down to the metal below.

Explosions crashed out all along the length of the *Undrider*, punctuated by the scream and snap of expiring void generators. The whole ship reeled as las-beams carved into overheated conduits and burned through metre-thick plate. The engines coughed and flared, beating erratically as if having a sudden coronary.

'Away now, evasive manoeuvre *jorva*,' ordered Jorundur calmly, all the while watching the hololith whirl and flicker.

The structure of the ship shivered as the *Undrider* launched into a steep, cork-screwing climb. More explosions thundered out, bombarding the bridge crew with debris. Cracks cobwebbed across viewports, quickly shuttered. Kaerls staggered to and fro across the chamber, labouring to reach nascent fires and douse them.

'Status, master,' Jorundur asked, all the while monitoring spatial positions.

Bjargborn, who'd nearly been knocked out of his throne by the repeated impacts, scrambled for data.

'Starboard weapons gone,' he reported. 'Lance gone. Six, no seven, hull breaches. We're leaking atmosphere.'

'What's this thing made of?' muttered Jorundur. 'Paper?'

Gunnlaugur braced himself against the steepling deck, compensating for malfunctioning grav generators.

'And the enemy?' he demanded.

The destroyer had shot wide, battered by the brutal broadside exchange. It was coming round for another pass, but more clumsily than before. A long trail of gases plumed from its underside.

'Its voids are down,' said Bjargborn, scanning the auspex data. 'Still got weapons. Still got engines.'

'It can kill us,' said Ingvar quietly. 'We can't kill it.'

Jorundur whirled around.

'I'm just getting started,' he glowered.

Ingvar turned to Gunnlaugur.

'We have to withdraw, *vaerangi*,' he said. 'We can't fight this.'

Gunnlaugur looked back at Ingvar.

'Withdraw?' he asked. His voice betrayed astonishment. For a moment, it looked like he had no idea how to react.

More explosions hammered out from the lower decks. A whole row of cogitators exploded, their screens flinging shattered crystals across the decking. A choir of warning klaxons broke out, overlapping one another in a discordant hymn of despair.

'There's no shame in this,' Ingvar said. 'We might still outrun it, but we can't kill it. We have no weapons left.'

At that, Gunnlaugur gave a grim laugh.

'You've been away too long,' he said. 'We have plenty.'

He glanced briefly at the hololith, calculating, before turning to Jorundur.

'Take us in again, close as you can, fast as you can. Then burn like Hel away from it. Don't care where, just don't die on the way in.'

Jorundur grinned knowingly. 'That is understood.'

Gunnlaugur turned to face the rest of the pack. They looked back at him expectantly, sealed in their suits of armour, draped in pelts, daubed with ritual bloodstains, etched with runes, hung with wolf's-teeth, wyrd-totems and fate-forged blades.

'Come, brothers,' he said, his thick voice snagging with anticipation. 'I wish to show you something.'

* * *

Gunnlaugur jogged down the corridors leading to the frigate's hangars. The lumens failed before he got halfway; his helm compensated instantly. The broken thuds of his pack's massed bootfalls resounded down the narrow space after him. He filtered out the incessant klaxons and warning beacons, only hearing the clinks of weapons against armour, the ragged, expectant breathing, the tinny grind of power armour servos.

The *Undrider* was, in all but one respect, a substandard vessel, something that he should have been ashamed to go to war in. It had one thing, though – one thing that made it more than useful.

'So what is this?' came Váltyr's voice over the pack-wide comm. 'What are we doing?'

He sounded uneasy, like he should have been informed. Váltyr was always on the look out for slights.

'We're here for this,' said Gunnlaugur, reaching a pair of thick security doors. He punched a switch, and they eased open with a scrape of pistons.

On the far side of the doorway was a yawning chamber the size of the Thunderhawk hangar. The metal of the walls was blackened, as if lined with carbon. Huge lifting claws hung from the roof, shaking slightly as the *Undrider* took more hits.

In the centre of the chamber was a slingshot launch mechanism – two hundred metres of track-lined tunnel heading straight out into the void, softly illuminated by a heart-red glow.

At the far end of the track stood two closed sets of armour-plate doors. At the near end, sunk into floor level and squatting amid scorched rockcrete buffers like a lumpen, ugly twin-hulled avatar of the Imperial brutalist aesthetic, was the reason they'd come.

'Blood of Russ,' breathed Baldr.

'A Caestus,' said Olgeir, sounding impressed. 'Glorious.'

Gunnlaugur laughed as he strode over to the control console and activated the remote launch authorisation.

'Strap in quick,' he said. 'Jorundur's sending us out, and he won't like waiting.'

A Caestus Assault Ram was a common sight on Adeptus Astartes capital ships, rarer on escort-class vessels like the *Undrider*. Unlike the versatile Thunderhawk gunships, which were almost three times as large, a Caestus was built around a single operational principle. Its twin hulls were heavily armoured and reinforced with plates of ceramite, ridged and braced to absorb enormous impacts. Its chunky thrusters had afterburners designed to hurl it into blistering straight-line speeds. Its weapon complement – twin-linked heavy bolters, wing-mounted missile launchers, magna-melta heat cannon – all faced ahead, concentrating their destructive power into a single point.

A Caestus, launched into the void and carrying its full complement of ten Space Marines, could survive a direct hit at full speed with the unshielded hull of any battle cruiser in the Imperium. That was fortunate, as it could do very little else. It was less a vehicle, more a projectile.

The two embarkation ramps clanged open. Ingvar and Baldr clambered into one; Váltyr, Olgeir and Haflói the other. Gunnlaugur took his seat in the tiny cockpit, set back at the rear of the ungainly craft. It was an awkward, cramped fit, doubly so once the metal ribs of the impact cage descended across his chest.

The hull booms closed with the hiss and snap of locking bolts. Gunnlaugur primed the engines, feeling the whole vessel shudder as the thrusters broke into life.

The launch chamber rocked again, buffeted by more incoming fire from the void-battle outside. One of the lifting claws separated from its supports and came crashing down beside them, crunching into a tangle of metal fingers and cracking the rockcrete floor.

Gunnlaugur glanced down the long launch tunnel, watching as the external blast doors opened, one after the other, exposing star-flecked blackness beyond.

'Brace for launch,' he ordered, seizing the rudimentary flight controls and tensing for the explosive launch. Piloting a Caestus in such conditions was like riding a whirlwind – he'd be able to nudge its trajectory a little before impact, but not much more than that. 'The Hand of Russ be with–'

The ram exploded into movement, leaping forwards as if kicked. Its engines swelled into a crescendo of flaming, roaring thunder, deafening even over his helm's aural dampeners.

Gunnlaugur slammed back in his seat. The launch tunnel screamed by in a rush of motion-blur and the Caestus shot clear of the *Undrider*'s hull. Stars wheeled before them briefly, marred by trailing fronds of smoke and fire.

Then the destroyer's bloated hull swept up to meet them, racing into range at frightening speed. Jorundur had timed the burst well – they were heading straight amidships, angling under the jumbled forest of armour plating and into the engine levels. A storm of las-fire cracked around them, some of it impacting on the Caestus's hull, rocking it even as it careered towards its target.

Gunnlaugur prodded the vessel's course down by a fraction, aiming for an already-damaged section of hull-plate. He let loose with the missile launcher, then the heavy bolters, blazing away at the projected impact site.

The sun-hot magna-melta was the last weapon to fire, just as the destroyer's bulk overshadowed them, racing up out of the void like a cliff-face of adamantium. For all his conditioning, Gunnlaugur couldn't resist gritting his teeth together, clenching his jaws tight as the hull hurtled in close.

The smash was colossal. The Caestus blazed into a raging core of melting, boiling metal. For a microsecond it plunged straight through the magma, barging aside disintegrating columns and armour plate. Then it rammed square against a solid bracing rib and reared upwards. Momentum dragged it onwards, scraping and tearing through chunks of steel and adamantium, boring away into the reeling heart of the destroyer's wounded flank.

Gunnlaugur was hurled forwards in his seat, barely held in place by the thick metal bars across his chest. Massive, fleeting explosions flared up around the assault ram, turning the forward viewer into an orange soup of flame.

The bracing rib bent, twisted, then broke, bringing a fresh mass of crumbling superstructure raining down on the still-moving assault craft. Its engines cut out suddenly, and their roar was replaced by the shriek of tortured metal and the whistling rush of escaping air.

Slowly, grindingly, the Caestus slid to a halt, wedged deep within the bowels of the enemy ship like a bullet lodged in the muscle of its prey.

Gunnlaugur released the cage and blew the door-locks. More incendiaries went off, clustered around the hull booms to clear a space for the descending crew ramps. His cockpit hatch flew open and he clambered out, reaching for his thunder hammer as he scrambled free of the Caestus's up-ended chassis.

Around him lay a collapsing, howling, blazing maze of destruction. The Caestus had blown a huge hole in the side of the destroyer, carving away whole chunks of hull structure and exposing the ragged ends of broken decking. A gale of oxygen rushed over him, extinguishing the myriad fires that laced the collision site. Shattered lumens flickered and swung from severed brackets, throwing grotesque and leaping shadows over the ruins.

Behind them, back at the end of a cone-shaped tunnel of molten ironwork, was the void. In front of them was the ship they had come to murder.

Gunnlaugur activated *skulbrotsjór*, and blue lightning arced across its adamantium head.

'Time to go,' he growled, hoisting clear of the Caestus and grabbing hold of a section of broken decking to brace himself.

The rest of the pack emerged from the hull booms. They hauled themselves away from the upended Caestus, seizing what spars and braces remained intact around them and climbing upwards through the devastation. The air had gone but the ship's artificial gravity remained, allowing them to orientate themselves and pull free of the tangled wreckage.

They formed up again on the next deck, the first place that retained some semblance of a floor, walls and ceiling.

'That was... invigorating,' said Olgeir, shaking a crust of debris free of his shoulders. *Sigrún* sat comfortably in his two hands, sweeping the area in front of them casually. The rest of the pack fanned out, their helm lenses glowing red in the unsteady gloom.

A large open space stretched away from them, echoing and empty. What parts of it remained intact had the look of a cargo hold – the floor was rockcrete and the walls were iron. Dark, fluted columns studded the expanse, each one terminating in pointed arches against a ridged ceiling. The vacuum made it silent and as cold as Morkai's breath. Nothing lived, nothing stirred. The faint vibration from the engines against their boots was the only indication that this wasn't a dead ship already.

On the far side of the chamber, thirty metres away, were six huge cargo shafts, each one barred by reinforced shutters.

Baldr knelt down, peering at the floor. He scraped a patch of still-glowing dust clear.

'Tank tracks,' he said, looking up at Gunnlaugur. 'A vehicle depot.'

Gunnlaugur nodded, swinging *skulbrotsjór* back and forth and rocking his head from side to side. The cramped passage in the assault ram had compressed his spine – he needed to flex his limbs.

'To the bridge, then,' he said.

As he finished speaking, one of the shutters began to rise. A sickly green light, lurid like marsh-gas, tumbled out from under it, dissipating quickly in the darkness. Black shapes, blurry through the fog, moved back and forth on the far side.

'Not just yet,' said Váltyr with relish, spinning *holdbítr* in one hand before bringing it up into guard. 'Here come the crew.'

Chapter Seven

Jorundur staggered, keeping his feet with difficulty. The mortals around him did less well. Those strapped into their chairs were flung viciously against their bonds. Those who were unsecured were hurled from one wall to the other, landing with the crack and snap of broken bones.

A sheet of flame rippled across the observation dome, overloading half the hull-mounted sensoria and masking for a moment the horrendous punishment the *Undrider* had just taken on the close pass. A gallery on the far side of the chamber twisted and sagged as its supports cracked. Shouts, some of pain, some of urgent command, blended into the background noise of explosions and disintegrations.

'Assessment,' Jorundur commanded, gripping the back of the command throne as the *Undrider* tilted precipitously.

Bjargborn struggled to speak. Something, shrapnel perhaps, had hit him in the face and his cheeks streamed with blood.

'Uh,' he mumbled, his speech slurring. 'M-multiple impacts. Hull breached on four, no five, levels. We're depressurising. No, we're not. Not everywhere.'

Jorundur glanced at one of the few functional pict screens, taking in its data quickly.

'Did we hurt it?' he asked, more interested in the damage he'd done than that which he'd sustained.

Bjargborn called up the sensoria reports. His hands trembled, but he was working hard to hold it together.

'We did,' he reported. Even in his battered state, he sounded proud of that. 'Pretty bad. See for yourself.'

Bjargborn switched the rear-view feed to the throne-mounted screens.

Jorundur saw the destroyer falling away from them, its nearside flank bursting with quickly-extinguishing spot fires. Whole sections of hull-plate had been driven in. A swarm of sparking fragments tumbled around it in the void. It looked like it was having trouble coming around, and rolled awkwardly in space like a beached *hvaluri*.

'And the assault ram?'

'They're in, lord,' said Bjargborn. 'Out of locator range, but they're in.'

As the master spoke, Jorundur caught sight of the ingress wound made by the Caestus – a jagged hole in the destroyer's side, laced with glowing shards of molten metal.

He felt a small surge of satisfaction. He'd aligned the ram well. Gunnlaugur had better remember that when it came to the mission assessment.

'We've done what we had to,' he said. 'Now get us away from that thing.'

Around him the command chamber slowly returned to something like a functioning space. Men still lay prone on the floor, streaked with blood, but the servitors just kept on working. Kaerls, many of them limping or cradling broken arms, moved to douse the fires and shore up the worst of the damage.

For all that, Jorundur knew the situation was still balanced. The *Undrider* had gone into the broadside in worse shape than the enemy and had come out of it badly mauled. The damage it had sustained already might well prove fatal, even without the continued attentions of a pursuing ship.

He felt the broken judder of the engines kick it again, thrusting the *Undrider* away from the combat zone. The movement felt sluggish, as if only half the usual levels of power were online.

Bjargborn read his mind.

'They've holed the enginarium,' he said. He'd managed to find a rag to wipe his face with, and blood smeared across his chin. 'We won't outrun them for long.'

Jorundur nodded and glanced at the hololith tactical display. The enemy was recovering too. The destroyer began to turn, angling back to match course with them. Its speed had been dented too, but not by as much.

'Give me what you can, master. Stay within range of the planet. Any weapons still functioning?'

Bjargborn gave a hollow laugh.

'A few,' he said. 'Enough to chip their war-paint.'

Jorundur didn't find that amusing.

'We'll trust to speed, then. Find it from somewhere.'

Bjargborn turned back to his pict screens, a furrowed look on his bloody face. He knew their only chance of picking up speed lay with the hundreds of enginarium workers down in the forge-hot belly of the vessel, striving against hope and reason to restore the titanic drive mechanisms to health. For all he knew they were already dead, their bloated corpses tumbling through space in their wake.

Jorundur kept watching the ship-signal on the hololith as it completed its turn and came after them.

'Out of interest,' he asked, feeling like he already knew the answer, 'can we still make warp?'

Bjargborn smiled sadly. 'Without a Geller Field?'

'Just asking.'

It had been a hypothetical question; while the pack was on board the enemy ship there was no question of leaving them. Jorundur liked to know all the options, though, just for the sake of completeness.

Whatever you're doing in there, he thought, watching the destroyer's shadow loom larger on the hololith, *do it quick.*

They had once been human. They weren't any more.

They still had the carcasses of human-flesh, and still wore the robes and uniforms of human soldiers, but they had passed beyond their old state and into something new, something abhorrent, something debased.

For Ingvar, the most striking aspect was the smell. The fighting soon took them beyond the ruined vehicle depot and into pressurised areas of the ship, and after that the stink of it pressed in on him. A thousand aromas jostled against one another like swine in a herd – decaying offal, mould, pestilence, the rich tang of recent death, the metallic stench of old blood. He could pick out every strand. He could taste it like sour milk at the back of his throat.

Over the past decades he had become used to xenos fighting. The smell of an alien was always so utterly bizarre that disgust barely registered; engagement with it was a rational matter, something to be processed and filed away for reference.

And so he had forgotten the uniquely sickly fug of fallen humanity, the cocktail of scents that hovered on the edge of familiarity before plunging into chasms of filth, all of it too close to home to be indifferent to.

A human wore his scents like an autobiography, describing his journey through the labours of sanctioned life and into damnation. It picked out traces of old ways – the fabric of uniforms, the sweat of mortal glands, the rotten breath swirling out of mouths black with caries. There were smells of the descent – the flush of fear, the frothy residue of mad euphoria, the dull ache of coming malady. Then, finally, the stink that came with the falling itself: pox, bloat, sore, tumour, pus-streak, glisten-tight sac, ulcerous gobbet of slime, residue of bile, liver-green effluent of gristly, metastasising organ. It all piled up on top of itself, multiplying like a nest of blowflies on a corpse, intensifying in the dark and the wet, redounding to the glory of the false god that revelled and rolled in such muck.

The ship was pregnant with bodily horror. In every chamber, down every corridor, behind every bulkhead and compartment more of it lurked, ground hard into the spongy mass of the floors and dripping like afterbirth from the sagging ceilings. The creatures that had once been human waded through it all to meet them, dragging scrofulous limbs through slurries of liquidised flesh and breaking the scum-crusts that floated atop standing pools of fermenting saliva.

They had lost much, those once-humans. Their eyes were milky orbs, shuttered with cataracts or clawed into blindness by frenzied fingernails. Their exposed skin was grey and vomit-yellow and clustered with berry-red sores that wept trails like bloody tears. Their distended stomachs swung low and heavy, wobbling free of chafed leather belts and spilling over knock-knees and bowed legs. Their jaws lay slack on blubbered necks, laced with sulphurous, trembling strands of viscous spittle. Clouds of biting flies swarmed over them, clogged in the fatty clefts of their quivering hides, tumbling out of sleeve-ends to buzz and plop into the liquid below.

But they had gained much, too. Their rotten muscles were strong. Their addled flesh sliced without bleeding, closing up on wounds instantly. They gurgled and murmured as they came, immune to fear, immune to pain, lost in a universe of syrupy infection. They had forgotten what it was like to yearn for health and cleanliness, for all that remained was the sticky embrace of plague. They cavorted in it, sweeping up the filth and waft and musk in both hands until nothing but a blurred miasma of cankerous foulness remained, swirling around them in billows of seamy vapour.

They had forgotten their names, their ages, their purposes.

They were the lost. They were the damned.

Ingvar raced through the twisting corridors alongside his brothers, charging into the oncoming horde with clean, fast strokes. Grey hands reached out to him and he cut them clear at the wrists. Fingers tugged at his armour, grabbing the pelts that flew around him, scrabbling to get at the joints of his helm and gorget.

He kept moving, kept working. His sword dripped with a thick layer of mucus that clung to the metal, weighing it down. Plasma and creamy dollops of fat splattered across his armour, slowly dribbling down the overlapping curves of ceramite.

The others laboured just as hard. He could see Gunnlaugur ploughing on ahead, hurling the head of his thunder hammer around, crashing it through semi-living flesh, annihilating it in bloody bursts and plastering the walls with scraps and flecks. Váltyr fought more clinically, aiming *holdbítr* for the neck, the eyes, the skull. The corpses that tumbled away from him did so cleanly, their released heads splashing into the knee-deep slime, their outstretched hands scrabbling at nothing.

Over on the flanks, Olgeir reaped whole swathes of corpses, firing in disciplined bursts from his heavy bolter. Diseased flesh exploded into spinning fragments, laced with clots and cysts like biological frag grenades. Baldr and Haflói used their bolters, backing up Olgeir's volleys with pinpoint strikes that burst skulls, punched chests, spilled mottled guts.

Progress was slow. The once-humans could be cut down, only to drag themselves back up. They clogged the claustrophobic corridors and access routes, shambling into battle in close-packed crowds. Some hefted blunt hand weapons – mauls, warhammers, spiked clubs – and others carried guns. They were outlandish things, those guns: rusting, oil barrel-shaped blasters with glowing cabling and feeder vials of toxins. Others hurled gas grenades, each stuffed with nerve-agents and flesh-eaters. The poisons they used were potent, strong enough to melt the walls around them in hissing pools of steam, but still they marched through it all, wheezing and streaming but staying on their feet.

Ingvar hauled his blade around, swinging it two-handed, barely registering as it ended the tortured existence of another glass-eyed mutant. More came to replace it.

'This is taking too long!' he warned Gunnlaugur.

The Wolf Guard didn't seem to hear him. Gunnlaugur fought on, scything his hammer upwards and hurling broken bodies into the ceiling. They fell back to the floor in a slapping rain of body parts. Further back, the echoing roar of *sigrún*'s discharge picked up frequency. Olgeir was having to expend more bolter-rounds than he wanted.

Váltyr swivelled on one foot, kicking a stumbling mutant in the face. His boot wrenched the creature's spine clear of its shoulders in a shower of fractured bone and fluid. Then he switched back to the blade, gutting two more before taking a single stride forwards.

'How many of these things,' he asked, his breath getting short, 'does it take to run a ship?'

Ingvar nodded grimly.

Thousands. Tens of thousands.

They would be crawling down from every deck, leaving their stations and slithering into creaking transit shafts. They would be shuffling up from the bilges, thick with oily slime on their fingers. They would be emerging from demented apothecarions, their organs hanging out and their faces bandaged with dirty swaddling. They would just keep on coming, unable on their own to seriously threaten the armoured giants that walked among them, but capable of slowing them, holding them up, throttling their progress.

'Too many,' Ingvar said. 'We need to speed this up.'

He reached for a frag grenade at his belt, cleared space around him with a vicious blade-sweep, then hurled it down the corridor. It sailed over the heads of the oncoming horde, bouncing from the slime-slick walls before falling among them.

The explosion rocked the confined space, crashing out and hurling severed bodies in all directions. The blast wave swept along the corridor, slamming dismembered corpses headfirst into the foaming effluent. A wave of whirling gore flew back at them, dropping around them in messy, liquid slaps.

That broke the horde's momentum. The front ranks staggered, dragged down into the slime by the weight of those falling behind them.

Olgeir stepped up to take advantage.

'Watch your backs, brothers,' he warned, then opened fire.

Sigrún thundered out, vomiting a thick hail of mass-reactive rounds. The bolts punched deep into the reeling mass of pustulent flesh before detonating in a ragged line of destruction, ripping diseased meat apart in bleeding slabs.

As the echoes died away, Gunnlaugur surged back to the front, ploughing into the shaken heart of the enemy, immense and battle-roused, his hammer whistling around his shoulders in incisive arcs. Váltyr and Baldr were close behind, crashing through what remained of the mutant horde with growing space and freedom.

Of all of them, though, it was Haflói who went in hardest. He sprinted right into the press of once-humans, screaming battle-cries through his helm-vox. His bolt pistol bucked in his right hand; the left clutched a double-bladed axe. He leapt straight past Gunnlaugur, slamming bodily into the morass of corruption beyond, lashing out like a berserk of the Old Ice.

Olgeir struggled to keep up with him.

'Whelp!' he roared furiously, trying to summon him back.

It did no good. Even Gunnlaugur laughed to see it – the Blood Claw, limbs flailing, giving into his bloody rush of primordial kill-urge.

'Fenrys!' Hafloí cried, pounding and slaying with artless abandon.

The mutants broke then, assailed on sides and faced with the twin storms of Gunnlaugur's massive presence and Hafloí's crazed one. Those that had survived the initial assault began to limp away, shrinking back into the stinking shadows or sinking into the murk at their feet.

'Hjolda!' roared Gunnlaugur, wading after the fleeing horrors.

The pack hunted the remnants down the corridor, following its organic twists and turns as it snaked into the heart of the corrupted ship. The retreat became a rout, a killing ground, an exercise in raw butchery.

They fought on until reaching an intersection with a vertical transit shaft, running up from the lower levels and soaring away into the heights. The iron doors that had once guarded it from the corridor were shattered.

'They've destroyed the lifters,' observed Baldr calmly, wrenching the head of a milk-skinned mutant from its rash-red body.

'So they have,' replied Gunnlaugur, shaking his hammerhead free of a ropey necklace of entrails. 'Then we climb.'

'Hel,' swore Olgeir, preparing to hoist *sigrún* across his back. 'How far up?'

Váltyr kicked out with his boot again, driving in the eggshell-thin skull of a blinded, crawling mutant.

'Not far,' he said coolly, walking up to the shaft. 'But rein in your protégé. He's getting carried away.'

Hafloí had ignored the transit shaft and had surged ahead down the corridor, lashing out to either side of him with bolt pistol and axe, shrieking and cursing.

Ingvar was closest, and went after him, grabbing him by the shoulder and dragging him back. Hafloí whirled on him, for a moment looking like he'd take on anything.

'*Easy*, hot-blood,' warned Ingvar, keeping *dausvjer* en garde. 'Don't make me use it.'

Hafloí stared at the sword for a moment, bristling with aggression, before finally lowering the axe.

By then Gunnlaugur had moved into the shaft, swinging clear of the broken gates and into the red-tinged darkness beyond. The others followed him, leaping like grey ghosts into the abyss.

The shaft was immense. It dropped away below them into an angry crimson swirl of choking fumes. The deep boom of the destroyer's engines drummed up from its base, echoing eerily from the many-columned walls. Iron gargoyles stared out across the void, their leering, daemonic faces warped into grotesque, bloated expressions of loathing.

Pipework, rusting electronics, mouldering mounts and braces all criss-crossed the metal-plate surface, affording plenty of handholds. Everything was draped in a slick, sticky layer of slime, making the surface treacherous. For all that, the pack surged up the shaft like rats running up a hawser, going quickly even as the fragile ironwork cracked and crumbled under their armour's weight.

'*How* far up?' repeated Olgeir, falling behind as his heavy bolter slowed him down.

Gunnlaugur gave him no quarter. The pack clambered up the levels. Eerie noises pursued them: moans, creaks of tortured metal, whispered voices just under the edge of hearing. The filth in the air got thicker, making their helm filters strain. A pale green mist tumbled down to meet them, emerging from beast-mouthed outlets protruding from the shaft walls.

Gunnlaugur reached the summit first. Massive, twisted iron cables hung from the roof of the shaft, swinging and clanking in the rising stink. They would once have hauled elevator cages up from the depths; now they dangled free, like nooses.

Near the top a narrow ledge jutted out into the abyss, above which were a pair of heavy doors surrounded by two swollen pillars of warped and cracked stone. Gunnlaugur grabbed hold of the ledge and dragged himself up on top of it. He seized his thunder hammer, pulled it back and hurled it two-handed at the join.

The doors crashed inwards in an explosion of blue-white lightning. Gunnlaugur charged through the gap, closely followed by the others as they reached the ledge and hauled themselves over the top.

On the other side of the doors was a huge chamber. Its roof was curved like a ribcage of burnished bronze and glazed with translucent crystal. Beyond that was the void, half visible through smeary panes. Pillars of veined marble jutted up from a floor swimming in greasy, bubbling matter. Gantries ringed the central command throne, all dripping long lines of clear fluid from rust-edged walkways. It was stiflingly hot, and the air hummed with the drone of corpse-flies.

On an Imperial frigate, a bridge that size could have accommodated over two hundred crew members. On that ship, only one remained at its station. No room was left for anyone, or anything, else.

Perhaps once the creature had sat on a command throne like a normal human, legs planted on the floor and hands resting against the arms. Maybe the mutations had burst out quickly after that, blooming like overripe fruit and tumbling forth across the available space. Or maybe it had been sitting there for centuries, slowly bulking out, slowly consuming everything around it, squeezing all other life from the chamber until it alone squatted there, wobbling with sores and lesions, hemmed in on all sides by the creaking walls of its starship cage.

Whatever the process, it had become colossal. Its lower limbs had long since been swallowed up by its expanding girth, the bulk of which rippled like gelatine across the floor. Webs of ink-dark veins pulsed under the trembling surface of its skin, pumping sluggish blood around its gigantic structure. Waves of blubber folded up against grimy cogitator banks, surrounding them, enveloping them, sinking down over them. Strands of sinew stretched directly from its obese flanks and locked into signal connector nodes. The frail network of tendrils shivered as the thing drew shuddering breaths.

It no longer occupied the bridge. It *was* the bridge.

And it stank. It stank of suppurating fat, of boiled fish, of rotten fruit, of confined and intensified putrescence. When it moved, waves of foul odour wafted across its vast body. Fluids glistened in the crevices between fatty tissue. Mucus spilled across slick patches of taut skin and bubbled over scabby patches where abscesses had ruptured.

A tiny head still surmounted the mountain of blubber, a vestigial remnant of a human skull and face. It was eyeless and hairless, with flared nostrils and a long whiplash tongue. It screamed at them, and flecks of yellow spittle splattered down a cascade of trembling chins. Tiny arms, wasted and scrawny, thrashed against its sides.

Baldr gazed up at it.

'That is impressively foul,' he murmured.

Ingvar stood at his shoulder. *Dausvjer*'s energy field spat and shimmered, throwing electric light across the face of his armour.

'Then we end it, brother,' he said, bringing the blade to bear in unison with his pack-brothers, 'and send one more lost soul back to Hel.'

'Energy spike, lord!'

The kaerl's report rang out across the command chamber. On the realview feed, Jorundur watched the destroyer's forward lance power up, sparkling like ball-lightning in the darkness of space.

The *Undrider* was racing as fast as its savaged engines would carry it, but the enemy had clawed back much of the space between them. Las-fire flickered from its forward array, too inaccurate to cause much more damage, but with increasing intensity.

It would soon find its range. After that, the brief game would be over.

'Any signal from the pack?' he asked.

'Nothing,' said Bjargborn.

The man's voice was tense. The pressure of the chase was telling.

'Then we are out of time,' said Jorundur. 'Give the order.'

Jorundur had only partial faith in the plan they'd concocted. Engin-seers working down in the weapons levels had somehow managed to dredge up a semblance of a working weapons grid. He had no idea how: he'd heard Bjargborn over the comm talking about re-routing the output from the lance mechanism to burned-out lascannon coils under the warp core, which had meant precisely nothing to him. Whatever they'd done, it had been difficult and dangerous. He'd heard the screams of the tech-priest himself as one attempt had failed, incinerating an entire gen-erator module and blowing lumens on every deck in the ship.

Now, though, they had it working. A single volley, that was all – a lone burst of shots sent spiralling away aft, hoping against hope to score a decisive hit on the destroyer's forward lance housing. If they managed to disable that, then they had a chance to live a little longer. A small one, but a chance.

Jorundur had waited until the last moment before authorising the strike. The odds of even hitting the destroyer's lance were low, but if they somehow managed it, an infinitesimal risk existed that they would do more than just knock out the weapon itself. A starship lance was a huge repository of volatile energies – a direct hit might cause an overload, sending mutually reinforcing explosions rushing back up into the ves-sel's innards and destroying the whole thing.

That would save the *Undrider*, but wipe out six-sevenths of Járnhamar. The decisions were fine ones, each soaked in danger.

'Order all non-weapons crews to prepare for saviour pod evacuation,' said Jorundur, his eyes fixed on the glowing hololith before him. 'If this fails, tell them to move quickly.'

'By your will, lord,' said Bjargborn, his fingers dancing over the throne's controls as he distributed the instructions down the chain of command.

One, the few surviving servitors, plugged into a terminal close by, turned its pallid, slack face towards them.

'Weapon primed, lord,' it intoned dryly.

Jorundur's eyes never left the hololith.

'Fire,' he commanded.

A crackling boom rang out from the lower decks, echoing up from the depths as if something huge had collided with the frigate and was now ploughing up through the ship, deck by deck. The command chamber shook, dislodging a stone image of Russ from the ceiling. It shattered on the floor in a cloud of shards, nearly killing the kaerls working nearby. Red lights flickered across the consoles, reciting a baleful litany of over-loaded relays and burned-out translocators.

That was the price of a final, defiant volley. Jorundur watched as the makeshift array opened up, stabbing a tight cluster of las-fire aft towards the closing destroyer. For an instant the barrage blazed brilliantly, a nanosecond's worth of hard, clear energy, then it was gone.

The *Undrider* shuddered. The arrhythmic growl from the engines cut out entirely, then shakily resumed. Cracks ran up the walls around them, and more loosened debris scattered across the marble.

'Did we hit it?' demanded Jorundur, peering intently at the viewers.

The destroyer hadn't lost speed.

'We did, lord,' reported Bjargborn. He sounded like he barely believed what his auspexes were telling him. 'Direct hit, forward lance.'

A second later, and the damage became obvious through the realview-ers. The destroyer's prow was burning, masked by an inferno that raged in defiance of the vacuum around it.

'Blessed Allfather,' breathed Jorundur, gazing at the destruction. He turned sharply to Bjargborn. 'I want detailed readings on that ship. Power build-ups, secondary damage. You get *anything*, you tell me.'

He was already planning what he'd do if a chain reaction took hold. He might be able to get the *Undrider* in close again, but only if the enemy had lost control of its remaining weapon batteries. They couldn't sur-vive another broadside. He started to calculate the distances, the relative speeds, what remained of his hull armour.

'Energy spike, lord!'

The report came from the same kaerl as before, in exactly the same tone.

'That's imposs–' started Bjargborn.

Jorundur's head snapped back up. He looked out at the realview feed.

'They can still fire,' said Jorundur grimly.

The gap between the ships had closed further. Jorundur saw the ener-gies snap and fizz across the lance's muzzle, only temporarily disrupted by the volley they had sent into it.

Bjargborn's face was locked into horrified unbelief. Part of him was still searching for something – some mistake, some reading that had eluded him. Anything but the truth that now confronted them.

The chase was over. The *Undrider* was seconds from destruction.

'We can source more power,' Bjargborn said, his fingers and eyes moving quickly. 'We can–'

Jorundur laid his gauntlet heavily on the mortal's shoulder, silencing his desperate attempts to find a last-gasp solution.

'They're firing,' he said. 'Get to the pods. Now.'

Bjargborn looked up at him for a moment longer, his unwillingness to leave evident.

Then his shoulders slumped.

'This is the master,' he announced over the ship-wide comm. 'Leave your posts. Leave your posts now. Take the saviour pods. Go swiftly, and the hand of Russ be with you.'

Jorundur released him.

'Well said. Now *run*.'

The chamber was already emptying. Kaerls unstrapped themselves from their stations and sprinted across the deck, streaming towards the lifters that would carry them to the banks of saviour pods.

Bjargborn made to do the same. The chamber shuddered as the first stabs of las-fire cracked into the *Undrider*'s structure.

'And what of you, lord?' he asked, still deferent even as the ship began to come apart around them.

Jorundur smiled, already moving.

'Look to your own, master,' he said. 'I can handle myself.'

Then the lance fired – a brief, silent stab of immense energy out in the void – and everything turned to fire.

Chapter Eight

Gunnlaugur *roared*.

The bellow of raw aggression made his lungs burn and the bridge around him tremble. He whirled his hammer around his head, picking up tremendous amounts of momentum before loosing his fury at the horror before him.

Around him, his pack did the same. He saw Hafloí launch himself into action with typical reckless abandon. He saw Ingvar and Váltyr work off one another, the two of them forming a seamless wall of swordplay. A rain of bolts punched into the creature's bloated withers, puncturing the translucent skin and exploding in wet, muffled slaps.

Fighting it was like fighting a sea of living fat. Sword-edges snagged on it, gripped by the cloying matter. Hafloí's pistol-rounds seemed to do no more than pock-mark it. Only Olgeir's heavy ammunition made much headway – his relentless barrage had carved a vast, weeping gash in the mutant's putrescent hide.

Gunnlaugur's thunder hammer was the next most effective weapon. Its charged head could shear swathes of juddering flesh away, ripping it up and throwing chunks clear. He felt like a reaper of old, striding into the mouldering heart of the beast and carving his way towards its heart.

The sensation did him good. He could lose himself in his battle-anger. The doubts and trials of the past few weeks meant nothing in the heat of combat; all that existed for him then was his fury, unleashed on the flood.

Hjortur had been the same. The old Wolf Guard had been an immense presence to fight alongside. He'd howled to the sky while charging in close, his axe whirling. It had looked messy, but that was all artifice. No Sky Warrior fought inexpertly, not once they'd emerged from the testing ground of the Blood Claws. The battle-cries, the posturing, the bravado, the howls and growls, that was all to chill the blood of the enemy, to stir the ancient spirits of murder, to loosen the amber-eyed wolf within.

To kill, kill, and kill again. That was what he had been bred to do. That, in the end, was what they had all been created to accomplish. A Space Wolf was an axe-blade, a sword-edge, a hammer's head. Life offered nothing finer for those who understood that; only misery awaited the Son of Russ who queried that purity of purpose.

His gripped the handle of *skulbrotsjór*, relishing the familiar weight and heft of it in his armoured hands.

'*Deyja, hrogn af Helvíti!*' he thundered in battle-cant, hacking and sweeping, feeling the muscles of his mighty arms sing.

The creature responded. It did so blindly, erratically, all the while screaming from its grotesquely tiny head. New growths burst out from its innards, glossy and shining like embryos. Polyps emerged from pores, bursting in clouds of foul-smelling gas. Ragged jaws opened up all across its body, splitting the skin and exposing concentric rows of black teeth.

One bursting polyp caught Haflói full in the face. He staggered back, clutching at his facemask, hacking uncontrollably. Baldr got himself entangled between two snapping pairs of flesh-jaws, and a mountain of blubber rose up over him, quivering with the anticipation of drowning him in a tide of corpulence.

Ingvar broke free immediately and waded towards Baldr, slicing through sweeps of jellied meat with his lightning-arced blade. That blunted the effectiveness of Váltyr's attack, and the blademaster was forced backwards before a snaking forest of barbed, poisonous feelers.

Gunnlaugur snarled. The pack's momentum was faltering.

The head. Always strike corruption at the head.

He glanced up, spying the raging, wailing skull of the creature as it flailed around in a spittle-laced fit. Three metres away, and nothing but jaws and adipose horror in between.

'Russ guide me,' he whispered, crouching down and tensing. The pistons in his power armour geared up, responding to his physical and mental cues. He gripped his thunder hammer two-handed, feeling the shaft vibrate as the lightning-crowned head whined up to full power.

He launched himself into the air, propelled by his enormous strength and boosted by his armour. As he swept towards the creature's shrunken head, he raised *skulbrotsjór* high.

At the last moment the creature sensed the danger. Its blind head snapped towards him, screaming hatred.

Then Gunnlaugur landed. The thunder hammer plunged downwards, cleaving straight through the monster's skull and boring through what remained of its upper body. Gunnlaugur heard bones snap and organs splatter. The screaming broke off abruptly, replaced by the sick splat of watery flesh-sacs bursting and the stench of disruptor-scorched skin.

Gunnlaugur's weight carried him down. He plummeted into the heart of the beast, cutting through with the still-burning *skulbrotsjór*. Waves of blotchy, greasy fluid crashed over him, dragging him under, enveloping him in a clutching swamp of sucking, ruined tissue.

He kept fighting, feeling the pressure of the beast's headless carcass press against him. Curtains of visceral slime washed down his armour, smearing his helm lenses. It felt like being thrown into an ocean of slops and foetid offal.

The pressure built up. Gunnlaugur felt his grip on his hammer slip and struggled to hold on. The tide of blubber rose over his head, burying him in cloying, suffocating bulk. Moving his limbs became difficult, like swimming against a riptide. He raged on, hearing his thunderous battle-cries become muffled as slick nodules of flesh pressed against his helm.

Then, just as it was getting tricky, the pressure released. The walls of fat and stink abruptly shivered, quaked, and began to fall apart. Gunnlaugur heard the snarls and howls of his pack coming for him. His hammer whipped around in front of him, cutting cleanly through the rapidly diminishing press of bloody brawn and sinew.

His head burst free, dripping with gore-flecked sludge. He saw Olgeir wading towards him, the great one using his bulk and strength to rip the creature apart.

He was using his *hands*. That made Gunnlaugur laugh – a brutal laugh of joy in battle.

'*Hjá*, Heavy-hand!' he roared, greeting the arrival of the heavy weapons specialist with a slopping salute of his gristle-dripping hammer.

Then he saw the others, all cutting and slicing their way towards his position. In the face of that combined assault, what remained of the vast creature melted and shuddered away, sliding into a foaming, bursting morass of shapeless tallow.

Olgeir extended his gauntlet to Gunnlaugur, seizing him and dragging him clear.

'That was a mighty leap, *vaerangi*,' he said.

Gunnlaugur broke clear of the last of it, his armour caked in gobbets of slime. Now that the thing was dead, the euphoria of the kill was waning fast, giving way immediately to a fresh sensation of danger. The floor under his feet was trembling.

'What of the ship?' he asked.

'This *is* the ship,' said Baldr grimly, standing knee-deep in a bubbling pool of blubber. 'We need to leave.'

Even as he spoke, that truth became obvious. The horror's residual flesh was blackening fast, hardening and stiffening as if scorched by fire. The tendrils it had used to link to the ship's corrupted spirit snapped, severing the arteries of control.

Marsh-gas lumens above them flickered and died, plunging them into darkness. From far below, the destroyer's engine-growl halted, restarted, then halted again, as if the entire vessel were having a massive coronary. Corroded pipes running up the glistening walls of the bridge burst open, showering the space in oily spurts of coolant.

Gunnlaugur shook off the last stringy lengths of sinew and started to move.

'The whelp?' he asked.

'He'll live,' said Ingvar, supporting Hafloí as the pack began to withdraw. The Blood Claw's helm was cracked half open, exposing a raw mass of bloody flesh beneath. He was breathing, though, and the wound was already clotting.

'Can we make the Caestus?' asked Baldr, bringing up the rear as the pack hastened out of the bridge and into the gloomy corridors beyond.

'We'll see,' said Gunnlaugur, picking up the pace as the bridge around them began to convulse. 'But if we can't, pray that Old Dog's still flying the *Undrider*.'

The *Undrider* was broken, impaled by a scything column of energy. Whole sections of hull peeled free, shearing clear of the stricken core and rolling slowly planetwards. A fuel tank breached, causing a fireball to roar through the containment cages and sweep through the lower decks, raging thirstily as it destroyed ammo dumps and power storage cells.

Some of the crew had made it into saviour pods, jettisoning free of the dying ship even as the lance-strike burned through it. The cloud of tiny vessels – little more than teardrop-shaped caskets of adamantium – burned their way into Ras Shakeh's atmosphere, lighting up like torches as they spiralled down to the surface.

Jorundur saw none of that. His last clear view of anything had been

Bjargborn's head being blasted apart by a leaping crackle of electric discharge. Then the command chamber had collapsed around him, bursting into a sun-hot cloud of flying crystal shards and powdered marble.

His armour absorbed much of the impact, but he didn't go unscathed. The servos in his right leg-plate buckled, and he crushed his left wrist against something heavy as he landed, twenty metres away from where he had been standing. The impact was bone-jarringly hard, sending radial judders down his spine and causing him to black out momentarily.

He moved like an automaton after that. His survival instincts propelled him even as his mind remained blurred and sluggish. He clawed his way free of the wreckage, somehow finding the half-destroyed doors at the rear of the command chamber and dragging himself through them.

The escaping atmosphere howled around him into the burning void, dragging detritus with it. Jorundur crawled onwards, his senses gradually returning to clarity. He could feel pain burning all over his body. His retinal display listed all the ways his battle-plate had been battered and dented. The only important factor was its air-tight seal, which appeared to be intact. Jorundur's breath echoed raggedly in his helm, and he could already taste the staleness of the oxygen recycled through his suit's filters.

More crashes rang out, roaring up from the flame-ridden bowels of the frigate. Everything around him seemed to be in motion – the walls of the corridor shook, rolled and buckled. Wall sections further down broke open, revealing the glow of swelling fires beyond.

Jorundur clambered to his feet and started to run. Keeping his feet on the rolling deck was difficult, even with his preternatural balance. He slammed into the nearside wall, staggering away from it. Then the floor began to give way.

He leapt ahead, landing heavily on a firmer patch as the metal walkway tumbled into ruin. Gouts of fire-flecked smoke poured up from where the floor plates had been, filling the narrow space with choking waves of smog.

'Hel,' he spat, feeling his body protest as he pulled himself back into motion. 'This is *absurd*.'

He limped, crawled and lurched onwards, buffeted by the raging destruction around him. The corridor gave way to an intersection, then to an access tunnel, then an open hallway with a crumbling roof and jagged crevasses snaking across its floor. Explosions shook the walls, multiplying into an overlapping orgy of demolition. Bodies were everywhere, hurled on top of one another, stuffed into blocked service hatches, hanging from stairwells, all beginning to burn as the growing flames lapped at them.

When Jorundur finally reached his destination he barely recognised it. Sheets of blue-tinged fire coursed down the melting entrance passage. A whole segment of outer hull had peeled away over to his right, exposing dizzying patches of emptiness. He had a brief glimpse of stars striated with flying lines of wreckage. There was no sign of the enemy destroyer, and he briefly wondered why it hadn't closed in for the kill yet. The ground beneath him rippled like water, snapping pressed-steel panels as if they were made of plexiglass.

He broke into a limping run, racing over the disintegrating floor and skirting past igniting piles of fuel tanks. The ship was coming apart around him. He felt his footfalls growing lighter as the grav generators gave out.

'*Skítja*,' he swore as he tumbled forwards, careering into a pile of ammo cases and sending them flying. Unable to arrest his forward momentum, he blundered on, slewing through the half-open shutters of the entrance passage and into the huge space beyond.

Once through, he skidded along a wide, open patch of buckling rockcrete. He had the vague impression of an enormous vaulted roof above him, zigzagged with growing cracks. The lack of air made everything strangely balletic – a choreographed dissolution in total silence.

Ahead of him was the gulf into the void. He saw the starfield beckoning, broken only by lines of spinning debris. He'd made it to the outer skin of the *Undrider*, beyond which there was nothing but empty space.

For a moment he thought he'd be carried straight out, shooting clear of the collapsing structure and somersaulting into vacuum.

He avoided that by a hand's breadth. He shot his intact left hand out to catch the trailing edge of the landing gear as he sailed past it, grunting from the effort. His gauntlet closed over the metal strut, arresting his outward trajectory with a jerk. Once secured, he began to haul himself back up, struggling against the hurricane of flying wreckage.

He looked up, seeing a familiar grey cockpit looming over him. For all its bulk, it was already beginning to slide towards the void as the docking clamps holding it in place twisted and snapped.

Jorundur grimaced, and started to pull himself towards the entrance hatch.

'No you don't, you ugly bastard,' he said through gritted teeth. 'Not… *yet*…'

The plague-ship was dead and drifting, locked into a steadily accelerating tilt towards the planet below. The animating presence lurking at its heart was gone, and like a vast body suddenly bereft of its brainstem the whole vessel began to go haywire.

Ingvar ran hard, keeping Hafloí on his feet and trying not to lose ground with the rest of the pack. Together they tore through the warped labyrinth of the ship's gruesome interior, going as swiftly as the cramped space and treacherous footing would allow. The route they'd taken to reach the bridge was closed to them – blocked by a furious, acidic inferno belching out of the ship's tortured innards – and so they'd been forced to make their way down through the narrow capillaries of the destroyer's crew decks.

It was hard to believe that the ship had once been designed by the hand of man. Once, many thousands of years ago, it would have been a creation of iron and adamantium, proudly bearing the insignias of the Imperial Navy on its golden prow and commanded by mortal officers bearing the sacred aquila on their breasts.

After millennia of corruption, little remained of that. Every surface had been warped and twisted, curled away from its original purpose and compelled into new, troublingly carnal forms. The narrow airways were thick with spores, and the spongy floors were clogged with filth. Every metal strut and beam was thick with oxidisation. The machinery, all of it ancient and arcane in its own right, had morphed into bizarre techno-biological hybrids, quivering with organesque appendages and glossy with cascades of dribbling fluid.

When it started to break open, it did so like a body. Blood coursed down from the sagging ceilings; pus pooled in the torn gaps between wall sections, oozing like infection across a scabrous hide.

'No signal from the *Undrider*,' reported Baldr, leaping over a dissolving patch of hissing floorspace. 'Nothing at all.'

The plague-ship suddenly lurched hard, throwing them against the pulpy walls. The narrow tunnel started to shiver more violently.

'Out of interest,' asked Váltyr, struggling to keep his feet, 'how close are we to re-entry?'

'You had to ask,' grunted Olgeir.

The pack pressed on, going as fast as the treacherous conditions permitted. With every step, the stench and filth intensified around them.

Eventually they burst out of the tunnels and into a larger domed chamber. It had been set into the side of the ship, and its exterior wall was entirely taken up by a multi-faceted window in the shape of a giant eye. The place might once have been a viewing gallery, built in an age when starships carried more than purely military crew.

Now it was a charnel house, a rotting canker of accumulated foulness. Death-bloated corpses hung from the roof on rusting hooks. Maggots carpeted the floor, wriggling across a sickening floorspace of mouldering cadavers. Bleached skulls protruded from the festering mass, barely visible under the clouds of flies that droned around them.

As they entered, the heaps of putrescence stirred. Bodies, clad in robes of mildewed sackcloth, twisted to meet the intruders. Their cowled faces were masked by obscenely long rebreathers, and their round eye-lenses glowed lime-green in the dark. Like the mutants they'd seen earlier they carried toxin weapons in their bony hands. Oblivious to the slow doom encompassing their ship, they limped towards the pack, chattering to one another in half-breathed, sibilant voices.

'Slay them!' thundered Gunnlaugur, kicking aside the heaps of decaying body-parts to get at them. 'Slay them all!'

Olgeir's bolter opened up again, sending severed limbs spinning and bouncing across the chamber.

Ingvar didn't follow the order. Dozens of the creatures had already risen; many more were stirring. There would be hundreds before long, drawn from every stinking hole and pit in the ship by the sounds of battle.

They were running out of time. Soon the ship would begin to roll into the planet's atmosphere and the whole structure would burn. Gunnlaugur would never admit it, but they'd left it too late to reach the Caestus. They'd still be fighting their way towards it when the first flames began to lick along the destroyer's hull.

Hafloí struggled to free himself from Ingvar's grip. Though still spore-blind and bleeding, he wanted to fight. Ingvar didn't let him go.

'Bastard,' Hafloí slurred groggily.

Ingvar ran another sweep via his helm-mounted sensors, searching for some sign that the *Undrider* had survived.

He got nothing: the frigate was gone. Ingvar felt his heart sink. Gunnlaugur's gambit had been too risky; they should have withdrawn when they'd had the chance.

He was about to give up, to return to the fight, when something suddenly registered. He picked up a signal in the void, moving fast, closing on their position.

The way it flew was familiar. Ingvar smiled.

'Brothers!' he roared, dragging Hafloí over to the huge window. 'We have to leave! We have to leave *now!*'

They didn't listen. They couldn't listen: they were already hard-pressed by hordes of grave-mutants. The whole chamber crawled with them – snaking down from the meathooks, burrowing up from the butcher's piles, shuffling into the chamber from corridor orifices.

Ingvar turned to Hafloí, and activated *dausvjer*'s disruptor.

'Hold your breath, whelp,' he said. 'This is going to hurt.'

He lashed out with the blade, shattering the window. The sword's energy field exploded and the iron frame cracked outwards. Foul air exploded through the breach, wrenching the rest of the window free and blowing the contents of the charnel chamber out into the void.

Ingvar was ripped out first, shooting clear of the destroyer's hull in a tumbling rain of crystal and iron. He kept a tight grip on Hafloi's cracked helm, squeezing it tight in his gauntlet and trying to stem air-loss.

A messy spume of spinning bones and cadaverous flesh shot out after them. Among the spreading fog of decay tumbled the grave-mutants, clutching wildly at nothing and gasping for air through their useless masks. The armour-sealed Space Marines came along with them, protected from the shock of exit and oxygen loss though powerless to halt their ejection.

'What in *Hel*?' demanded Gunnlaugur over the comm, sounding choked with rage as he rolled clumsily through space. 'What are you *doing*?'

'Look up,' replied Ingvar calmly.

Vuokho swooped in close, manoeuvring expertly on its retros as beams of las-fire flickered around it. It hovered over the expanding cloud of falling bodies, swivelling on its axis and opening the frontal crew-bay doors.

'Six of you,' came Jorundur's sour voice on the pack-wide comm, dripping with irritation. 'This could take a while. For Russ's sake, try not to thrash about.'

The two vessel-corpses carved their way into Ras Shakeh's upper atmosphere, lighting up in vivid trails of flame.

One was the *Undrider*, barely more than a semi-coherent collection of melting metal plates.

The other was the plague-ship. Its core integrity remained intact until the full force of re-entry hit. Its swollen underside began to glow rust-red, then orange, then eye-watering white. It exploded shortly after that, spreading a network of burning debris across the skies of the planet below.

Gunnlaugur watched both ships burn from the sanctuary of *Vuokho*'s cockpit. Since being recovered, his mood had blackened. He'd always found it difficult to come down from the fearsome endorphin-high of combat. This time, though, it was doubly hard. Jorundur had sensed it, and for once attempted no acerbic comment. They sat together in silence, watching the wreckage below them twist and blaze.

All across the control console, *Vuokho*'s machine-spirit sent them angry warnings of imminent systems failure. The gunship had taken a lot of damage from the enemy's close gunners. Just making planetfall would be an achievement.

The whole pack was subdued. Hafloí had nearly died. Váltyr shared Gunnlaugur's anger with Ingvar, convinced that they could have fought their way to the Caestus before it was too late to launch. Baldr and Olgeir had said nothing about it, though even Heavy-hand had found little to smile about after his recovery.

It had been victory, of a sort. They were alive, the enemy was dead. Somehow, given the carnage, given how close it had been, it was hard to see things that way.

He overruled me.

Gunnlaugur suppressed the thought, knowing where it would lead. Dealing with Ingvar would have to wait

He turned to Jorundur. The two of them were alone, sitting side by side; the others had remained in the crew compartment below.

'So,' he said. 'Tell me. What was that?'

'Only guesses, *vaerangi*,' said Jorundur.

'Any signal from the planet?'

'Still silent.'

Gunnlaugur looked down at the Thunderhawk's scrolling auspex readings. He saw patterns of conurbations down on the surface – sprawls of industrial cities, web-like traceries of roads, the puckered mass of mountain ranges. Some of it was burning; trails of black smoke stained the atmosphere across a whole band of urbanised terrain.

'No orbital defences,' he said. 'One ship couldn't have taken them down. There must have been others.'

Jorundur looked sceptical. 'Then why aren't they still here?'

'They did what they came for – landed forces, then moved on. We saw empty depots on the destroyer. It stayed behind. A sentry, perhaps, overlooking the planetary assault.'

Jorundur nodded slowly. 'Perhaps.'

Gunnlaugur scrutinised the auspex feeds. Their resolution wasn't enough to make out much detail, but the damage on the surface was hard to miss.

'There's fighting down there,' he said. 'Movement. I can see it. If we're getting no readings, then they're being jammed.'

'We have to land,' said Jorundur. 'We're losing power. Soon we'll lose our hull. Here are the drop coordinates we were given.'

Gunnlaugur watched as the picters scanned across to them. He saw a blurry urban splash of pale grey against red earth. He saw two concentric walls, and what looked like massive defensive installations arranged in terraced rows. There was no burning around those walls; the nearest sign of destruction was hundreds of kilometres to the south-west.

'Looks undamaged,' he said. 'Take us down. Broadcast encrypted landing clearance on the secure comm. I'll get Olgeir up here to man the guns – we might need him.'

Jorundur started to move the heavy control columns, and the gunship's battered muzzle dipped towards the world's curve.

'What are you expecting?' he asked, trying to lighten the oppressive atmosphere.

'I don't know,' said Gunnlaugur, sinking back into his seat and falling silent. 'I really don't know.'

11
THE WOUNDED HEART

Chapter Nine

Sister Uwe Bajola rose before sunrise, as she always did, and went to the west-facing wall of her cell, as she always did.

In the hour of deep-red shadows, before the full day's heat properly arrived, her mind was clear and her body was calm. Routine calmed it further. She had always appreciated the familiar rhythms, the mechanical purity of repetition. In times of trial they had a particular value.

She opened the gahlwood door and padded out onto the balcony. She took a deep breath. The air was already warming. It tasted of sand.

Bajola leaned on the balcony and felt the last of the night's breeze press against the cotton of her shift. That was pleasant, for the short while it lasted. Though raised on a world of unrelenting sun, her melanin-rich skin as black as her battle-armour, she had never quite come to terms with Ras Shakeh's climate. Something about the sunlight was wrong. It burned, but did not warm; it dazzled, but did not illuminate.

She bowed her head, running a hand absently over her cropped hair. Such thoughts, such ingratitude, were unworthy.

Cleanse my soul, she mouthed, reciting the words in her head, remembering how they'd looked on the parchment when she'd first learned them.

Cleanse my soul;
Clear my mind;
Enable my body.
Grant that my station may serve;
Grant that my strength may suffice;
Grant that my life may give honour;
Grant that my death may earn it.

They were beautiful words. They comforted her; they always had. She closed her eyes for a moment, enjoying the quiet of the pre-dawn. In the distance she heard the *erh-erh* of klohawks. The scents of the city rose to meet her: gently warming rockcrete, dried spices, burning oil, gahl trees turning their speared leaves to face the rising sun.

Only in the hour before dawn was the city of Hjec Aleja restful. As the flaming orange sunrise tipped over the western horizon, the manufactories would start up again, the dust-crawlers would begin to move, the garrisons would empty and refill as the watches were cycled.

Until then, she could watch the place sleeping, cooled by the long night, the toils and strains and nightmares subdued for a while, if not forgotten.

Her balcony was high up, near the summit of the Third Spire of the Cathedral of Blessed Alexia, so she could see a long way. Her deep brown eyes ran over the cityscape as it unfolded below her.

She saw tight-packed streets with tiled roofs, arranged in a haphazard maze of overhanging eaves. No thoroughfare in Hjec Aleja ever ran straight. When she'd first arrived she'd assumed that was an accident. Only later had she discovered the myriad superstitions of the planet. A straight road let in mirage-spirits, she had been told. Keep the way crooked, and they can't find the thresholds.

Stupid beliefs they were, probably heretical, but tolerated for so long that opposing them had long ago been abandoned. Bajola knew that de Chatelaine would have loved nothing more than to purge the world of its theological untidiness – it was a shrineworld, after all – but even she had to bend when faced with something ground so deep, so, impervious, like the endless red dust that you could never scrub from your fingernails or keep from caking on your lips.

Besides, the people of Ras Shakeh worshipped the Emperor fervently enough. They could be forgiven their eccentricities, which even the canoness allowed were harmless.

In any case, now that the horror had arrived, such things had ceased to be important. Bajola screwed her eyes up, gazing into the rusty haze of the horizon, wondering when that empty land would first fill with the cloud-blight of marching soldiers.

Soon. All the strategeos told them that, shaking their heads as they looked into their tactical projections. Progress had been astonishing since the landings: unreasonably fast, unreasonably brutal.

When she had been younger, newly inducted into the Orders Famulous and sent out into the void on her first diplomatic missions, Bajola had been troubled by what she saw of the arch-enemy's work. Why, she had wondered, did the Emperor, the omnipotent Master of Mankind, permit such terror to exist in the universe? He must have been capable of destroying it, just as he had once destroyed the heresy of his greatest son.

The error of that thinking had led to castigation fairly swiftly. Canoness Reich, her first superior in the Order, had been unequivocal.

'What do you want, child?' she had demanded, fixing her with those biting, ice-blue eyes. 'A life of comfort? What d'you think would become of us then?'

She'd leaned over to Bajola, jabbing her in the chest with her bronze augmetic finger.

'We'd become fat. We'd become corrupt. Conflict keeps us lean, fit, pure, the way we were meant to be.'

Bajola had been more easily cowed then. Reich had been a formidable woman.

'He orders the universe as it should be. Welcome the test, child. Welcome the knowledge that the void harbours terror. Without terror, there are no heroes.'

It had been easy to say, and easy to believe. Now, watching the sun rise over a doomed world, waiting for the ranks of terror to close on the last city, the aphorism felt hollow.

Bajola was not so easily cowed now. She was capable of making her own mind up.

Grant that my life may give honour;
Grant that my death may earn it.

A first sliver of gold broke over the distant ridge of the Djarl peaks. Almost immediately the air began to feel hotter.

She could have stayed there for a long time, gathering her thoughts before the day's labours began. When her comm-bead disturbed her, buzzing into life as she watched the first amber rays of sunlight angle through the mountains, it was an irritation.

Early, for a summons.

'Bajola,' she acknowledged, moving away from the balcony and slapping the railing's dust from her hands.

'Sister Palatine,' came the response. It was Callia, one of de Chatelaine's aides. 'The canoness demands your presence. Hall of the Halicon, twenty minutes.'

Bajola smiled. Typically terse.

'On my way,' she said. 'Did the canoness say what it was about?'

The link cut dead. Either Callia was being rude, or she was ferociously busy. The latter was more likely.

Bajola walked back into her cell. Not much to look at – a narrow bed with no covers, a devotional pict of Saint Alexia, a metal-bound chest containing her robes, a bolter hung on the wall from iron brackets and draped in embroidered benedictions.

Her eyes lighted on the weapon. It had an ugly, blunt aspect. Even though she'd long since left the Order Famulous behind and embraced the way of the Wounded Heart, she'd never learned to love the core tool of her adopted trade.

Get over it, she thought to herself, pulling the shift over her head and starting to dress. *You'll be using it again soon.*

When she arrived at the Hall of the Halicon, the place was in a frenzy of preparation. That was unusual. Ever since fighting had broken out, the grand ceremonial space had been virtually unused, its marble surfaces surrendered to the drifting, gritty air.

Now hundreds of labourers were at work, polishing statuary, rolling out long crimson carpets, hanging banners with the bloody symbols of the Wounded Heart sewn in crimson and gold thread.

As soon as she saw that work, Bajola's spirits rose a little. She knew who had been summoned. So perhaps they had made it. Perhaps it would be a whole battle company of them. That would be something worth seeing; it might even turn the tide.

She couldn't see the canoness. She walked up the wide stairway, feeling the first pricks of sweat at her neck, trying to catch a glimpse of de Chatelaine in the milling crowds.

The Hall was an obscene place, a vulgar display of power and indulgence that sat uneasily with Ras Shakeh's windswept emptiness. Bajola hated it, the canoness hated it, everyone who worked in it hated it. Unlike the white-walled structures in the rest of the city, the Hall had been constructed from a dark-veined stone that sucked in the sunlight during the day and made the interior shimmer with close, sweaty heat.

Its bulk was out of all proportion to the older buildings around it. Rings of corded pillars supported an ornate panelled ceiling of stuccoed cherubs and milk-faced saints. Incense burners swung from the vaults above, staining the patterned floors with saccharine aromas. Golden statues of heroes stood in ranks down the echoing aisles, their melancholy, smug faces turned to the starry heavens for inspiration.

The Order had not been responsible for the Hall's construction. Cardinal Tomojo-Kech had built it seven hundred years ago, demolishing a more suitably austere priory that had stood on the site since the Order had first come to Ras Shakeh in the 37th millennium. No one knew how much it had cost to ship such huge quantities of precious commodities to such an isolated place. Perhaps the extravagance had been what had cost Tomojo-Kech his head during the Jericar Purges; perhaps not. It was always hard to know.

His legacy had lasted, though. The Halicon citadel, of which the Hall was the major part, dominated the mountain city of Hjec Aleja, squatting atop the rocky outcrop at its heart and gazing out across the plains with overblown grandeur. All roads in the city led there, sooner or later, snaking up the narrow causeways and switchbacks until they emerged at the Plaza of Triumph, two hundred metres above the ochre plains and baking under the sun.

Bajola preferred the cathedral, her own demesne, set outside the inner walls of the city and placed within the teeming outer hab-districts. It was where it ought to be, close to those who needed it, allowing the priests to minister to the faithful rather than sweat away in Tomojo-Kech's folly up on the mountain.

Bajola pushed her way through the crowds, smelling their odour of sweat and incense, before catching sight of the canoness at last.

Alexis de Chatelaine saw her coming and nodded sharply in what passed for acknowledgement with her.

'You're late,' she said.

'Forgive me,' said Bajola, bowing. 'The streets were clogged.'

De Chatelaine pursed her lips. 'Word has got out already. I don't know how. The masses will always find a way. If we could tap that, turn their ferreting curiosity into something useful, I would not fear losing this war.'

The canoness was a clipped, severe figure. Her silver hair, cut into a sheer razor-bob, framed a hard-edged face made old by a lifetime of devotion. Her lips were thin and her flesh was roughened from both the sun and age. De Chatelaine scorned cosmetic treatment and so looked every year of her one hundred and forty-two winters. For all that, her movements gave away her essential vigour. She could still fight, and Bajola knew her will was as starkly unbending as ever. She dominated the space around her, tall and spear-lean in night-black armour-plate, trimmed with pale ermine and decorated by the crimson cracked heart device in pearl and ruby.

'They heard more than I did,' admitted Bajola.

'Then I shall enlighten you, child,' said de Chatelaine. 'Emperor be praised, our summons have been answered. I could almost have given up, but that would have been a failure of faith, would it not? The Wolves of Fenris have sent their forces, just as their Great Wolf promised. The timing is propitious. They have already given battle to the enemy and have emerged victorious. Now we are tracking them. They will be here within hours.'

Bajola placed her hands together and bowed her head. A mix of emotions surged through her – she had begun to insulate herself against the possibility that they might not come.

'How many?' she asked.

'I do not know. I fear not many. But recall this: a single warrior of the Adeptus Astartes is worth a hundred Guardsmen. In the cause of morale, his value is even higher. They will kill at a rate that even our Celestians cannot match.'

'So I have heard. Let us hope the stories are true.'

'Of course they're true,' she snapped. 'I've fought with them before. Watch your thoughts, Palatine.'

Bajola bowed in apology. It was something she'd become used to, when speaking to the canoness.

'I mean no disrespect,' she said. 'But our service has been with the Adulators, who are steeped in our ways and are on close terms with the holy orders of the Ecclesiarchy. These are the Wolves. I have heard... things.'

De Chatelaine's expression softened a little.

'So have I,' she said. 'Who has not? But these are the instruments the Emperor chooses to make available to us, and so, by necessity, they are the right ones.'

Bajola sometimes found de Chatelaine's ramrod faith touching, almost juvenile. To admit that, though, even to herself, was dangerous.

'That is so,' she said. 'I look forward to meeting them.'

'You will do more than that. I wish you to work with them. You will be our conduit. I trust that meets with your approval.'

Bajola felt a brief twinge of surprise. 'Of course,' she said. 'But, I–'

'You were of the Famulous before you joined us,' said de Chatelaine. 'The diplomats. I take it you have retained some of those skills. We will need them.'

The canoness lowered her voice, moving her head closer to Bajola's.

'Matters have not always gone well between the Church and the

Wolves,' she said. 'You know this, and they will not have forgotten it. I am not a fool, Palatine: I am aware of the potential for strife, and I wish to limit it. We will have to find some way of working together if we are not to end our days on this dust-blown rock.'

She placed her gauntlet over Bajola's hand. It was a strangely protective gesture from a battle-hardened woman.

'Do not let me down, Uwe,' she said. 'You will be the voice of calm that smooths the way between us.'

Bajola swallowed her discomfort. Working with the Wolves directly had not been something she'd considered. Unlike the canoness, she had long since got used to the idea that they weren't coming. It was a complication, though maybe one she should have forseen.

She bowed. 'By His will,' she said.

When she raised her head again, de Chatelaine was no longer looking at her. The commotion in the hall was growing. From the Plaza outside came the noise of Shakeh Guardsmen shouting something in Haljeha, something about an incoming ship on the horizon.

'Earlier than I expected,' said de Chatelaine, fixing her green eyes on the ornate entrance gates as if she could peer through them. 'Perhaps I should not be surprised.'

She took a deep breath, and released Bajola's hand.

'Prepare yourself, Palatine,' she said. 'The Wolves approach.'

They were, and they weren't, what she'd imagined.

Seven of them strode through the Hall gates, shaking the dust from their armour as they came. De Chatelaine had used what little time remained to her well, and the audience chamber was as clean and well-ordered as could have been hoped for. Lines of Guardsmen stood to attention along either aisle, their uniforms scrubbed clear of the worst of the grit and bloodstains.

Squads of Battle Sisters stood beside them, far more imposing in their pristine black power armour. Bajola felt a swell of pride just looking at them. Some of her sisters had returned from the front mere days ago, carrying stories of horror with them. They stood to attention in neat ranks, eyes gazing straight ahead, betraying nothing but rigid, silent resolve.

De Chatelaine waited for the Wolves at the far end of the chamber. A marble dais of wide steps led up to a blood-red leather-upholstered throne surmounted by a gaudy tableau of angels and writhing serpents. The canoness had chosen not to make use of that, but stood at the base of the stairs, clad in her regulation battle-plate. A small coterie of aides, including Callia and Bajola, clustered around her.

Bajola watched the Wolves approach. She surprised herself by feeling a faint tremor of unease. Not fear, exactly; more like tension, as if an attack were imminent. The warriors in grey exuded a palpable atmosphere of intimidation. It rose from them as they moved, flowing from their limbs like musk, hanging in the air behind them.

She studied them as they neared, moving her eyes from each one to the next, soaking in as much information as she could and storing it away, just as she had been trained to.

Observe. Retain. Scan for weakness; watch for strength.

Their leader was obvious. He walked with a fighter's rolling gait. He wore his full armour minus the helm, and it made him massive. His head was bald and marked with tribal tattoos. A matted grey beard tumbled across his breastplate. The hair looked filthy, as if it had been dipped in a bucket of boiling lard and the slops had been left to dry.

They were all dirty. They stank of rotten meat. Their chipped battle-plate was smeared with blood and grease and grime. They were hirsute and grim-faced, save for one: a younger-looking warrior with flame-red hair and a raw weal running crossways the length of his face. That one could almost have passed for human.

She had expected them to look savage. She had expected the grinding whine of power armour, the clanking bone-totems, the back-slung weapons with runes carved finely on the blades.

She hadn't expected the stench. She hadn't expected the sheer aura of belligerence, the thick expressions of surly violence in their amber eyes.

They were beasts. They were beasts clad in the rags of humanity, given a veneer of civilisation to mask the deep animal within.

As she was wont to, as she always did, she found herself wondering why the blessed Emperor would have created and given sanction to such things.

The answer came to mind almost immediately.

Because they are needed.

Bajola noticed that one of them carried himself differently to the others. His eyes were grey, not golden. His exposed face was equally marked by scarification and tribe-marks, but he walked taller, with less swagger. He was contained, wrapped up in himself. The others let their souls spill out in front of them, betraying their essential core of menace, glorying in the dominance they so casually projected.

The grey-eyed one did not.

Once, a very long time ago while serving with her old Order, Bajola had witnessed a squad of Ultramarines accompanying an Inquisitorial retinue. She'd been awe-struck by them – their discipline, their confidence, their reserve. The grey-eyed warrior carried himself a little like they had done. That was strange. She wondered whether anyone else had noticed. She even wondered whether the rest of his pack had noticed – such subtle signals were hard to read and easy to miss.

The leader drew up before de Chatelaine. At close quarters he was immense, a mountain of brutal energy encased in dirty ceramite.

'I am called Wolf Guard Gunnlaugur,' he announced. 'Of the Great Company of Ragnar Blackmane, of the Rout of Fenris.'

His voice was harsh, a grating thrum of pit-deep hazard.

'You are welcome, Son of Fenris,' replied de Chatelaine. Her voice was dry and clear. If the canoness felt any uneasiness in his presence, she didn't show it. 'We are grateful to the Great Wolf for sending you. We are grateful to you for coming.'

Gunnlaugur grunted. 'Glad you're pleased to see us. That ship up there wasn't.'

'You destroyed it,' said de Chatelaine. 'That was your first great service to us. We shall not forget it, it was a mighty deed.'

'Mighty? I lost my own. That is a great shame to have hanging on my shoulders. We were not expecting to have to fight our way down.'

The canoness gave him an apologetic look.

'Yes, I am aware of that,' she said. 'If there had been any way of warning you–'

'There wasn't?'

'If we had been able to reach you, to help you, do you not think we would have done it?'

Bajola appreciated de Chatelaine's skill. The canoness spoke evenly, matching the Wolf's blunt challenges with calmness. It was not easy to quarrel with one who would not rise to it.

Gunnlaugur fixed her with his black-pinned gaze for a long time, assessing, appraising. Bajola half expected him to start sniffing.

'Tell me what has happened here,' he said at last.

'I fear you will not like it,' said de Chatelaine. 'You have landed in the middle of a war, Wolf Guard. Until you had arrived, I would have said it was one we could not win. Even now, I am not sure how long we have left.'

Gunnlaugur didn't look troubled by that. If anything, Bajola thought she caught the gleam of something like excitement in his eyes.

'We are here now,' he said. 'Anything is possible.'

After that, the conversation moved to the canoness's private chambers. The troops in the Hall dispersed, sent back to their barracks and bunkers where they could exchange wild theories about what they had just seen. Only de Chatelaine and her entourage – a dozen officers and officials – and the seven members of Gunnlaugur's pack took their places in the heavily shielded room behind the dais.

The ornamentation was less elaborate there, though the chairs had gilded backs and the polished table was formed of a priceless darkwood that didn't grow natively on Ras Shakeh. The walls were scrubbed plain and the floor was bare stone. Sunlight angled in from rows of half-blinded windows. Even with screens in place, the glare added to an already uncomfortably hot space.

The two parties took up places on either side of the table. The chamber had been fitted out with the largest, most sturdy set of furniture they had been able to find, but still the Wolves looked almost comically ill at ease when seated. Bajola guessed that they would have preferred to stand, but they didn't insist.

In their own way, they were making an effort. That was encouraging.

'So, the situation,' said de Chatelaine, pressing her hands together on the tabletop. 'The Adulators withdrew their defensive presence from here six months ago. By that time the cover they offered us was little more than token. We frequently went for months with no significant strike force within range. I was unhappy with the situation, as was the Chapter Master, but it became apparent that no easy resolution existed. The Ras subsector contains over thirty-nine inhabited worlds and has a population in excess of ninety billion souls, so merits more than cursory attention. But the Adulators have many concerns, and I believe that garrison work does not greatly appeal to them. Perhaps that is true of other Chapters too.'

Gunnlaugur listened intently. Bajola watched him drink the information in. She'd heard that Space Marines possessed eidetic recall. Then again, she'd heard many things about them, not all of which could possibly be true.

'You will be aware of plans to use this subsector as a staging post for a new crusade into lost space,' she went on. 'When I first learned of the proposals, I knew the process of organising such an undertaking would last decades. Nonetheless, the idea put us on the stellar cartograph, so to speak, and gave me leverage in my quest for more permanent defensive arrangements. Ancient pacts between the Ras subsector and the Fenrisian zone of protection were uncovered. I was informed by my scholiasts that the treaties had no current validity. I responded that anything was worth a try.'

Despite himself, Gunnlaugur smiled. It was a curious gesture. The Wolf

Guard had an elongated jawline, crammed with overdeveloped denti-
tion, especially the canines. His smile was more like a dog's growl, with
the lips pulling back and the fangs jutting forwards.

Even their expressions of amusement, it seemed, served as a challenge.

'My motives were sound,' said de Chatelaine. 'We are not immune to
the blights of heresy and sedition here. The problem has been growing, and my sisters have been fully occupied over the past few years.
We destroy one nest, another emerges. These heretics worship sickness.
I have witnessed men expose themselves to crippling disease, revelling
in their decay. The appeal of that eludes me, but then we do live, do we
not, in a fallen galaxy?'

At the mention of plague-cults, a low murmur of recognition passed
among the Wolves.

'The heretics,' Gunnlaugur said. 'They brought the war.'

'No, not them. They kept us occupied, but we never let them flourish
for long. Do not think that my sisters are afraid to use their flamers, Wolf
Guard, for they are not.'

Gunnlaugur smiled again. Against all expectation, he and the canoness
seemed to be finding each other's company agreeable.

'The enemy came from outside the subsector,' said de Chatelaine. 'The
cults here did nothing more than prepare the ground for them. The ships
must have arrived in-system before we sent our request for aid to you,
but back then we had no inkling of their presence. It was a large fleet, and
our defences were so paltry and undermanned that we stood no chance.
We quickly lost what orbital grids we possessed. We prepared our cities
for bombardment, assuming that destruction was what they wished for.
It was not so. They landed forces – we do not know how many – and the
majority of the fleet moved on. The ship you encountered was the only
one they left behind. As we speak, dozens more are no doubt ravaging
the rest of the subsector.'

Bajola watched de Chatelaine's expression grow tighter, more self-
conscious. The canoness had taken the blame for the war on her own
shoulders, and the ruin of her world pressed heavily on her. The fact that
she had acted with the utmost propriety at every stage made no difference. De Chatelaine had exacting standards, and did not exempt herself
from them.

'It happened so quickly,' she said, almost to herself. 'Too quickly. They
have already overrun our industrial heartland. We have lost our population centres, our manufactories. A few hold-outs remain, but we receive
word of capitulations every day. This planet is going dark. Two weeks
ago I ordered the withdrawal of all remaining forces to this zone. We

have succeeded in holding the city since then, but we know they are coming for us. Everyone here knows it.'

She smiled dryly.

'This is the planet you have landed on. I had hoped to show you an exemplary shrineworld, one from which the legions of the Emperor would march out to fresh conquest. Believe me, I am sorry that I cannot do that.'

Gunnlaugur leaned back in his seat, and the wooden chair creaked alarmingly under him. He hacked up a gobbet of phlegm, leaned over and spat on the floor.

'War has a way of following us,' he said. 'Truth be told, we like it that way. We get bored without it.'

De Chatelaine's advisers looked disapproving. Bajola could understand why – they had all suffered enormously; the savage in front of them was making light of it.

She stole a glance at the grey-eyed figure sitting at the far end of the pack. As her eyes lighted on him she caught him looking directly at her. She averted her gaze quickly, half embarrassed, half irritated.

He is studying me, just as I am studying him. Do I seem as outlandish to him as he does to me?

'If war is what you wish for, you will have no shortage of it on Ras Shakeh,' said de Chatelaine. Her expression had become severe again. The canoness disliked flippancy in most things; in the face of the horror that had come to her world, it bordered on obscenity. 'Though perhaps I have not adequately conveyed the scale of what faces us.'

She turned to Callia.

'Replay the footage from Jedaj,' she said. 'That may prove instructive.'

Callia nodded, rose from her chair and moved over to a wall-mounted projector. She adjusted the controls and the blinds slid down the windows. At the far end of the chamber, against a bare whitewashed wall, a picter image flickered into life.

'We retrieved this material six weeks ago,' explained de Chatelaine. 'It was taken by a defender of the ore-processing plant at Jedaj, five hundred kilometres south of here. I am not sure why he took it, nor why it survived. Perhaps he wanted a record of what had happened, or perhaps the enemy wished us to see what they are capable of. My first inclination was to destroy it, but I decided against it. It is not easy viewing, but then I am sure you are used to such things.'

As she finished speaking, the footage crackled into life. It was shaky and motion-blurred, as if the images had been shot from a helmet-mounted picter. The first pictures were dark and grainy, indicating night-vision enhancement.

Bajola hadn't seen the footage before. She'd been offered the chance when it had first come in, and had declined, guessing what was on it. She shifted in her seat, watching the images with a heavy heart. She had no great wish to keep watching.

A few seconds afterwards, an audio track kicked in: a man's breathing, heavy and panicked. The picter-view leapt around wildly as he moved his head. It showed an industrial complex at night – tangled pipes, rows of generator-coils, huge cooling towers. The dark sky beyond was mottled with smoke, the kind of dense, greasy pall that comes from burning promethium.

The man with the helmet-picter was running, making the picture shake and jerk. Others ran with him, all in Shakeh Guard uniforms, all carrying lasguns two-handed.

'Holy Emperor,' the man mumbled, snatching the litany between his ragged breaths. 'Holy Emperor. Holy Emperor.'

It wasn't clear where the men were running. Explosions sounded in the background, muffled and tinny on the recording; no doubt deafening to them.

Other shouts intruded – men's voices, curdled with fear and disbelief. 'Holy Emperor. Holy Emperor.'

The Guardsmen opened up with their weapons. Bright lines of lasfire scored the night, overloading the pict-stream and blanking the feed. When the images resumed the men were running again, faster this time.

Something flitted across the picter's lurching visual field, just glimpsed for a second: a bloated face amid the far darkness, pale as corpse-light, grinning, stalking towards them.

'Holy Emperor. Holy Emperor.'

The man's panting got more urgent, more uncontrolled. More lasbeams flashed off.

The view swept round suddenly. A semi-ruined wall emerged from the smog, gaping with black holes where munitions had exploded. Unidentifiable shapes were moving in the shadows beyond, twitching and rocking and jabbering.

'Grenade!' screamed one of the Guardsmen, out of view.

The picter lurched to the floor. A riot of static hissing broke out as explosions maxed-out the audio filters.

Then the man started moving again. Audio resumed. He was whimpering from fear.

'Holy… Emperor… Holy… Emperor…'

Someone screamed from behind him, a garish sound of animal horror, high-pitched and keening. The Guardsmen all started sprinting, their formation gone, firing off random rounds into the dark, leaping and stumbling over blast craters underfoot. One of them was hit by something. The view jerked over to him for an instant – his face white with terror.

'Don't leave me!' he squealed. Something with spidery limbs was crawling up his leg.

'H-holy... Emp... eror!'

The men kept running. They stumbled through what looked like a bombed-out manufactorium. Huge machines were still running inside it, clanking and spinning and roiling in the darkness. Screaming started up again, a whole chorus of it. It seemed to come from all directions, from the mouths of all of them, echoing from the jagged wall-remains.

Objects hung from the roof, twisting in the grainy gloom. The view briefly slewed upwards, exposing a shaky snapshot of man-shaped bundles suspended on corroding meathooks, some shuddering like marionettes, some glistening wetly.

'H-h-ho... Hol...'

Bloated, grinning horrors crept up out of the shadows. Las-fire downed some of them, knocking them back to the ground with gurgling pops. Others kept on coming. They had swollen faces in the flickering light, the skin stretched tight and held in place by iron pins. They laughed as they scampered, a low, throaty *hurr hurr hurr*.

The picter was shaking badly now, shuddering so hard it was hard to make out what was going on. The horrors must have got in amongst them. Everything dissolved into a jumbled succession of sickening images – flesh being cut, eyes being pulled, stomachs bursting.

In a brief flash of clarity, a devilish face reared up dead centre, laughing so hard its lips split open. Its eyes stared wildly, cat-yellow and weeping with pus. It reached out with needle-tipped fingers. The whine of a circular saw started up somewhere close by.

'Ho–! Hol–! Empe–! Ach! Nnngh!'

The Guardsman's frenzied litany collapsed into a jerking, frothing shriek. Blood splashed across the picter's lens, coating the image with a splash of red. It shook violently, rocked back and forth by its bearer's spasms.

Then it went dead, replaced by a fizzing wall of white noise.

A few seconds later it resumed.

The image was swinging back and forth like a lazy pendulum. The sound had gone. Blood on the lens made everything smeary and indistinct. The viewpoint was higher up, as if the picter were suspended a long way above the floor.

It showed a manufactorium crawling with movement. Hundreds of enemy troops scuttled between machines like swarms of roaches, clambering over one another, chittering and cavorting. Huge, distorted creatures stalked among them, stomachs ballooning and flesh glimmering with corpse-light.

Something else approached the lens. A single, glowing eye peered up, lodged in the centre of a rusting, tusk-jowled helm. Massive pauldrons rose up out of the murk, each one studded with gleaming entrail-loops. The edges of twin cleavers could be made out, glistening, steadily dripping.

For a moment the armour-clad titan just stared at the picter. Then it reached up. The last image was of a gore-splattered gauntlet closing over the lens.

After that, static.

Callia cut off the feed. The window-blinds slid up, letting sunlight flood back into the chamber.

Bajola looked down at her hands. They were damp with sweat.

'That is what our troops have been fighting, Wolf Guard,' said de Chatelaine. 'They were heroes just to stand their ground, do you not think?'

Gunnlaugur gazed back at her steadily. He didn't look entirely unmoved by what he had seen. That was to his credit, Bajola thought.

'They were,' he said.

The atmosphere in the chamber was subdued. One of de Chatelaine's counsellors, a scholarly man named Arvian Nomu, looked faint, and gripped the edge of the table tightly.

'That thing at the end,' Gunnlaugur said. 'You know what it was?'

'I do,' said the canoness.

'How many of them have landed?'

'That is our only confirmed sighting.'

Gunnlaugur snorted, his nostrils flaring. He looked pensive. 'Your troops can't kill it,' he said.

De Chatelaine nodded. 'I know. I hope yours can.'

Gunnlaugur didn't smile that time, which surprised Bajola. Until then, his casual confidence had seemed inexhaustible.

'We can kill anything,' he said. 'That's what we do.'   .

He turned towards one of his warriors, a lean-faced killer with a long-sword strapped to his back. They exchanged a brief, significant glance.

'Just depends how many there are,' he said bleakly.

Chapter Ten

Three hours later, with the sun burning high in the sky, Váltyr walked up a tight spiral stairway, his shoulder guards grinding against the stone walls. He emerged onto a small square platform at the summit of one of the Halicon's many towers. The city and its surroundings flowed away from him in every direction, falling down the long, broken mountain ridges before giving way to kilometres of featureless ochre plains. The distant horizon was hazy, masked by a pale screen of dusty grey.

The arch of Ras Shakeh's sky was a deep, royal blue. Its earth was dull orange, like rusting iron. Everything shimmered under a beating, constant wall of heat. No breeze stirred the air. No animals called, no birds sang.

He paced over to the battlements running around the edge of the platform. Olgeir was already there, peering over the edge, his huge gauntlets gripping the sides.

'Planned it out, great one?' asked Váltyr, coming to join him.

Olgeir didn't reply immediately. His amber eyes ran across the warrens of streets below. His cracked, pierced lips moved soundlessly, as if he were calculating angles, strengths, numbers.

The Halicon squatted at the summit of the mountain city. Beyond its walls lay the upper city, an orderly collection of red-tiled chapels, memorials, habs and admin blocks. Groves of spear-leaved trees grew in shaded courtyards and the sound of running water could be heard from under their eaves. The sigil of the Wounded Heart was prominent on the larger edifices, hanging limp on unmoving banners. A few landing stages were dotted amid the tight-packed buildings, ringed by defence lasers and servitor bays. *Vuokho* sat on one of them, still leaking smoke, still looking barely functional.

The upper city was protected at its perimeter by a winding circuit of high, thick walls. Defence towers studded the battlements at fifty metre intervals, each one bristling with lascannon turrets and swivelling missile launchers. Only one gateway broke the enclosure of those walls – the Ighala Gate, a blunt bastion of adamantium and granite that hunkered darkly to the west of the Halicon's bulk. The Gate was a mini-citadel all on its own, dank, angular and forbidding. Just like the towers on either side of it, weapons clustered all over it. Some of the bigger guns looked like recent additions, cannibalised from overrun installations and bolted into place for the attack they all knew was coming.

Beyond the Ighala Gate was a narrow bridge that stretched out across a plunging, debris-choked gully. The ravine was a natural cleft in the mountain that ran around the upper city, dividing the two halves of the settlement and adding to the effective height of the inner wall. The cleft was too deep for infantry to negotiate unaided and lay tightly under the shadow of the tower guns. Váltyr grunted with approval when he saw that. It was a killing ground, a formidable barrier for any army to cross.

On the far side of the ravine was the lower city, a much larger straggle of far shabbier buildings. That was where the bulk of Hjec Aleja's population lived their lives, clogged up against one another in close-packed hab-towers. The urban landscape ran down through a series of terraces, each one teeming with jostling, multi-storied estates. Váltyr could see very few major transit arteries; the streets were narrow, winding and overlooked.

Few structures of note existed in the tangled morass of stone beyond the inner walls. Only one caught his eye – the Cathedral of St Alexia, a gothic basilica with three gargoyle-encrusted spires. Its trio of spikes rose up into the clear air, casting long shadows over the houses below.

Much further out, tiny with distance, was the outer perimeter wall. Like the inner barrier it was buttressed with defence towers and studded with fire-points. A second armoured gatehouse stood on the outer rim, as lumpen and gun-covered as the Ighala Gate.

After that, nothing – just desiccated scrubland, dissolving slowly into rust-coloured desert. A lone road wound steadily westwards, its broken rockcrete surface marred by blown dust.

Váltyr looked at it all carefully, taking his time.

'This is no fortress,' said Olgeir eventually.

'No,' said Váltyr. 'It isn't.'

'You know how many troops they have here?'

'Tell me.'

'Thirty thousand regular Guardsmen. A few thousand armed militia. Less than a hundred Battle Sisters. A few dozen tanks and walkers. One crippled Thunderhawk. And us.'

Váltyr nodded, chewing over the figures. All that was left of a planet's defences after just a few months of war. Not much to boast about.

'Arm the civilians?' he suggested.

'They have been armed,' said Olgeir, in a voice that gave away how useful he thought that would be. He leaned over the parapet, hawked and spat. The spittle flew a long way down before hitting anything. 'I've seen better defended asteroids,' he concluded.

'We should strike out,' said Váltyr, running his eyes along the horizon. 'Blood them before they get here.'

Olgeir grunted in agreement.

'Gunnlaugur's already planning it. The canoness is unhappy. She wants everyone behind the walls, waiting for them to get there.'

Váltyr looked down at the inner ring of defences.

'We could hold this upper level, perhaps,' he said thoughtfully. 'The bridge is a choke point, and those walls look solid. But the outer rim… I don't know.'

Olgeir nodded. 'There's no way we can hold the perimeter. Too long, too low. But she wants to, all the same. They won't let the cathedral fall without a fight.'

Váltyr couldn't blame them for that. It was their cathedral.

'We're going to need to clear some space, then,' he said. 'We can't move anything through those streets.'

'Aye,' said Olgeir. 'I've been planning it. They've got earthmovers and plenty of manpower. We need trenches, ones we can get burning. The one thing they'll do is keep on coming. We could soak up thousands if we organise it right.'

Váltyr didn't say what he thought.

It won't be enough.

'Do they have flyers?' he asked.

'Apparently not.'

'That's something.'

The two of them fell into silence again. Váltyr felt himself sweating under the relentless glare of the sun. He could have put his helm on and

let it regulate his temperature, but that felt like an acknowledgement
of weakness. De Chatelaine had said that most of the fighting on Ras
Shakeh had taken place at night, and he could see why. Even the damned
would struggle to march under that unbroken heat.

'I tell you, Heavy-hand,' he said at last. 'I already hate this place.'

Olgeir chuckled. 'That bad?'

Váltyr thought for a moment.

'Actually, it is,' he said, letting his irritation get the better of him. 'I
mean, what in Hel is this? This is a backwater, a rock. If we're going to
die here, I want to know why. We won't get a saga for this. Not a decent
one. Why would *anyone* fight for this?'

Olgeir shrugged. 'Can't answer that, brother,' he said. 'But you can see
it as well as I can. This isn't just a raid – they're here to take this world.
Others, too. This is organised. There's method in it.'

'What can be here that they would possibly want?'

'Something worth sending a fleet for. Seems to me this is about
occupation.'

Váltyr shook his head. Olgeir's judgement was normally good, but that
felt wrong.

'The Sisters,' he said, changing the subject. 'They sent distress calls?'

'For weeks, they say,' said Olgeir. 'They don't know if any got through.
We're months away from anywhere with an army.' He chuckled darkly.
'Face it, we're on our own.'

Váltyr pushed back from the railing and stretched his arms out, feeling
the muscles flex.

'Then I need to get out of here and find something to kill. I'd just
started to find my rhythm.'

Olgeir nodded appreciatively. 'You and me both,' he said.

Váltyr looked into the distance, and the empty land gazed back at him.
To the west, the horizon's haze had taken on a faint greenish tinge, like
mould spreading across water.

'That's where they'll come from,' he said.

Olgeir nodded. 'I can smell them already.'

Váltyr felt an itch run across the palm of his sword-hand then. It missed
the weight of *holdbítr*.

'Soon, then,' he said softly, clenching his fist tight and gazing intently
at the pall of sickness on the world's edge. 'Very soon.'

Gunnlaugur sat alone. The chamber he'd been given by the canoness
was the finest in the citadel: the walls had been hung with silks and the
floor had been covered in a series of finely woven deep-pile rugs. He'd

had them strip all that away, exposing the stone and plaster. Only two chairs remained; the rest had gone.

He struggled to shake his black, surly mood. He'd arrived at Ras Shakeh expecting no greater enemy than tedium. Though he would only have grudgingly admitted it, even to himself, a little tedium would have been welcome. It would have given time for the pack to bed in, for Ingvar and Haflói to find their places, for everything to settle into the old rhythm.

Instead they had been plunged into a world on the edge of ruin. The *Undrider*, with its thousands of loyal souls on board, had been lost. Those that had made it to the saviour pods had crashed down onto a planet enveloped in a nightmare. None of them had made contact since *Vuokho* had landed at Hjec Aleja. That disaster alone wore away at his conscience. In the scant moments he'd had to himself since making planetfall, he had run the events of the brief orbital battle over and over in his mind. Perhaps he could have handled it better. Perhaps his desire to get into combat may have overruled tactical sense.

Or perhaps not. The choices, and the time to make them, had been limited. It was always easy to second-guess decisions made in the heat of battle.

So why am I so troubled by this one?

He knew the answer.

A soft chime sounded at the door.

'Come,' he growled.

Ingvar entered. The warrior's expression was hard to read. Not contrite, exactly; not spoiling for a fight. He must have known what was coming, but he made no concessions to it.

He came to stand before Gunnlaugur. His face was a mask of calmness.

That alone pricked at Gunnlaugur's pride.

You are a Son of Russ! Show some mettle!

'So why did you do it?' Gunnlaugur asked, looking up at Ingvar from under heavy lids.

'I tried to warn you,' said Ingvar. 'It was the right thing to–'

'It was not your call.' Gunnlaugur's voice remained low, animated by a low, snarling threat-note.

Ingvar took a breath. 'I saw Jorundur approaching,' he said. 'It was the right thing to–'

'Blood of Russ, don't treat me like a fool!' Gunnlaugur swept up out of the chair. They stood facing one another, barely a hand's width apart. Gunnlaugur's face was hot with anger; Ingvar's remained still.

'What has *changed* in you, brother?' Gunnlaugur growled. 'You spoke against me on the bridge. You didn't want to attack that ship.' As he spoke, as he remembered it, the whole thing became harder to understand. 'We had a chance – one chance – for the kill. Why would you not take it? Why would you *ever* not take it?'

Ingvar's grey eyes didn't flinch.

'I didn't speak against you,' he said. 'We had to consider alternatives. The tactical options had not closed down.'

That was not language Gunnlaugur had heard from Ingvar before. It was not language he had heard from any Sky Warrior.

'Speak plainly,' he muttered.

'We could have withdrawn. We were faster. They had seen us before we saw them, and so had the advantage. Given space, we could have used our speed to more effect. An alternative to boarding might have presented itself.'

'You're saying I was wrong.'

Ingvar shook his head. 'No. You are *vaerangi*. But it was my duty to point out alternatives.'

Gunnlaugur looked at him with furrowed brows. The language Ingvar was using, the tone of it, it was all unsettling.

He wouldn't raise his voice. He wouldn't fight him.

'You've changed,' he said again.

'You say it like it's something to be feared.'

Gunnlaugur looked away, spat on the floor, then rubbed his hands through his matted mane. Something like sickness churned within him.

'I fear nothing.' He flexed his fingers, as if to clutch at his weapon. Fighting was easy, straightforward. That was what he knew how to do. 'Do you remember Boreal V? Do you remember how we ravaged that world, you and I? That was fighting. That was how I remembered you, when you were gone.'

As he spoke, Gunnlaugur let the memories revive within him. He saw Ingvar and he alone amid a sea of howling, tearing blood-cultists. His hammer had whirled with abandon that night, hewing at the damned in droves. Ingvar's sword had never moved faster, never slain with more deadly accuracy. They had stood back to back, isolated in a sea of death-lust as the sky burned above them, fighting in the purest way possible – two battle-brothers, their lives in each other's hands.

Gunnlaugur had expected to die then. He had not been sad about it: a death on Boreal would have been a fitting end. Sagas would have been sung of two Sky Warriors, elbow-deep in the blood of the fallen, their sacred duty discharged and their honour unstained.

When Hjortur had eventually fought his way to their side, raging and flailing with the others in tow, it had almost been a disappointment.

'I remember all our fights, brother,' said Ingvar. For the first time, his voice had something like emotion in it.

'Then *act* like it,' said Gunnlaugur, whirling back to glare at him. 'Act like you're back amongst your own kind, like you belong here.'

Ingvar's grey eyes were unmoving. 'I would die for Járnhamar,' he said, his voice intense. 'I always would have. You know this.' He took a step towards Gunnlaugur, his own fists twitching as if he wanted to clench them.

Your anger is stirring. Good.

'But I learned *so much*,' Ingvar said. His eyes flickered strangely, as if his attention were elsewhere. 'I thought that I would learn nothing, but I was wrong. We think of ourselves as the bravest, the fastest, the strongest. We laugh at the others. We're wrong. We blunt our own weapons. There are other ways. Some are better.'

Gunnlaugur listened with disbelief. 'Better? That it? Better than the savages from the ice-world who bred you?'

'You're not listening,' Ingvar snarled. Another spark of anger flickered across his face. 'Your mind is closed. It has always been closed.'

Gunnlaugur swept in close, fangs bared, his whole body bristling.

'Do not *dare* to lecture me,' he warned darkly, his hot breath on Ingvar's face. 'We are not equals, Gyrfalkon, ready to brawl in the straw to settle this. This is my pack. You will accept that, or by the blood of the ancients I will *break* you.'

They stood, face to face, both of them tensed for the first move. Gunnlaugur felt his blood pumping around his system, ready to flood into primed muscles. He could see the fury in Ingvar's expression, the desire to lash out, the pungent spike of kill-urge.

Heartbeats passed, thudding heavily in rib-fused chests.

Then, slowly, Ingvar backed down. His eyes lowered. His gauntlets uncurled.

'You are right,' he said quietly. 'You are right. I recognise my failing. I will be sure to correct it.'

Gunnlaugur watched him pull back from the confrontation. For a moment, he couldn't believe it. He had been ready to fight, poised for the explosion of movement. It was a struggle to come down from that. His blood still thundered in his arteries, thick and vital.

I was ready to humiliate him. I was ready to prove myself.

With effort, he forced himself to relax.

Would I have won?

It was hard to find the right words. For a moment longer, they faced one another in silence.

'Listen, brother,' said Gunnlaugur at last, making his voice ebb, pushing it to lose its edge of violence. 'We can fight together like we used to. I want this. But it cannot be the same. I need to know that you will follow an order. I need to know that you will follow me.'

Ingvar nodded. He looked suddenly withdrawn, unsure of himself, as if he'd got close to blurting something out and had only hauled it back at the last minute.

'You are *vaerangi*,' he said again. 'I never challenged you for that.'

Gunnlaugur suddenly felt like he'd missed something, like he'd mistaken Ingvar's meaning somehow.

But it was too late to argue back. He'd stamped his authority, just as Hjortur would have done. That was the important thing.

'Then we are clear,' he said. 'We understand one another.'

'We do.'

Gunnlaugur took a deep breath. In another age he might have reached out then, clapping Ingvar on the shoulder with his gauntlet, behaving like the battle-brother he'd once been. Now, though, the gesture felt strangely inappropriate. He kept his distance.

The air hung heavily between them, tense and febrile. It pressed against his temples. Nothing would clear it; not anger, not remorse.

'We need to work with the Sisters,' Gunnlaugur said, moving awkwardly on to strategic matters, hoping that would salve the nagging unease in his mind. 'They've been working hard on the defences here, but there are too few of them. They don't understand what's coming here.'

Ingvar listened carefully, saying nothing more. He looked chastened, but with an edge of defiance still in his bearing.

'There are things we can do, ways we can strike back,' Gunnlaugur went on. 'But the canoness has her own priorities. The cathedral is one. It's madness to try to hold it, but they won't pull back. I want you to go there, see how defensible it is, assess how viable a stand would be.'

Ingvar nodded. 'By your will,' he said. 'But that isn't all, is it?'

'The Sister Palatine. That's her domain. You saw her observing us at the council, thinking we didn't notice. She's the liaison the canoness has chosen. If they want to observe us, then we can do the same.'

Gunnlaugur looked at Ingvar seriously.

'It won't be easy, working with them,' he said. 'We both have a hundred reasons to distrust one another. So get close to the Palatine, learn how they operate. By the time the enemy get here I want us to be working like hand and gauntlet. You understand?'

Ingvar bowed. 'It will be done,' he said.

Gunnlaugur nodded. 'Good. And after that we'll fight together, you

and I. That will cleanse all this bad blood. It will be like Boreal V again –
pure, uncomplicated, as it ought to be.'

He could hear himself sounding forced, trying to erase the memory of
his anger. It didn't convince him; he doubted it would convince Ingvar.

To his surprise, though, the Gyrfalkon looked at him almost gratefully,
as if he'd been handed a way back. That was something to seize on.

'I would like that, *vaerangi*,' he said. 'Like Boreal again, you and I.'

Vuokho stood on the landing platform, its shell blackened from re-entry.
The length of its blocky hull was scored with damage taken on the
approach to the plague-infested destroyer. Even while their warship had
been dying around them, the enemy gunners had maintained a thick
defensive barrage, one that had sorely tested Jorundur's skills in evasion.

He cast an expert eye over the damage, and his face wrinkled in disgust.

'How do they *do* it?' he asked, talking to himself. 'They can hardly see,
hardly breathe, their hands are tentacles. How can they pull a trigger, let
alone hit things?'

After the void-battle, the descent into Ras Shakeh's atmosphere had
been difficult. One system had blown after another, gradually knocking
out all of the gunship's flight aids and turning it into little more than a
wedge of gliding wreckage. By the time he'd finally got it down, *Vuokho*
was more dead than alive.

'So will it fly?'

Jorundur turned to see Hafloí walking towards him. The Blood Claw's
face was a mass of scabs and inflamed flesh. Even his enhanced body had
struggled to cope with the poisonous wound he'd taken, and his short
trip into the vacuum hadn't helped.

But he was healing well. Gunnlaugur had been right – the whelp was
tough.

'No, it will not,' said Jorundur, turning back to the pitiful heap of
wreckage before him. 'I've seen the tech-servitors here and what they can
do. We may as well start building a new gunship from scratch.'

Hafloí joined him and gazed along the Thunderhawk's long flanks.

'Doesn't look too bad,' he said.

Jorundur laughed in his dark, throttled way. 'Fine,' he said. 'You try to
fly it.'

Hafloí bristled. 'I might,' he said, his scabby chin jutting.

Jorundur snorted, a grim sound that cut out abruptly.

'Listen to me,' he said, jabbing his fist at Hafloí's chest. 'You do not
touch it. You do not go *near* it. You do not even think about going near it.
Gunnlaugur himself wouldn't take it without checking with me.'

Hafloí looked shocked for a moment, then laughed in turn.

'You're serious?' he asked. 'You think I want to fight you for this heap of junk?'

Jorundur scowled. 'It's not at its best,' he said. 'It was never ready.'

Hafloí turned back to face it. 'We could still use it,' he said, musingly. 'Get this in the air, and we'd murder them. You know the enemy doesn't have flyers?'

Jorundur rolled his eyes. 'I see. Perhaps, then, you'll tell me where we can locate a replacement drive chain, and thruster housings, and retros?'

Hafloí didn't rise to the bait.

'I've seen these things fixed on a battlefield. This city has workshops.'

'Crewed by morons.'

'How do you know? You just got here.'

Jorundur shook his head. Hafloí's persistence annoyed him. The whelp was young, full of the confidence and optimism that youth brought. He hadn't been part of the pack five minutes and already he was offering his counsel.

Had he been like that himself, once? It was centuries ago. Hard to recall.

'Why are you so interested, anyway?' Jorundur asked irritably, walking up to the frontal wings and running his hand along the chipped metal. 'You'll be on the front line with the others, shrieking and hollering like you did on that destroyer.'

Hafloí grinned. 'Maybe,' he said, following Jorundur. 'Or maybe I'll be right here with you, in the cockpit, running the battle cannon.'

Jorundur snorted. 'You could handle that?'

'I've been trained.'

Jorundur looked at him scornfully.

'Training's one thing. If you can keep your aim while the gunship's being shot to shards and the air's burning and your dying crew's screaming in your ear and you've got blood running down your chest and arms, then I'll be impressed.'

He patted *Vuokho*'s chassis.

'This thing has taken down Titans,' he said proudly. '*Titans*. Don't tell me how to look after it. I'll work on it, even if I have to rewire those servitors myself.'

Hafloí nodded. 'Then I'll fly it,' he said.

Despite himself, despite trying hard not to, Jorundur laughed out loud.

'*Skítja*, lad, no you won't.'

He looked up at the cockpit. The metal around the armourglass panes was cracked. He knew that most of the instruments inside were burned out and that the machine-spirit had been reduced to a barely perceptible flicker haunting the automatic motive system.

'It'll be a miracle if we get it ready in time,' he said. 'A miracle. And, believe me, despite all the saints and angels haunting this place, I'm far too old to believe in miracles.'

Haflói smiled.

'You might be,' he said, his voice full of arrogance and confidence and challenge, just as it should be. 'I'm not.'

Chapter Eleven

Baldr didn't know where he was. *Away* was the best approximation, and that was good enough for him. The pain in his temples, hammering away since the engagement on the plague-ship, had become a problem.

Lack of sleep had exacerbated it. A Space Marine could go for days without sleep, using his catalepsean node to prolong that even further. That didn't mean that it was comfortable. Given enough time the symptoms of sleep deprivation kicked in just as they did with mortals. Fuzziness, heaviness in the limbs, slower reaction times, poor judgement.

He needed to rest. Escape from the warp hadn't helped as he'd hoped it would. It might do, in time, but Ras Shakeh's hot, dry air didn't make it easy. The sunlight was harsh, reflecting painfully from the deep-coloured landscape and flashing from glass and metal.

So he'd gone down, right into the bowels of the Halicon. Below the ostentatious entrance halls, the citadel's chambers became cooler and darker. The lumens were set low and many had been turned off, pooling shadows in the corners of the corridors. To begin with there had been plenty of people around – robed officials, Battle Sisters hurrying from one duty to another, Guardsmen. Now, deep in the basement, the numbers had thinned out.

He was alone again. It felt good.

That fact surprised him. For as long as he could remember, Baldr had revelled in the close fraternity of Járnhamar. They had welcomed him when he'd joined, Ingvar in particular. He'd slotted in well. He couldn't match Váltyr for sword-play or Gunnlaugur for brute force, but his aim with a bolter was the best of them. There had been times on the battlefield where it had felt like he'd known where each enemy would be before they did. On his day, Baldr's shells found their marks with uncanny, unerring precision. It was all so easy, all so effortless.

So his torpor, his lack of self-command, that concerned him. For a brief time, during the fighting on the plague-ship, he'd been able to forget the pain throbbing behind his eyes. Only on the descent to the city, with the Thunderhawk shaking and rattling around him, had the pain returned.

Contemplating such weakness angered him. He would have to learn to master it. He was a Son of Russ; pain should be easily overcome.

He kept on walking, descending dusty stone stairs, striding down long, bare corridors, passing by empty doorways leading into empty rooms.

Motion helped. Coolness helped. Being alone helped.

He heard the whimpering late. If he'd been in his right mind, he would have detected it far earlier. As it was, his senses blunted by the angry throb in his skull, he nearly missed it entirely.

He stopped, listening carefully. It came from further down. At the end of the corridor a tight spiral staircase descended through a circular well-shaft of stone. The tiles on the walls around it had come loose; several had shattered across the floor. Dust lay heavily on the remains, a thick, undisturbed layer. No one had walked that way for some time.

He heard it again. A faint, breathy exhalation, ripe with pain.

He tensed. Something about the noise made the hairs on his body stand up. He drew his bolter silently and moved towards the stairs. Getting down them silently was impossible – the metal railing snagged against his armour. Before he'd reached the bottom, he heard something scuttling away from him.

The dark closed in. His eyes compensated immediately. He moved away from the stairs and walked further into the shadows.

He was in some kind of basement vault. The arched roof was low, barely high enough for him to walk without stooping. The floor was bare earth, old and loamy. He guessed he'd reached the foundations of the citadel. A familiar stench – sweet, cloying – hung in the dusty air.

He moved his head carefully, sweeping the space ahead of him. The earth was disturbed, as if an animal had suddenly stirred and raced off into the dark. The nearside wall was clear, but the opposite end of the basement was piled with old metal crates, most of them broken and gaping.

Baldr paused, listening, sniffing.

It was behind the crates. It didn't make much noise, but it had to breathe. He heard its lungs straining, pulling hard on dank air.

He guided his bolter muzzle over to where the sound came from, and fired.

The explosion of the shell's release broke the silence. At the same time, the crates burst apart, hurled away from the walls as something broke from cover. Baldr's round detonated harmlessly into the wall, blowing a crater in the stone.

He had a brief glimpse of something running at him, scampering across the floor like a giant, bloated insect. It moved incredibly fast.

Baldr fired again, hitting it this time. It flew back away from him, its limbs splaying, a thin shriek echoing around the vaults.

He went after it, stowing his bolter as he moved. It twisted around and leapt back up at him. He saw a grey, gaunt face leer up out of the dark, snapping at his own with black jaws.

His fist shot out, seizing it by a scrawny, stringy neck and pinning it to the floor. He felt sinews break and bones snap under his grip.

It still lived. Its hands clawed at him, scraping his armour in a frenzy of useless scratching. It spat at him, sending a stream of thick, lumpy spittle into his face. It thrashed, screamed and writhed under the pressure of his gauntlet.

Baldr looked at it in disgust. Its flesh hung in flaps from its bony frame, withered and wasting. Sores clustered thickly around its lips, tight and pus-filled. It was almost naked, its exposed skin covered in lesions and tumours. Its eyes were sunken deep into an emaciated skeletal face, both dull with cataracts. Its tongue was long gone, chewed away in the wretch's madness, and its screams were formless and choking.

For all that, it had once been human. Baldr recognised the remnants of a scholiast's robes hanging around its loins.

He squeezed his fingers together. For a moment longer the thing hung on, its blind eyes popping, its hands clawing.

Then it went limp. Baldr withdrew, wiping the smear of stinking spittle from his face. He could almost taste the corruption in it, like long-rotten fruit.

He drew himself up, gazing down on the crumpled corpse of the scholiast. Its mouth hung slack, exposing inflamed gums and the blackened stump where its tongue had been.

It reeked.

He activated the comm-stud in his armour collar. The link, which he'd severed earlier, sparked back into life.

'Fjolnir,' came Gunnlaugur's voice. He sounded preoccupied and irascible. 'Where have you been?'

'Clearing my head,' said Baldr. 'Where are you now?'

'With the canoness. My chambers.'

'I'll see you there,' said Baldr, stooping to scoop up the remains of the diseased cadaver. He turned back to the staircase, his tread heavy. 'She'll want to see this too. Warn her that we have a new problem.'

He cut the link. As he climbed, tucking the limp bundle of limbs under one arm, he could already feel his headache getting worse.

Ingvar walked down the narrow streets from the Halicon citadel to the cathedral. To do so he had to pass through the Ighala Gate, jostling with the crowds that milled under its narrow portals.

The experience was uncomfortable. Mortals disliked being in such close proximity to him – they pulled away when they saw him coming, staring with open mouths as he passed – but under the shadow of the enormous arches there was too little space for them to escape.

He ignored their stares, partly for his own comfort. Decades of operating on secret missions with Onyx had desensitised him to unaltered human presence. He had become more comfortable with the select few who, like him, had been elevated into positions of prominence: Inquisitors, Imperial agents, senior Adeptus Mechanicus priests, his fellow warriors of the Adeptus Astartes.

Mortals were different. Whenever he caught their expressions they showed the same thing: fear. They were terrified of him. Children ran away, screaming. Adults worked harder, but he could see the anxiety clearly enough in their staring eyes, their trembling fingers, their sudden, pungent aroma of fight-or-flight.

Ingvar knew Gunnlaugur wouldn't have worried about that. Perhaps he was right not to. In any case, it was just one more difference that had grown up between them.

He strode down from the gate, over the bridge and into the lower city. The streets there were hotter and closer than those above the Ighala bastion. The buildings were shabbier, though more brightly decorated. Pennants displaying the Hjec Aleja coat of arms hung limply from doorways, their colours fading as the sun beat down on them. The smell of spices – cloves, cumin – rose from the baked earth, as if generations of use had stained it forever. Voices rose and fell from hab-units around him. The conversations sounded brief and subdued. Very little laughter rang out from the narrow windows. An atmosphere of tension, of low-level fear, of weariness, had sunk into the entire place.

People went about their business as they must have done before war
had come, but their tight, febrile movements betrayed their anxiety.
Ingvar had seen such things often on other worlds and in other battle-
grounds. Humans would maintain a familiar rhythm for as long as they
possibly could, pottering around, concerning themselves with triviali-
ties while the forces of Hel crouched just over the horizon. The pretence
could only ever be half successful – they all knew their world was about
to change – but then what else were they supposed to do? Food still
needed to be prepared, water needed to be fetched, clothes needed to be
laundered.

Eventually the press of crooked streets opened up into a wide square.
On the far side of it rose the sheer walls of the cathedral, sweeping up
into the sky in a series of ever-narrowing layers of stony gothic ornamentation. Its three spires jutted dramatically, soaring far above the roofline
of the houses around, thrust up from the overlapping tumble of slate
and stone like an immense iron-tipped trident.

The courtyard at its base was shaded and thronged with people, all of
whom were waiting patiently in long, huddled queues. At the head of
those queues stood priests of the Ecclesiarchy in earth-brown robes. One
by one the people received a blessing from them and were sent away.
Ingvar watched them bow before the clerics, their heads bobbing low
over the ground. They had the sign of the aquila waved over them and
a few words of High Gothic muttered. Then they went away, a look of
quiet satisfaction on their otherwise haunted faces. They slipped back
into the shadows of the narrow streets, quickly disappearing.

Ingvar watched the process repeat itself. The mortals paid him little
attention here. Their attention was fixed on what they were doing; if they
caught sight of him watching them, they didn't show it.

'Do not despise them,' came a woman's voice.

Palatine Bajola drew alongside him. She wore her ceremonial robes –
ivory cotton, trimmed with red and gold. Her ebony skin stood in stark
contrast.

'Why do you think I would?' he replied.

'You are superhuman,' she said. 'They are human. They suffer fear. I am
told you do not.'

Ingvar watched the queues shuffle. Just as at the gate, he could smell
the undercurrent of uneasiness.

'How often does this happen?' he asked.

'Priests are here every day between dawn and dusk. They are kept busy
the whole time.'

'And it does some good?'

Bajola paused before replying.

'If you mean that those people sleep a little at night and are able to go about their business without falling prey to waking nightmares, then yes, it does. It you mean that the Emperor will spare them from the coming horror and allow them to live their lives in peace, then no, it does not.'

Ingvar turned to face her. 'Do you receive the blessing?' he asked.

Bajola smiled. 'They wouldn't dare. They assume I have all the faith I need.' She gestured towards the cathedral. 'You are here to see me, I take it. We should go inside.'

'And do you?' asked Ingvar, staying where he was.

'Do I?'

'Have all the faith you need?'

Bajola hesitated.

'We will find out, I guess,' she said.

The interior of the cathedral was cool even while the streets outside sweltered. Its vast nave ran north-south, lined with dark rows of basalt columns. Sunlight angled in through narrow stained-glass panes depicting stylised images of saints and warriors, throwing intense coloured swatches on the chequerboard marble floor. The high altar was simple – an obsidian block of stone over which hung war-banners of the Wounded Heart and the Shakeh Guard regiments. An imposing cast-iron representation of the Emperor Manifest on Earth smiting the Great Serpent Horus had been mounted above that, glinting wetly in the gloom.

Few people moved around in the dusty shadows: scholiasts, a priest, an old penitent crawling towards the altar on his knees. The faint sounds they made were amplified amid the soaring spaces. Aromas of incense and human sweat rose from the stone.

Ingvar took it all in. He could appreciate Bajola's pride in the place. It was a serious building, a place of devotion, unlike the grotesque pile of the Halicon that the canoness occupied.

She led him through a side door and up into her private chambers. The room they ended up in was high on the south-facing front, lined with crystal-paned windows that gazed out over the city below. Several chairs stood waiting, all of which she ignored. That was considerate; Ingvar guessed his armour-clad weight would have cracked most of them.

'They call you the Gyrfalkon,' she said, leaning against the far wall and smiling at him. 'What is that? No one has been able to tell me.'

'You cannot guess?'

'A bird, I would have said.'

'You would have said right. One of the few that can dwell on Fenris. It has grey plumage, thick against the cold. They are good hunters. Then again, everything on Fenris is a good hunter. If it is not, then it dies.'

Bajola looked amused. 'So why you?' she asked. 'Because you are a good hunter? Or is it some dark secret of your Chapter?'

Ingvar shrugged. 'My brothers are not overly imaginative,' he said. 'My eyes are grey. I had a reputation for speed with the blade, once. They liked the sound of it. I don't know.'

Bajola nodded, as if he had confirmed some suspicion she had of him. 'You are not quite like your brothers, I think,' she said.

'They might agree with you,' he said. 'Why do you say so?'

Bajola evaded the question.

'Tell me about yourself, Gyrfalkon,' she said.

'What purpose would that serve?'

'The canoness asked me to get to know you,' she said. 'You have been asked to get to know me. If you like, we could dance around one another for days, trying to gather information by stealth. Or we could put aside those games and talk. Enough, at least, to keep our superiors happy.'

Bajola had a polished, worldly air that Ingvar had not seen from the other Battle Sisters. She and de Chatelaine, it was obvious, were cut from very different cloth.

'You are not quite like your sisters, I think,' he said.

Bajola laughed. It was deep, spontaneous laugh, almost like a man's.

'That much is true,' she said. 'But tell me of the Wolves. If we are to die here together, I'd like to know who I'm dying with.'

Ingvar looked away from her, past her shoulder, out through one of the windows. Ras Shakeh's deep blue sky shone with heat and light. A world more removed from Fenris would have been hard to find.

'We are Járnhamar,' he said slowly, as if to help himself remember. 'That is the pack-name. A pack may last for many generations, and we have fought together for a long time. Gunnlaugur, Olgeir, Váltyr, Jorundur and myself are the surviving founders. Baldr came later. Hafloí, the pup, barely yesterday. That forges a bond. It is not easily broken, though it can be strained.'

'I noticed,' said Bajola. 'You and your leader, you see things differently.'

Ingvar shook his head.

'Not really,' he said. 'Not about the essentials.'

He snapped his head towards her suddenly, baring his fangs, snarling. He was pleased to see that, for all her poise, she started.

'We are both of the blood of Asaheim, Sister,' he said, smiling at her hungrily. 'Neither of us is tame.'

'I never thought you were,' said Bajola, recovering herself and looking irritated.

'Gunnlaugur has led the pack for fifty-seven years,' Ingvar went on. 'Longer than the lives of most of your Guard captains. He knows what he's doing. I would trust my life to him. I have done, many times.'

'Still. You see things differently.'

Ingvar's eyes narrowed. Bajola was bold. He couldn't decide whether to be impressed by that.

'He's proud,' he said. 'He's got much to be proud about. But time changes things. It changes perspectives.'

'What changed yours?'

'I have been away from the home world. Our old Wolf Guard died while on campaign. I left Fenris before Gunnlaugur took over from him. It was a long time before I came back.'

'How long?'

Ingvar smiled wryly, calculating. 'Nine weeks ago.'

Bajola let out a long breath. 'Holy Ophelia.'

'We're adjusting.'

'I don't doubt it,' she said. 'What happened to your old Wolf Guard?'

'Greenskins,' Ingvar said, simply.

She didn't need to know the details – the long assault on the chain-fortresses of Urrghaz, the void-pursuit, the final confrontation with the orks above the gas giant Teliox Epis. She didn't need to know that Hjortur's body had never been found – an insult unworthy of the old warrior and a sad loss of gene-seed. At the time, that detail had seemed strange; now it was just a piece of history, embedded in the archives of the Valgard and mourned in the sagas.

'I'm sorry,' she said.

Ingvar shrugged. 'Don't be. It was his time. He lived a good life, a warrior's life.'

Bajola looked thoughtful. 'You are a fatalistic people,' she said. 'I have heard this before, from others who have had dealings with you. Now that I meet you, I believe it.'

'We live amongst death on Fenris. From birth we are surrounded by it. It comes suddenly, the crack of an ice-sheet, the gush of flame. You cannot defend against such things. You learn to accept it: the way of things, fate. The wyrd.'

'I could not live like that,' said Bajola. 'I have a... problem with fate.'

Ingvar didn't reply immediately. Bajola watched him all the while, holding his gaze with her brown eyes.

'I've been doing all the talking,' Ingvar said. 'This has been an uneven bargain.'

Bajola smiled, and lowered her eyes. 'Fair enough,' she said. 'What do you want to know?'

'I could ask you the same things you asked me,' he said. 'You sit ill with your comrades. I have never heard one of your kind talk like you do. I wonder what forces created you. I wonder what forces brought you here. You are as unlikely a presence on this world as we are.'

Bajola gave a slight nod of acknowledgement, as if to say *Well read.*

'I was trained by the Ordo Famulous,' she said. 'I accompanied Hereticus Inquisitors on high-level missions and arbitrated in the disputes of planetary governors. If you're interested, I speak twenty-nine dialects natively, six hundred more via lex-implants. I learned to read the state of a man's soul through a single gesture. Once you read a man's soul, you control him. At least, that was what the Inquisition taught me.'

She sounded almost wistful as she reeled off her accomplishments.

'I assume, though,' she said, 'that you think little of the Inquisition.'

'It is always dangerous to assume,' said Ingvar. 'Your story is half-told. The Order of the Wounded Heart is militant, not ceremonial.'

Bajola looked weary. 'Ah, yes. The Wounded Heart prides itself on its burn-tally.' She looked down at her hands, pressing her fingers together in a loose cage. 'Why did I join them? It was not enough, in the end, to spend my days talking. I felt that I was wasting myself. I saw the effects of wars but never participated in them. I was a mouthpiece for others, never speaking for myself.'

She looked back up at him. An edge of defiance danced around the edge of her expression.

'I was advised against the transfer,' she said. 'They told me I wasn't right for the Militant Orders. But there are ways of getting what you want if you try hard enough, even in the Adepta Sororitas.'

'So I see,' said Ingvar. 'And you never regretted it?'

The defiance in Bajola's face faded, replaced by a more familiar resignation.

'I regret plenty,' she said. 'I regret that this world is so damn hot, so damn arid. I regret that it will soon be put to the sword, and that so many will die. If I had stayed in the Ordo Famulous my life would have been easier, and probably longer.'

Then she flashed a smile at him again – a knowing smile, one that spoke of a capacity for mirth that had not yet been extinguished.

'But do I regret standing on my own two feet and learning to fire a bolter?' she asked. 'No, not at all. Turns out I'm good at it.'

In that instant, in those few words, Ingvar felt he knew all he needed to know about Uwe Bajola. It was hard not be impressed, given the circumstances.

'That makes two of us, then,' he said.

'Where did you find this?'

Gunnlaugur could hear the low fear in the canoness's voice. The corpse lay twisted on the pristine floor of her chamber, stinking of rotting fish. Its unseeing eyes glared up at the ceiling, already beginning to decay from the inside. Its neck was swollen, bruised and oozing.

'In the foundations,' said Baldr. 'Right under your feet.'

To Gunnlaugur's eye, Baldr didn't look too good either. He seemed tired, distracted. His hair hung lankly around his forehead, which was strange. Of all of them, Baldr was normally the one who looked least like a savage.

First Ingvar, now him, thought Gunnlaugur. *What is wrong with them all?*

The canoness turned her face away from the corpse, her nose wrinkling.

'It is – it *was* – Scholiast Geriod Nerhm,' she said, drumming her fingers together. 'He's been missing for several days. I had assumed... Emperor forgive me. I had assumed that he'd deserted. Some have tried that, knowing the heat will kill them quicker.'

Gunnlaugur studied the heap of suppurating flesh at his feet. The signs of virulence were familiar enough; the scholiast's body could have been lifted straight from the corrupted heart of that plague-ship.

'Had Nerhm been exposed to the enemy?' he asked.

De Chatelaine shook her head. 'He was an official,' she said. 'He never left the citadel.'

'What of the rest of your troops?' asked Baldr, running a tired-looking hand across his forehead. 'The ones you pulled back?'

The canoness looked lost for a moment.

'I– I suppose so,' she said. 'We have regiments extracted from the war-zone, brought here to resupply. What was I supposed to do – leave them to be annihilated?'

Gunnlaugur pursed his lips. 'Have you seen any cases like this?'

De Chatelaine shook her head. Her expression was distraught.

'None,' she said, weakly. 'We didn't think to–'

'No, you didn't,' said Baldr, his voice accusatory. 'You've been fighting these things for weeks. There should have been quarantine for anyone coming from the front. Do you see what you've done?'

'Enough,' snapped Gunnlaugur. He had no idea why Baldr was behaving so harshly. Blame was pointless; given the speed and severity of the outbreak of war, it would have been impossible to screen everyone.

De Chatelaine's face, though, had gone pale.

'No, he is correct,' she said, looking haunted. 'We thought it was the right thing, to pull them back. We thought we were saving them. Oh, Holy Emperor...'

Gunnlaugur shot a furious glance at Baldr.

'It matters not now,' he said. 'We still have time. What medicae complement do you have?'

The canoness struggled to focus.

'Sisters Hospitaller, a few squads,' she said. 'The Sisters have training. We can run checks, set up quarantine for those in the garrisons.'

'Good,' said Gunnlaugur. 'Do those things. Are the gates sealed?'

'Not yet. We had hoped for reinforcements. The Twelfth Guard battle-group, heading north from the ruins of Bagahz. From reports, they're two days out.'

Baldr rolled his eyes. 'Do you not understand?' he said wearily. 'They *allow* them to survive. Carriers walk among them. You cannot let them in.'

'They cannot be abandoned.'

Baldr shot her a dark look. 'There are millions of people in this city, canoness,' he said. His voice was low but insistent. 'Some of them will already be infected. If we act now, we might keep it down, but if you let more in, this thing will spread. You will have dozens, *hundreds* of living corpses within the walls. Is that what you want?'

De Chatelaine looked down at the corpse, her drawn face riven with indecision.

'Seal the gates,' insisted Baldr, looking briefly to Gunnlaugur for support. 'Allow none to pass in or out. Then start the purges. You'll need flamer teams – everything contaminated must be destroyed.'

Still de Chatelaine hesitated. For the first time, Gunnlaugur noticed the deep lines of fatigue around her eyes. She'd been fighting without pause for too long.

'He's right,' said Gunnlaugur quietly.

Slowly, very slowly, de Chatelaine's chin lowered.

'It will be done,' she said. 'Leave it to me. We have allowed this into the city, we will purge it.' She sighed deeply. 'So they have got what they wanted. We will be cooped up here, unable to strike out, waiting for them like rats in a trap.'

'No, we will not,' said Gunnlaugur fiercely. 'We – the pack – we can still fight. We'll hit them on the plains, blood them, show them what manner of warrior defends the city. It'll give you some time.'

De Chatelaine looked unconvinced. 'I had hoped you would help us here,' she said.

'Right now they fear nothing on this world. When we have done with them they will fear plenty.' He grinned coldly, baring his long hooked fangs. 'It's what we're bred for.'

On another day, perhaps she might have resisted longer. The toll of her workload, though, combined with guilt, seemed to dilute her will.

'You will do what you judge best,' she said, her eyes flickering to the corpse lying on the floor before her. 'But if you go, just make sure you hurt them. Hurt them badly. For the first time since this thing began, I find myself wanting to see them truly suffer.'

She stared at the scholiast's body stonily. Then she recovered herself, and looked back up to the Wolf Guard.

'I have much to do,' she said. Her voice had recovered some of its steel. 'Purge-teams will be dispatched. We will root this out.' She shot him a wintry smile. 'If there's one thing we know how to do, it's burn.'

Gunnlaugur nodded. 'You will not be alone,' he said. 'While the sun shines, we fight here. After that, the pack hunts.'

De Chatelaine bowed. 'So be it,' she said. 'While the sun shines.'

Then she turned, pivoting sharply on her heel, and strode out of the chamber. Her boots clinked against the marble, echoing from her heavy tread.

After she'd gone, Baldr made to do the same. Gunnlaugur prevented him, raising a hand before his chest.

'Brother,' he said. The tone he used was firm. 'Speak to me.'

Baldr looked back at him. His complexion was pale, his eyes dull. He did not look sick, exactly. Drained, perhaps.

'About what?'

'You are not yourself.'

Baldr's eyelids twitched. 'I'm fine,' he said. 'The warp passage was… difficult. I will recover.'

Gunnlaugur didn't release him.

'Ingvar suffers like that,' he said. 'I have to worry about you both now?'

Baldr smiled. It was a distracted, snatched gesture. 'Don't worry about either of us,' he said. 'We're not children.'

Gunnlaugur's gaze didn't waver. 'I don't like to see you like this,' he said. 'It's enough that Jorundur is forever in foul temper. You were always the one I could rely on to keep your head. If something is amiss, tell me.'

Baldr hesitated. For a moment, he looked unsure of himself. His dull eyes flickered up to meet Gunnlaugur's, then away again.

'Seriously,' he said. 'Just warp-sickness. It will pass.' He took a deep breath, and rolled his shoulders. 'I need to hunt. To hunt properly. Void-war is one thing. It doesn't match the chase. You feel it too.'

Gunnlaugur nodded. He let his hand fall away. 'When night falls, brother' he said.

'Good.' Baldr's eyes alighted on the corpse. 'For now, though, work to do.'

Gunnlaugur grunted distastefully. 'Aye,' he growled, looking at the pile of pustulent matter at his feet. It would be the first to enter the furnace. Many more would follow. 'Summon the rest of them. Time we got started.'

Chapter Twelve

Ahlja Yemue woke up. Her eyes opened lazily, bleary with mucus. It was hard to open her eyes. She would have preferred to sleep. Sleep was all she had wanted to do for a while. The pain was less when she slept, even though the dreams were bad.

But she couldn't sleep. Not now. The itching compelled her. It made her limbs restive and her mind fractious. She needed to move. She had something to do.

Ahlja pushed her coverlet down. It smelled bad and was heavy with sweat. The mattress under her was damp and hot. The room around her was thick with flies.

That wasn't good. She didn't like flies. Why were they there? She should have cleaned up. She was a good cleaner, the most fastidious in her hab.

At some point the flies had got in and they hadn't left. She didn't remember when. Remembering anything was hard. Why was remembering anything hard?

She swung her feet over the edge of the bunk and tottered upright. She was thirsty. Her throat felt furry and baked. Swallowing was painful.

Ahlja looked at the window and winced. Strong sunlight burned away at the edges of the blinds. It looked like late afternoon outside. She shouldn't have been sleeping in the day. There was work to be done. It was lazy.

Work to be done. Work to be done.

Her mind seemed to run in circles. Whenever she tried to think of something new, the same old thoughts would cycle around and around.

Get up. Get up. Get up. Work to be done.

Ahlja shambled into the washroom. Her feet ached. They looked swollen. She wouldn't be able to squeeze them into her shoes. She'd have to go outside barefoot. That would be embarrassing. Helod would see her like that. She'd gossip about it. Hateful Helod. Why were her feet so swollen? Some misfortune must have occurred.

She reached the basin and stared into the cracked mirror above it. She didn't remember it breaking. It looked as if someone had thrown something at the glass, trying to shatter it.

Ahlja looked at herself.

Holy Throne. I look...

Get up. Get up. Work to be done.

She looked away. It wasn't nice, seeing all those things on her face. She rubbed her hands across her belly, feeling the flesh sway and bulge.

She was running to fat. Really, badly, running to fat.

She felt sick. She need to drink something. She needed to eat something.

She stumbled into the next room. No food there. Just her living area, tatty and smelly and buzzing with flies. The floor was covered in stains. One corner had a pile of drying, caking vomit in it. Other parts were worse.

I should clean this up. Very soon. Just need to find the time.

She kept walking, swaying heftily under her nightshirt, wincing as the material scraped across her lesions. Her feet trod through puddles of sticky liquid.

No time now. No time now. No time now.

She ran her hands over her hips. She felt the swollen curves there, pressing up against her nightshirt. So bloated, so uncomfortable, like something was trying to push its way out. How long had it been like that? She couldn't remember.

She did remember the man, though, the one who'd been helping her. He'd been nice. What was his name?

It doesn't matter. Work to be done.

She'd appreciated his kindness. He'd been very good to her, offering the balm that soothed the worst of the rashes and making the spiced tea that had cleared her head a little and patiently winding the bandages around her sores on her calves and arms and neck. He'd been there for her ever since she'd first got sick. He'd never left her. So attentive. So kind, even if he'd always smelled strange.

Perhaps that tea had made her stomach swell.

Ahlja pushed open the door and limped down the stairs. The air was cleaner outside her hab-unit. The communal corridor was free of all the muck on her floor. That was shameful. The others had got ahead of her. Helod would be gossiping already, holding her nose and pointing at her doorway with spiteful eyes.

It doesn't matter. Work to be done. Work to be done.

She reached the outside door and pushed against it. Sunlight flooded over her, blinding her, making her head throb. She felt dizzy and leaned against the frame. She could hear people talking and jostling around her.

They were in the street, those people. She'd gone out into the street wearing her nightdress. Why was she doing that? It was indecent.

It doesn't matter. It doesn't matter.

She kept walking. The sunlight hurt her eyes so she kept one hand over them. It was hard to walk. The stones in the street cut her skin. She felt the sores on her soles burst, popping open and spilling their fluids. She felt her belly sway. Throne, she really had got fat. It was embarrassing.

She heard people gagging around her. She opened her fingers a little, just a crack, to see what was going on. They were running away from her, or pointing at her with disgust on their faces, or laughing.

That almost made her stop. Why were they laughing? Why were they disgusted? Should she go back, clean herself up? Why was she even in the street in her nightshirt?

It doesn't matter. You have work to do. You have important work to do. They do not matter. They do not matter.

She kept going. She didn't like it when her mind cycled. If she just kept going, her mind cycled less.

Then she heard shouting. She heard a woman screaming, and she heard men crying something over and over again. She didn't like that. It upset her. She broke into a run, which was difficult on her cut feet and with her sagging belly.

Do it now. Do it now. Do it now.

Do what? Why was her mind cycling again?

She picked up speed, bumping and jostling against the walls around her. She stumbled over a drain-cover, nearly pitching headfirst into the dust of the road. The sunlight made it so hard to see. She didn't know where she was. Near the cathedral? She hoped so – she liked the cathedral. The priests had blessed her there, three times, maybe more. So hard to remember.

'Stay where you are!'

The voice was like a woman's, though horrifying; monstrously loud. Ahlja spun round, opening her fingers.

She saw a monster coming at her, running after her: a huge, tall monster, clad in black armour and wreathed in fire. She saw the monster carrying an enormous metal weapon that smoked and spat from its muzzle. She saw the people scattering away from the monster, breaking away from her, sprinting up the street, screaming and falling.

Do it now. Do it now.

Do *what?* She got very scared. The monster was almost on her. She dropped her hands from her face, squinting around her, trying to work out where she was.

She saw a holy brass aquila, hung up over the lintel of a doorway. She heard the hum of machinery behind rockcrete walls. She saw narrow, barred windows.

Then she knew where she was. She was outside the power plant, the substation that fed the district, no more than a hundred paces from her own little hab.

Do it now. Do it now.

The monster skidded to a halt in front of her. It was less than five metres away. Ahlja saw the horrific mask over its face, the swirling cloak, the cracked heart on its breast. It lowered its gun at her.

Suddenly, Ahlja knew what was going to happen. After so long being sick and bleary and muffled, she knew exactly what came next. She tried to swallow it down, but it was too late.

Well done.

Sister Honorata was thrown back as the subject exploded. The fat woman's foul body, riddled with its diseases and unnatural tumours, blasted apart with horrifying speed and force. Bile-laced flames cascaded up and over the walls around her, shattering brickwork, cracking metal, hurling masonry in all directions. The streetscape briefly became a blizzard of debris and fractured rockcrete.

It took a few moments for the carnage to clear. Smoke billowed up from the blast-centre, fed by smouldering piles of rubble. Puddles of blood boiled and bubbled amid the destruction. The power plant wall remained intact, though only barely. A gouge ran across its length, exposing metal shielding within.

Honorata picked herself up from the floor, tasting blood in her mouth. Her vision cleared. She hefted her flamer in bruised hands and advanced carefully towards the charred crater-edge.

'Notify,' she voxed into the comm, sweeping the muzzle of her flamer across the blast site. At either end of the street, terrified civilians were already emerging from behind whatever cover they'd been able to find. 'Another bomb-drone. Rejez-district power plant, intersection of Yemn main-route and south-west cathedral approach.'

'Understood,' same the reply from the Halicon. The comm-operator's voice was clipped. She sounded stressed. 'Damage report? Did you get it?'

'Negative.' Honorata stepped through the wreckage, listening and watching carefully. The equipment within the plant seemed to be working. The whine of the generators might have been a bit more strained than usual, but she was no expert. 'Target managed to detonate. Minimal damage, but get a tech-team down here. If this thing blows, we do have a problem.'

'Acknowledged. Support on its way. Remain in position, Sister.'

A fresh commotion broke out at the far end of the street. Honorata looked up. Some of the civilians had started moving again. Fresh shouting broke out.

Her eyes narrowed. She blink-activated her helm's zoom-lens. A crowd was forming, spilling into the street from the mouth of a big hab-unit further down. One of the civilians was moving strangely, reeling unsteadily on bowed legs. His grey tongue lolled from an open mouth.

'Negative,' she snapped, thumbing the flamer back into life. 'I've got another one. Just get that team down here.'

Then she broke into a run, screaming at the crowd to get out of her way, aiming the flamer carefully and judging when to fire.

She'd erred back then. She'd cared too much about collateral damage to open fire when she should have done. The time had passed for such sensitivity – things were getting out of hand. Plague-carriers were emerging from everywhere, bursting out of their stinking dens as if summoned by silent, coordinated commands.

So Sister Honorata ran harder this time, feeling the flamer weigh heavily in her gauntlets. Her jaw clenched, her finger rested easily over the trigger.

This time would be different. This one wouldn't live long enough to swallow.

Ingvar heard the distant explosions go off before Bajola did. He stiffened immediately, gauging direction. As he did so, another one detonated, closer to the cathedral, near enough for her to pick up.

'What is–' she started, but Ingvar was already moving.

'It's started,' he said grimly, striding over to the doorway.

Bajola came after him. She was out of her armour and carried no weapon.

'Already?' she asked. Her unguarded voice betrayed a note of unease. 'Last report said they were days away.'

Ingvar paused before the lintel and shot her a dry smile.

'Fought the plague-damned before, Sister?' he asked.

Bajola shook her head.

'They carry weapons other than cleavers,' Ingvar said. 'The contagion spreads. They'll plant seeds of sickness here, hoping they'll take root. They'll pump toxins into the air and poison your water. They'll recruit the slack-minded with whispered promises in the dark. They'll reduce this place to infighting and disease before they come in sight of your walls.' He reached for his helm. 'I've seen it before. This is where the battle starts.'

He lifted his helm into place and secured the seals. He saw proximity markers scroll down his retinal display overlaid with moving pack runes. His brothers were already on the prowl.

Strange. Gunnlaugur hadn't summoned him.

'Then I'll need my armour,' said Bajola, her expression hardening. The uncertainty in her gestures faded quickly, replaced by a tight, disciplined resolve.

'You will,' said Ingvar, turning away from her and striding out of the chamber. The stairs wound down in their well, twisting into darkness. 'You should seal the cathedral. You should clear those crowds too.'

Bajola followed him down.

'If you wait, we could fight together,' she said.

Ingvar halted. He turned to face her. Bajola looked suddenly self-conscious.

'I mean, we...' She trailed off. 'My armour takes time to fit.'

Ingvar gazed down at her. In his battle-plate he towered over her. She was a slight, slim woman. In her robes she looked impossibly frail.

He felt a strange impulse then, the first stirrings of something like... protectiveness. He felt that if she should come to harm he would regret it.

Unusual, to think that. Possibly unworthy.

'The fight has started,' he said, turning back. 'I cannot wait. If given leave, I will come back.'

Noises of running, of consternation and alarm, were already filtering up from the cathedral's nave.

Bajola hurried after him.

'We could use you here, Space Wolf.'

Ingvar winced. He was *Fenryka*, a Sky Warrior, a Son of Russ. *Space Wolf* was what off-worlders called them, transfixed by their totems and fang-tight jawlines and black-pinned eyes.

'If Hjortur were alive to hear you say that,' he said, 'he'd knock you cold, mortal or no.'

'Who?'

Of course. He'd not mentioned the name.

'Hjortur Bloodfang. The one who used to lead us. The one I was telling you about.'

Bajola stopped walking. Ingvar glanced over his shoulder and caught the look of surprise frozen across her features. For a moment, her ebony face looked almost grey.

'Mean something to you?' he asked.

Bajola shook her head. As she did so, another explosion rang out. It felt like it came from just the other side of the cathedral walls. The stone around them shivered, and lines of dust trickled down from the ceiling.

'You're right,' she said, pushing past him and hastening down the stairwell towards the doors at its base. 'This thing has started. We've talked for long enough.'

Ingvar followed her. He wasn't a fool. That had been recognition on her face. Such a thing was not quite impossible – Járnhamar had fought across hundreds of worlds and with dozens of allies – but it was almost vanishingly unlikely.

Bajola reached the doors and shoved them open. Just as she was about to go through, out into the body of the cathedral, she swivelled to face Ingvar.

'You got here just in time,' she said. Her voice had a strange, sardonic edge to it. 'Just before the fighting started. Strange, eh?'

Ingvar drew *dausvjer*. He could hear growing commotion from beyond the cathedral confines.

'It was my wyrd to be here,' he said. 'Just as it was yours.'

Bajola smiled dryly. 'Maybe you're right.' She looked squarely up at him. Her expression was an odd mix of defiance and amusement. 'I do need more faith.'

The smell of burning rose up into Ingvar's nostrils then, barely filtered by his helm's intake grille. Screaming broke through the bustling tumult of the crowds outside. He felt his heart-rate begin to pick up, already preparing for the exertions to come.

Her manner had become strange. There was no time now, but he would need to speak to Bajola again.

'When I am gone, seal everything,' he said. 'Begin your siege preparations. Kill any among you who show signs of plague. And clear those damn crowds.'

He pushed past her, out of the doors and into the nave beyond. Already his helm-display was giving him targets.

'And you'll come back?' Bajola called out after him.

'Count on it,' he growled, kicking *dausvjer*'s disruptor into life and breaking into a run.

Váltyr paused for a moment, driving the tip of *holdbítr* into the soft earth and leaning on it. The sun began to dip over the roofs of Hjec Aleja, presaging the end of the long, hot afternoon.

For all the sweat and grime that caked his exposed skin, he wasn't tired. He wasn't close to being tired. With the steady lessening of the heat the streets had become good hunting grounds. The contagion was in its first stages – still sporadic, still isolated – and its victims hadn't succeeded in grouping together in any numbers.

Still, the process had only just started. Parts of the lower city were already burning, sending dirty columns of smoke into the clear sky. Plenty of plague-nests still existed, fomenting filth and pestilence in forgotten corners. Váltyr knew, just as they all knew, that they were ready to burst, scattering their foul incubated contents into the seamy air.

Ahead of him stretched a series of tumbledown, metal-framed warehouses, all in various states of disrepair, all huge and blunt against the deepening sky. The streets between them were sunk in shadows and thick with brown dust. Their walls were caked with a scouring patina of drifting sand that lodged in the detail of the metalwork. Váltyr had already uncovered one cluster of plague-carriers nestled within the district; he was sure there were more. In such semi-derelict, barely patrolled parts of the lower city the conditions were ideal for the incubation of proto-mutancy.

He inclined his head a little, stilling his breathing, letting his armour-hum die down with inactivity, listening.

He didn't pick it up immediately. The noise was just on the edge of detection, buried deep, muffled by walls and hanging dust and distance.

But his ears, like those of all his brothers, were sharp. He smiled, bringing *holdbítr* back into guard, watching the metal glint as the blade whirled into position. Then he started, silently, to move.

He slipped along the narrow alleyway between two warehouses, and the shadows slid over him like liquid. Twenty paces ahead to his left a wall section was broken. He saw a corrugated metal panel peeled away from its housings, hanging like a flap of skin from a wound and shivering in the cooling air. The noise became clearer as he neared the source – rattling breath, irregular and rheumy, the soft brush of clammy skin against cloth. More than one pair of lungs was working. Bodies were huddled together, clustered tightly on the far side of the damaged wall.

Váltyr paused and sniffed, flaring his nostrils. The note of honeyed decay was unmistakable. Mortal sickness did not have that stench, not even when gangrene had set in or the flesh had turned rotten. The sufferers of such unnatural illness learned to love the sweetness. They no longer wanted to be cured. They would caress their own lesions and pustules, squeezing them gently and watching the bile ooze thickly between their fingers. Once that stage was reached, all they really feared was death. Death brought the end of the blissful pain, the suffering they'd come to love. Even in the misery of plague-raddled weakness they would fight to stay alive, just to stretch the odorous agony a little longer, just to revel in it for a moment more.

Váltyr crouched beside the breach in the wall, moving carefully, estimating numbers. A dozen, maybe, all close at hand, all unaware of his presence.

Easy prey.

With a sudden jolt from his armour, he pounced, bursting through the ragged gap and plunging into the cavernous interior. The clang of falling metal echoed as pieces bounced around him. He whirled around, catching sight of a cluster of plague-thick bodies huddled against the near wall, wrapped in filthy bandages and nuzzling against one another like a brood of rats. As soon as they saw him they broke, scampering and scuttling away on all-fours.

He was far, far quicker. The first one to die never made a sound – *holdbítr* cleaved her from head to waist in a single flashing stroke, carving through her ribcage and scattering it in a clatter of bones.

Another one darted across the floor at his feet, panting like a dog, frantic with fear. Váltyr twisted back to jab, and the mutant's swollen head rolled into the dust, neatly cut from his bloated body.

He never stopped moving, switching from one stroke to the next in the space of a thought, lashing out smoothly as more of the plague-bearers scurried for cover. Every strike was perfectly aimed and weighted: cleaving necks, cutting muscle, going for the efficient kill, the swordsman's deadly figures. The only sounds were his victim's strangled cries, ringing out into the darkness in an overlapping mess of surprise and terror.

'Nineteen,' he breathed, adding to the tally of the day. 'Twenty. Blood of Russ, more than I thought.'

The floor became sticky with blood. He slaughtered with ruthless speed, felling most before they'd got more than a few paces away from him. Only a few managed to break clear of the initial assault, racing off into the dark, squealing like startled swine.

He went after them, loping across the cracked rockcrete floor, holding his blade low. There was nowhere for them to go. Their shuffling, stuttering footfalls echoed into the open spaces, giving their location away. Váltyr swooped on the first runner, a man with weeping white eyes and a glowing rash around his obese neck. *Holdbítr* flickered and he collapsed to the ground, his sore-tight stomach carved open in a single gaping slash.

Váltyr swept across the warehouse interior like a vengeful spectre. He knew he was almost invisible to them in the dark, picked out only by his helm lenses, which hovered in the shadows, and the shimmer of his blade as it whirled.

He liked that. He liked to think of his enemies convulsing with terror even before he came into cutting range.

Three more were struck down in the next few seconds, their cries ended in sudden, gurgling coughs of blood-choked surprise. After that only one set of running feet still rang out across the floor towards the far walls. Váltyr sprinted after it, fixing his eyes on a lone, shambling mutant ahead.

He came within blade-range, hearing the plague-damned man wheeze with fear even as he drew his sword round for the killing blow. He could smell the man's corruption, his fear, his desperation to escape.

He brought *holdbítr* down savagely, fast as ever, watching the mono-molecular edge whistle towards its prey's spine...

...and miss.

Unbelievably, the plague-ravaged man leapt clear at the last moment, scrambling away from the blade. The killing-edge snicked his robes, slicing free a scrap of dirty fabric, but didn't cut into flesh.

Váltyr almost lost his footing. It was inexcusable. *Embarrassing.*

'I would have killed you *quickly*, little man!' he roared, thundering after his prey's scuttling outline. 'Now you *suffer!*'

The man moved incredibly quickly. His flesh looked wasted, all skin and bone under flapping robes. He reached the far wall of the warehouse and frantically scrabbled for a way out. He found one – a corroded metal door hanging by its hinges. He slammed into it and the lock broke open; then he tore through the gap and out into the alley beyond.

Váltyr spat a curse and followed him through. Once outside he swung around, expecting to see the man scampering down the narrow streets ahead of him. Instead the plague-bearer's body lay at his feet, twisted in the dust, his robes dark with blood and filth. Standing over the corpse, towering into the darkening air, was a warrior in pearl-grey armour carrying a mighty warhammer one-handed.

'Careless, brother,' admonished Gunnlaugur, shaking the blood from the hammer's head.

Váltyr bristled, his blood still pumping. 'He was lucky.'

Gunnlaugur gestured towards the warehouse. 'All cleansed in there?'

Váltyr nodded.

'Good,' said Gunnlaugur, sounding satisfied. 'I'll summon a burn-team.'

He pressed his boot to the man's sore-mottled skull, and pressed down. The bone caved in with a limp crack, splattering white-flecked gore across the dust.

'Walk with me, *sverdhjera*,' he said, moving off down the alleyway.

Váltyr followed him. The two of them strode back through the warren of dusty streets around the warehouses. Ahead of them, golden in the failing light, reared the outcrop of the mountainous upper city.

'Outbreaks everywhere,' said Gunnlaugur grimly. His armour bore the evidence of fighting – streaks of wind-dried pus and slime across his gauntlets and breastplate. 'It'll get worse once night falls.'

'The Sisters can cope,' said Váltyr.

'I'm sure they can.'

Gunnlaugur stopped walking and lowered his head.

'Have you spoken to the Gyrfalkon since we made planetfall?' he asked.

Váltyr shrugged. 'Not much.'

'What do you make of him?'

Váltyr hesitated before replying. Since the practice-duel on the *Undrider* he'd not given much thought to Ingvar.

'He fights like he used to,' he said.

'You think so?' asked Gunnlaugur. 'That's not what I saw.'

Váltyr sighed. 'What do you want me to say? If he's changed, we all have.'

Gunnlaugur remained motionless. It was impossible to read the expression behind his bloody helm mask.

'I wouldn't have blamed you if you'd spoken against him. Yours was the only rune-sword in Járnhamar. Now there are two. You need to know this, though: you are my blademaster, my right arm of vengeance. That has not changed.'

Váltyr didn't know what to make of that. He hadn't asked for reassurance. The fact that it was being offered at all gave him pause.

'Glad to hear it,' he said.

Gunnlaugur started walking again.

'We've got to get out of this city,' he muttered. 'Hunting this scum is weary work.'

'Just say the word, *vaerangi*,' said Váltyr, following him. 'We'll all follow you out.'

'No.' The finality in Gunnlaugur's voice was sudden. 'Not all of you. I don't want Ingvar with us. I don't want him questioning orders. I don't want him slowing us down. *Skítja*, I don't want him there at all.'

Váltyr didn't like hearing that. It was not the way of the pack: Ingvar had behaved strangely since his return, sure, but he had been back only a few short weeks. There was time for that to change, for his old self to re-emerge.

'Are you sure?' he asked. Gunnlaugur answered him with a snarl.

'It is my judgement,' he said. 'You, me, Olgeir, Baldr and the whelp – we'll conduct this raid. Ingvar can stay here with Jorundur and stiffen the resolve of the Sisters. Russ knows there's plenty to keep them busy.'

Váltyr shook his head. 'He won't like it,' he said.

'He doesn't have to.' Gunnlaugur swung his hammer menacingly as he walked. The head of it rolled like a pendulum in the gloom. 'But I need you to support me. I have your word?'

Váltyr didn't like that either. In fifty-seven years Gunnlaugur had never asked him to support anything. He'd just gone ahead and acted – that was the way of things. Now, without warning, that seemed to have changed. It was as if all Gunnlaugur's certainty, his famed pride and justified battle-arrogance, was eroding before his eyes.

For a moment, Váltyr felt like protesting, arguing Ingvar's case, standing up for the unity of a broken brotherhood.

But he didn't. He looked across at Gunnlaugur, noticing the pent-up frustration in the warrior's shoulder-roll, the over-tight grip on the warhammer, the almost imperceptible stiffness in his long stride, and thought better of it.

Perhaps it was for the best. A hunt – a clean hunt with no dissension – would clear the air.

'You always have my support,' said Váltyr, haltingly, trying to inject more certainty into his voice than he felt.

'Good,' said Gunnlaugur bluntly, sounding like he'd been given what he needed. 'Then let's get it over with. We meet at the Ighala Gate.'

'And then?' asked Váltyr.

Gunnlaugur let slip a low, snagging growl.

'Then we break out of this shithole,' he said, 'and bring Hel to the enemy.'

Chapter Thirteen

The great sun sank towards the western horizon like a smouldering ingot of gold, turning the sky bronze and setting the world's edge alive with fire. Shadows streaked across the rust-red of the plains, rippling over runnels of sand and merging in their broken lees. The air lost its heaviness; it remained hot, but the searing, beating oppressiveness of it lightened just a little.

In happier times, dusk was magical on Ras Shakeh, a time to light candles under the lintels of the doorways and file towards one of the city's one hundred and twenty-nine chapels to perform rites of devotion. Scents of cinnamon and gahl-oil would rise from braziers and thuribles, intermingling with the murmur and hum of voices lost in prayer and wonder.

Now, though, the coming of night was far from magical. Hjec Aleja burned with unholy fires now, punctured across its expanse by the immolation of plague-addled saboteurs. Pyres constructed before the chapel doors now smoked from the charred bodies of the damned. The roast-pork stench of smouldering human flesh hung like a cloud over the narrow roofs and winding streets.

Burning the infected was the only way to limit the damage. Keeping the flesh intact created foul cradles for the blowflies and maggots that spread the sickness. The Sisters worked methodically through the city's many districts, dragging those with signs of infection from their habs and administering the Emperor's Mercy. Civilians looked on sullenly, only partially aware of the dangers posed by the plague-carriers in their midst, resentful of the savage measures taken to keep the healthy intact. Rumours filtered up to the Halicon of riots in the poorer quarters, of families sheltering mutants in cellars and under floors, and fighting to keep them hidden from the burn-teams.

They were only rumours, but this was just the beginning. All knew it would get worse.

Olgeir stood on the ramparts of the Ighala Gate, just under the shadow of one of its many defence towers, and gazed out over the cityscape below. Unlike his brothers he had taken no part in the hunt. His energies had been devoted to the city's defensive preparations: shoring up wall sections, excavating fire trenches, demolishing paths through the tangle of buildings to allow the passage of arms. He'd worked tirelessly throughout the day, hauling and lifting alongside the mechanised transports, roaring at the mortal labourers and exhorting them to greater feats of sacrifice. Many of the men were already exhausted, thrown into construction work straight from active tours on the battle-fronts to the south and west.

Olgeir felt pity for them. He recognised their sacrifice, he could see the pain in their faces, he knew what some of them had already faced.

He gave them no quarter. Time was short, and the storm front was closing. With the Sisters preoccupied with containing the infection, much of the task of improving the defences had fallen to him. He'd embraced it, throwing himself into the heavy, draining labour as if he alone could somehow refashion the entire city in the few days that remained. He'd trudged up and down the lines of sweating labourers between the inner walls and the outer gate, marshalling them, bellowing for more supplies, physically clearing blockages and barriers when mortal endurance failed.

But even his strength was not infinite. As the last of the sun's rays sank below the horizon, he leaned on the stone walls of the soaring inner wall and felt the sweat rising from his body like steam from a horse's flanks. Every muscle in his huge body throbbed painfully, chafing at the input nodes where his power armour interfaced.

He let his shaggy head fall back and pulled in a long, long draught of night-warm air, feeling the smoky taste of it against the back of his throat. Above him, the stars gazed down, points of brilliant silver in a field of darkening nightshade.

'*Hjá*, great one,' came a familiar voice from further down the parapet, towards the Ighala gatehouse where more lascannons were being slowly winched into place.

Olgeir smiled as he turned to face Baldr. 'Good hunting?' he asked.

Baldr grinned. His face was speckled with gore and his long hair hung unplaited around his neck. His helm had been locked to his belt and his blade was sheathed.

'They're everywhere,' he said, drawing alongside Olgeir and looking out over the city below. 'Kill one, another runs from cover. It's thirsty work.'

Olgeir looked at Baldr carefully. He looked better than he had done when they'd made planetfall. His eyes had their old intensity back, like soft orbs of gold. Perhaps his cheeks looked a little more sunken than they should have, but his voice had recovered its calm, easy assurance.

'It suits you, brother,' he said. 'I'd begun to worry.'

Baldr sheathed his blade and leaned heavily against the stone railing. 'No need,' he said. 'But nice to know I have a nursemaid.'

Olgeir let a rumble of laughter escape his chapped lips. It felt good to let his lungs expand after so much heavy lifting. He stretched his arms out, feeling the muscles pull, loosening the stiff layers of hard flesh.

'Don't relax too much,' he warned. 'We'll be heading out again soon.'

Baldr nodded, looking eager enough. 'Aye,' he said, softly. 'Can't wait.'

He meant it. His face had a hungry look to it, one that hung around his grey features like a scent. He stared out across the twinkling cityscape as the dusk-lights were lit, beyond the outer walls and across the wine-dark plains beyond.

'You've been working hard,' Baldr said, scanning the earthworks that scarred the route down the outer gate.

Olgeir snorted. 'We could have weeks and it wouldn't be enough.'

'Still. You've done plenty.

Olgeir shrugged. 'The main gates are rigged with incendiaries,' he said. 'Once they break in, we'll burn their entire vanguard. After that they've got three layers of trenches to get across. We'll pump promethium into them once this thing starts – it'll take them a while to wade through all that. And this place has twice the armaments on it now. I diverted a whole stash they'd been planning to mount on the Halicon walls. No point keeping them there. If they get that far we'll all be dead and rotting.'

Baldr nodded thoughtfully.

'Good,' he said. 'Good. Much more to do?'

'Depends how long we've got,' said Olgeir. 'When the Sisters aren't burning plague-carriers they're training the civilians to shoot straight, which is worth doing, but they won't do much more than slow the advance.'

'I don't know. I've seen mortals learn to fight. These ones are scared enough. They know there's nowhere else to go.'

'True enough,' said Olgeir grimly.

Baldr's fingers drummed against the parapet railing. He pushed himself away from them, grasped the hilt of his sword, then released it again. His movements looked nervy, impatient.

'Where are the others?' he muttered, almost to himself. 'We should be going.'

Olgeir watched him warily. Perhaps his earlier assessment had been too optimistic. It was strange to see Baldr so transformed, so removed from his usual self.

'They'll be here soon,' he said cautiously. 'Brother, I mean no disrespect, but are you sure you're feeling...'

He didn't finish the sentence. He'd got so used to Baldr's calmness, his lack of fuss or drama, that finding the words to express concern was difficult.

Baldr looked back at him for a moment. It looked like he was going to say something, to unload some long-clutched anxiety.

'Heavy-hand!'

Ingvar's clear voice rang out across the parapet. Baldr spun round, the moment gone, his expression clearing.

'Gyrfalkon,' he said, clasping Ingvar's hand as he came to join them.

Olgeir greeted him in turn. Ingvar looked pleased to see both of them.

'Others not here yet?' he asked. Like Baldr, his face and armour were speckled with dried gore. He hadn't wiped it free of his matted hair or skin; the Wolves wore the blood of their enemies as marks of pride.

'You were always faster,' said Baldr. 'Many kills?'

Ingvar nodded. 'Crawling all over the Cathedral district.' He patted *dausvjer*'s scabbard. 'Not any more.'

Olgeir shook his head with disgust.

'That blade shouldn't sully itself with filth,' he said. 'The Sisters should have nailed this down themselves – they've had weeks.'

'They've done plenty,' said Ingvar. 'This is a shrineworld, the garrison here is tiny. Don't judge them too harshly.'

Olgeir chuckled. 'So she's got to you,' he said. 'You've gone native.'

Ingvar smiled. 'Not yet,' he said. 'But they can fight. You'll see it.'

'We'll all see it,' said Baldr.

The noise of more boots crunched along the parapet. Three more

warriors emerged from the shadows of the Ighala Gate tower. Gunnlaugur and Váltyr marched together; Haflói trailed behind. The Blood
Claw bore almost no trace of the wound he'd taken on the plague-ship.
Váltyr's expression was hard to read. He seemed tense, as if already preparing for the combat to come. Gunnlaugur's burly face was expectant
and heavy with kill-urge. He looked ready to burst out of the walls, ready
to plunge into the oncoming horde and smash it apart single-handed.

'Now listen,' he said, looking across the assembled pack. 'Here's what
we're going to do.'

Vuokho's innards spilled across the blast plate, patchily lit by scaffold-
mounted flood-lumens arranged around the perimeter. Whole engine
sections lay on the rockcrete, stripped down and exposed to the night
air. Oils and lubricants stained the ground in splatters. The landing
stage hummed with the low buzz of machine tools, the whine of drills,
the thud of rivet-guns. Welders threw dazzling arcs of blue fire across
the scene. Between it all, dull-eyed labourers shuffled into place to lift,
clamp, cut and fit.

They were all servitors, and they crawled over the gunship's carcass like
scavengers picking at the bones of a fallen giant. Some looked almost
species-normal, with only puckered grey skin and augmetic limb-units
giving them away; others were more machine than human, with mere
fragments of muscle and sinew stretched between jointed tracks and
thickets of cabling. They slaved silently, ignoring the sparks from the
welders as they burned against unprotected skin, never slowing, never
hurrying.

Jorundur clambered out of an inspection pit under the gunship's huge
underbelly and wiped his forehead. His skin was covered in streaks of
inky engine oil, his beard singed from the hot metal of the thruster
housings. He'd removed his armour and wore a filthy brown tunic that
exposed the burnished sweat of his arms.

He seized a rag from one of the more human-looking servitors and ran
it over his neck. His hair and beard hung lank about his gaunt face.

'Progress?' he asked.

The servitor looked back at him vacantly.

'Task at phase alpha, lord. Estimated completion: five local days. Parts
missing. List follows: two fuel-line regulator valves, three boost-plug
sleeves, one–'

'Spare me,' sighed Jorundur, throwing the rag back at the demi-human
workman. It slapped the creature full in the face and slid down to the
floor. The servitor didn't flinch.

'Blood of Russ,' swore Jorundur, limping around the apron to get a better look at *Vuokho*'s flanks. He felt stiff and awkward, a result of hours spent hunched over piles of crackling component-bundles. 'Hopeless.'

He stomped around to the cockpit. Its angular nose hung above him, still covered in re-entry burn and cracked from projectile impacts. One of the panes of armourglass was a shattered mess. That had been fun when it had happened, still barely into Ras Shakeh's troposphere and with the gunship falling fast.

He stood back, hands on hips. *Vuokho* was far from flight-ready. It was even further from combat-ready. Deep in his heart, he knew it would play no role in the battle to come. Even if he could somehow restore limited drive-function, the weapons would overload the second they were fired.

His time would have been better spent with the pack, hunting the plague-damned before their foulness spread further.

For all that, though, he couldn't let it go. It was all he had, his peerless mastery of airborne combat. Take that away, and it was hard to mask the truth: he was old. He'd missed his chance for the Wolf Guard, he'd missed his chance for the Long Fangs. All that remained for him was death in Járnhamar, no longer fast enough to evade it, no longer strong enough to see it off.

He could feel Morkai panting down his neck. At night, in the scant moments of sleep he allowed himself, Jorundur could feel the dark wolf's foul breath running down his spine. Only when he was in the air, wheeling and banking through the hammering fire-lanes and letting rip with the battle cannon, did the sensation leave him.

He hawked up a bitter gobbet of oil-tainted phlegm and spat messily.

'You and me,' he snarled, looking up at his beloved *Vuokho*. 'Ice and iron, I'll get you in the air again.'

He heard a faint cough, and whirled round.

A Battle Sister stood before him. She was dressed in full ebony armour, though her head was bare. Like all her sisters she wore her hair clipped short. Hers was silver-blonde, shorn close to pale skin. Frost-blue eyes looked at him uncertainly.

'What do you want?' Jorundur growled, irritated at the interruption. Being surrounded by mind-dead servitors was one thing; having living mortals sniffing around was another.

The Sister bowed.

'Callia, at your service, lord,' she said. She proffered a regulation food-tin, vacuum-packed with protein extracts. 'The canoness sent me. She thought you might have need of sustenance.'

Jorundur looked at the tin doubtfully. He could smell its bland contents through the metal. He briefly remembered the supplies that had been destroyed with the *Undrider* – raw meats of Fenris, blood-heavy and slick with fat; whole vats of *mjod*, frothing in the cold and as thick as bile.

He started to salivate, and swallowed it down.

'My thanks,' he muttered, snatching the tin from her. It looked meagre in his oversized hand, barely enough to sate a moment's hunger.

But she was right, and it had been good of her to come. He'd lost track of time and had little idea how long he'd been working.

Sister Callia looked up at the half-dismantled Thunderhawk. Her cool eyes soaked up the damage.

'It's not as bad as it looks,' said Jorundur, a little quickly, unable to stomach criticism of it even when it was half ruined and broken open.

'A mighty machine,' murmured Callia. Her quiet voice held no trace of sarcasm. 'Even before the war destroyed our few flyers, we had nothing so grand.'

She started to walk around it, heading under the cockpit's overhang.

Jorundur put the tin down and followed her. He couldn't decide whether to be annoyed or flattered by her interest.

'Four centuries,' he said, staying close. 'That's how long it's been in service.'

Callia turned to face him. 'And will it last a little longer?' she asked. Her face held a certain sadness, as if she'd long resigned herself to the destruction of all she cared about and now only concerned herself with making a decent fist of the last stand.

Jorundur rubbed his chin. 'Perhaps,' he grunted. 'Get me some better servitors, I might get it flying again.'

Callia gave a rueful smile. 'You have our best already. But I'll talk to the canoness.'

'Do that.'

Jorundur turned away from the gunship and looked at Callia. Her armour, though beautifully cared for and polished, bore the marks of recent use. Her greaves and cuirass were chipped down to bare metal. Like her sisters, she had been in action for a long time.

Callia noticed his gaze and seemed to guess what he was thinking. 'Burn-team duty,' she said bluntly. 'Next rotation in two hours.'

Jorundur nodded. He'd smelt the pyres.

'Did you get many of them?'

She nodded sadly.

'Too many.' She pursed her lips. 'Your brothers kill faster than we do. I saw them in action. They laughed when they returned, covered in blood they didn't bother to wipe from their armour.'

She looked down.

'I cannot laugh. These are my people. A month ago we were ministering to them. We told them a new dawn was coming, the start of a crusade. Even when the plague takes them I mourn that so many must die. I wonder at the way you Wolves delight in slaughter.'

Jorundur shrugged. 'Don't expect us to be like you,' he said. 'We were made this way. That's why you wanted us here, was it not?'

Callia looked back up at him, unabashed. 'The canoness wanted you here. Others of us – I will not mention names – were opposed. You have a reputation.'

Jorundur chuckled. 'A cultivated one,' he replied. 'You speak plainly, Sister. I like that. I'll return the compliment. Until I got here I thought you were all stuck-up bitches, wearing a pale mockery of our sacred armour and pretending to fight like we do. I thought you were pious and arrogant.'

Callia suppressed a smile. 'Stuck-up bitches,' she said, amused. 'That's... candid.'

Jorundur shrugged. 'I try to be. And don't be surprised – our memories are long. Fenris has been attacked by your kind more than once.'

'Not in living memory.'

Jorundur snorted. 'In *our* living memory. You may have forgotten, but we have not. We tell sagas of it. We sing of how we sent your priests home, their robes stripped from their backs and their warships breaking open around them.'

Callia sighed. 'I'm sure you do,' she said. 'But then you are a warlike people. Fenris has been attacked by the Inquisition too. You make enemies easily, it seems.'

'We make no enemies but Traitors and xenos. If others choose to get in our way, that's their business.'

Callia nodded, as if confirming something to herself. 'Perhaps that is what I meant.'

Jorundur paused then, suddenly concerned he'd caused too much offence. He wouldn't normally have been worried, but Gunnlaugur had given them all strict orders to keep the peace.

'But I speak loosely,' he said, smiling awkwardly and exposing his curved yellow fangs. 'You understand that? Forgive me. We are just savages – savages from an ice-world that breeds us cold and rude.'

Callia looked amused again.

'I'm not some prim schola maid,' she said. 'But thank you: I had not

expected such concern for my sensibilities. Especially as we are all such
– what were the words you used? – *stuck-up bitches.*'

Jorundur laughed out loud, hacking up phlegm from his dry throat
and coughing on it. He clapped Callia hard on the shoulder, and the slap
of unguarded flesh against power armour made his palm sting.

'I like you!' he exclaimed. 'Blood of Russ, has the galaxy no end of
wonder?'

Callia looked less sure.

'Maybe not,' she said, moving away from him smoothly. 'But I do have
duties waiting. I'll talk to the canoness about the servitors.'

Jorundur bowed, still smiling. 'It can wait,' he said. 'My work is drawing to a close for today.'

Callia raised an eyebrow.

'You need rest?'

'No, no. My brothers have had the hunting in this city all to themselves. They will be heading out into the dark soon, and it is time I took
up the burden on their behalf.'

Callia looked at him distastefully.

'You will relish killing our people as much as they.'

Jorundur gave her a crooked, semi-ashamed grin.

'Maybe more so,' he confessed.

Ingvar watched Gunnlaugur intently. The Wolf Guard spoke to them
all but wouldn't meet his gaze. He'd look at all the others, but not him.

He's putting something off. Something he doesn't want to tell me.

Ingvar felt his hearts sink. He'd hoped the exchange in the Halicon,
as difficult as it had been, had cleared the air between them. A state of
continued tension suited nobody.

But then Gunnlaugur had always been proud. He was a born warrior,
only happy with bolter in hand and prey in sight, never knowing how
to handle anything but combat. It wasn't so much that the Wolf Guard
didn't tolerate differing points of view, more that he didn't understand
how they could exist. The way of Russ, the brutal life of the hard ice, the
exalted state of the Sky Warrior, that was all there was for him. Just as
the Sisters fervently believed in the perfect godhood of the Emperor, so
Gunnlaugur believed in the perfect heritage of the primarch, frozen into
the annals of Fenris and sanctified by millennia of war.

Ingvar couldn't blame him for that. He'd thought the same once. It had
taken a lot to shake that faith.

*Tyranid-breed xenos, millions upon millions, turning the void into a living
hell, burning with hive-malice, dousing the light of Terra. The ships! They are*

like worlds, vast and swollen, disgorging living contents in columns of twisting, slavering frenzy.

We cannot fight them. They will come at us, again and again. There is no end to it. Callimachus, there is no end to it!

Ingvar forced himself not to remember. He forced himself not to see the Ultramarine's face turning towards him, stoic to the last, ready to enact the order he'd been given by Halliafiore. He forced himself not to see the agony in that face, hidden by Callimachus's peerless conditioning, his reserve, his unimpeachable honour.

The things they made us do.

He curled his fingers together, concentrating on the present.

'The canoness has restored partial mid-range auspex scans,' Gunnlaugur was saying. 'We have readings coming at us from all directions. The city is at the centre of a closing circle. Numbers are hard to estimate.'

'Take a guess?' said Olgeir.

'Thousands,' said Gunnlaugur sourly. 'Many, many thousands. The plague has spread. De Chatelaine thinks most of their troops are defenders who've succumbed and then mutated. That's why this thing's happened so fast. Every city they've taken has swollen their ranks. They conquer, they get stronger.'

'She was right: they do not wish to destroy this world,' said Baldr. 'They wish to possess it. For what?'

Gunnlaugur looked at him irritably.

'We don't need to know.' Still he avoided Ingvar's eye. 'Survival is the first task, vengeance the next. The armies have fractured as they near the city. Discipline is weak on the fringes, and one armoured column has come too far up the defiles to the south. That's the one we'll take.'

Olgeir grunted. 'What are we talking about? Mortals? Plague-bearers?'

'Both. Perhaps more.' A glint of anticipation lit up Gunnlaugur's features, sparking in his amber eyes. 'De Chatelaine picked up strange readings, ones they couldn't decipher. Something... interesting travels in that column.'

Ingvar felt mounting unease. A raid was one thing – taking out enemy troops before they could take up position made sense. Going after unverified targets was another.

He said nothing. It would only antagonise Gunnlaugur. The Wolf Guard had taken a blow to his prestige by losing the *Undrider*; a feat of arms against a worthy foe would redress the balance.

'How far?' asked Hafloí, flexing his fingers absently. His voice gave away his eagerness – he was chafing at the leash already.

Gunnlaugur gave him an approving look.

'If we leave now and move fast, we can engage before dawn.'

'No speeders?' asked Olgeir.

'Nothing that could carry us. We'll run.' Gunnlaugur grinned. 'Think of it brother: close pursuit, under the stars, nothing but the scent of fear between you and the enemy.'

Olgeir nodded slowly, a smile creeping across his scarred, ugly face.

'Pure,' he murmured.

'We kill them all,' said Gunnlaugur. 'Destroy everything. Hit hard, then withdraw. Allfather willing, that'll give the bastards pause. They already know something destroyed their ship – we can work on that doubt. It might even slow them, give us more time to cleanse the city.'

'They won't slow,' said Ingvar. The words came out of his mouth unbidden; he hadn't meant to speak. Immediately his eyes flickered up towards Gunnlaugur, but the Wolf Guard still avoided contact. Váltyr, standing to Gunnlaugur's right, looked uncomfortable.

'It'll hurt them,' said Gunnlaugur. 'And what's the alternative? Hole up here until they're clawing at the walls? Not the way of the *Fenryka*.'

Olgeir and Hafloí both growled in agreement. Ingvar could almost smell their hunt-readiness.

Gunnlaugur pulled himself to his full height. The runes on his armour flickered in the soft lights of the city, playing over the ceramite like tongues of flame. Despite the blood and slime that still caked his battle-plate, he looked savagely magnificent, the very embodiment of a *vaerangi*.

'We were brought here for a reason, brothers,' he said. 'Time to show them what it was.'

'And Jorundur?' asked Ingvar.

Only then did Gunnlaugur look directly at him.

'He's staying here,' he said. 'As are you, Gyrfalkon.'

For a moment, Ingvar didn't believe it. He felt sure he'd misheard.

'You mean–' he started.

'I mean you're staying here.'

Gunnlaugur's voice was cold. His amber eyes didn't waver.

Ingvar felt sweat break out across his palms. For the space of a heartbeat he couldn't say anything, sure that if he tried he'd unleash something he'd regret.

'Why?' he asked thickly, keeping himself under control with difficulty.

'The plague worsens. The Sisters need help.'

That was ridiculous. The Sisters had been trained for such work; they were very, very good at it.

Ingvar looked over at Váltyr. The blademaster averted his eyes.

'Is this your doing?' he spat. The anger in his voice rose to the surface.

Váltyr stirred then, looking like he wanted to rise to the challenge. He was cut off by Gunnlaugur.

'Enough,' he said, letting threat-notes bleed into his speech. 'The city is burning. I will not abandon it.'

Ingvar crushed his fists into tight balls.

It was a humiliation. Punishment for what happened on the plague-ship.

I need to know that you will follow an order.

Or a test.

Ingvar stared directly at Gunnlaugur. For a moment their eyes met, one pair golden, the other as grey as winter sleet. When he spoke next, his voice was sharp with bitterness.

'You want me to waste my blade here on filth that can barely stand? So be it.' Ingvar raised his chin, looking proudly back at the Wolf Guard. Jocelyn himself could not have expressed such disdain. 'I will scour the citadel. When you return, expect to find it cleansed and ready for your arrival.'

He swept his gaze across the rest of the pack. Olgeir was dumb with surprise; Baldr almost distraught. Hafloí returned his gaze coolly. Váltyr looked torn between shame and defiance.

Then he turned, not waiting for Gunnlaugur to dismiss him, and strode away from the pack, back towards the defence tower. He could feel his cheeks burning from the fury that coursed through him, bubbling under the surface like magma under a thin crust of rock.

After he'd ducked under the doorway and started to descend the stairway down to the next level he heard footsteps clattering on the stone behind him. For a moment he thought, or hoped, they were Gunnlaugur's. When Baldr grabbed him by the shoulder it was a disappointment.

'You have been wronged,' said Baldr.

Ingvar twisted round to look at him. Baldr's face was white with shame. His eyes looked sunk deep into his flesh and an unhealthy pallor hung in their shadow.

Ingvar wondered how he'd not noticed that earlier.

'It is nothing,' he said.

'Olgeir is arguing with him. Come back. Fight with us.'

Ingvar smiled, despite himself. He could hear Heavy-hand's booming voice from the parapet above, remonstrating futilely.

'You are my true brother,' he said. The worst of his anger subsided, giving way to a low, sullen feeling of misuse. 'But do not do this. He is *vaerangi*. It is his judgement, and his anger is with me, not with you.'

Baldr looked pained. 'It is unjust.'

'It is not.' Once the first flush of humiliation had passed, Ingvar began to see what Gunnlaugur was doing. It was not the way that Callimachus would have run his squad, but it had a certain, brutal logic. 'Follow Gunnlaugur, just as you have done. You do not help me by defying him.'

Baldr hesitated. He looked lost.

'I do not understand,' he said. 'You were like blood-kin.'

'We were. We may yet be again.' Ingvar reached down to the soul-ward at his breast, the *sálskjoldur*, and lifted it up. 'But *this* is the mark of brotherhood. I cherish it. Do not fear for me.'

Baldr's eyes followed the pendant as it twisted in Ingvar's grasp. He looked suddenly wistful, as if part of him regretted losing it.

'This is one raid,' he said. 'One raid. After that the true battle begins, and we will come together then: you, me, Gunnlaugur, like it used to be.'

Ingvar nodded. 'I yearn for it,' he said, with feeling. 'For now, though, let him have his way. Blood the enemy, just as he wishes. He needs a victory, one that will banish the shades of the *Undrider*. Deliver that for him and he will forget his pride.'

Baldr reached up for the soul-ward and pressed it back against Ingvar's breastplate. His grimace was wry. When he looked at Ingvar, the meaning in his expression was plain.

It should have been you.

'As you command, though it pains me,' he said. 'Hunt well, Gyrfalkon.'

Ingvar bowed. 'Hunt well, Fjolnir. I will look for you with the dawn.'

Then Ingvar turned, hastening down the stairs and away from the pack. As he did so, despite his words to Baldr, a part of him hardened, tightening with a resentment that he knew would not easily unravel.

Chapter Fourteen

The pack left the outer gate as the first moon rose. It cast a fragile silver sheen over the still-warm landscape. They broke into a run as the massive doors clanged closed, loping easily in loose formation. The city quickly fell away behind them, retreating into the north as they sped. The five warriors dropped into a steady rhythm, their limbs working in unison, each casting a deep-black shadow on the dust beneath them.

Gunnlaugur set the pace. He'd strapped *skulbrotsjór* to his back, lacquered down his straggling hair and beard and donned his helm. Like the others, his battle-plate was still layered with the patina of combat. The rune of destruction, *turza*, was still visible on his helm's forehead, cut deep by the Iron Priests and inlaid with iron. In the moonlight it glowed dully, making his snarl-masked visage seem marked with the sign of ancient magick.

He drove the others hard. The physical exertion helped to clarify his mind. He felt his hearts beating in slow unison, fuelling the huge furnace of his body. He drew air into his barrel-chest in long draughts, feeling the gritty dryness of it drag deep into cavernous lungs.

The pack went silently. Olgeir was brooding, still angry at Ingvar's exclusion. Váltyr was similarly unquiet, though he'd voiced no objection. Haflói was the only one in high spirits. He'd let out a whoop of battle-joy on leaving the city, but hadn't repeated it after no one else had joined in.

'What's the matter with you all?' he'd grumbled once they were under way. 'Lost your voices when your hair went grey?'

That had made Baldr laugh, but it had been a stifled sound. After that they had run without speaking. They might have been predators indeed, grey-clad and draped in strange hides and bones, striding out across the wide emptiness in search of victims.

Gunnlaugur didn't blame Hafloí for his irritation. Back when he'd been a Blood Claw himself he'd raced into battle with death-oaths thundering from his hoarse throat. He'd laughed as readily as he'd cursed, exuberant at the raw power unleashed within him by the Helix. Hjortur had been the same, and under his leadership Járnhamar had been a raucous, brutish juggernaut of noise and hot blood.

Gunnlaugur didn't remember when that exuberance had begun to fade. Perhaps it was fatigue – the pack had been on engagement after engagement for nearly a century with only snatched periods away from the front. Even the furious energy of a Sky Warrior had its limits.

Gunnlaugur found himself growling as he ran, his hot breath snagging throatily. It was an animal sound, a primeval note of slow-burning frustration. He had found it hard to endure words of reproach from Olgeir, who was the most generous of them, the one most ready to laugh off tension and still dissent with a cuff or a laugh. It had been hard to endure Baldr's weary looks and Váltyr's doubts.

For all that, he couldn't regret his decision. Ingvar had to learn his place in the hierarchy. It was a matter of precedence, of power. From Járnhamar, to Blackmane's Great Company, to the Rout, to the Imperium itself: everything depended on hierarchy, on the establishment of command. Without the iron gauntlet of discipline everything fell apart, leaving the defences open to the predations of the enemy.

In time, things would be more like they had been, but only once order had been re-established. Matters had been left to drift. He was *vaerangi*, the inheritor of an ancient and noble battle-role. Even if he wanted to loosen things a little, to cut the others some slack, he couldn't.

It wasn't personal. It wasn't about self-doubt, jealousy, or the spectres of the past. It was about duty, about leadership.

Above all, it wasn't about Ingvar. He was certain of that. It wasn't about Ingvar.

I'd want a blade of his pedigree in the pack. If he challenged me, I'd beat him down.

Arjac's words came into his mind unbidden, like a waking dream. He remembered the way the Rockfist had spoken to him: like a father to a son. The memory affected him strangely. He couldn't remember his birth-father at all. It was all so long ago.

If fate brings you and Ingvar back together, the pack will shape itself around both of you, one way or another.

Ah, but there was the rub. Gunnlaugur had to control the pack. He had always needed to control, to fashion, to mould, just as Rockfist moulded soft metal into his killing blades.

Pride makes you strong, stripling.

Yes, that was so. It had always been so. It had been the cause of his rise from the mass of other warriors, the thing that had first caught Hjortur's eye. His pride did more than make him strong. It made him unbreakable.

We only live for the pack: that is what makes us deadly, what makes us eternal. Nothing else matters.

And that was also true. Gunnlaugur had always known it. He had always lived it. What had Ingvar done for Járnhamar, compared to him? It was Gunnlaugur who had held the pack together after Hjortur's death, making it stronger, tempering it and keeping a grip on the raging spirits within. Could Ingvar have stood up to Tínd when the black temper came on him? Would Ingvar have kept Jorundur's bitterness in check, or managed Váltyr's need for validation at every turn?

But this wasn't about Ingvar.

Ahead of him, the plains stretched away into darkness. Gunnlaugur checked the locator readings on his lens-display, blink-clicking to cross-reference with the coordinates de Chatelaine had given him. On the southern horizon the land began to pucker up like scar tissue, breaking into a mass of higher ground riven by snaking gorges. The wind from that place had a taint of foulness.

Gunnlaugur checked proximity readings. Just on the edge of sensor-range, he saw the cluster of runes he'd been hoping for. They glowed red against the filtered darkness of the desert around him.

He adjusted course and picked up speed. The pack swung automatically along with him. He could hear their low breathing, the dull thud of their boots against hard-packed dust.

'That one,' he said, pointing over to the mouth of a wide defile that opened out onto the flat land. It was thick with shadow, unlit by the low moon.

They would come through there. They would come incautiously, believing the land cleared of defenders. They would stride proudly out, waddling from plague-distended torsos, wheezing from corruption, living only to spread the infection that fizzed and coursed through their swollen veins. They would bring their engines of war with them, each one laden with long-forbidden biological weaponry and marked with the ruinous symbols of dark gods.

Gunnlaugur kept running. His breathing picked up, not from fatigue but from expectation.

Skulbrotsjór felt light across his back; it would feel lighter in his hands.

Ingvar walked through the empty streets, his mood as black as the sky above him. The boom and clang of construction still echoed into the night as more guns were hoisted into position and more streets were cleared of clutter for supply-lines. Few mortals left their hab-units after dark; those that did so wore the tabards of the Shakeh Guard or the battle-plate of the Wounded Heart.

Ingvar ignored them. He went quickly, descending from the Ighala Gate and down into the lower city. The stars were vivid, masked only by drifting smoke from the pyres. He could still hear noises of combat from all over the city, distant and unremitting. The Guards' las-weapons were silent, but the sporadic reports of the bolters and flamers used by the Sisters broke the tense blanket of fear like hammer-blows.

Hjec Aleja was gripped by foreboding. The smell of death was everywhere. Civilians, Guardsmen and Ecclesiarchy officials all suspected one another, hurrying to report every observed flesh-sore, overheard cough or suspected rash. It made for a wild, drum-tight air of interlocking suspicion.

Ingvar cared for none of that. The canoness could worry about the city; he had other concerns.

The cathedral reared above him into the night. The lights around it had been doused, making it ghoulishly forbidding. The courtyard where pilgrims had queued for blessing was empty, the stone flags carved up by the tracks of crawlers. Heavy bolters had been mounted up on the spires, jutting out from the stonework like huge snout-nosed gargoyles. Sandbag walls had been heaped around the doorways, all of which were braced with bands of steel and ringed with hastily thrown-up defensive barricades. Shakeh Guardsmen manned all those entrances, huddling around tripod-mounted lascannons and squat-throated mortars.

They shrank back as Ingvar approached the main gates, not daring to challenge him. They could see the grim look in his eyes as he emerged from the cloying darkness.

He pushed the doors open and walked into the echoing nave. It was deserted. His footfalls echoed down the long space. He could smell mouldering incense, left unburned in caskets or strewn across the stone. Ahead of him, hung in darkness, was the statue of the Emperor.

Ingvar's eyes lighted on it for a second. The representation was highly stylised. The Allfather's face was hidden behind a golden mask carved in the likeness of a young man. It was handsome, almost cherubic. That might have been Imperial orthodoxy – the Emperor in the prime of vigorous youth striking down the upstart Warmaster – but Ingvar doubted it had any basis in fact.

Then again, who alive could know what had taken place in those days of fire and loss? Who was to say the Emperor had not worn a mask of gold as he prepared to face Horus the Betrayer for the first and last time?

History had faded into myth, just like the sagas of Fenris told over and over in the firelit halls of the Aett. No one outside the inviolate sanctums of Holy Terra had set eyes on the Emperor for nearly ten thousand years. Perhaps even the fabled Custodians did not see him as he truly was. Perhaps they only saw a shell of what he had been, or a screen of illusion projected by his indomitable will, or rushing visions of glory and redemption streaming from his immortal throne.

In the Cathedral of St Alexia on the shrineworld of Ras Shakeh, though, he would always be just as he was in a million other gloomy temples of the Ecclesiarchy: young, vital, indestructible.

Human.

Ingvar looked away and headed to the stairway leading up to Bajola's chambers. He could already smell her presence; she had been on the stairs recently. As he neared her rooms, he heard the clamp and drill of armour being put in place.

He pushed the door open and swept inside. Bajola whirled round to face him, shock written across her face. Her attendants, three young women of the Sisterhood in black robes, reached for their weapons.

'Leave us,' growled Ingvar, staring at Bajola.

He hadn't drawn his blade. His hands were empty. Bajola's attendants trained las-pistols at him; one of them aimed at his head, the other two at his hearts.

Surprise ebbed quickly from Bajola's face. She clipped the last buckle of a replacement cuirass into place, then placed a calming hand on the nearest of her attendants.

'You may go,' she said. Slowly, they lowered their weapons.

Ingvar waited for them to leave. His eyes never left Bajola as they filed past him and into the stairwell beyond.

'If you wished to resume our conversation, you could have picked a better time,' said Bajola, reaching for her helm and checking the connector bolts.

'What do you know of Hjortur Bloodfang?' asked Ingvar.

This time there was no recognition in Bajola's features, no brief flicker of guilt. Instead, she shot him a weary look.

'Not now, Ingvar,' she said.

'You recognised the name. It meant something to you. Why was that?'

Bajola shook her head irritably. She reached up and fixed the helm over her head, twisting it in place with a hiss of seals.

'Not now.'

In her armour, she cut a very different profile to the last time he'd seen her. The battle-plate bulked her out, making her both taller and broader. The plates of ebony ceramite were lined with silver and picked out with blood-red detailing. The power generator at her back let out a grinding hum of electronics, just as his did. She carried a boltgun, just as he did.

Ingvar blocked her passage.

'Did you serve with him?'

Bajola exhaled in exasperation. 'I need to leave,' she hissed. 'Get out of the way.'

'You were shocked. I saw fear in your eyes. You're not the only one trained to recognise deception.'

Bajola blurted out a cynical laugh. 'Oh really? Who taught you? Some ranting shaman?'

Ingvar didn't move an inch.

'The same people who taught you. Don't test my patience, Sister. It has been a trying night.'

Bajola's finger strayed to her bolter's trigger. Ingvar found himself wondering just how fast she was.

'You are–' she started, but never finished.

The floor rocked suddenly, and cracks sped across the stonework. A muffled boom broke out from far below, followed by another.

'Throne, Space Wolf, get out of the way!' she shouted, looking ready to open fire on him where he stood.

He hesitated for a second longer, but then more explosions went off, all from far below, shivering the walls.

'We'll take this up later,' he said, finally standing aside.

'Fine,' she said, pushing past him and heading into the stairwell. 'For now, make yourself useful.'

Ingvar followed her.

'What's going on?' he asked, breaking into a jog to keep up with her as she raced down the spiral of stone.

She didn't turn, just kept her eyes fixed ahead. When she replied, her voice was cold.

'I don't know yet,' she said. 'But whatever it is, it's in the crypt, and it's started.'

Baldr crouched down low amid the rocks, his head hammering, his palms sweaty, his breath shallow.

The short-lived respite had ended and the pain had returned. Sealed in his armour, he was able to conceal it from his brothers, but the sensations were getting worse; it felt like something was stretching his muscles and pulling them from the bones. At times he had to bite down not to cry out.

He clutched his bolter two-handed, willing something – *anything* – to happen. He needed to move, to burst into action again, to force his aching limbs to stretch. Bodily exertion helped. Combat was even better. It allowed him to direct the pain away from him, to focus it onto the enemy and turn it into something useful.

He didn't know why the pain ebbed and flowed, but he could guess, and those guesses made him uneasy. In the warp he had been close to the raw stuff of the ether. In the city it had been strongest while in the presence of the ether-blighted; only when their unholy contagion had been staunched did the agony abate a little.

Now, as the enemy crawled towards them once more, searing needles of fire in his temples were blazing again. The touch of the ether would be heavy on them too. Baldr remembered what Gunnlaugur had said.

Something interesting travels in that column.

Not for the first time he thought of the soul-ward he had given to Ingvar. He'd been fighting with it for so long that he'd still not got used to its absence. The pain had got worse since he'd given it up.

He didn't regret handing it over; it had been the right thing to do.

Still, the pain *had* got worse.

He clutched his bolter more tightly, pressing the outline of his gauntlets into his weapon's grip. He could feel his flesh push up against the inside of the ceramite. His armour's inner membranes felt hot, even in the coolness of the desert night. His tongue was swollen in his mouth, and his throat was raw.

'Here they come,' warned Hafloí over the comm.

Baldr stiffened, peering into the darkness. His hearts were already drumming from the pain. Their rate picked up further, fuelled by hyperadrenaline seeping into his system.

His body knew combat was close; as ever, it worked to make him ready.

Like the others, Baldr was perched up one side of the ravine wall, half covered with rock and rubble. Gunnlaugur and Váltyr were on the far slope, lodged amid piles of chest-sized boulders about ten metres up from the gorge floor. Olgeir was crouched on the same side as Baldr, further back and higher up, the better to get an angle for *sigrún's* deadly delivery. Haflói was at the forefront, his young eyes employed to get advance warning of the approaching column.

All of them were virtually invisible. They had dug in deep, and their matt armour blended with the stone of the ravine sides. Even though Baldr knew where his brothers had concealed themselves he could barely make out their outlines against the stone. Only his helm-display showed their location: glimmering red runes overlaid on the fractured, tumbling terrain.

'Hold position,' growled Gunnlaugur. His comm-filtered voice was thick with anticipation. He wanted to move. When he did so, it would be like a dam bursting.

Baldr gritted his teeth. Sweat ran down his cheeks.

Then they came into view.

A few hundred yards to the south of the pack's position the ravine took a sharp turn to the west. They emerged from around that corner, creeping across the level valley floor like a slowly encroaching swarm of bilge-vermin.

Baldr narrowed his eyes, letting his helm's lenses zoom in and pick out the detail.

The troops in the front ranks were lightly armed. They were mortal, with poorly-fitted carapace armour pieces bolted over civilian uniforms. Some went helmless, exposing bald, grey-skinned scalps to the atmosphere. Others wore heavy iron gas masks. Pale green illuminations swam behind their visors, glowing in the dark like bobbing corpse-lights. They came in loose bands, walking unguardedly and swinging their weapons. The squads were small – twenty, thirty troops.

More detachments followed. Soon hundreds of them had entered the ravine, some limping, some misshapen, all of them carrying hulking carbines or strange canister-fed gas-guns. They filled the valley floor from side to side, kicking up clouds of dust as they tramped onwards.

Baldr winced as the stench of them assailed his nostrils. His eyes watered, and he felt his gorge rise uncomfortably.

Let me slay them. By Russ, let me slay them all.

More troops followed the vanguard. Some of those were clad in heavier armour. Banners swung above the host, rocking to the rhythm of the march, each one clanking with necklaces of skulls. Fell symbols had been bleached into the tattered fabric. Baldr made out three leering, bloated death's heads nailed to an iron frame; three circles, riddled with worms and shedding maggots; the eight-pointed star drawn in dark brown blood.

Those symbols made his head worse, and he looked away.

'Hold position,' repeated Gunnlaugur.

The first of the gas mask-wearing troops began to draw level with Haflói's position. They marched onwards without pause, not one of them looking up. Baldr started to make out the *hurr hurr* of their massed phlegmy breathing. Those whose faces were exposed displayed nothing but a blank, semi-blinded torpor. It looked like they were sleepwalking into battle. Insects buzzed around their shoulders. The stink of old vomit rolled around them in a cloud of drifting spores.

Then, back at the turn in the ravine, the first of the chem-tankers crawled into view. Another emerged, following in convoy, then another. Their huge tracked chassis were lit up by marker lights that slowly blinked in the darkness. They churned along at walking pace, their enormous engines throwing up clouds of red-tinged soot from rusting smokestacks. The cylindrical tanks they carried were crusted with corrosion and streaky with leaking lubricant.

Slowly, grindingly slowly, the tankers crawled onwards. More followed, each as bulky and cumbersome as the first. They were vast, towering over the hordes of infantry around them and swaying laboriously atop immense tracks. Steam gushed from bronze valves jutting along their flanks. Tangled masses of piping ran all over every rusting surface, twisting and clogging like a jumble of varicose veins splayed across muscle. They belched fumes and retched smoke, wallowing and grinding as they hauled themselves towards the front line. Their spines were serrated with the bronze-spiked maws of cannons and flail-launchers.

As they drew closer, the earth began to tremble underfoot. Six tankers in total ground their way down the ravine, each one surrounded by hundreds of mutant troops. Baldr saw hideous growths on some of the marching guards – obscene flopping bellies bursting open with disease, lashing tentacles spilling out of the cracks between armour plates, hooked hands dripping with trembling lines of fluid.

Baldr heard Gunnlaugur's heavy breathing over the comm.

'When the lead tanker draws level, we break,' he ordered. 'Váltyr and I'll take the first, Haflói and Baldr the second. Olgeir in support. Then we work down the line, one by one. Understood?'

The confirmations came in order. Baldr barely whispered his response, fearful his tight-clenched jaw would give him away. It felt like his blood was boiling in his arteries.

The first chem-tanker inched its way towards the invisible line

Gunnlaugur had drawn across the gorge. Baldr watched it come, willing it to move faster, feeling his innards churn and his temples throb while his body remained static. The glowing lights of its drive-unit swam closer, surging up through the clouds of smoke and spoor, juddering and leaking, trailing acrid tangs of chemical poison. Every riveted panel of it, every piece of armour-plate or looped tubing was raddled with decay and degradation. It was a wonder the thing moved at all. Lurid flickers strobed along its straining bulk, exposing stringy lattices of mucus hanging from each joint and piston-housing.

Finally the leader passed Haflói's vantage. Baldr's breathing got faster. He heard the faint clunk of Olgeir bringing his beloved *sigrún* into position. He detected movements on the far side of the ravine as both Váltyr and Gunnlaugur adjusted stance, ready for the pounce.

He felt sick. In the final few seconds that remained, he scanned the host marching in the valley below, scouring it for the source of his sickness.

Something interesting travels in that column.

He saw nothing but rank after rank of shuffling plague-bearers, their sore-puckered mouths hanging open, their feet dragging in the dust, their empty eyes fixed ahead. Some of them wore the remnants of Shakeh Guard uniforms.

Then Baldr heard the comm-link crackle open. When he heard the order, the relief was overwhelming.

'The Hand of Russ be with you, brothers,' said Gunnlaugur, his savage voice alive again. 'Slay freely.'

Ingvar and Bajola descended quickly, bypassing the cathedral's nave and heading deep into the underground levels below. Bajola led, travelling swiftly and surely through the switchbacks and twists. Her lighter armour was an advantage in the cramped tunnels of stone, and more than once she nearly left Ingvar behind.

The chambers and passageways under the marble floor formed a labyrinth of dank, claustrophobic spaces, thick with old dust and mouldering with the stale air of centuries. Ingvar caught fleeting glimpses of age-withered statues set in arched recesses. He saw leathery purity banners hanging over granite altars, barely moving even as he brushed past them.

'How in Hel did they get down here?' he asked, working hard to keep up.

A fresh storm of bolter-fire snapped out ahead of them, fractured and overlapped by the echoing chambers. They were close.

'Throne only knows,' said Bajola, her voice tight.

She swerved around a many-columned pillar crumbling from age. A dull red glare of firelight swept over her, turning her black armour the colour of old blood.

Ingvar rounded the pillar after her, drawing *dausvjer*.

Ahead of them lay carnage. An arched chamber stretched away from where they stood, its vaulted roof lost under a pall of smoke and underpinned by lined ranks of granite pillars. Flames roared furiously from its far end, licking up along blackened walls and rippling across the floor like spilled liquid. Huge, squat objects stood between the pillars, as square and solid as devotional altars. They were all on fire, sparking and raging like igniting melta-bombs. Portions of the roof had fallen in further back, and metal struts dangled precariously amid the roaring blaze. Gouts of thick smog curled up against the arches, raining flakes of soot.

Two Battle Sisters had arrived before them. They were retreating in the face of the inferno.

'Where are they?' roared Bajola, grabbing one of them by the shoulder and hauling her round to face her. Her voice was furious.

The Sister nodded towards the fires.

'Dead already, Palatine,' she reported grimly, nodding to a scattering of blackened bodies lying on the stone near the edge of the fire.

Bajola edged over to one of the corpses, keeping her bolter raised, raising one hand against the heat. She kicked it over with her boot. A flabby, slack-skinned mutant rolled onto its back, its sightless eyes staring up at the ceiling. One whole side of its body was burned into scarring from the flames. Its eyes were gone, leaving empty orbits. Even in death, its blubbery face retained a brutish expression of fervour.

Ingvar drew alongside Bajola.

'How did they get in?' he asked again. He could feel the tremendous press of the flames even inside his armour.

Bajola shook her head. 'Did you not hear me the first time?' she said. She squatted down beside the plague-bearer's corpse and looked more closely into its face. 'I have no idea.'

More Battle Sisters arrived. Orders for dousing agents were shouted back up the line. The stone roof above them began to crack and blister.

'We cannot remain here,' said Ingvar, watching the growing wall of flame lick up across the vaulting.

'Too late,' breathed Bajola, no longer listening. Her voice was distant, broken. 'All destroyed.'

Ingvar stared into the heart of the inferno, letting his helm-lenses adjust to the light and heat. More bodies lay amid the flames, crackling and bursting. Some were little more than slivers of flesh, blown apart by the bombs they'd been carrying. Others, more intact, lay amid the altars like slaughtered cattle. Sparks flew from the boxes as they burned, interspersed with flickering arcs of electrical lightning. The iron sheaths that had encased them were melting, buckling and distorting.

'What is this place?' Ingvar asked.

Bajola clambered to her feet, shrugging off his outstretched hand irritably. Her helm-masked face turned to his. Even though her expression was shielded by the black ceramite, he could sense her frustration.

'If you had not delayed me...' she started, then trailed off.

More explosions sounded at the far end of the chamber, fuelling the firestorm. Fragments of granite fell from the ceiling nearby, shattering as they slammed into the ground.

Bajola gazed one more time into the inferno.

'Too late,' she said, sounding defeated. 'Damn you, Space Wolf.'

'What is this place?' Ingvar pressed.

'What does it matter now?' she said, her voice a hoarse whisper.

She turned away from him and started to walk.

'All destroyed,' she said. Ingvar watched her go. 'All destroyed.'

Chapter Fifteen

Gunnlaugur broke, flinging himself from the fragile skin of debris that had sheltered him. His hammer lashed round, leaping into his grasp as if alive, and the disruptor field snarled into life.

Váltyr broke from cover beside him and burst down the slope. He went silently, swiftly, uttering no battle-cry.

Gunnlaugur's momentum carried him down. He leapt and skidded down the long scree incline, swinging the hammer in arcs to build momentum. He felt his blood pump in his temples, swelling the veins with heat and fervour.

The need for secrecy had passed; he could unleash his true self.

'*Fenrys!*' he bellowed, and the sacred, battle-sanctified words echoed from the ravine walls and called back to him in a dozen new, overlapping voices. '*Fenrys hjolda!* Cower and scream, slaves of darkness, for the blades of the Wolves are upon you!'

He heard Olgeir answer him with a slamming volley of heavy bolter-rounds. The explosive shells lanced into the front ranks of Guardsmen, immediately causing havoc around the lead tanker. Dozens of troops went down, clutching at their exploding bodies futilely and tumbling into the dust. Some of them tried to respond, scrabbling for their weapons and looking for something to fire back at.

By then it was too late. By then the pack was among them.

Gunnlaugur crashed into a knot of milling troops, hurling half a dozen of them into the air with a single blistering sweep of *skulbrotsjór*. Their broken bodies thudded back to earth before they'd even had time to cry out.

'The Blood of Russ!' he roared, scything the hammerhead back and throwing more corpses into the night. He swung *skulbrotsjór* two-handed, leaning into the devastating strokes, whirling on his axis like a typhoon of destruction, carving his way deep into the mass of marching bodies.

The still of the night exploded into a rage of flashing las-light and clattering bolter-fire. Gunnlaugur saw Váltyr turning and leaping, veering past incoming lines of fire effortlessly as he sliced through the meagre defences. He left piles of twitching corpses in his wake, each of them mortally cleaved by a single stroke.

Gunnlaugur grinned. That was astonishing skill. It was arrogant. It was *beautiful*.

By then the rest of the pack had joined in the carnage. He could hear Hafloí's echoing cries of rage and frenzy. He could see the Blood Claw's favoured axe glittering in the moonlight, already flinging blood around it in long splatters. He saw Baldr break from cover and charge, his bolter thundering, screaming ancient death-curses from the Old Ice as he rampaged. His voice was the most terrible of all. It sounded almost demented.

The defenders loosed off rounds into the dark – panicky shots, poorly-aimed and badly timed. Some were already scrabbling up the ravine edges, desperate to escape the sudden, horrific attack of the grey terrors that had exploded into them.

Gunnlaugur turned on his heel, slamming *skulbrotsjór* hard into the midriff of a wide-eyed plague-carrier. The force of the blow ripped through the mutant, sending remnants of its bisected body tumbling backwards in a cloud of blood and spores. Gunnlaugur switched back savagely, taking the head off another one. They couldn't get away fast enough – there was no room. The thunder hammer became heavy with strips of gore, the flesh cooking into frazzled slivers on its sparking disruptor. Gunnlaugur waded through them like a reaper of old, slaying in crushing strokes, spinning and crushing and cracking. He towered above them, his heavy power armour making him twice the bulk and heft of even the largest of them. His hammer flew freely, travelling in unstoppable arcs, moving around him in a halo of annihilation like those of the mythic Iron Gods.

Váltyr was the first to gain a foothold on a chem-tanker. He sprang up from the clutching hands of the mutants, kicking out as he rose and breaking the jaw of a reeling cleaver-carrier. He seized on a railing that ran along the swollen flanks of the toxin tank and clutched it fast, his boots searching for purchase.

By then the enemy had begun to respond. They surged towards the invaders, swarming around the beleaguered chem-tankers. Their aim got better, and Gunnlaugur felt the hard jab of las-beams glancing from his breastplate.

He roared with laughter, shrugging them off like rain.

'That's better!' he thundered, crashing through the press of bodies around him, flattening any who came within the ambit of the thunder hammer. Another half-dozen hapless mutants were crushed, smashed or ripped apart, their bloated entrails sent spinning into the night. 'Try harder! Come on, try *harder*!'

They did. They screamed at him, hurled their corroded blades at his face, clutched at his ankles as he trod them into the blood-clotted dust, grabbed at his arms as the hammer-blows blurred past, loosed thick barrages of las-fire to try to bring him down.

The task was hopeless. Olgeir's withering torrent of heavy ordnance blew apart any nascent defensive positions. Hafloí's assault cut deep into their reeling ranks, preventing any rally further back. Váltyr's terrifying efficiency was just unanswerable.

But the one that really scared them was Baldr. Gunnlaugur, busy with his own slaughter, only caught snatches of what was going on, but it sounded like Baldr had gone completely berserk. He heard him shrieking like a banshee of legend, and the sound of it chilled his blood. He wondered what it was doing to the enemy.

'What in Hel's wrong with Fjolnir?' voxed Váltyr breathlessly, working his way along the tanker's toxin-cylinder, swatting down the defenders that crawled all over it and beginning to climb higher.

'He's certainly having fun,' replied Gunnlaugur, kicking through the stomach of an obese waddler and vaulting over the corpse. The chem-tanker's tractor unit loomed through the dust-flurried murk, its cab-lights glowing like a cluster of insectoid eyes. 'Concentrate: let's bring this down.'

He lashed out with the hammer, clearing a two-metre circle around him. Three mutants were sent spinning under the tracks of the tanker. They had plenty of time to scream as the treads slowly ground them to a pulp.

Gunnlaugur leaped, pulling clear of the crowds and landed on a coolant duct on the tanker's muzzle. It was riddled with oxidisation, and whole chunks of it came free in his grip as he climbed up to the cab.

Gunnlaugur whipped his hammer round and mag-locked it to his back, hauling himself up the front of the titanic vehicle.

Some of the enemy tried to follow him up, but most were picked off by Olgeir's ever-present curtain of supporting fire.

'My thanks, Heavy-hand,' voxed Gunnlaugur as he reached the cloudy armourglass of the cab windows. He was enjoying himself.

'Bring them pain,' replied the great one cheerfully.

Gunnlaugur reached up with his fist and smashed the closest pane. A bloom of thick, green smoke tumbled out, streaming down the front of the tractor unit like spilled sick.

He grabbed the frame and hauled himself up. Inside, the chem-tanker's crew were hard-wired into fleshy command thrones. Eight of them sat in a cramped space stuffed with throbbing, pulsing mountains of semi-tissue and pseudo-machinery. Tentacles ran from rheumy glands, interfacing with thickets of dirty metal cables. Fluids gurgled in translucent sacs, filtered through pinned-open bodies and sent churning down long tubes into the innards of the vast machine.

The crew turned to face him as he clawed his way inside, letting fly with screaming wails of impotent hatred.

'Right, then,' he snarled as he pushed himself through the shattered windscreens and thudded to the cab's floor. He drew the thunder hammer. 'Who's first?'

They screamed at him in unison. With a shrug he started to swing, crushing what remained of their mortal skulls and punching through their etiolated innards. They shrieked as they died, locked into position, forced to watch as Gunnlaugur worked his way down the line. As each one died the whole chem-tanker shuddered. The growl of its engines became a stuttering whine, and the clouds of smoke billowed ever higher. As he neared the end of the line Gunnlaugur felt the chem-tanker change direction, reeling on its axis and starting to crush its way aimlessly across the ravine floor.

'Time to leave, *vaerangi*,' came Váltyr's voice over the comm.

'Already?' said Gunnlaugur, breaking the neck of the last shrieking crew member and pushing his way to the far side of the cab. 'Hel, you work fast.'

He glanced back at the carnage left in his wake. Fluids, pink with blood and blotched with inky lubricants, swilled across the metal-mesh floor. Eight raw carcasses slumped amid a tangled mess of fizzing cabling and shattered ironwork. The last of the pale marsh-gas drifted loosely away, no longer fed by its belching feeder valves.

Gunnlaugur grunted with satisfaction, then smashed through the far end of the cab wall, pummelling a huge, ragged hole in the armour plates. He thrust himself through the gap, hanging clear of the cab-edge. The huge machine was still ploughing onwards, though its progress was now directionless. Dozens of milling defenders were dragged under the tracks as they tried to get out of the way. He could still hear Baldr's frenzied screams and Hafloí's battle-cries. The two of them had already destroyed their chem-tanker, which blazed in a mass of lurid chemical flames against the far wall of the ravine.

Gunnlaugur saw Váltyr leap from the tanker's lurching spine, hurling himself a long way clear and landing expertly amid a swarm of glow-eyed mutants. Gunnlaugur tensed, ready to do the same.

Then the krak grenades went off.

Váltyr had clamped them all along the toxin-tank, just as Gunnlaugur had ordered him. They exploded in sequence, rippling along the bulbous sides of containers, spraying the noxious contents in all directions.

The chem-tanker bucked, shuddered and ignited, hurling Gunnlaugur clear of the cab. He crunched heavily to the ground several metres away, his shoulder guard driving deep into solid rock, his helm cracking against blood-wet rubble.

He picked himself up in time to be doused in a spray of flesh-eating acid from the broken chem-tanks. It cascaded down his armour, instantly dissolving the blood and slime from the surface and eating through the pelts that hung from his shoulders.

The mortal troops around him were not so well protected. They screamed in chorus as their flesh was scoured from the bone, a riot of shrieking, gargling sobs that only ended when the acid ate down to the vocal cords.

When the torrent finally died out the scene around the smoking tanker was horrific – bodies in all directions, skinless, eyeless, with exposed bone and shrivelled flesh. A thick soup of dissolved organic matter, tinged grey with foamy scum, lapped over the rocks of the valley floor, bubbling and babbling as it drained deep into the dry earth.

The chem-tanker itself, driverless and burning, swayed on, finally crashing into the far side of the ravine and bursting into toxin-edged flames, just like its companion further down the gorge.

Gunnlaugur shook the last of the acid from his burly frame before striding out to find Váltyr. As he walked, his boots crunched sickeningly through half-eaten bone. The silence from Olgeir's heavy bolter told him that Heavy-hand was climbing down to join in the close combat. Four tankers remained before their night's work was done.

Gunnlaugur was glad of that. He was enjoying himself.

'Ahead of schedule, bla–' he started, just as something huge went off over by Baldr's position. It was an explosion of sorts, but it lit up the ravine edges with corpse-glimmer and sounded like a strangled scream. He tensed immediately, the hairs on his arms raising.

Then Hafloí's voice came over the comm. It didn't sound like it normally did – it was urgent, tight, serious.

'Support,' Hafloí gasped, his words clipped with pain. 'Blood of Russ, support *now*.'

Gunnlaugur took up *skulbrotsjór* again, his mood switching instantly. Even before Hafloí had finished he was already running.

Ingvar and Bajola stood facing one another in her chambers, just as they had done on their first meeting. The night was old by then, heavy with smoke and the fatigue of a city under siege. Lights could be seen from the vantage of Bajola's spire-windows, bleeding across the whole expanse of the lower city. They were not wholesome lights – they were pyre-glows, or searchlight beams, or the sudden flashes of las-volleys in the dark. Those lights were accompanied by similarly unwholesome sounds: crackling flesh, the thudding of running feet, screaming in the dark.

Unlike at their first meeting, Bajola did not remain standing for long. She slid into a hard wooden chair, scratching it with her armour as she slouched wearily. She let her unfixed helm fall from her hands, and it rolled across the stone floor.

'When did you last sleep?' asked Ingvar.

'I don't remember. You?'

'Four days ago.'

Bajola snorted. 'Explains your mood.'

Ingvar walked across to the far side of the room, near one of the narrow windows.

'This place was meant to be a respite.' He smiled to himself. 'Garrison work.'

'You want to sit?' she asked.

'I'm fine.'

Bajola gave him a sardonic look.

'Always on duty, never at rest,' she said. 'You *never* get tired? You never just want to stand back, for a minute, to look away from it all and forget that you're the Emperor's finest and that you're needed all the time and everywhere because, well, we're all so much weaker than you?'

Ingvar leaned against the stone wall behind him. In truth, he wasn't immune to fatigue. If things had been less straitened he would have welcomed the chance to recover himself, to reflect on how to handle Gunnlaugur when he returned, to prepare for the trials ahead. But those things were luxuries.

'What was that place?' he asked for a third time.

Bajola's face fell. 'The archive room. Not something you'd think much of – just a bunch of data-cores and repository banks, sealed and categorised.' Her brown eyes went hollow. 'The history of an obscure shrineworld, its succession documents and transaction records.'

She looked up at him.

'It was our story here,' she said. 'One of the things I was charged with defending. Now all gone, and before the enemy has even arrived at the gates.'

'Could it not have been moved to the Halicon?'

'It would have taken a whole convoy of heavy transports, and they had all been assigned other tasks.' She shook her head resignedly. 'I made my decision. De Chatelaine will ask the same questions when she hears of it. It will be one more failure in her eyes. She was never convinced of the wisdom of taking me on, this will reinforce that view.'

Ingvar found himself surprised by Bajola's deflation. When they had first met she had seemed so lively, so defiant. It was strange: in her fragile robes she had been strong; encased in power armour, she was diminished. Perhaps she might have been better off staying in the non-military cadres.

'They're only records,' he said. 'None of your troops were hurt.'

Bajola let slip an empty laugh.

'Only records,' she said. 'I don't suppose you keep any, on Fenris.'

'We do.' He tapped the side of his helm. 'The skjalds recite the sagas. We commit them to memory. We pass them on. Every one of us knows the myths of the past.'

'Myths.' Bajola's tone was scornful.

'All of us use myths, Sister. Some are stored on data-slates, some come from the mouths of skjalds. Your way has its strengths. Its weaknesses are obvious.'

Bajola smiled wryly. 'Nice.'

Ingvar clasped his hands before him. The blood on them had blackened from the heat of the archive chamber.

'You know why I came,' he said.

Bajola nodded. 'You think I'm keeping something from you.'

'You recognised his name.'

Bajola reached up and rubbed her scalp with her gauntlet. Her short, wiry hair was flecked with ash.

'I did.' Some of her old defiance glistened in her eyes.

'How?'

Bajola laughed.

'You think he kept it secret?' She shot him a sidelong glance; it was almost flirtatious. 'You are a boastful people, Space Wolf. You brag about your conquests from one end of the Imperium to the other. Do not be surprised if others hear you.'

'It had significance,' said Ingvar. 'You had heard it before.'

For a second longer, Bajola held his gaze. Her dark skin, the same ebony as her armour and sweaty from exertion, glistened in the low light of the chamber.

Then she lowered her eyes.

'I have seen many secret things,' she said softly. 'Never intended for my eyes, but one does not spend so much time with the powerful and not catch glimpses of their affairs.'

Ingvar listened intently.

'It is said that Fenris makes enemies easily,' said Bajola. 'You do not know the tenth of it. There are inquisitors who would gladly see your world virus-bombed into poisonous slush if they could only find a way to do it. Other Chapter Masters, too. And, yes, the Ecclesiarchy harbours some with no love for your brethren. That is no secret: our forces have clashed before, they may do so again.'

Bajola's voice was low but firm. She spoke like an agent delivering a report to her superiors, much like she must have done many times while in the Orders Famulous. Ingvar remembered how he'd been required to speak when in Halliafiore's presence, and how long it had taken for him to knock the rough cadence of Juvykka from his speech. The results had been much the same.

'There was a document,' Bajola went on. 'I only saw it once, but I was in the business of memorizing things then. It had names on it, most of which are irrelevant. Hjortur Bloodfang was among them. I remember thinking the name was absurd, but that was before I had had dealings with others of your kind.'

'What was it for?'

'A briefing note, prepared for the senior cardinal of my jurisdiction, one of dozens that would pass his desk every night. Such things had many purposes. It might have been in relation to diplomatic embassies – unlikely, in this case – or problems with military liaison, or some clandestine matter that I would not have been aware of.'

Her voice was steady, calm, assured.

'That's all?' Bajola nodded.

'My guess: it related to communication between Fenris and the Ecclesiarchy that was kept quiet. Such things exist, you know. Perhaps Hjortur was the conduit.'

Ingvar remembered how Hjortur had been – his frothing bravado, his thundering anger – and almost laughed out loud. Subtlety had not been his strong suit.

'I find that unlikely.'

Bajola looked equivocal. 'Well, you knew him,' she said. 'But at some point his name came to the attention of a cardinal of the Ecclesiarchy, one who wielded considerable power. I have seen stranger things in the galaxy, but not many. If you do not know why that is then I cannot help you.'

Ingvar drew in a long breath, tasting the last of the soot that still clung to his vox-grille. He turned Bajola's words over in his mind. Silence fell across the chamber, broken only by the sporadic noises of trouble still rumbling across the city outside.

'There is no lie in your voice,' he said eventually. 'But you are not telling me all you know.'

Bajola half smiled – a strange, almost melancholy gesture – and leaned back in her chair.

'You're wrong,' she said. 'But even if you weren't, I won't take lectures from you about that.'

Ingvar raised an eyebrow under his helm. 'Which means?'

'You understand me,' said Bajola. 'The Imperium we both serve and love is built on secrets. We use them to clothe ourselves, to wall ourselves in, and I swore vows never to disclose the secrets I was given to guard. I swore never to reveal the identity of those who conferred such privilege on me, nor those whom I was charged with protecting. Those vows were not lightly made. The secrecy that binds me is as sacred to me as your sword is to you.'

She looked at him, and her eyes sparkled knowingly.

'You are no stranger to secrets, Ingvar,' she said. 'You did not tell me what took you from Fenris for so many years, though I can guess, and if I am right you could not tell me even if you wished to. No force on this planet could compel you to speak, no matter how much I might desire to share the terrible sights you keep locked in your never-forgetting mind.'

She leaned forwards in her chair. Her face lost its spectre of dry amusement and became earnest again.

'For all that, I do not doubt that you are a servant of the Emperor and a loyal ally. You could extend the same courtesy to me.'

Ingvar didn't respond immediately. He watched the way her body moved – the confidence of it, the heaviness of her limbs, the comfort of knowing she was in her own demesne and surrounded by her own kind.

Her chin jutted proudly. She held his gaze, looking up into his death-snarl mask fearlessly.

A rune-signal flickered into life on his retinal display. Jorundur wanted to see him about something. Ingvar dismissed it. The Old Dog would have to hunt alone for a little longer.

He reached up, released the air-seals and twisted his helm free. He mag-locked it to his belt and ran his fingers through sweat-stiff hair. The long tresses flopped over his armour's gorget.

He pushed himself away from the wall and advanced on Bajola. The disparity in their sizes was almost comical: his bulk, augmented by thicker plate and heavy pelts, dwarfed her slender frame.

He stood over her and lowered his head towards hers.

'I have no doubt of your loyalty,' he said. His voice was a low murmur, one that resonated in his chest and echoed from the stone around him. 'If I had, you would be dead where you sit.'

His eyes bored into hers. For the first time, he saw a flicker of fear in her sleek features.

'I will fight alongside you, Sister,' he said. 'I will serve the cause of this world as if it were the cause of my own, and before the end of this thing you will learn truly why I bear the name I do and what it means.'

His grey eyes went flat.

'But know this: my brothers are more than blood-kin to me. If I discover your silence has led to harm befalling them, I will come after you. Wherever you are, I will hunt you, and what the *Fenryka* hunt they find.'

He grimaced, his leathery flesh creasing away from his fangs.

'You would not like me as much then.'

To her credit, Bajola retained eye-contact. She blinked once, then again, but never looked away. When she replied, her voice wavered but did not fail.

'Then I thank the Throne I have nothing to hide,' she said.

Chapter Sixteen

Hafloí fought with two weapons, just as he did whenever he could, his axe in his right hand and his bolt pistol in his left. Older warriors, those who had honed their craft over centuries, would eventually settle on a preference for blade or ranged work, but he intended never to specialise. He enjoyed the interplay between axe-strike and pistol-kick, doling out death in equal quantities as he rampaged through the enemy. He relished the thick cut-and-drag of the metal on diseased flesh; he took delight in the action of the bolt pistol as it tore up body-armour and ripped through vehicle plate.

He'd opened his throat since Gunnlaugur's order, giving in to the urge that he had always had to shout and holler and whoop with the raw joy of killing. That had been how it was in his old pack, all of them flame-haired neophytes led by the brutal *vaerangi* Oje Redclaw. They'd taken joy in their work, laughing like savage children in the heart of battle, pushing every limit that was set for them, racing out to be the fastest, the most deadly, the strongest, the best.

Járnhamar was different. He'd known it would be, but still the shock of it had been hard to get used to. From the long, hard training sessions back on Asaheim he'd learned just what it took to be a Grey Hunter. Olgeir was as strong as a mountain, Váltyr as quick as a snake, Jorundur as wily as an ice-drake. One on one they were all more than a match for him. Their sinews had hardened, their muscles had tempered, their combat-skills had been honed and honed again.

And yet, for all that, they were missing something. Their joy had gone. They had all been fighting too long; the Long War had made their spirits shrivel even as it had toughened their bodies.

Hafloí kicked out, plunging his boot into the reeling forehead of another plague-bearer. He loosed a single shot to halt the charge of another, jerked his axe-blade round harshly to decapitate a third. Flecks of blood circled him like debris swirling around a star, thrown up by the vicious hack, thrust and fire of his relentless movement.

One chem-tanker already smouldered, its fuel tanks ruptured and its toxin-cylinder leaking. He could hear that the other one – the one taken on by Gunnlaugur and Váltyr – was reeling. The hordes of plague-raddled mortals had shaken off their shock and now lumbered into combat, but they had little with which to combat the unleashed wrath of the Wolves.

'*Hjá*, brother!' Hafloí roared to Baldr, leaping clear of a las-volley before blasting the firer's head open with a return shot. 'The next one waits!'

Baldr was worrying him. On Fenris, Baldr had always been serenely, irritatingly in control. Olgeir had called him the quiet one, the calm presence at the centre of the pack.

Now Baldr was shrieking, ripping into the enemy with a stark energy that surpassed even his own. Hafloí had never seen another *Fenryka* fight like it. Baldr's movements were fast, too fast, careless and slapdash. If the enemy had been more competent he might have been in trouble; as it was, his sheer brutality was enough to daunt the trapped and panicked host of misshapen and plague-twisted. They were terrified of him, falling over themselves to flee his haphazard sword-strokes.

'Forget this filth!' Hafloí called out again. 'The tanker!'

No answer came over the comm. Baldr's breathing was thick and wet, more like the wheezing of a dog than a man.

Hafloí spun round, swinging his axe to clear space amid the milling host of mutants, looking up briefly to gauge the shape of the battle.

Further down the ravine the remaining four tankers had slowed, grinding to a near-halt as the gorge-slopes descended into chaos around them. Their towering drive-units reared up above the swirling melee, underlit by eerie green glows, their engines churning as they struggled to change course.

Hafloí glanced over at Baldr one last time. He remained busy slaughtering those around him, lost in a mist of blood and fury.

'*Skítja.*'

Giving up on him, Hafloí kicked into movement, sprinting after the next chem-tanker, firing at any plague-bearers who barred the way ahead and cutting down any who got too close. He wasn't sure what he'd do when he arrived. He might vault up into the cab and take the tractor-section down, or maybe go for the engines with kraks. In any event it would be a worthy kill to add to his name, something that might gain him a little more respect from the warriors around him.

He'd like that. For all their lack of mirth and vigour, for all their dreary fatalism, he'd still like their respect.

He was barely ten metres away from the chem-tanker when he saw the Traitor stride out from the shadows. If he'd been more experienced he might have sensed him earlier, though the fug of human filth clogging the ravine floor made it hard to pick out individual aromas. He might, though, have noticed the ever-heightening terror in the mortals he cut down so easily and seen that they weren't just scared of him. As it was, consumed by the combat around him and fixed on the target ahead, he only saw the Traitor once he had lumbered into range.

Once, he must have been like Hafloí: a loyal Space Marine of the Impe-rium decked in blessed power armour. Now he had been altered, had grown, bloating and twisting as the slow arts of the warp had worked their baleful influence. His ceramite plate was thick with poxy encrusta-tion, like polyps of dirty coral layered over rotting stonework. He trod ponderously on huge, cloven hooves, and necrotic flesh burst through wound-like gouges in his breastplate and cuirass. A sweaty stink of fear hung over him, and hosts of flies followed his every movement, billow-ing around him like a shroud.

Inexperienced as he was, Hafloí knew well enough what he faced.

Plague Marine.

His helm had once been an old Mark I issue but it had been ravaged almost beyond recognition. A dull green light spilled from hollow lenses, leaking across the decaying snarl of the vox-grille. A fused mass of tortured ironwork rose up over his shoulders, studded with loosely nailed skulls and pulsing with the ghost-flicker of unnatural energies. He carried a heavy glaive two-handed, and phosphor-dim witchlight glim-mered over the pocked blade.

As soon as he saw the Traitor, Hafloí felt his battle-joy transmute to blind rage. Deluded mortals were one thing; fallen brothers were another.

'Allfather!' he roared, charging towards the Traitor, loosing a hammer-ing barrage of bolts from his pistol and twisting the axe-head to swing.

The Plague Marine did not move fast. He could not match Hafloí's pace and energy, and his reactions were sluggish.

But he did not need to move fast. As the Blood Claw closed in on him, cracking a dozen rounds against its fist-thick battle-plate, the Traitor raised his glaive and levelled the point at him.

'*Maleficaris nergal,*' he whispered in a glottal, sibilant wheeze.

Haflói never saw the bolt hit him. He had the briefest impression of savage fire bursting across him, tinged with lime-green flickers and stinking of ethanol. The next thing he knew he was on his back, hurled five metres away, his armour half embedded into the earth below. His bolt pistol had been knocked clear and he only barely clasped on to his axe.

He tried to rise and instantly felt agony flood through his limbs. Witchlight rippled across his armour, playing across it like mercury sliding on steel. He felt his flesh tighten, his energy draining away. He tried to cry out, but his mouth had dried to a husk. Through a filmy haze of pain and disorientation he saw the Plague Marine loom over him, pointing the tip of the glaive at his neck. A hot-metal stink of fell magicks competed with the rank odours of decay.

The Plague Marine gazed down at him. His gestures were laborious, made as if wading through tar, but the power he exerted was crushing. Haflói weakened further, his lungs burning as he tried to breathe. He felt his axe fall loosely from his grasp.

'Just a child,' whispered the Traitor, musingly.

His voice was extraordinary – gurgling thickly through bubbling layers of saliva and mucus, broken into overlapping tones and breathy echoes as if a thousand other voices jostled for prominence within his blank helm. No particular malice permeated it, just a kind of long, tired sadness. The air itself seemed to sag in his presence.

Haflói couldn't move. He stared up at the Plague Marine, watching the glaive hover above his neck. He could feel his skin creasing under his armour, crinkling with unnatural weariness. He fought against it, tasting sorcery at the back of his throat like a bitter gall, swallowing it down and coughing, but the vice did not loosen.

Haflói knew then the measure of his foe: a witch, steeped in the twisting, changing ways of the warp's touch, a warrior as far beyond him as he was to the milling crowds of diseased cattle that marched alongside the chem-tankers.

'Just a *child*,' repeated the sorcerer, shaking his head sadly before pulling the glaive back to swing.

The rain of bolter-shells came from hard over to the right, peppering the witch's armour-plate and rocking him back on cloven heels. He staggered, lost in a bursting torrent of splintering ceramite. The glaive was knocked out of position.

'*Fenrys!*' came a bellowing, half-demented voice.

With the sorcerer's hold broken, Haflói managed to lift his head a little.

Baldr was charging across the ravine floor, his sword drawn, his bolter blazing. Tattered scraps of pelt flew around him as his limbs pumped.

The sorcerer responded, moving as slowly as before. His rotten armour seemed to absorb the power of the bolts, rippling like sludge as the shells detonated. The impacts clearly hurt him, but still he was able to lumber around to face Baldr's attack.

Haflói could barely move. He felt as if centuries of ageing had taken place in seconds, making his limbs frail and his bones weak. He tried to retrieve his axe, and the effort made him gasp.

Baldr closed in on the witch, and the two of them fell into combat. The Plague Marine's movements were still slow, but somehow he managed to parry Baldr's flurry of expert strokes. It was as if time itself sloughed to a halt around him, dragging everything down into a pit of torpor.

'You are no child,' observed the sorcerer softly, gurgling away as Baldr's sword clanged against the rusty glaive.

Baldr ignored him, cracking him back several paces. His strikes were wild and florid. He'd discarded his bolter and now threw his sword around two-handed.

The sorcerer levelled the glaive and the Hunter smashed it clear in an explosion of sparks. Baldr's movements were still erratic, but some dark, urgent fury seemed to animate him.

'You should not be here,' said the sorcerer, pushed back again and parrying sluggishly. 'Why are you here, Son of Russ?'

Baldr pressed home the attack, cutting and lashing. Haflói could hear his grunts of effort, the heavy breathing. He was fighting furiously just to stay alive.

Haflói reached again for his axe, dragging himself across the rocky ground towards it. As he crawled nearer, he saw the first pair of glowing eyes emerge from the gloom. A plague-mutant stood before him wearing a heavy gas mask over its sore-thick face and holding a spiked morning star on a looped chain. More of them shuffled into view, edging forwards nervously, clutching flails, cleavers and meathooks in liver-spotted claws.

Haflói managed to snarl, to clench his fists and clamber to his knees. That forced them back, squealing with fright, but they didn't break. Haflói knew that if they rushed him now he'd be in trouble. He tried to snarl again, but the noise died in his throat as his energy drained away.

Then, from behind him, the ravine suddenly exploded into light, a riot of lightning-white illumination that raced up the rock-face on

either side and threw everything into eye-watering definition. Hafloí
was briefly dazzled by it before his helm-lenses darkened; the mutants
fell back, clawing at their faces and shrieking madly.

Hafloí twisted round to see the sorcerer bathed in a sick corona of vivid
energy, cracking and curling around him like a billowing cloak. Baldr
was suspended in mid-air above him, wreathed in the same whipping
coils of power, his whole body clenched in spasms of pain. His head had
jerked back, locked in a silent scream, and his arms were thrown wide.
The sorcerer held his glaive up, using it to feed more power into the
ether-summoned aegis.

'Do they even know what you are?' asked the witch, sounding genuinely curious. 'Why have you never told them?'

Hafloí watched as Baldr writhed in pain. He tried to rise, to run again,
to do *something* to break the deadening fatigue clamped on his limbs.

He failed, his strength giving out, and fell back to his knees.

'Support,' he gasped into the vox, forcing the words through clenched
teeth. It was all he could do to spit them out, let alone rise again. 'Blood
of Russ, support *now*.'

Gunnlaugur sped past the broken shell of the tanker, his boots churning the earth as he sprinted. He needed no locator mark to spy Baldr's
position – he could see the witch-lightning crackling around a silhouetted core of brilliance. The stink of sorcery hummed in the air, rank and
putrid.

'*Hjolda!*' he thundered, charging directly towards the source.

Váltyr and Olgeir tore along beside him, their blades flashing brightly
in the unnatural light.

The sorcerer saw them coming. Gunnlaugur thought he heard him
speaking – a whispered voice saying something to Baldr – but then the
corroded helm swivelled to stare directly at him. The swathe of ether-
energy surrounding Baldr gave out and the Hunter crashed to the ground,
his head lolling like a corpse's.

The sorcerer angled the glaive at Gunnlaugur, and the Wolf Guard felt
the sudden build-up of dark power.

It was too late. Gunnlaugur pounced, his hammer held high and
spitting with raw plasma. His enormous body, still streaming flecks of
burning acid from the tanker's immolation, coursed through the air,
massively, unstoppably.

Gunnlaugur slammed *skulbrotsjór* down. The warhammer connected
with the sorcerer's helm, shattering the diseased ceramite and driving
on in.

The witch reeled, bludgeoned to the ground. He tried to swing his glaive up but Váltyr darted in close, lashing *holdbítr* around and severing the sorcerer's arm at the elbow.

Olgeir piled in next, throwing wild, heavy blows with both gauntlets, pummelling in a blind rage. He was screaming death-curses; in such a fury he was all but unstoppable.

Gunnlaugur swung again, hurling *skulbrotsjór* across hard, working it like a pile-driver, pistoning the energy-wreathed hammerhead into the Traitor's throat and sending him sprawling on his back.

The Plague Marine was incredibly tough. Even in the face of that onslaught he somehow hung on. He reached for his glaive with his remaining hand, scrabbling after it as the blows came in.

Váltyr worked as smoothly as ever, switching hands and dancing in close. He chopped down on the sorcerer's free arm, cutting the sinews cleanly and ending his desperate reaching for the glaive. Olgeir seized the witch's broken legs and hauled him across the ground towards Gunnlaugur, pinning him face-up.

That left Gunnlaugur to land the killing blow. The Wolf Guard swept the hammer up a final time, gazing with disgust into the bloody mass of what had been the Plague Marine's head. He could see a puckering mass of warty flesh looking back up at him, as pale as milk and rimmed with red. He saw one filmy eye blinking and the remnants of a crushed jawline hanging loose. Blood bubbled up from under torn flaps of crusty skin, dribbling down into a shattered gorget.

The Traitor tried to speak.

'You don't know–'

Gunnlaugur brought the hammer down, and *skulbrotsjór* cleaved the sorcerer's skull with a thunderous clap of discharged energy. A sheet of pale flame shot up, raging across all three warriors before gusting out with a boom and rush like storm-wind.

The sorcerer's body shuddered, spasmed, and slumped into stillness. The three Wolves broke away from it, panting hard, weapons raised, watching for any deception.

None came. The Traitor's body lay broken, its eerie light gone, its throaty breathing stilled.

Gunnlaugur turned away, moving quickly to where Baldr lay. He stooped down, cradling the Hunter's head in his hands.

'Brother,' he whispered. 'Fjolnir. Speak to me.'

Váltyr crouched down beside them. He withdrew a handheld auspex from his belt and ran it over Baldr's limp form.

'Alive,' he said. 'But unconscious. The Red Dream has him.'

Olgeir limped to join them. He was still breathing heavily and one gauntlet was cracked and sparking.

'What's that on his armour?' he asked.

Baldr's breastplate and helm were coated in a film of luminous slime. It glowed in the night, an after-echo of the storm unleashed by the sorcerer. Olgeir leaned down to wipe it clear.

'No,' said Gunnlaugur, grasping Olgeir's wrist. He could hear Baldr's shallow heartbeat, just on the margins of detection. Morkai circled closely. 'Not yet.'

He looked up, searching for the whelp, and saw Haflói crawling towards them. The Blood Claw's plate was scorched white, his pelts and totems ripped away.

Váltyr went over to him, hooking a hand under his armpit and dragging him to his feet.

'What happened here?' he asked.

Haflói tried to answer but the words were just a mess of croaking. His head lolled loosely on his shoulders, his boots scraped for purchase in the dust.

Olgeir started to move, fingers flexing, bristling for more violence.

'Four left,' he muttered darkly, watching the remaining tankers slowly reversing down the length of the ravine, putting as much distance as they could between them and the Wolves. Their mutant entourage retreated with them, going warily with their weapons raised, staring nervously at the carnage they'd stumbled into. 'Give me leave, *vaerangi*. Give me leave to take them.'

Gunnlaugur followed his gaze. His first instincts were the same. A cold anger seized him, spurring him to take up the hammer again. They had killed the sorcerer. All that remained were the witch's vermin, ripe for slaughter.

He glanced at Váltyr. The blademaster slowly shook his head.

Gunnlaugur drew in a deep, reluctant breath. Váltyr was right. Baldr was teetering on the edge of death; the whelp was out of action. The hunt was over.

'No, Heavy-hand,' he said, his voice catching with frustration. 'No, not now.'

He laid Baldr's head on the ground and got to his feet.

Around them, the valley floor was a scene of pure devastation. Scores of bodies lay draped over the rocks, broken and bleeding by the Wolves' assault. Two toxin-carriers had been destroyed. What remained of the enemy detachments were hurrying back the way they came.

Gunnlaugur's gaze settled on the Plague Marine's corpse. The body smelt even fouler in death than it had in life. Maggots dropped, still wriggling, from the gaping chasm of a shattered chest. The witchlight had died, sinking into nothing with the death of its master.

'We'll burn the gene-seed,' said Gunnlaugur bleakly, reaching for his thunder hammer. 'Then we return. Olgeir – you and I will bear Baldr. Váltyr will take the whelp.'

Olgeir started to protest. Gunnlaugur ignored him. He withdrew a long dagger from a sheath at his thigh and stalked over to the sorcerer's corpse. As he walked, he heard the crackle of flames and smelled the chemical tang of boiling toxins.

It was destruction, but not what he'd hoped for. The pack's resources were limited; he had damaged them further.

Pride. All for pride. The Gyrfalkon should have been with them.

Haflói staggered up to him. The Blood Claw could barely stand, let alone walk.

'My thanks, *vaerangi*,' he rasped, blurting the words out from behind a heat-whitened vox-grille.

Gunnlaugur nodded curtly. He should have said something in reply, but the shame, the sick guilt of it, prevented him.

They would have to leave soon. They would have to trawl back across the desert, going as fast as they could, fleeing before the wrath of the pursuing host. That wasn't victory; that was disgrace.

All for pride.

He bent over the sorcerer's stinking cadaver, gripped the knife in his fist, and started to cut.

The night's hunt had come to a close and the dawn was close. Ingvar walked up onto the walkway atop the city's inner wall and leaned against the rockcrete parapet. He looked west, out across the encircling plains. The night sky was dark still, a cool, near-black purple studded with stars. Behind him the upper city rose up in tiers of glimmering light, pockmarked by smoke from the pyres. At the summit, proud and ugly, hunched the Halicon fortress, floodlit gaudily as the siege labourers crawled over it.

His body ached. Soon he would be entering his fifth day without sleep. He'd noticed his reactions slowing, just a little, probably imperceptibly to mortal senses but clear enough to him.

That wasn't good enough. He'd have to work harder.

He rested his weight against the rough-cut stone and smelled the cool air. The scent of the city surrounded him – dust, sweat, spices, embers. He smelled the leaves of the trees as they swayed in their courtyards, and the oily burn of crawlers hauling material down to the bulwarks, and, faintest of all, the slowly growing tang of corruption, wafting across the plains and over the walls.

They were closing in, coming at the city from all directions, their ranks swollen with the newly-dead and plague-infested. By the time they arrived the air would be thick with their filth, buzzing with clouds of blowflies and making the citizens cough and retch.

He sniffed again, trying to guess distances.

Close, now. This would be the last night that the air was clear.

A locator rune blinked softly on the edge of his retinal feed indicating the presence of Jorundur climbing up to meet him. Ingvar smiled to himself. The Old Dog had been busy during the night, stalking through the shadows after the infected with a brutal zeal. Some life in him yet, it seemed.

Ingvar strolled along the parapet towards the nearest defence tower, wondering whose tally was the higher. He guessed his was, though you could never tell with Jorundur, who had a habit of surprising.

Jorundur emerged from the tower's doorway and sloped onto the walkway. He went helm-less, just as Ingvar did, and his lean face carried a rare grin of enjoyment.

'Thirteen,' he announced.

Ingvar bowed his head. 'Eleven,' he replied.

Jorundur laughed. 'Had trouble finding them?' he asked.

'The Sisters have been busy,' admitted Ingvar. 'I think this thing has finally been contained.'

Jorundur grunted dismissively. 'Until the rest of them get here,' he said, leaning heavily on the parapet edge, just as Ingvar had done. He stared out at the pre-dawn dark, wrinkling his hooked nose and frowning. 'Any signal from the pack?'

Ingvar shook his head, resting his elbows beside Jorundur's. Being reminded of the rest of Járnhamar out hunting, pursuing the genuine threat rather than mopping up the last dregs of sabotage, was still an irritant. He hid it poorly.

'Still sore, then,' noticed Jorundur. 'Ice and iron, I don't envy Skull-hewer.' He laughed again, his more usual cynical snort. 'All your egos, jostling together like pups in a litter. Who'd try to command you? Not me, even if they begged.'

Ingvar smiled. 'I think your time may have passed,' he said.

'I think you might be right,' said Jorundur. 'Allfather be praised.'

He spat on to the parapet and sniffed noisily.

'So how's your friend?' he asked. 'I made a friend of my own this night, you know. I reckon I could learn to stop despising the Sisters, given a little more time.'

'Palatine Bajola is fine,' said Ingvar. 'The cathedral was hit. She took it personally. Her troops burned a lot of things to make up for it.'

'Careless,' said Jorundur. 'Is she sloppy? Will she be a liability?'

Ingvar pursed his lips. 'I don't know,' he said. 'The Battle Sisters are tough. They'll fight like wildcats to keep the enemy away from the Halicon. But her? I'd like to think so.' He paused, thinking back to their exchanges. 'I don't know, though. She's a strange one.'

Jorundur snorted, as if to say *you can talk*.

'How bad was it hit?' he asked.

'They got into the crypt. Took out the archives, wiped everything out. That was it.'

Jorundur gave him a sidelong look. 'The archives?' he asked.

'Yes. What of it?'

Jorundur thought for a moment, his hollow cheeks bulging as he ground his fangs together. 'Nothing.'

Ingvar turned to face him. 'Speak to me.'

Jorundur shrugged. 'Perhaps they just got lost.' His old, shrewd, yellow eyes glittered in the dark. 'But you never asked yourself why, given the choice, they went for a bunch of scrolls in a basement?'

As Jorundur spoke, Ingvar felt a sudden pang of unease. He didn't reply.

'I mean, that place is covered in guns,' Jorundur went on. 'Really big guns, ones we'll need. The bomb-drones, they've all been directed towards the sites that would hurt us – ammo dumps, power plants, comms towers. Think about it. You get a gang of them inside that cathedral, what are you going to tell them to do: head up to the batteries and bring them down, or torch the archives?'

He shook his shaggy head.

'Maybe that's what they wanted,' he said. 'I just find it surprising.'

Ingvar felt a sick sensation in the pit of his stomach. He gripped the edge of the parapet, and the fingers of his gauntlet sent hairline cracks running across its surface.

'They were trapped,' he said. 'It was their only target.'

Jorundur looked unconvinced. 'If you say so.'

Ingvar pushed back, away from the edge.

'I should go back,' he said.

I swore vows never to disclose the secrets I was given to guard.

Jorundur reached out, grabbing him by the wrist and holding him back.

'And do what, Gyrfalkon?' he asked.

Ingvar whirled to face him, but couldn't find the words to reply. He had nothing concrete, no suspicions, no theories, just the renewed sense of missing something important.

It was my wyrd to be here. Just as it was yours.

'I don't know. Yet.'

He started to push clear of Jorundur's grasp when his comm-feed crackled into life. De Chatelaine's voice emerged over the non-secure channel.

'Warriors of Járnhamar,' she said, sounding both concerned and angry. 'Your presence is requested at the Halicon. Urgency, please, would be appreciated.'

Ingvar paused. 'What is it?' he asked.

'Communication from Gunnlaugur. He's coming in now, carrying casualties. The apothecarion is prepared. We will do what we can.'

Ingvar shook his head furiously. '*Skítja*,' he swore.

Jorundur was already moving, his cynical face hardening as he made his way to the tower portal. Ingvar hesitated for a moment, torn between conflicting priorities.

Gunnlaugur, you fool.

'Can you give me more information?' he asked, lingering on the parapet. 'What has happened?'

He heard de Chatelaine exhale impatiently.

'Forgive me, but your brothers can inform you better than I,' she said, her voice sounding almost peevish. 'I have many things to detain me. You are on the walls? Look up, Space Wolf, and I'm sure you will understand.'

The link cut out abruptly. Startled by her tone, Ingvar turned and peered out across the night-shrouded plains. Jorundur, halting before the portal, did the same.

Right on the edge of vision, across to the far horizon where the wide, flat landscape broke into ravine country, the perfect dark had been broken. A long, thin line of green polluted it, glowing softly in the night. It hadn't been there a moment ago. Even as Ingvar watched, it grew in intensity, as if hundreds of tiny candles had been lit in the shadows.

It was still far off, but clearly visible. The faint strand seemed to stretch from north to south without a break.

'So many,' breathed Ingvar, everything else forgotten for the moment.

Jorundur drew alongside him.

'Aye,' said the Old Dog, his expression grim. 'So they're here at last. Now it gets interesting.'

III
THE BLIGHTED

Chapter Seventeen

Gunnlaugur lowered Baldr's torso onto the metal-slab operating table. Olgeir swung the Hunter's legs over the far end, arranging them on the stainless steel surface with painstaking care.

A man in a white tabard hurried up to the table, his hands stuffed with a thick bundle of cutting equipment.

'Leave him!' snarled Gunnlaugur, twisting round and shoving the man away. The mortal fell heavily, upending a metal container full of empty syringe cases. 'This does not concern you, human.'

His mood was black still, fuelled by shame. The long trek across the plains had been hellish – a limping, straggling race in the dark, every jarring step risking more damage to Baldr's battered body. As the night had waned the lights had started to follow them: a few at first, then hundreds more, always a long way behind, but growing like a canker across the horizon.

He'd longed to turn then, to bare his fangs and charge straight back into the pursuing horde, losing himself in the pure exertion that would help him forget.

Instead he'd set his jaw and staggered onwards, his arms hooked under Baldr's shoulders, the dead weight of his battle-brother dragging him down.

None of them had spoken during the journey back. Olgeir's harsh breathing had become more and more strained as he'd struggled to haul Baldr's bulk on top of *sigrún*'s. Váltyr had had his own hands full keeping Hafloí on his feet. Between them they had cut a sorry sight, limping back to the safety of the city with the pursuing stench of the enemy curling at their heels.

Now, back in the Halicon, they were surrounded by fussing, useless mortals, stumbling over one another to offer their fussing, useless assistance.

The apothecarion was cramped and cluttered with equipment. It had six operating bays, each one designed for human dimensions, all reinforced for power-armoured occupants thanks to the Sisters' presence. Baldr lay on one, Hafloí on another. Pristine white tiles reflected the glare of overhead lumen-bars, pitilessly picking out the damage on their battle-plate. Hafloí's armour was the colour of bleached bone. Baldr's was mottled and streaked with dark green growths, as if lichen had sprouted from the joints.

'Get out,' ordered Olgeir, gesturing to the remaining mortal staff. All four of them, including the functionary Gunnlaugur had knocked to the floor, scurried to comply. The apothecarion was then occupied solely by Wolves – Gunnlaugur, Váltyr, Olgeir and the two invalids.

Váltyr twisted his helm off, hurried over to Baldr and began to work. He was no Priest, but of all of them he had the deftest hands and greatest knowledge of the Apothecary's art.

'He lives still,' he said, gently prizing the vacuum seals from Baldr's helm and unlocking the catches. 'I can feel his primary heart beating.'

Gunnlaugur started to prowl back and forth, unable to stay still. He felt like a caged bear, bursting with energy but unable to do anything. He removed his helm and shut off the comm-line to de Chatelaine. He yearned for answers, but knew asking for them would be futile: Váltyr needed to work at his own pace, undisturbed and unhindered.

Olgeir remained unmoving, his huge arms crossed, brooding. For once he had no words of encouragement to offer.

Hafloí, left alone on the next slab along, pushed himself up onto his elbows and peered over at Váltyr's work. The whelp was still weak but had already regained some measure of control. He could speak again, and his strength was gradually returning.

Gunnlaugur no longer worried for him; Baldr was the concern.

'This… *stuff* is resistant,' said Váltyr, grimacing as he tried to clear the residue of slime from Baldr's facemask. 'It has some life of its own. It's got under the seals somehow, I think he's absorbed a lot of it.'

He withdrew a steel cylinder from his armour, unclasped it and took out a long scalpel. Working quickly, he cleared the algae-like filth from the gorget-join of Baldr's armour, where the torso met the helm. The lumpy substance clung to the armour, stringing out viscously against the blade edge.

'He was not himself,' croaked Haflói, still sounding disorientated. 'He was screaming, Gunnlaugur. Did you not hear it?'

Gunnlaugur said nothing. He remembered how Baldr had been during their last conversation. He remembered how he had been on the warp-transit.

Should I have probed more, asked more questions?

If so, it was too late now. The knot of guilt in his stomach tightened.

So many errors, one after the other.

'I'm removing the helm now,' said Váltyr. 'We can't leave it on him, the airways are all but clogged fast.'

Gunnlaugur stopped pacing. He came over to the slab and rested his knuckles on the metal. Olgeir stayed where he was, silent, watching intently.

Váltyr pulled gently, releasing the helm's locking mechanism. It came free with a dry hiss of escaping air.

Gunnlaugur felt his hearts sink. Baldr's face was the colour of his armour – pearl-grey, sinking to black under his open eyes. His mouth was open, revealing a dark tongue lolling loosely amid gaping fangs. His breath was sulphurous, making Váltyr gag as he withdrew the diseased helm. Sores had broken out around Baldr's white lips, tight with pus and ringed with angry red inflammation. His cheeks had sunken, and his clammy skin had a greenish tinge to it.

'That is not the Red Dream,' said Olgeir slowly.

Váltyr said nothing. He looked even paler than usual.

Gunnlaugur sniffed, flaring his nostrils and drawing in the noxious stench. Corruption was generally easy to detect – it was over-sweet, layered with the subtle flavour of the warp.

He couldn't be sure. Baldr looked much like any of the plague-bearers he'd killed in the city. That thought alone made his stomach tighten.

'Speak to me, Váltyr,' he said.

The blademaster ran his hands through his hair, smoothing down the sweat-matted mass of grey. His movements were stiff; like all of them, he was tired.

'I don't know,' he said eventually. He looked up at Gunnlaugur. 'If he were mortal, then... But he's one of us. I don't know.'

Olgeir growled in frustration and uncrossed his arms, balling his great fists impotently.

'*Skítja*,' he snarled. 'I've seen filth like that on men I've killed, and–'

Hafloí tried to get to his feet, and failed.

'He was *screaming*, Gunnlaugur. Something was wrong. He was–'

'You don't know–' started Olgeir.

'Enough.'

Gunnlaugur's stare swept around the apothecarion, cutting them short. Silence fell, broken only by the soft workings of the chamber's equipment.

Gunnlaugur's chin fell to his chest. It was hard to clear his head, to think what to do – emotions boiled away within him, still too raw to dismiss.

'No one enters this room but us,' he said at last, his voice deliberate. 'One of us remains here at all times, watching over him. We say nothing of this to the canoness. As far as she is concerned, we are tending to a fallen brother's wounds.'

He looked up, fixing each of them in the eye.

'For now, we do nothing. We watch, we wait, we hope. But if he is taken by plague, if his spirit turns…'

He hesitated, then drew in a deep breath.

'If he turns, I will do it. I began this, I will end it. That is my judgement.'

He continued to stare at the others, as if daring them to disagree. Hafloí was too weak to object; he seemed to go limp again, resting his head on the slab. Váltyr looked gaunt, but nodded.

Olgeir held out the longest. His scarred, ugly face remained twisted by unhappiness. He looked down at Baldr's diseased features, then up at Gunnlaugur, then back to Baldr again.

Then even his mighty shoulders sagged. He nodded resignedly.

Then the door to the chamber slammed open. They snapped round as one. Váltyr drew *holdbítr*; Gunnlaugur seized the hilt of his hammer.

Ingvar halted where he was, framed in the doorway, shocked by the reaction.

'What's this?' he asked.

'Close the door,' hissed Gunnlaugur. Váltyr sheathed his blade.

Olgeir pushed past Ingvar and Jorundur, shutting them in. Only then did Ingvar catch sight of Baldr's body on the slab.

'Allfather,' he swore, rushing over to the table.

'Don't touch him!' warned Váltyr.

Gunnlaugur interposed himself between Ingvar and Baldr's body, grasping the Gyrfalkon's forearm.

'He is in the Red Dream, brother. Be careful.'

Ingvar's eyes went wide as he saw Baldr's face.

'That is no Red Dream,' he said. 'What happened?'

Gunnlaugur maintained his grip.

'They had a sorcerer,' he said. 'Baldr bore the brunt. He may yet recover.'

Ingvar angrily shook off Gunnlaugur's grasp and shoved his way to the slab-edge.

'Recover? Blood of Russ, he's infected!'

'We don't know that,' said Váltyr.

Ingvar rounded on him.

'What more evidence do you need, blademaster?' he asked, his voice wild. 'Look at him!'

'We will wait,' said Gunnlaugur, watching Ingvar carefully. 'He may yet–'

'What did you *do*?' demanded Ingvar. 'Why was he taking on a witch unaided?'

Gunnlaugur suppressed a flare of anger. Ingvar's face was lurid with accusation; it provoked him, but he knew the cause of that.

'Watch yourself,' he warned, pinning the words on a low, growling note. 'You weren't there.'

Ingvar laughed out loud, though the sound was bitter.

'No, I was not! You saw to that. Why was that, *vaerangi*? What did you fear from my being there? That I'd show you up again?'

The room burst into movement. Olgeir came over, hands spread, trying to calm the others. Váltyr muttered something inaudible, glaring darkly at Ingvar. Hafloí tried to speak, but his dry throat betrayed him.

Gunnlaugur rounded on Ingvar, keeping his temper in check by a hair's breadth. He could feel his heart-rate picking up, his blood pumping angrily.

'Say no more, Gyrfalkon,' he ordered, glowering menacingly. 'If you value your hide, say no more.'

'Not this time!' cried Ingvar, eyes staring. 'I held my peace before, I walked away twice – not again.'

He shrugged off Olgeir's restraining hands and squared up to Gunnlaugur.

'You *knew* there was something hidden in that column,' he said, his eyes blazing. 'You knew it! But still you went after it, hungry for the glory you needed.'

Gunnlaugur felt his restraint slipping. Ingvar's mood was febrile and his words pricked at him like dagger-tips.

'Damn you to *Hel*, Skullhewer,' Ingvar raged. 'You *killed* him. Are you proud now? Has that sated your need for bloodshed?'

Ingvar swung in close, so close that the spittle from his invective flew into Gunnlaugur's eyes.

'You killed him, you *fool.*'

The dam broke.

Gunnlaugur launched himself at Ingvar, barely even feeling Váltyr's futile attempt to rein him in, throwing himself forwards and butting him viciously on the forehead.

'You *want* this?' Gunnlaugur roared, throwing a punch with his left fist. It connected brutally, hurling Ingvar back and sending him reeling. 'You *want* me to destroy you?'

Ingvar crashed into a trolley full of medical instruments. They spun and clattered to the floor as he careered on backwards. Gunnlaugur went after him, fists swinging, aiming for the head.

Ingvar pushed back, shoulders down and arms wide, crunching into Gunnlaugur's waist. Ingvar wrapped his arms around him and heaved, arresting the Wolf Guard's momentum and nearly upending him.

They rocked back, locked together, smashing machines and sending them skidding into the walls. Gunnlaugur twisted out of Ingvar's embrace and hurled him aside. Ingvar slammed heavily into the apothecarion's far wall, cracking the stone and spitting blood onto the floor.

Before Gunnlaugur could close, Ingvar came back at him, fists whirling. The two of them traded a flurry of bludgeoning punches, each one landing with the force of jackhammers. Ingvar was quicker, cracking two ferocious blows against Gunnlaugur's right side, but Gunnlaugur fought as if possessed, his eyes blazing with a dark, enraged energy.

He crunched a deadening strike into Ingvar's face, hurling him back against the wall. Then he piled in, lunging madly, roaring curses as his arms flailed.

By the time Olgeir and Váltyr finally dragged them apart both of them were panting hard and covered in blood. Gunnlaugur's forehead carried a long gash and streaks of deep red coursed freely over his beard. Ingvar's face was swollen and purple, his lips split and one eye half closed.

For a moment they both stared at one another, breathing heavily. Gunnlaugur felt his whole system blazing with energy, urging him back into the fight. The veins at his throat throbbed. His fists were still tight-clenched, aching to fly again.

Hafloí's jaw hung open, as if he couldn't quite believe what he'd seen. Váltyr looked weary of it all; Olgeir concerned.

Only Jorundur was unmoved. His sour laughter broke the heavy silence.

'It happens at last,' he said dryly. 'Better now than when the walls are on fire. So is that it? Can we move on now?'

No one had any appetite to answer. Gunnlaugur remained poised, his fists raised and blood pumping. The discharge of fury had felt good while it had lasted. It had been building up for days, poisoning him, polluting everything he did.

Ingvar glared back at him. He'd taken a battering; brawling had never been his strong point. He was still angry, but something else lurked behind those stony features.

Shame, perhaps. Or maybe sorrow.

He glanced momentarily towards Baldr's unmoving body, and something seemed to snap within him.

His shoulders slumped.

'Brother, I–' he started.

'Say nothing,' ordered Gunnlaugur, still primed, still snarling. He pulled himself to his full height, ignoring the slowing trickle of blood that ran down his cheek. 'Say *nothing.*'

He turned his gaze to Haflói, who still wore an expression of shock. No doubt he was used to Blood Claws settling things in such a way, but Hunters were another matter.

'Can you walk yet, whelp?' demanded Gunnlaugur.

Haflói seemed briefly uncertain, but nodded.

'Good,' said Gunnlaugur. His senses were returning. He felt clarified. 'The canoness will be wondering where we are. We need to go.' He shot a savage look at Ingvar. 'We'll settle this later. For now, survival.'

The pack looked back at him. They listened. In a strange, primitive kind of way he'd established his authority again.

Is that the best we can do? he thought to himself, not knowing how he would answer that, if pushed. *Is that really – still – how these things are done?*

'Stay with Fjolnir,' Gunnlaugur ordered Ingvar. 'Let your blood cool while you're in here. He needs guarding, and I'll not have the Sisters discovering this.'

Ingvar nodded curtly, his expression torn between residual belligerence and the sullen acceptance of defeat.

Then Gunnlaugur swung round to the rest of the pack. The flow of blood raging around his system banished the weariness of the night's work. There would be time to reflect on his choices later; for now, battle called again.

'The rest of you, with me,' he said, reaching for his helm. 'We have a war to fight.'

* * *

With the departure of the pack, the apothecarion fell into near-silence. Baldr remained prone on the slab, his face grey and pallid. Unseeing eyes stared up at the ceiling, their pupils shrunk into mere specks of black. Even the golden irises, normally so vivid and reflective, looked washed out.

After a while Ingvar came over to stand beside him. His own face, a criss-crossed mass of bruises and lacerations, scarcely looked healthier than Baldr's. He stooped, resting his hands on the edge of the table and bringing his head down closer to his brother's.

Grief marked his severe features. He felt suddenly older, as if the cares of centuries had only then chosen to etch themselves on his genhanced flesh.

'Brother,' he whispered, as if speaking to him could bring Baldr out of the grip of his deep coma.

If he died there, it would be a terrible death, one every Son of Russ would shudder to hear of. No glorious last charge, no defiant stand, just slow capitulation to corrupting poisons within the walls of a mortal fortress.

Ingvar's body ached. He could feel the blood on his skin thickening into scabs. Already the brawl seemed like a trivial, stupid thing; something born out of grief and guilt, something to be put aside and forgotten.

Some things, though, were more important.

'Brother,' said Ingvar again. He reached for the soul-ward at his breast. Despite Gunnlaugur's furious assault it remained intact, as did the Onyx skull beside it. 'You should not have given me this. It was yours, and I should not have taken it back.' His eyes lowered. 'But it was freely given. Is that not the way of our kind? To seal blood-debts with trinkets? I thought it was a way back for me. That was why I took it.'

Ingvar's eyes flickered out of focus, their gaze uncertain.

'I believed I could come back. I truly believed it. I wear them both now – my two lives, intertwined, interdependent. I thought I could keep them in balance.'

He looked around him then, as if suddenly nervous others might be listening. The apothecarion gazed back at him, deserted, echoing with antiseptic emptiness. Baldr's blank expression registered no change.

Ingvar lowered his head further, keeping his voice to little more than a hiss.

'I have to tell someone,' he said. 'If we are both to die here, far from the ice and unmourned, I have to tell someone. You will not remember. No vow is broken.'

Baldr's face was unmoved, locked in the rigid grip of paralysis. His sickly features seemed carved from granite.

Ingvar paused, poised over what felt like a precipice. Heartbeats passed; his own strongly, Baldr's almost undetectably.

'I no longer believe, brother.'

Ingvar's voice almost broke as he spoke those words. His hands gripped the side of the table. Horror filled his heart, horror that he had spoken such a thing out loud. Until then he had never done so, not even in the privacy of his cell's solitude. The psycho-conditioning of the Adeptus Astartes was so ferociously strong.

But not unbreakable.

'I no longer believe,' he said again, more firmly.

It was less terrible the second time. Like unlocking a door into a hidden chamber of forbidden secrets, more thoughts spilled out, tumbling after the first one. He had broken the taboo; the totem had been cracked. After that, anything was possible.

'We were seven,' he said, no longer staring at Baldr's static features but seeing things far away. 'Just like Járnhamar, we were seven. Callimachus of the Ultramarines, Leonides of the Blood Angels, Jocelyn of the Dark Angels, Prion of the Angels Puissant, Xatasch of the Iron Shades, Vhorr of the Executioners, Ingvar of the Space Wolves. We were Onyx Squad.'

Ingvar smiled softly.

'We did not call ourselves that. Halliafiore gave us the name. He gave us our missions. He gave us plenty.'

As he spoke he heard the faint noises of the apothecarion machinery working around them – the hum of rebreathers, the drip of saline valves, the slow click of medicae-cogitators. The chamber itself seemed to be listening to him.

'For a while I held on to the past. I kept to the old ways, I walked the path of the ice. I learned to doubt slowly. Callimachus was patient. I think he liked me, for all the pain I gave him. He believed I would see the virtue of the *Codex* if I could be shown how it worked. He was right about that, at least at first. It was painful to see myths unravelled. Do you remember when we used to laugh at other Chapters? Of course, *we* were different. Nothing so hard, so cold, as the soul forged on Fenris.'

Ingvar bowed his head lower. He stared at his own clenched fists.

'To do what we do, we have to believe. We have to believe there is no alternative, that our destiny is sacred, set apart from the start. That is what we are told in every saga and forced to learn by every Priest.'

Ingvar reached up for the soul-ward again, clutching it tight and straining the chain around his neck.

'But what if the myths are broken?'

He remembered Bajola's contempt.

Myths.

'I have seen things, brother. I have seen star systems burning. I have heard the screaming of a billion souls. All of them, screaming. We couldn't shut it out. I still hear them.'

Ingvar's right hand started to shake. He let go of the soul-ward and clamped his gauntlet firmly against the steel.

'There are weapons, Fjolnir, things you would not believe. There are devices so powerful that even to speak of them outside the Deathwatch is to earn execution. Only Callimachus could have been trusted to give the order to use them. He would have done his duty even if it meant tearing out the heart of his own primarch. Could I have done it? I do not know. But he did. He gave the order, and we used those things on our own kind, burning them into atoms so that the Great Devourer would not be able to feed on their corpses.'

The cogitators ticked gently. Baldr's chest rose and fell. The rebreathers hummed.

'Then we had to watch it come. The Shadow, so vast it might have been another star system in motion. We had to watch it move over us, blind to our presence, day after day, huddled away from its wrath, watching its living ships ply across the void, watching them crawl into the warm heart at the centre of the galaxy.'

Ingvar shuddered at the memory.

'Endless,' he whispered in horror. '*Endless.*'

Baldr's ashen face showed no tremor of recognition. He lay limply, locked in a sealed world of pain.

'After that, after seeing that, I no longer believe,' Ingvar said again. The third time, it was almost easy.

He straightened slowly, pushing himself away from the slab.

'If there is to be victory, brother, I cannot see it. I cannot remember how it feels to keep my blade in hand, glorying in my service to the Allfather. All I see is the living ships. All I see is what they made us do.'

His voice cracked again.

'I thought I could come back. I thought I would remember again once I was among you. I do not blame Gunnlaugur for pushing back, he is as lost as the rest of us. I blame myself for hoping.'

He smiled again, a pinched, wistful narrowing of the lips.

'And I blame you, Baldr. You fed my hope. As long as you remained as you were in my mind's eye – so calm, clear, so noble – coming back did not seem impossible. But it is. I understand that now.'

He wiped a thickening trail of blood from his upper lip. He could feel his broken skin beginning to swell.

'You must fight this. You still have a place here. If I fight for anything now, it is for that. I would see you restored before the end.'

Ingvar leaned down again for a final time, bringing his lips close to Baldr's ear, ignoring the stink of putrescence.

'Remember how you were. Remember the way you smoothed the way between quarrelling brothers. You always commanded your animal spirits so much better than we did. Remember that strength. Do not die here, brother. Remember yourself.'

Baldr made no response. His open eyes stared sightlessly at the ceiling, their lustre gone.

'Remember yourself,' he said again, his voice a quiet urging. 'I no longer believe, but you must do. For the sake of what is left of this pack, you must believe.'

As Ingvar spoke, he felt the first spike of tears at the corner of his eyes.

It might have been fatigue. It might have been shame, or frustration. It was weak, out of character; but then so much of what he had done had been out of character, and for as long as he could remember.

Ingvar bowed his head.

'For the sake of us all,' he said, his voice soft and pressing. 'Come back.'

Chapter Eighteen

They came with the sun. As the sky turned rust-red, then flesh-grey, then a clear, deep, cloudless blue, the plains began to fill with the armies of ruin. Slowly at first, as the advance units crawled across the dust, then with growing frequency as the main detachments caught up and the day waxed towards noon. They went warily, watchfully, before finally digging in several kilometres clear of the walls.

Canoness de Chatelaine watched them from atop the fortifications of the Ighala Gate. As the hours passed, she watched the air turned brown from the clouds of dust they threw up, and smelled the hot, putrid stench of their bodily corruption. The sun beat down, making her sweat even within her armour.

Callia stood beside her, as well as six of her Celestians in their dark battle-plate. All along the walls, running away from the gate-bastion in either direction, Guardsmen and Battle Sisters had taken up positions behind the battlements. The Guardsmen wore full-face gas masks and sealed carapace armour. Few of them spoke. Few of them moved. They stood quietly, expectantly, nervously, watching.

'Word from the Wolves?' asked de Chatelaine, her eyes fixed on the gathering army out on the plain.

'On their way, canoness,' said Callia. Her voice was more nervy than usual.

'Their wounded?'

'One warrior. He remains in the citadel. The others will fight.'

De Chatelaine nodded. 'Good. For what it is worth, good.'

She couldn't summon up much more than a token enthusiasm. This day had been coming for months. It had filled her dreams every night since the plague-ships had first appeared above her world. In her heart she had never believed victory to be possible. Now, seeing what the enemy had created and was capable of deploying, that belief became a certainty.

Privately she had always doubted that Gunnlaugur and his savages really understood just what volume of horror had been unleashed on Ras Shakeh. Perhaps their raw confidence was just an act, a show of defiance in the face of inevitable defeat. Perhaps they truly believed they could turn the horde back. In either case, their arrogance had only a superficial charm.

'Nothing remains to be done,' she said coldly.

It was true. The outer walls were fully manned and the defence towers stocked with huge quantities of ammunition. The engineering works in the lower city had been completed. Fire lanes had been gouged through the interlocking network of shadowy streets; pits had been dug in concentric lines ready for the promethium that would be pumped into them at a moment's notice. Explosive lines snaked their way through the hab-units and gun-clusters, ready to be ignited as the enemy reached them.

De Chatelaine felt a soft swell of pride as she cast her eyes over what had been achieved. Her Sisters had laboured well, keeping the spread of contagion down and mobilising the workforce. The Wolves, particularly the big one with the scars, had accelerated the work enormously, but the bulk of the lifting had still been done by mortal soldiers under her command. Given the time they had had to work in, and the conditions, it was an achievement worth taking pride in.

She ran the numbers through her mind one last time. Twenty thousand Guardsmen were on the outer perimeter, almost all stationed along the walls or in the defence towers. Sixty Battle Sisters stood with them in ten-strong squads to stiffen their resistance. A reserve line of ten thousand Guard and militia, plus the few mechanised units they possessed, were posted within the terraces of the lower city in staggered detachments. Six Sisters were billeted in the cathedral with Palatine Bajola, with the remainder of the Sororitas contingent up in the Halicon, together with the final five thousand Guard troops, ready to oversee the withdrawal to the citadel should they be forced into a last stand at the summit.

De Chatelaine lifted her helm and looked out again at what faced them. The enemy had dug in several kilometres out, far beyond the range of the guns on the perimeter wall. Her helm-lenses zoomed in as she squinted into the hot light.

Their formations were huge. Battalions of infantry, each one many hundreds strong, marched up out of the dust. They arranged themselves in ragged squares, each one headed by contagion-mutated command squads bearing rough-hewn standards and skeletal trophies. The air around them was thick with a screen of dust and spore-clouds. The troops wore a motley collection of armour – rusting iron plates, looted Guard uniforms, strangely warped and merged creations of bolted metal and stretched sinew.

De Chatelaine couldn't zoom in close enough to see their faces, though she knew well enough what they would be like: listless, bloated with tumours, the flesh pressing out from the stitched joints in their leather hoods and gas mask-helms, stained green from the clouds of filmy murk that swam behind their eyepieces. Some of those troops would have been landed from the plague-ships; others were new recruits, infected and enslaved during earlier fighting. They were all equally lost now; only death, in some cases for the second time, would release them.

Already the host of plague-bearers comfortably outnumbered the defenders on the walls and more regiments were arriving all the time. She saw huge, slab-sided troop carriers smoking and rolling into position, vomiting more diseased soldiers from their flanks before shuddering back away from the front line to ferry more in. Plumes of noxious smog rolled and boiled amid the drifting dust, staining the clear blue of the sky with a wash of swimming filth.

De Chatelaine swept her gaze back and forth, scouring the front line for signs of more formidable fighters. She knew they would be there, somewhere, stalking amid the endless ranks of mortal fodder. She'd seen footage of great striding horrors, each three times the height of a man and almost impervious to pain or damage. She'd heard stories of hovering drones that buzzed across the battlefield spreading gouts of flesh-melting blooms, and swarms of fist-sized insects that latched on to faces and bit through flak-jackets.

She saw none of those things. They were being held back at the rear of the gathering host, ready to be unleashed when the defences were reeling under the weight of attacking numbers.

De Chatelaine smiled thinly. It was what she would have done, given the luxury of such overwhelming force.

And of course there was the matter of the Plague Marines. She knew that one had been destroyed by the Wolves; she doubted it was the only one. Perhaps only a handful had been landed, or perhaps dozens had.

No way of knowing until the fighting started.

'We've been waiting too long,' said Callia grimly. 'I find myself wishing for it to begin.'

De Chatelaine nodded. 'Which is why they will linger.'

'Maybe this time will be different.'

'No. They wish for our fear to grow.'

Even as she spoke, a strange, half-audible noise drifted across the plains towards them. At first it sounded like the eddying drift of the desert wind. Then it clarified – a whispering chant, hissed through broken lips and filtered by spore-thick rebreathers. Thousands of voices were murmuring in unison, mournfully repeating the same words over and over again.

Terminus Est. Terminus Est. Terminus Est.

'The end,' said Callia. 'They are telling us that this is the end.'

De Chatelaine listened. 'Maybe,' she said. 'Or perhaps it has some other meaning. Who knows?'

She spoke deliberately lightly, as if it mattered not what jabbering nonsense those pustulent mouths spat out. For all that, the mournful repetition quickly became grating. It preyed on the nerves, irritating like the sting of a gadfly. The army kept up the chant, whispering and chattering like ghouls.

She straightened, pushing her shoulders back and keeping her spine straight. That was how she intended to stay until the fighting began – standing tall, looking the enemy in the eye.

'Ensure the mask drills are broadcast,' she ordered. 'Check the secure comm-lines to Bajola and the perimeter. And unfurl the standards – it is time we matched their faithlessness with the symbols of devotion.'

Callia bowed, and hastened to obey.

De Chatelaine let her go. She would have to think of more things to give her to do. She would have to think of more orders to issue to all of them, keeping the entire city busy lest it lapsed into a fearful paralysis. In truth, though, there was nothing left to do. Everything that could have been done had been done; all that remained was to wait.

Terminus Est. Terminus Est.

De Chatelaine edged forwards, making sure she was visible on the parapet to the troops lining the terraces below her. It would be important to stay visible, to give them a signal that she was with them.

The air around her felt muggy and oppressive, even more than usual, as if thickened and curdled by the poisons leaking from the enemy.

Terminus Est.

The words were strangely familiar, though she couldn't quite think why. She turned her mind from them, trying not to listen. It would be important not to listen.

Terminus Est. Terminus Est.

She gritted her teeth, forcing herself to think of other things.

All that remained was to wait.

Váltyr hurried down through the streets, heading for the outer walls. Olgeir went with him, striding in his purposive, unhurried, rolling gait.

The pack had split. Gunnlaugur had gone to the Ighala Gate to consult with the canoness. Hafloí and Jorundur were heading to the northern edge of the perimeter zone to stiffen the defences there. Váltyr and Olgeir had been assigned to the southern half. With the city surrounded on multiple fronts, the defenders were stretched thin.

Váltyr briefly wondered if it had been the same in every city that had been destroyed. Perhaps each of them had put in place hasty defences, working until their fingers bled to erect barricades and fire-trenches, hoping against hope that it would be enough.

As the two of them moved towards their positions, loudspeakers blared out repetitive messages to the populace.

Keep your gas mask on at all times. Ensure your armour is sealed. Check your fall-back routes and muster points. Do not leave your post unless ordered to do so. The Emperor protects the faithful. Remain strong, and the righteous will prevail. Keep your gas mask on at all times. Ensure your armour...

Olgeir had spent the time since leaving the apothecarion cleaning and oiling his heavy bolter. Huge loops of ammunition hung from his burly frame, interspersed with graven rune-totems promising destruction for the faithless. His battle-plate still bore the acid-burns from the ravine but he'd stripped the tattered remnants of his pelts from his back.

'You are quiet, great one,' said Váltyr as they walked.

Olgeir sniffed. 'Not much to say.'

His rolling voice was subdued.

'Perhaps not,' said Váltyr.

Neither of them wished to speak of recent events, though in truth there was little else on their minds.

They passed quickly from the shadow of the Ighala Gate and down through the Cathedral zone. Mortal soldiers scurried around them the whole time, hauling ammo gurneys or hefting lasguns. They had stopped staring at the Wolves a long time ago. Their faces were hidden behind masks, but their movements were hurried and anxious.

'How long do you think this perimeter will hold?' asked Váltyr as they approached the lowest terraces. He tried to keep his tone light, but it sounded forced. 'You helped build it.'

Olgeir snorted. 'If we'd had more time, maybe a day or two,' he said. 'As it is? A few hours.'

Váltyr looked around him.

'Aye,' he said ruefully. 'Looks about right.'

They strode across what had once been a narrow, tree-lined courtyard. The hab-units around its edges had been demolished to clear space for a lascannon emplacement on the northern edge. Old tiles and cobbles had been dumped in a rough embankment around the lascannons. Shakeh Guardsmen crouched on the far side of it, surrounded by stacks of las-guns and spare power-packs. Some were methodically going through their last weapon rites in order to placate machine-spirits. Others were praying. Others just squatted in the heat, their limbs listless, waiting for their world to come crashing in on top of them.

'It will be hard on them,' said Olgeir, halting for a moment.

Váltyr nodded. 'It will.'

Olgeir gazed around him. The surviving walls of hab-units and person-nel bunkers seemed to shake in the heat.

'I worked with them,' Olgeir said. 'They are good people. I think they will fight well enough.'

Váltyr listened warily, wondering where he was going with this.

Then Olgeir shook his head dismissively. 'It is a shame they will die,' he said. 'I could have done things here. With more time, we could have made them as tough as kaerls.'

As he finished speaking, a low, brushing noise broke out across the city. From every tower balcony and gate lintel around them, banners suddenly unfurled, sliding down the stone and hanging limply in the unmoving air. Váltyr looked over his shoulder, back up at the imposing bulk of the Ighala Gate, just in time to see two immense standards unroll on either side of the yawning entrance arch. Each one was black, lined with pearl-white and gold. One displayed the emblem of the Wounded Heart in deep crimson; the other had the Imperial aquila emblazoned in gold.

Similar devices unfurled across the entire city. Hjec Aleja was a cer-emonial site, full of processional hangings, regimental standards and ritual tapestries; when they were unravelled all at once the effect was startling: blank stone and rockcrete was replaced by a rippling sea of ebony, white, gold and crimson. The immortal images of the Imperium and the Ecclesiarchy came into being, picked out starkly by the unforgiv-ing sun, staring out defiantly at the sea of blasphemy beyond the walls.

For a moment, faced with that spectacle, Váltyr forgot the reality of the tactical situation. He saw the dazzling array of icons, all of them created by a world whose only purpose was to venerate the Imperial order. He saw the pride that had gone into their making. Ras Shakeh was not a rich planet, it was not a beautiful one, but it had always been pious.

Olgeir grunted with approval.

'Good people,' he said again, as if that had proved his point.

The two of them started moving again, Olgeir striding out, Váltyr following on, his hand on the hilt of his blade. He felt a mix of emotions, including ones he rarely indulged. For once, the forthcoming combat was not something he looked forward to as an abstract exercise. With Baldr's fall, it had gone beyond that, becoming something more personal.

Most strangely, and against all the odds, he found himself sharing some of Olgeir's sentiments. As things had transpired, he regretted the ruin that would come to Ras Shakeh. They had already fought hard for it; they would fight harder for it before the end came.

The people had earned that. With their dogged resistance, their artistry, their loyalty, they had earned the right to one last battle.

He remembered hating the planet, and found he could no longer do so.

It is a shame they will die.

Hafloí limped along behind Jorundur. They were near the outer walls, surrounded by the bunkers and resupply depots of the perimeter defence forces. His limbs still felt like they were atrophied inside his armour. Váltyr had told him it would pass. Hafloí wondered how he could be so certain.

'You could slow down,' he complained.

'And you could keep up,' Jorundur retorted, not changing his pace. 'I thought you were capable of fighting?'

'I am,' said Hafloí sullenly. 'This is walking.'

Jorundur stopped and turned to face him.

'They're linked,' he said acidly. 'Tell me truly, whelp: if you can't swing an axe up there, you're no good to me.'

Hafloí scowled under his helm. 'I can swing an axe fine,' he said. His voice held a growling edge to it, just as Gunnlaugur's so often did. 'Just get me into position and let them come to me.'

Jorundur looked at him for a long time, as if judging whether that was wise.

'Your armour's burned white,' he observed. 'That's not going to change. Perhaps we should give you a name to remember it by. Witch-marked?

White-pelt?' He shook his head. 'Never been gifted at such things. Baldr would have known what to suggest.'

Haflói felt a twinge of pain. 'Deed names are for heroes,' he said. 'I won't take one.'

The memory of what had happened in the ravine was still raw. He'd fought a thousand times against the scions of the Dark Gods and had never been so easily swatted aside. If he'd just been a little quicker, a little wilier or a little more experienced, Baldr might not be lying on a slab in the heart of the Halicon.

He expected Jorundur to respond with sarcasm. To his surprise, the old warrior reached out to him, resting his gauntlet on his warp-whitened armour.

'You're young, whelp,' he said. His dry voice was as warm as it ever got. 'You fight well. Váltyr told me he'd have struggled against that witch if he'd been up against him. It took three of them to take him down. *Three*. And one of them was Gunnlaugur, who can kill anything that lives. So you have nothing to be ashamed of.'

The kindness was so unexpected, so unusual, Haflói didn't know how to respond. For a moment he thought Jorundur might still be mocking him somehow, masking a jest with honeyed reassurances.

'Doubt is the killer, Haflói,' Jorundur went on. 'Let it under your guard, and it will murder you. I've seen you use your axe, and you've got a mighty future ahead of you.' The Old Dog's voice drifted a little, as if he were remembering something else. 'Don't doubt. I'd hate to see you not fulfil your potential.'

It was then that Haflói knew he wasn't mocking him. He watched Jorundur standing before him, somehow hunched and crabby even in his ancient battle-plate. Those last words had been heartfelt.

Then Jorundur withdrew his gauntlet and started walking again.

Haflói hurried to keep up with him, feeling the muscles in his calves throb. He struggled to think of something to say.

'So what of *Vuokho*?' he asked, suddenly remembering the Thunder-hawk sitting up in the citadel.

Jorundur laughed. 'Still hoping, eh?' he said. 'Forget it. It's back in one piece, but we ran out of time. It wouldn't get off the landing pad. And if it did, it would crash soon after.' He chortled darkly to himself. 'A shame. I'd have enjoyed opening up with the cannon.'

Haflói sighed. 'Aye,' he said. 'And I'd have enjoyed flying it.'

That made Jorundur laugh again.

'Where is this nonsense coming from?' he asked. 'You're a fine warrior, but you're no pilot. Trust me, I've trained plenty. You've got muscle where your brain should be. You'd burn a Thunderhawk into the ground as soon as look at it.'

Hafloí began to feel reassured. That was more like it – the old sarcasm was back.

'So you think,' he said, wincing as his damaged muscles protested against the work he put them to. 'I'd have enjoyed proving you wrong.'

As he spoke, they reached the broad expanse of cleared earth on the inside curve of the walls. Dozens of Shakeh-liveried troops milled around at the base of the fortifications, hauling materiel or barking orders to one another. Ladders ran up from the ground level towards the summit, more than twenty metres up. Hafloí could see figures moving between the various gantry levels on the walls' inside faces. Long chains ran down from the parapets above, ready to lift the heavy ammo-crates chewed through by the fixed bolter turrets on the battlements. Everything was in motion, a bustling energy that spoke of nerves and resolve. Hafloí could smell the sweat of the workers even though their sealed armour and rebreathers. They would be sweltering in their chem-resistant outfits.

Jorundur moved to one of the many ladders leading to the parapet, then paused as he gripped the metal.

'Last time I'm asking,' he said. 'Are you fit for this?'

Hafloí briefly saw Baldr's grey face, laid out on the slab, eyes open but unseeing. *They* had done that to him. He hadn't been strong enough to prevent that then, but there was always vengeance.

He flexed his arms. Still painful, but some of their old suppleness was returning.

'Think I'd tell you if I wasn't?' he said. 'But worry not, old one.'

He drew his weapon and hefted it loosely.

'I can swing an axe fine.'

De Chatelaine smelled the Wolf Guard's approach before she saw him. His aroma hadn't improved with the passing of time. The musk that always hung around him had been added to by the remnants of those he'd killed: she could detect the dry tang of crusted blood, the slowly decaying residue of slaughtered flesh, the musty stench of residual acid-eroded furs, so incongruously worn in the full heat of the sun.

She waited for him on the platform above the Ighala Gate, standing where she had done since the first enemy troops had crawled onto the plains before her. She heard his heavy tread coming up the stone steps behind her. She knew that Space Marines could move stealthily when they chose to, but for the most part their movements seemed to her heavy, almost clumsy.

They were such crushing, blunt instruments. Each individual among them was capable of slaying hundreds of lesser troops. They had passed so far beyond the capabilities of mortality that they were more like living tanks than lone soldiers.

And of all the Chapters that might have answered her summons, the Wolves were the most incongruous of all; a weird mix of mutation, superstition and backwardness that would have long since been purged from the Imperium if it hadn't been for their other qualities: unshakeable loyalty, terrifying combat prowess, sheer bloody-mindedness.

De Chatelaine smiled silently to herself. Despite everything, despite all she'd expected, she couldn't help but appreciate their uniqueness. Dealing with the Adulators had been easier. They had been courteous, predictable and efficient. But – Throne forgive her – they had also been mordantly dull.

'Canoness,' came Gunnlaugur's greeting.

De Chatelaine turned away from the vista before her and inclined her head gracefully.

'Wolf Guard,' she answered. 'How fares your wounded warrior?'

Gunnlaugur drew alongside her. The two of them stood together at the Ighala's summit. Below them spread the tumbling face of the lower city. Beyond that sprawled the enemy army, now bloated into a foetid sea of bodies that lapped in all directions, staining the earth into blackness. Their numbers had long since become uncountable.

'He lives,' said Gunnlaugur. His expression was masked by his helm. 'One of my pack tends him.'

De Chatelaine placed her hands together before her.

'Good,' she said. 'Then your raid was a success.'

Gunnlaugur didn't reply immediately.

'They had a witch with them,' he said. 'A sorcerer. We killed it.'

'So I heard,' she said. 'The first such abomination to die on this world. Let us hope it will not be the last.'

Gunnlaugur growled his assent. 'Trust in that.'

Out on the plains, the low whispering had never stopped. It still rolled across the thickening air, repeated in overlapping, husky, phlegm-thick voices. The sound was impossible to get used to; de Chatelaine couldn't block it out or forget it was there. That was, presumably, the point. She forced her mind not to fixate.

'*Terminus Est*,' she said. 'Does it mean something to you?'

Gunnlaugur nodded slowly. 'It does,' he said. 'It is the name of a ship.'

As soon as he said it, de Chatelaine knew he was right. She dimly recalled stories, old stories, legends of drifting hulks in the deep void crewed by nightmares.

'So why do they say its name?' she asked.

'I do not know.'

De Chatelaine looked at him shrewdly. 'You do not know, or you will not tell me?'

Gunnlaugur seemed to consider that for a while. Eventually, he spoke again.

'The mutants that pollute your planet are scions of Mortarion,' he said. 'The Traitor Marines that walk among them are of his Legion, the Death Guard. Their captain has many names and many faces. Some are legendary, some remembered only by the souls of those he has slain.'

Gunnlaugur's voice dropped low, audible only to her and the Celestians in attendance.

'In the annals of our order he was once Calas Typhon of the Dusk Raiders. Now he is called Typhus.' The contempt in Gunnlaugur's voice was almost physically tangible. 'The *Terminus Est* is his flagship.'

'Why do they call out its name?' asked de Chatelaine. 'Is he here? Is that it?'

Gunnlaugur made a strange, twisted noise. For a moment de Chatelaine thought he was choking on something. Then she realised he was laughing.

'If he were here, Sister, this world would already be smouldering ash,' he said, before turning his dust-lined lenses to her. 'They say I am proud, but I am not stupid. Some foes are beyond all but the mightiest of us.'

He looked back out over the plains.

'No,' he said. 'His brothers lead this attack, but he is not with them.'

The canoness couldn't draw much comfort from that. The forces against them were so immense that the presence or otherwise of one warlord, no matter how dreadful, seemed to make little difference.

'Then I do not understand why they chant,' she said.

'Neither do I,' said Gunnlaugur. 'But if his name is invoked here, then this battle is a part of something larger. The *Terminus Est* has been hunted for millennia. Whenever it draws clear of the warp it is the harbinger of some great terror.'

His tone was sombre. The ebullience that had coloured his words on arrival seemed to have faded.

'I have the sense of something unfolding,' he said. 'I have the sense that long-prepared plans have been mobilised. This world – your world – had the misfortune to be in the way of them.'

'Misfortune?'

'Fate, then.'

De Chatelaine unclasped her hands. Absently, her right strayed to the grip of her holstered bolt pistol.

'Nothing you say makes me optimistic, Space Wolf,' she said. 'For a long time, even after they began to march on us here in Hjec Aleja, I was optimistic. I prayed that some outside force would come to deliver us. When you arrived, I thought it might be you.'

Gunnlaugur snorted in amusement. 'We haven't started on them yet.'

'But you yourself do not believe it.'

'Oh, I do,' said Gunnlaugur, at last injecting some resolve into his deep voice. 'We all believe. That is what makes us who we are.'

He held up his gauntlet and turned it in the sunlight. The grey ceramite was criss-crossed with scratches, scorches, gouges, chips and bloodstains.

'These are just tools,' he said. Then he tapped his finger against his chest, just over the angular markings on his breastplate. '*This* is what makes us *Fenryka*. We believe. If any one of my pack wavered in that, even the closest of my battle-brothers, I would disown him. When the urge comes on us, when we enter the fight, none of us doubts. Not for a second. That is Russ's legacy.'

He clenched his fist before lowering it.

'Some things are eternal,' he said. 'When this thing starts, I will enter battle in the full certainty that I will crush them utterly.'

De Chatelaine laughed. She wasn't sure whether that was because his words inspired her or because they were ludicrous. In any case, it felt good to release some small portion of the tension she had carried with her for so long.

'And you would say the same even if this Typhus were here?' she asked.

Gunnlaugur nodded. 'I would. And you would see then what contradictory creatures we are.'

De Chatelaine inclined her head amusedly. 'I already see that,' she said.

They stood together after that, watching the clouds of dust drift across the plains. The sun was at its apex, hammering down over defender and besieger alike. Smoke wafted lazily up from the enemy lines. It was hard to make out what they were doing. In the far distance, the hazy outlines of huge vehicles could just be made out. Some looked like bloated artillery pieces; others like massive fuel tankers.

'So Typhus is not among them,' said de Chatelaine, musingly. 'But they are led by one from his Legion. Who, I wonder?'

'Do not worry on that score,' said Gunnlaugur, his voice bleak. 'We will know it soon enough.'

Chapter Nineteen

The first sign of change came with the sounding of klaxons out on the plain. A few blared out, braying tinnily, then others joined them. The banners hanging over the legions of diseased troops twitched, then started to sway as their bearers broke into the march. Great booming gongs rang out from beaten hammers of brass. The cloud of drifting soot split and severed, fractured by the sudden movement of thousands of troops.

All along the battlements, Guardsmen immediately tensed, hoisting their lasguns onto the parapet edge and staring through the sights. The twin barrels of the bolter turrets swung into position, angling at the terrain before the walls. Warning chimes sounded throughout the city, echoing along what remained of the narrow spaces and courtyards below.

Váltyr watched it unfold with a calm, expert eye.

'The first wave,' he murmured, watching the front ranks of mutants start to creep across the dust-pan towards the outer gates.

More dust kicked up as the legions picked up momentum. The entire expanse of desert seemed to be shifting. Regiment after regiment began to move, lumbering heavily into motion, still whispering the same words, maddeningly repeated far beyond the tolerances of mortal sanity.

Terminus Est. Terminus Est.

Shielded behind the front ranks of infantry came the crawling siege engines. They hauled their way through the muck and murk, belching smoke and venting gas. Some carried rusty toxin vats on their backs, just like the ones destroyed in the ravine; others dragged along multi-barrelled artillery pieces, their snouts corroded and dry with ancient rot and metal cancer; others were tottering creations of iron scaffolding and ramshackle ladders, topped with grapple-claws and chain launchers. Dozens of them emerged out of the preternatural fog, then dozens more.

Stand firm, defenders of Hjec Aleja!

The recorded voice blasting from the vox-casters along the wall was more hectoring than reassuring.

The Immortal Emperor protects! Aim true, hold fast, and no creature of darkness shall pass these walls! Preserve your power-pack! Fire only on command!

Olgeir grunted. 'If they don't kill that man, I will.'

Váltyr didn't smile. 'They're coming within range of the wall guns,' he said. 'So slow. This'll be a slaughter.'

'Aye. But it'll soak up bullets.'

The enemy host picked up some speed, stumbling from a limping stagger into a half-paced jog. They never launched into battle-cries, just kept up the eerie, incessant chanting. As the heavy sun slammed down on them, feeding the sweaty, stale fug of their sickness, they hissed and wheezed in unison, their dull eyes gazing stupidly.

All along the parapet, lascannon feeder units whined up to full pitch. Their long barrels swivelled into position alongside the squat heavy bolters.

Váltyr glanced over his shoulder, up to the Ighala Gate fortifications in the distance. He could see the canoness standing at the summit of the gatehouse. Gunnlaugur had left her side, no doubt heading down to the perimeter before the storm broke against it. De Chatelaine looked isolated up there, her cloak hanging heavily in the airless heat and the metal lining of her battle-plate glinting. She raised her arm, and a thousand pairs of eyes all across the city waited for the signal.

For a moment her fist hovered motionless, raised above her like a salute. Then it fell.

The wall batteries opened up. The stone beneath Váltyr's feet trembled as serried lascannons, heavy bolters, sabre platforms and mortar launchers unleashed their contents. Blinding spears of energy lanced out from the city's edge, shooting clear of the smoke-choked discharge of missile launchers and heavy ordnance.

The front rows of enemy infantry disappeared behind a rippling wave of exploding earth. The cracks and booms of secondary detonations rang out, drowning out their whispering and replacing it with a hammering chorus of mechanical devastation.

More volleys followed, loosed in a steady rain of destruction, tearing through the oncoming horde and miring its advance into a bloody, dust-swirled morass.

Hundreds died in those opening seconds. They just kept marching through it, swinging their scrawny arms even as they staggered into the heart of the maelstrom. Not one of them turned back, not one of them hesitated.

Váltyr felt disgust rise in his gorge. He had seen men used callously on battlefields by the Imperium in the past, but the rank slaughter in front of him went far beyond that. There was malice in it, a casual destruction ordained by powers that loathed humanity and delighted in its degradation. Somewhere, in some forsaken vault of eternity, ruinous intelligences laughed to see such wanton suffering inflicted on their own servants.

For all that, the tactic was not mindless. The lascannons had to pause between barrages to allow the power units to be recycled. Bolter turrets needed reloading, mortar arrays took time to replenish. The crews worked quickly, getting their weapons firing again as soon as they could, but the tiny gaps created opportunities. Enemy infantry, their masks glowing with a dull-edged resolve, clambered across smouldering blast craters and trod down the sagging bodies of the slain. They kept on coming, inching closer with every pause in the firing. Eventually the gun crews were forced to angle their barrels down, ratchet-notch by ratchet-notch. The filthy tide of broken bodies and tangled metalwork edged closer, metre by clogged metre, their progress bought dearly amid the hammering rain of las-beams and bloody bolt-shells.

Through breaks in the growing screens of dirty smoke, war engines could be made out, grinding towards the walls in the wake of the sacrificial infantry. Their heavy treads rolled over the corpses, crushing the stacked cadavers into a slurry of brown-frothed slime. Every so often a lascannon would get a clear shot and one of them would burst into green-edged flame, collapsing into ruin as other weapons zeroed in. But for every one that was downed many more crept nearer, slowly crunching and snapping their way through the pools of twitching, necrotic flesh.

Váltyr drew *holdbítr*. Olgeir hoisted *sigrún*. The two of them stood on the wall's edge, watching the first of the big machines draw into range. Alongside them on the parapet's length, mortal troops held their lasguns tightly, blinked into their sights and tried not to seize up too much. The few Battle Sisters among them stood silently, patiently, like ebony statues of lost saints.

'The Hand of Russ be with you, Heavy-hand,' said Váltyr.

Olgeir nodded. 'And with you, blademaster. Reap a swathe.'

Váltyr flourished his blade. Even in the dull, smog-thick air the metal flashed brilliantly, polished to a glass-clear sheen.

'I intend to,' he said.

The dusk was hours away but the sky darkened swiftly. A dilated pall the colour of sour plums soared up from the horizon, blotting out the light of the sun. Rearing towers of airborne ash snaked out, bleeding up from the skirts of the boiling hordes as they advanced. Lightning, picked out in lurid green, flickered under the ragged hems of the racing clouds, closely followed by the dull roll of unnatural thunder.

The air, already hot, became stiflingly humid. Insects swarmed up from the plains and began to plague the battlement level of the walls. They clustered around the air intakes of the Guards' chem-suits, buzzing furiously as their swollen abdomens jammed in the mechanisms. Gun crews began to leave their stations, choking, slapping and clawing at their gas masks. The intensity of the defensive barrage fell away.

'Stay where you are!' roared Gunnlaugur, striding up to the edge of the broad gun platform that perched over the outer wall gatehouse. He was surrounded by hundreds of Guardsmen, all manning one of the dozens of bolter-mounts that lined the ornate bulwark. Despite the droning mass of biting insects they laboured on as best they could, dragging fresh crates to the gaping gun-breeches and spinning elevating wheels two-handed.

By then the enemy had almost reached the walls. Their losses were still incredible, but with every passing minute the gap closed by a few paces more. Some of the mutants even managed to loose grappling hooks or hurl spiked incendiary bombs up at the defenders. Such futile attempts did little more than scrape the foundations of the city's perimeter, but the fact they'd got so close, and so fast, was sobering.

Gunnlaugur grasped the lip of the platform's railing and leaned out over the raging tumult below, craning for a better view. The siege engines were getting closer, wrapped in thick coats of oily smoke. The first flickers of enemy las-fire started to spike upwards from ground level. As bigger guns were dragged into range, that trickle slowly grew more disruptive.

Hjec Aleja was completely surrounded. The plague-host stretched away in all directions, devouring the open land and turning it black. The pale stone of the city turned scab-brown under the gathering smog and the golden lining of the banners lost its lustre. Lumen banks began to flicker into life across the walls and defence towers, but their light was quickly muffled in the dense murk.

Gunnlaugur stood defiantly above it all, poised atop the beleaguered gates like some ancient sea captain at the prow of his wave-cutter.

Ahead of him, vast and wreathed in underlit gouts of steam, a tottering mobile tower rig emerged from the gloom. It reached up to the level of the battlements, dwarfing the ranks of marching mortals before its huge segmented tracks. Its flanks were formed of an intricate skein of interlocking iron webs. Banners of crudely stitched human hide fluttered in its wake, still bloody and unscraped, bolted to the scaffold with metal pins. As Gunnlaugur watched, a row of bronze-throated cannons rolled out along the tower's top tier, each one already smoking from its baleful contents.

'Bring it down!' he thundered at the crews around him.

They tried to. Two lascannon stations found their target, sending beams tearing through the superstructure and nearly sending it crashing back to earth. Somehow, the siege tower kept on coming, teetering and rocking.

Then, with a glottal roar, the tower's cannons returned fire. Shells screamed across the exposed gun platform, whistling across the space at head height. Gunnlaugur, ducking under the barrage, saw Guardsmen hit full on, hurled into shreds of flesh as the barbed missiles exploded. Metal shards flew out from the shells in bursting clouds of spinning debris, scything through body armour and cutting into stone. Trails of vomit-yellow mucus flew out from the exploding ordnance, clinging to whatever it splattered across and eating at it like acid.

In that single volley half the gun stations had been taken out. The rest of them had mauled crews and only slowly scrambled to respond.

Gunnlaugur kicked back to his feet. He raced over to the nearest heavy bolter turret – an open platform with a single twin-linked gun mounted on a swivel-plate. He grabbed the two-handed grip, spun the barrels round and opened fire. Twin columns of mass-reactive shells blazed straight back at the tower's approaching summit.

The line of cannons blew up one after the other as the stream of bolts flew into their gaping maws. Skeletal figures clinging to the tower's structure fired back at Gunnlaugur, concentrating las-beams at his position. Those shots that hit him glanced from his armour, scoring it but not penetrating. Gunnlaugur weathered the storm, firing all the time, holding firm as the long chain of shells spun through the bolter's feeder mechanism.

By the time the heavy bolter clicked empty the other gun crews were recovering. Stark white las-beams and solid projectiles hammered into the reeling siege tower. With a sighing crack, the spine of it broke, sending the top level crashing down to the smoke-filled plains below. Ammo-dumps stored inside ignited with a whooshing bang, and a thick bloom of orange flame raced up the tower's cracked sides. It reeled on its tracks, hanging precariously for a moment, then toppled, breaking up into burning shards as it disintegrated over the jostling throngs below.

Gunnlaugur looked around him. Three more war engines were approaching, each as large as the first one, crushing and tearing their way through the legions that pressed around them. At ground level, heavily armoured plague-bearers in dull black armour were hauling what looked like huge bomb carcasses towards the barred gate entrance. The volume of fire aimed up at the battlements was growing all the time.

He drew his bolter grimly, trying to gauge just how long the defences on the perimeter could hold before retreat became inevitable. The task was already nearly hopeless, like trying to hold back a storm-tide of the Helwinter.

'Hold fast!' he roared defiantly, picking his next target out and opening fire again. The familiar hammering clatter of his bolter rang out across the growing cacophony of the battlefield, adding to the steady crescendo of rage and fury. 'In the name of the Allfather, hold fast!'

Ingvar heard the blasts from far off. In the sanctuary of the Halicon's apothecarion they were little more than dull rumbles. Some of the larger impacts made the walls vibrate, sending hairline cracks along the cement between the tiles.

He started to pace around Baldr's table, his fingers twitching. The mood of despair that had fallen over him following the brawl with Gunnlaugur had faded, replaced by a burning impatience.

He should be out there, standing with his brothers. Watching over Baldr in the Halicon was a waste.

He paced some more, resisting the urge to draw his blade. The sterile air of the apothecarion tasted stale as he breathed it.

I should be out there.

He blink-clicked a comm link to Olgeir.

'How goes the fight, brother?' he asked.

The feed was crackly and static-filled. He heard the thin background buzz of what must have been explosions, the low roar of bolter-shells loosing.

'Ingvar?' Olgeir's voice was strained. 'What do you want? We're a little busy here.'

'Where are you? I should be with you. I'll come to your position.'

The feed broke off briefly, overloaded with white noise, before re-establishing.

'...ere you are. Blood of Russ, Gyrfalkon, do not leave him. You saw what he looked like.'

Ingvar clenched his fists in frustration, glancing over to where Baldr lay, as immobile as ever, his flesh as torpid as rotting meat. There had been no change. If anything, he looked worse.

'This is madness,' hissed Ingvar, starting to walk again. 'Send the whelp back. You need my blade there, brother.'

Olgeir didn't reply. The link boomed briefly with more explosions, followed by a series of drawn-out screams. Ingvar heard a mortal voice shouting something in the background.

They're coming through! Throne, they're coming through!

When Olgeir finally spoke again, his thick voice was punctuated by panting, as if he'd broken into a jogging run.

'Do *not* leave him,' he said, breaking off to fire another hammering volley before starting to move again. 'You hear me? At this rate we'll be back with you within the hour anyway – they're all over the walls. Stay at the Hali–'

The link snapped out.

Ingvar cursed, his fists still balled. He drew in a deep breath, trying to stay calm. It was hard to resist the urge to move, to prowl across the confines of his prison like a caged beast, to do *something*.

He glared at the door. The lock mechanism could be crushed from the outside, sealing Baldr in. He hesitated, torn between duty and desire.

He looked back at Baldr. The fallen warrior's cheeks still bore a greenish hue. It seemed to be intensifying, as if whatever filth had been shoved into his system were breeding away within him.

That was an uncomfortable thought.

Ingvar went back over to the slab, studying Baldr's pale face. Flecks of foam had collected at the corners of his mouth, speckled with blood. They shivered as his shallow breaths came and went.

Ingvar sniffed. Just as before, the tang of the warp was clearly detectable. That, though, could have been down to the residue of the sorcerer's art, clinging to the armour like bloodstains on a corpse. In itself, it was no proof.

If Baldr had been mortal, Ingvar would have killed him without another thought.

But he wasn't mortal. He was one of them.

As Ingvar stood there, his mind racing, more muffled booms rang out from far away, making the floor shudder. They seemed closer than the last ones.

'Forgive me, brother,' said Ingvar, straightening. 'But could you stay here, knowing the battle had come at last? I will return for you.'

He started to move away, then hesitated, looking over his shoulder. For a moment, just as he'd turned his head, he thought he'd seen a flicker of movement in Baldr's eyes – a momentary tremor of peeled-back lids.

He stared for a little while longer, scrutinising Baldr's prone outline.

Nothing. Baldr lay as still as graven image in the halls of the Jarlheim. The algal tinge around his cheeks and jawline remained as unsettlingly deep as before.

Then Ingvar grasped his helm from his belt.

'Forgive me,' he said again, backing towards the exit as he donned the red-lensed, snarling facemask. 'If Gunnlaugur wanted one of us to sit this out, he should have chosen the whelp.'

I need to know that you will follow an order.

He paused at the doorway, his fingers resting on the stone frame.

'I *will* return,' he said.

Then he pushed the door open, and headed out into the dark.

The volume of incoming fire steadily cranked up. It became intermittently dangerous, then solid, then devastating. As fast as the enemy artillery was knocked out by the defenders, more guns were hauled into place. Brass cannon-pieces, their barrels carved into snarling devil maws, bludgeoned the walls remorselessly, hammering away with incendiary bombs, shrapnel-bursts and tumbling vials of toxic sludge. The last were the worst – when they exploded amid the defenders their contents ate through armour with terrifying ease, melting flesh and popping eyes.

The parapets were aflame, burning in all quarters where the torrid mix of accelerants and chemicals ignited. The air shimmered with heat and noise and fear. Gouges had been blown out of the upper levels by the artillery barrages, cracking open the reinforced rockcrete and sending blocks of it crashing into the city beyond. Teams of enemy sappers, covered by ferocious quantities of las-fire and spore-grenades, had already gained the base of the walls and were pitilessly hacking away at the foundations. Several siege towers had reached their targets, cranking open drawbridges and spilling hordes of masked horrors onto the battlements. Each sally so far had been repelled, but more towers kept on coming, emerging out of the poisonous smog with remorseless frequency.

Jorundur stood on the battlements, firing his bolter two-handed. He worked stoically, almost in silence, fully absorbed in what he was doing. The mortals working alongside him continued to fight even as the defences crumbled around them. They all knew the cost of surrendering the walls and clung on to them tenaciously, firing in disciplined barrages while their comrades were cut down by the rain of chem-bombs and shrapnel bursts.

Hafloí was different. He marched up and down the parapet, firing his bolt pistol with abandon and brandishing his axe flamboyantly.

'That all you've got?' he roared, spreading his arms and taunting the enemy. '*Skítja*, you *disgust* me! Come up here and test your arms on *me!*'

Jorundur had seen the mortals break into laughter as Hafloí had strutted past them, despite the unfolding horrors around them. His relentless rain of insults, challenges and expletives was having an effect on them. They saw his brazen lack of fear, and some of it rubbed off on them.

Jorundur smiled wryly. That was good. He swept his bolter muzzle around, looking for targets in the murk. Down on ground level he saw a huge, slack-bellied monster lurching towards the walls, its yellow skin hanging in bags from an obscenely stretched skeleton and what looked like a massive limpet mine cradled in its arms. Claw-fisted infantry shambled along in its wake.

He took aim carefully, adjusting the bolter a fraction as the walls shook beneath him, and fired. The creature's head exploded in a burst of bone and jellied matter. The mine crashed to the floor at its feet and went off, sending a shuddering boom radiating out through the troops around it.

Even as that assault crumbled into disarray Jorundur searched for the next one. His concentration was distracted, however, by a horribly familiar surge and crackle from behind him. He immediately pushed back, leaving the battlements and moving to the inner edge of the walkway. The stink of discharged ether filtered up from the city below, mingling with the myriad other stinks polluting the smoggy air.

Hafloí had heard it too and broke away from his posturing. He seemed to be moving freely again.

'You sense that?' he asked, his voice tightening. 'I thou–'

'Hush,' snapped Jorundur, listening carefully.

He didn't have to wait long. From below, down at street level in the lower city, a chorus of screaming started up, punctuated by the wet rattle of bolter-fire.

'They've teleported behind us,' said Jorundur grimly, slamming a fresh magazine into his bolter and preparing to jump. 'Stay here and hold the walls.'

But Hafloí had already leapt, throwing himself clear of the parapet and plummeting down to the ground below.

'Damn him,' muttered Jorundur, following him down. He hit the earth hard and staggered from the impact. His armour servos whined as they compensated, pushing him back upright.

The scene on the ground was fluid. Ahead of him, twenty metres away, rose the nearest buildings. In between them and the walls was the wide area cleared by the engineers, clogged with barricades, ammo-crates, spare weaponry and reserve defence squads. Men were running back from the line of buildings, turning to fire sporadically. Something was in the maze of alleys beyond – Jorundur could hear the noise of walls collapsing, mortals crying out in terror, gunfire rattling.

Hafloí sprinted towards the source of the noises, his axe already whirling. Jorundur struggled to keep pace with him.

'Wait!' he roared, knowing it would be pointless but fearing what the Blood Claw would do. Hafloí was hungry to make up for his failure, and his blood was up. That was a dangerous combination.

Hafloí disappeared into the shadows of the streets. Jorundur raced after him. By the time he caught up, Hafloí was already in combat.

Jorundur burst into a steep-sided courtyard overlooked by burning habs. The floor of it was a cracked mess of rubble and bodies, strewn with torn limbs and crushed weapon barrels. In the midst of it stood a lone Plague Marine, his armour still swimming with shimmering ether-residue, his power claws nearly black with boiling viscera. Two pale green lenses glowed in the murk as he swung round to face the raging Blood Claw.

Jorundur aimed his bolter but Hafloí blundered into the way. Jorundur circled round to the left, closing in to try to get a clear shot.

He never had the chance to fire. As he watched, stunned into inaction by what he was seeing, Hafloí took the Plague Marine apart.

Hafloí's speed, his fury, his power – it was phenomenal. He fired with the pistol at close range, chipping and cracking the monster's crusted power armour, all the while hacking with the twin blades of his hand-axe. The Traitor was strong, just as all his kind were, but he had no answer to the sheer pace of the attack. Hafloí's movements became a blur of velocity, a whirlwind of hammer-blows and axe-bites.

The Plague Marine tried to respond, hauling his bloody claws in broad sweeps, but Hafloí never gave him a chance to bring his greater strength to bear. He ducked under the lunging claws, thrusting up and twisting his axe round in a tight arc. Then his body spun around, propelling the blade across in a glittering line. It severed the Plague Marine's neck just above the gorget. The strike was perfect – angled between the hard armour plates and dragged through the flesh beneath with staggering power.

The Traitor crashed to the earth, his lopped neck oozing a thick mixture of pus and heartsblood. Hafloí stood in triumph over it, his boot crunched onto the enemy's swollen breastplate, his axe raised high.

'*Fenrys hjolda!*' he roared, throwing his head back and howling to the fiery heavens.

Jorundur found himself momentarily lost for words.

'Blood of Russ,' he breathed, stalking over to Hafloí and gazing at the damage he'd done. 'A mighty kill. Where did you learn to do that?'

'From watching you,' replied Hafloí, his voice savagely cheerful. 'You're a miserable pack, truth be told, but I've learned a few tricks.'

Jorundur was about to reply when fresh screaming echoed out into the false night. He looked up, over the roofs of the buildings to where the walls loomed.

Plague-bearers had got onto the parapet at last. He could see them swarming along the battlements and grappling with the Guardsmen, overwhelming them through sheer force of numbers. Further along the walls, gouges had been opened up in the stonework as the big artillery found its range. Flames coursed up the flanks of the beleaguered defence towers, snapping and writhing like nests of serpents. The stink of warp-energy remained strong, indicating that other Plague Marines had been dropped behind the defensive lines. Above it all boiled the clouds of flies and chem-spores, whipped up into a thick airborne pall of madness and disease.

The line was breaking. Once that truth became evident the vox-casters blazed out again, matched by the shouted commands of the surviving unit sergeants.

Fall back! Back to the inner walls! Fall back! Back to the inner walls!

As soon as they heard the order men began to pull away from their posts, trying not to break into a headlong run, firing steadily in retreat at the hordes of bloated, twisted mutants that swarmed through every gap and breach in the burning defences.

Jorundur stowed his bolter and drew his power axe. He thumbed the disruptor field on and its blue-edged crackle snarled into life.

'Time for blades, I think,' he said, striding back towards the approaching enemy. 'Your axe and mine, White-pelt.'

Hafloí laughed harshly, falling in behind.

'Fine,' he said. 'But you *have* to think of a better name.'

Chapter Twenty

Gunnlaugur did not leave the gatehouse until it was falling apart around him. The walls on either side were breached and broken, and the ground beneath the arches was teeming with a crush of enemy troops, all hacking at the heavy metal doors and stacking piles of explosives against them. Las-blasts lanced up at the parapets, undeterred by any return fire now that the last of the bolter turrets had been taken out. Grappling hooks were flung up; siege towers clunked heavily against abandoned wall sections and disgorged their contents onto the walkways.

Still Gunnlaugur stayed where he was, his feet planted firmly on the keystone of the gate's central arch, his hammer swinging around him in bloody curves. He was alone; the mortals who had stood with him had either fled or had died. Mutants, plague-bearers and blight-skinned cultists all rushed at him, lashing with flails and morning stars and meathooks. He cut them down in broken droves, hurling spine-snapped bodies from the battlements and sending them crashing back down into the sea of straining flesh below.

'For the honour of Russ!' he roared, crying out each time *skulbrotsjór* connected. '*Heidur Rus!* The hammer of the *Fenryka* is among you!'

They were not daunted. Oblivious to the carnage being reaped among them, they kept on coming, crawling on all fours just to get their blades into striking distance. Clouds of pestilence buzzed and droned about their heads, the insects feeding on the gaseous flesh of the dead as eagerly as they sucked on the blood of the living.

Only when the gates were finally broken did Gunnlaugur fall back at last, sweeping the parapets clear with a final, mighty strike of his crackling thunder hammer. He felt the basalt columns beneath him shudder as the gate's adamantium doors were driven in, and heard the thick crack of stone coming apart amid the rush of explosions.

In a final act of defiance, he stood atop the crumbling archway and brandished *skulbrotsjór* to the lowering heavens. The sky was as dark as night, broken by green lightning dancing along the underbelly of unnatural thunderheads. The stench of fear hummed in the burning air, but Gunnlaugur Skullhewer stood tall, silhouetted against the raging flames that now whipped along what remained of the walls.

'I *defy* you!' he thundered, swinging *skulbrotsjór* in ritual sweeps of denunciation. 'Only death awaits you! I, Gunnlaugur of the Rout of Fenris, will bring it down upon you! For the Allfather! For Fenris!'

Then the gatehouse started to collapse, reeling on its supports even as a straining tide of plague-bearers began to surge through the cracked doors.

Gunnlaugur backed away, retreating to the inner edge of the ruined archway as it yawed and buckled beneath his feet. He flung himself clear, falling hard and crashing into the throngs of mutants that had already broken through, crushing several under his heavy armour and scattering many more.

Then he started to run, slamming aside any laggards who got in his way. Behind him, the archway slowly collapsed in a sighing, slipping landslide of stone and metal, sending up thick plumes of dust and glowing from within as the fires took hold.

A low roar of triumph rose up from the host still on the far side of the walls. They swarmed over the broken and burning masonry, trampling their own just to be in the forefront of those breaking in.

Gunnlaugur never looked back. He had held the line for as long as possible, giving time for the mortals to fall back to the next circle of defence. That was how it had been planned – staged withdrawals, each one extracting as much pain from the attackers as possible.

He ran along the wide thoroughfare that Olgeir had helped excavate, hearing the broken patter of thousands of calloused feet as the horde swept after him. Ahead of him lay the first of the trenches. He could see defenders on the far side of it manning the spewing promethium ducts. They were waiting for him to cross before igniting the blaze.

'Do it now!' Gunnlaugur roared, picking up his pace and sprinting towards the defensive cordon. 'Light it now!'

They complied immediately. Flamers angled down into the trenches and opened up. Jets of fire kindled in a clap of acrid ignition. A swaying wall of flame shot down the length of the trench, swiftly rearing up into a surging barrier. The valves stayed open, pumping promethium into the inferno and feeding the conflagration.

Gunnlaugur felt the enormous heat pressing against him as he neared the trench. He put on a final burst of speed, building up momentum, before leaping through the glowing furnace and bursting clear onto the far side. The few remains of flammable material still draped across his armour exploded into flame.

He ripped them free, letting the final sparks die on the ceramite. He could hear screams of frustration coming from the far side of the barrier as the pursuing horde skidded to a halt, suddenly cut off.

Gunnlaugur turned to the lines of Guardsmen waiting in ordered ranks behind the veil of fire, their weapons poised and ready.

'Do it,' he snarled.

The front line released their volley in perfect unison, sending a wall of las-beams lancing through the sheets of flame. The screams of the damned rose in intensity as shots found their targets. Even when firing blind through the inferno, the press of bodies in the street beyond made it impossible not to hit something.

With the barrier secure for the moment, Gunnlaugur walked away from the lines of Guardsmen, letting them rotate ranks to keep up the pressure. As he moved clear of them he saw Váltyr waiting for him. The blademaster's armour was blackened from fire.

'Dramatic,' Váltyr said.

Gunnlaugur grimaced. It was as close as he was likely to get to a smile. 'Speak to me,' he said.

'Plague Marines are inside the walls. Olgeir sighted one and went after it. The whelp killed another.'

Gunnlaugur started. 'Hafloí?'

'He's bragging about it already.'

Gunnlaugur shook his head wearily. He let his hammerhead lower, barely noticing the disruptor-cooked flesh-slops sliding off it.

'These won't hold them long,' he said, looking over his shoulder at the burning trenches. 'Are all fronts falling back?'

Váltyr nodded. 'We need more time. We killed obscene amounts on the walls, but they just keep coming.'

'Then I'll stay down here with Olgeir and the Old Dog. We'll make them pay for the passage of the lower city. Go to the Ighala Gate and put it in readiness. Call Hafloí back too and get him to replace Ingvar on the watch – the Gyrfalkon's stewed in there enough and we'll need his sword.'

Gunnlaugur glanced up at the distant Ighala Gate, towering precipitously above the burning city.

'That's the key. If we can hold the bridge a while this is not yet over.'

Váltyr gestured towards the cathedral, looming into the smog over to the left of their position. Its triple spires still spat with mounted gunfire. Once the last of the defenders pulled back to the inner walls it would be a lone island in a sea of ruin.

'What do we do about that?'

Gunnlaugur shrugged. 'That's up to the Sisters. If they've got any sense they'll pull out while they still can, and I'd welcome having their flamers with us on the inner walls.'

'And if they try to hold it?'

Gunnlaugur hefted *skulbrotsjór* once more, swinging it loosely around him. The noise of battle was already growing again.

'Not my concern,' he said, striding back towards the raging front line. 'I have Traitors to hunt.'

Bajola crouched down beside the altar, her bolter ready. The six surviving Sisters of her detachment did similarly, cradling flamers. The roof shuddered as incoming fire speared into the cathedral defences. What remained of the Guard units assigned to the place had withdrawn inside the doors, taking up positions within the aisles and nave.

Bajola said nothing. She had given all but one of the orders she would give. Her troops had fought with commendable resolve, slaying far more of the enemy than she would have predicted possible, holding them back from the precincts even as the surrounding barricades had been destroyed or were abandoned. Her Sisters had been in the forefront of every bloody melee and firefight, remaining in position until the last of the regular troops around them had been slain and the enemy was swarming through the breaches.

Sister Jerila had been the first to die, surrounded by clouds of exploding toxin-grenades and assailed by arm-length blood leeches that cracked her armour open and slithered underneath. Sister Honorata had been next, charging headlong into a whispering knot of grotesque plague-bearers, giving time for the Guard units with her to retreat into the cathedral's nave. Sisters Alicia and Violetta had both fallen during the final assault on the great gates, cut off at the last and swarmed over by hundreds of grasping, tearing claws.

Bajola had never truly been proud of being a member of the Wounded Heart. Her feelings about the militant order had always been complex, defined by the compromises she had made to leave her old life behind.

No longer. As she waited for the final assault every fibre of her body was proud. She saw the faces of the slain in her mind's eye, their fierce beauty and their unbending will, and felt like one of them at last. At last she had no doubts, no regrets.

Well, one regret perhaps: that she had not broken her vows and told Ingvar the truth. The Space Wolf deserved to know, even if the knowledge would only pain him and could not possibly do any good now. But that moment had passed; Ingvar was gone, no doubt fighting along with the rest of his malodorous brothers somewhere in the burning ruins of the lower city. She had made her choices, and had learned a long time ago not to give in to the corrosion of remorse.

In any case it was too late for remorse. The end was coming.

Grant that my station may serve.

Her lips moved slowly as she silently ran through the motions of the litany. At the end of the long nave, fifty metres away in the dark, she could see the gates still standing closed. The noise of the battering rams crashing against the barred metal tore at her heart. Every strike was like a body-blow, knocking the life out of the place she had never truly loved before that day.

It was ironic. Only on the verge of its destruction had she fully appreciated the austere majesty of the structure she had been charged with defending. There was a lesson in that, somewhere. Something for one of de Chatelaine's homilies; a pity, then, that there would be no more of them.

Grant that my strength may suffice.

The doors shuddered again, cracking along their full height. Another strike hammered home, cobwebbing the struts and beams with spreading fractures.

Bajola crouched lower, shifting her gun's muzzle a little, gauging where the first break would come. She could feel the sick tension in those clustered around her. They all knew this was last line of defence; no further fallback positions existed. Above them, hanging high in the shadows, the golden mask of the Emperor gazed serenely down on them, untroubled by the carnage unfolding under His spreading arms.

Grant that my life may give honour.

Another strike landed and the right-hand door was driven in, shattering and swinging back against the pillars. The jabber and hiss of mutant troops burst into the cold serenity of the interior. She heard the roar and crackle of flames, smelled the foetid reek of plague-riddled flesh under decaying armour plate.

Grant that my death may earn it.

As the horde spilled through the broken doorway at last, tumbling into the sanctified space of St Alexia's holy precincts with the sick light of debauchery in their weeping eyes, Bajola spoke at last. She gave the final order, the one she had been saving for the final extremity, the one she had been preparing in her mind over the last hour of desperate fighting.

'The altar will not be surrendered,' she said calmly, fixing her aim on the first of the horrors to break the holiness of her domain. 'Die well, Sisters. Our bodies may be broken, but our souls are secure.'

Scholiast-Majoris Iaen Rahmna hurried along the corridor between the Halicon's prayer-scroll librarium and the incense stores. The canoness's private chapel was running low on supplies, and with nine scheduled services on the slate there was a faint chance future ceremonies would have to be truncated.

For some people such an apparently trifling matter would not have seemed important, especially given what was happening in the city at large. Some people, not blessed with Iaen Rahmna's meticulous attention to detail, would have long since ceased to care about the niceties of ritual. They might have seen the armies of darkness eating their way slowly through the lower urban zones and despaired of ceremonial propriety. They might even, in their weakness, have taken up a weapon and turned it on themselves, knowing that their life's work was now useless and decades' worth of careful prayers to the immortal Emperor of Mankind had been in vain.

Thankfully, no such people were in charge of the canoness's ecclesiastical affairs. Under Rahmna's management the thirteen chapels and sanctuaries dotted all across the citadel still worked faultlessly. The world might be ending around them, the Sisters might all have been called away to the battles outside, but the rituals would carry on. If the cardinal himself were to walk through Rahmna's gilded doorways and into one of his thirteen chapels and sanctuaries, he would witness a perfectly orchestrated suite of devotional chambers, all perfectly stocked, all ready for the priests to undertake their solemn ministry.

And of course the familiarity of the routines was a distraction. It helped Rahmna to function. It helped to keep him from giving in to the fear that threatened to suffocate him every time he heard the echoing boom of the explosions getting nearer. It prevented him from remembering that he hadn't slept properly for two weeks, or that three of his staff had succumbed to the plague and had been executed by Sisters Felicia and Calliope before his very eyes.

Keeping busy was important. It staved off the worst of the nightmares. It kept his hands occupied and gave him no time to think about retrieving the laspistol he'd stowed under his bunk for emergencies.

That was the coward's way out. And for all that Iaen Rahmna was officious, prim and completely in thrall to routine, he was no coward.

The corridor was empty. His robes rustled softly as he walked. Aside from the diffuse hum of noise coming from outside the citadel, no other sounds disturbed his mechanical thought processes.

The only departure from orthodoxy was the route: he'd had to take a detour, heading deep into the lower levels to avoid Sergeant Ehre's squads milling about in the assembly rooms. The Guardsmen were making a fearful mess there, overturning priceless cabinets and dragging their heavy equipment across polished marble towards the doorways. Rahmna didn't really understand why they were bothering. If the enemy got as far as the Halicon citadel then surely it was all over. Better instead to remain faithful, to attend to the services, to pray.

He went as swiftly as he could. The lower levels smelled bad and the lumens flickered every time a big explosion went off. Rahmna wasn't even sure what the chambers down here were used for. Food storage, perhaps. Or maybe medical facilities for the Halicon staff. Yes, that was it – the chambers on his left were part of the medicae's domain.

Ahead of him he saw a door hanging loosely on its hinges. He slowed down, unsure what to make of it. He could hear the dim humming of medicae cogitators from the other side of the wall.

He stopped walking. Something about the open doorway unnerved him. The metal panels bore long, raking marks, as if huge claws had been dragged along them.

He looked over his shoulder, his heart beating. Then he looked back. He wondered what to do. It would take him a long time to find another route.

He pressed on. His imagination had always been vivid; his superiors had castigated him for it many times in the past and he had laboured hard to curb the excesses of his mind's eye.

He went as quickly as before, padding softly in sewn leather shoes. The open doorway approached, framed by the angled outline of the broken door.

He passed by hastily, not daring to look inside. He could smell a thick aroma of something like human sweat, though it was rancid and laced with other more musky elements.

Rahmna almost reached the far side before his eyes flickered involuntarily to the left. It was just the merest glance, a fleeting vision of what lay within.

He didn't scream. The shock was too great for that. A knot of panic twisted in his stomach and burst up his throat, choking off the cry of surprise that he wanted to make.

'L-lord,' he managed to blurt, wondering, despite it all, if the etiquette was to bow. 'I did not–'

They were the last words Iaen Rahmna ever spoke. A flailing storm of green-tinged lightning forked out at him, catching him in the face and bursting his skull apart. His headless body slammed into the far wall of the corridor. For a moment the corpse hung there, impaled on sparking fronds of ether-energy, twitching and kicking, before the lines of force finally snapped out. Rahmna's corpse slid to the floor, crumpling into a heap of smoking robes.

A little later, Baldr emerged through the doorway, breathing heavily. His eyes were glassy, his skin pallid and greasy. Thin lines of drool ran down from the corners of his mouth, viscous with clotted mucus. His gauntlets glowed with a pale witchlight, dancing across the armour-plate like a will-'o-the-wisp. His battle-plate had darkened, crusting with scab-like patches that throbbed and pulsed. His head drooped low, his jaw hung loosely, his arms were limp.

His feet dragged along the ground as he moved; his breath vaporised in foul trails of mist as he breathed. He seemed unaware of where he was or what he was doing. He looked up and down the corridor, halting before moving off again.

Only when he limped back in the direction Rahmna had come from, stepping carelessly on the dead man's legs and crushing the bones, did his sallow-eyed stare pick up something a little like resolve. A lime-green lustre kindled under his heavy lids. Strands of phlegmy saliva trembled on his lips.

'Terminus,' he breathed, his voice as dry and whisper-quiet as corpse candles gusting out. 'Terminus Est.'

When Váltyr reached the Ighala Gate it was lit red by fire. The bulwarks and gothic fortifications danced with the flickering light of flames, turning the stone into a seething patchwork of shadow and reflection. The twin banners on either side of the main archway leading into the upper city were torn and punched with holes from long-range ordnance. Guns arranged along the embattled parapets drummed a heavy return rhythm of fire, throwing round after round back into the contested suburbs below.

Váltyr paused at the head of the bridge, watching the last of the retreating columns of soldiers hurry across the span and into the shadow of the gates. They looked exhausted, their feet dragging and their shoulders hunched. Five hours had passed since the outbreak of hostilities and there had been no let up since; just a grinding, hammering, relentless assault that had kept on coming no matter what resistance had been put in its way.

He turned away from the bridge and looked back the way he'd come. The land immediately in front of him had been cleared to give targets for the wall gunners. It ran gently downhill without obstruction, a bleak, open plain of rubble, dust and blast craters.

Half a kilometre further down, the surviving buildings of the lower city started to cluster tightly together. They fell away from Váltyr's vantage in ranks of terraces that ran over the uneven slopes of the mountain. Olgeir's concentric rings of trenches were all lit far below, throwing their fuel-laced blaze into the mix of raging fires from incendiaries and las-blasts. The lower circles had already been breached, in some places by plague-bearers throwing themselves into the fire in such numbers as to create bridges from their smouldering carcasses. Those barriers that remained would not buy the defenders much more time; the enemy was advancing on every front, creeping up through the ruins like a cancer penetrating a body. Only in a few isolated places, where squads of Battle Sisters or individual Wolves had taken them on in counter-attacks, did the advance halt for more than a few moments.

As Váltyr watched the encroaching devastation, Hafloí strode up out of the flame-licked darkness, limping across the broken landscape. He looked weary, and his bleached armour bore signs of recent damage.

'*Hjá*, whelp,' said Váltyr. 'You gained a skull for your weapon belt.'

Hafloí snorted disgustedly. 'Wouldn't touch it,' he said. 'Smelled worse than the Old Dog's breath.'

Hafloí drew alongside Váltyr, turned and looked out over the same vista. His breathing was heavy, his movements stiff. For all the Blood Claw would never admit it, he was at the limit of his strength and still affected by the wounds he had taken in the ravine.

'You know what the *vaerangi* wants of you now?' asked Váltyr.

Hafloí nodded. 'For me to take my turn by Baldr's side. To free up another rune-sword for the final fight and sit the rest of this out.' He shook his head. 'Don't worry, blademaster. I know it must be done.'

Váltyr looked at him quizzically. 'You're not going to fight it?'

'Would it do any good?'

'No.'

'There you are, then.'

Váltyr laughed. 'You're growing fast, whelp,' he said. 'You surprise me. Soon your hair will be as grey as ours.'

'When Hel melts,' muttered Hafloí, turning away and stomping up the slope towards the bridge.

He was one of the last to cross it, still limping slightly but with his shoulders back and his spine erect. He was even learning to walk like a Grey Hunter.

Váltyr smiled to himself. The new blood was welcome. Of all of them, only Hafloí still had the unconscious, arrogant assurance that a Sky Warrior ought to have. Olgeir retained much of his old bravado, and Gunnlaugur in the right mood was still an unstoppable kill-engine, but even they had learned to temper their fury as the centuries had played out. Baldr had never lost his aura of self-command, not until this mission, but that was moot now.

Váltyr himself had never possessed that innate confidence. Despite all the psycho-conditioning, all the training, all the long decades of success, he had never quite been able to convince himself that he deserved his place among the honoured of the Rout. His matchless prowess with the blade didn't mask that. He knew he pushed his reputation too far, testing it too often, forcing others to take him on. He was aware that they resented it, thinking that he delighted in humiliating them and proving his superiority.

They were wrong about that. The duels, the tests – they were a compulsion rather than a desire. He had even begun to wonder whether he wanted to be beaten, just once, just so he could look himself in the eye in the mirror and know truly that his limits had been reached.

That was the strange thing about success. It was useless in disproving the nagging, whispering notion he'd been unable to shake ever since ascending into the Blood Claws: that he was a fraud, that he wasn't quite as good as his results indicated, and that one day he'd be found out; that one day, when it really mattered, he'd let the pack down.

Váltyr, like all his brothers, was immune from fear in battle, but he'd never been immune from that anxiety. No matter how hard he trained, no matter how deadly he became in the practice cages, the quiet voice in his mind would never quite go away.

It is good that we are always forced to fight, he thought grimly to himself, watching the city burn below him. *It prevents us spending any time with ourselves.*

The last of the mortal troops, some dragging their wounded behind them, crossed the bridge. The enormous doors under the central arch slowly ground together, leaving only a narrow gap for the Wolves to slip through. After that, when they were all in, the breach would be sealed.

Váltyr walked down the shallow slope, away from where the bridge met the cleared land. Ahead of him, still a long way off and half shrouded by smoke and night shadow, lay the jagged, toothless line of buildings. Many were little more than skeletal ruins, bombed empty and glowing like angry coals. The rest were deserted, dark and hollowed out, their old inhabitants slain or cowering behind the inner walls. From beyond their see-saw profile came the dull roar of battle, a distant sighing like the surge of the ocean.

He sniffed. Something unusual laced the air, mingled amid the melange of foul smells rising from the lower city as if purposively concealed there. The hairs on his forearms rose.

He walked further down, his boots crunching through the rubble, drawing steadily closer to the line of ruins. Visibility was poor, even with his superb eyesight: the air had been turned into a miasma of spores and smoke.

'Whelp?' he voxed into the comm, wondering how far Haflof had moved away.

No answer came. The Blood Claw's channel was unobtainable. That was strange; perhaps interference from the electrostatic in the air.

Váltyr drew to a halt, sword in hand, peering into the gloom. For a few moments more he saw nothing beyond the penumbral silhouettes of the ruins backlit by a lurid red-green sky.

'Will you stand against me, I wonder?' came a voice from the darkness.

Váltyr tensed. The voice was astonishing – a thick, wet purr of indolent malice that seemed to rise from the ground around him. It was like Gunnlaugur's, only deeper and more throatily resonant. After-echoes of the words hung amid the spores, whispering on in a faint chorus of weary mockery.

'Show yourself,' snarled Váltyr, keeping his blade raised.

'And it is a question to be asked,' slurred the voice, 'what valour still resides with the Emperor's lapdogs?'

The curtains of darkness seemed to sigh aside. A brume of ash and filth shuddered away, exposing a lone warrior standing beneath the shadow of the ruins.

As soon as Váltyr laid eyes on him his hearts started thumping. Killurge surged through his bloodstream, spiking his muscles. His pupils dilated under his helm and his lips pulled back in a fang-thick sneer.

'Contact,' he voxed over the pack-wide channel. 'Ighala Gate. One got past you, Skullhewer.'

He had no time for any more.

The Plague Marine lumbered closer, emerging from the darkness like a sepulchral leviathan hauling clear of the deeps.

The Traitor was huge, far taller and broader even than Olgeir. His armour might once have been Terminator plate, though the centuries had ravaged, swelled and altered it. The plates had fused together and thickened, merging into a leathery hide of scaly, semi-jointed segments. Raw flesh pushed and burst through the remaining gaps, bleached and glistening like fat. A long cavity ran across the monster's torso exposing glossy loops of entrails within. Every surface was crusted with a bizarre mix of rust patches and angry lesions, as if the substances had fused halfway between organic and inorganic matter and become prone to the infections of both.

The creature strode through the rubble on two massive cloven hooves, and each cumbersome tread sank deep into the earth below. Two immense fists carried thick-bladed cleavers. One blade ran with a constant drip-feed of blood; the other slopped viscous trails of pus. Cloaks of black-bellied insects swirled around the blades like shrouds. Two long tusks curved out from the creature's distended jawline, each one wet with thin layers of saliva. A single eye sat amid a domed helm, glowing green through a jagged frame of broken ceramite.

Váltyr recognised the profile. This was the monster that had been in de Chatelaine's vid-footage.

'We had not expected Wolves here,' the Traitor said. Just as the witch in the ravine had done, he sounded only marginally interested. 'Your presence, though, makes this turgid exercise just a little more consequential.'

Váltyr held his ground. He wondered how long it would be before Gunnlaugur could respond to the summons. He guessed that the Death Guard champion far outmatched him. He might outmatch all of them.

'We were fated to be here,' said Váltyr calmly. He let his muscles fall into their habitual loose state of readiness. He would need to be as fast as he had ever been. *Holdbítr* trembled momentarily in his grip, like a stallion eager for the hunt. 'We were fated to halt this.'

'Perhaps,' said the creature, coming to a halt a few metres before Váltyr. He loomed above him, bloated and immense. 'You were always fatalistic souls.'

Váltyr studied his enemy closely, trying to spy weaknesses in its twisted armour.

'Know this,' he said proudly, seeing none. 'I am called *sverdhjera* of Járnhamar. A thousand souls have been extinguished by my blade.

When you greet your gods in the cold tombs of Hel, tell them Váltyr of Fenris was the one that ended you.'

The monster bowed.

'An honour, Váltyr of Fenris,' he said, with no obvious irony. 'To return the courtesy, I am named Thorslax the Blighted, exalted of the plague-host of the Traveller. I have walked both mortal and immortal planes since the days when your ruddy-cheeked primarch drank oaths to the Throne of Terra and pretended to be more savage than he was. I too have killed more men than I could ever count.' The creature chuckled mordantly. 'It grows tedious, after a time. Everything grows tedious. That is the curse of this war. I long for it to be over.'

He raised his twin cleavers and they shed their gruesome coating like runnels in a storm.

'And it *will* be over, Space Wolf,' he said. 'Do you not guess what is happening here? This is the beginning, the first stirrings of the plague that will consume the galaxy. You cannot stop it now. It starts here, and on a hundred other worlds, but it will all end in Cadia. All that remains for you is the slow death that follows the sickness. You have all been sick for too long. Let us end the agony.'

Váltyr allowed the abomination to speak. He had heard such screeds before and paid the detail little heed.

'Finished?' he asked, assuming the stance, bringing *holdbítr* into guard. 'Then make the first move.' He smiled coldly, feeling the first pulses of joy in his lethal craft. 'I always allow my prey the first move.'

Chapter Twenty-One

Ingvar tore through the night, veering between the ruins at full tilt. Since passing under the Ighala Gate and breaking into the lower city he'd only had one destination in mind. It reared above the houses as it always had done, vast and forbidding, striking up into the roiling clouds like a three-pronged claw.

The streets belonged to the enemy now. The serried tides of the damned crawled up through the burning remnants of what had once been Hjec Aleja's main urban zone. The main body of the enemy host marched relentlessly towards the Ighala Gate, driving in huge columns through the devastation. Fringe detachments peeled off from the main assault, loping through the wavering firelight and looking for defenders still breathing under the rubble.

Ingvar skirted around all of that, hugging the shadows and keeping to the lesser paths, breaking into combat only when he had to. When it came, his fights were quick and brutal – a dozen precision strikes from the spitting edge of *dausvjer* leaving the burst corpses of the damned lying face-up in the gutter.

Only as he neared the cathedral did the volume of enemy troops increase again. They had swarmed across the supplicants' courtyards and broken through the main doorway. Most of them were glass-eyed, shabby plague-bearers, still clad in the rags of their old Shakeh uniforms, but some, the ones who had landed from the plague-ships, were more heavily mutated, their outlines now only faintly human.

They didn't see him coming, occupied as they were with trying to push inside the cathedral to join the slaughter.

Given space in which to work, Ingvar picked up speed, leaping over the smoking remains of a gun emplacement and burning through into the courtyard beyond.

'Fenrys!' he roared, and his hoarse voice rang out into the night.

Taken by surprise, the enemy troops scattered before him. Only the most corrupted, those whose minds had been turned into slurry by the long, numbing years under the sway of dark gods, had the will to turn and fight.

It did them no good. Ingvar ripped through them, unleashing the full flood of his fury for the first time since boarding the plague-ship. He whirled around, punching a broad furrow into the midst of the crowds, breaking ribcages, cutting through paunches and snapping scrawny necks. Dausvjer's energy field blazed, throwing electric-blue sparks dancing across the morass of slack-skinned, pox-gnawed bodies.

He hewed a bloody path towards the gates, his progress barely slowed by the knots of fighters around him. More of them ran, scampering back into the shadows to huddle out of sight of his wrath; those that remained died quickly. As he passed under the shadow of the cathedral's ornate frontage, Ingvar kicked the last of them aside and crashed headlong through what remained of the doors.

The scene inside the nave was one of rampant desecration. Sacred icons had been ripped down and trampled over. Graven images of primarchs and cardinals had been cast to the floor, shattering against the marble. Smears of vomit and excreta were strewn over the walls, belched up by obscene, obese mutants with tiny piggish eyes and orbicular bellies. Shakeh's regimental standards had all been shredded and fires had been started all along the aisles, kindled on the flesh and fabric of the slain and catching on the timber of candle-racks and portrait frames.

Mutants ran amok, careening over upturned fonts and altars, shrieking and spitting and laughing in high, gurgling voices. Insects swarmed noisily over the growing pits of filth, scuttling freely across the stone, spilling from the eye-sockets of corpses and bursting from their stomachs.

Only at the high altar was there still a flicker of resistance. The banner of the Wounded Heart had been nailed to the pillar behind the dais, just under the baroque sculpture of the Emperor defeating Horus. It was riddled with bullet-holes and charred around the edges, but the black and red sigil could still be made out. Heaps of bodies, the majority of them mutated or swollen with disease, piled up high on every side, a testament to the tenacity of the defenders' last stand.

'For the Allfather!' Ingvar bellowed. His voice surged up into the vaults, echoing in the dark spaces and resounding down the long aisles.

The mutants turned from their slaughter. When they saw him coming – crackling with the tight burn of his energy weapon, his lenses blazing red like fresh-cut heartsblood, his massive armour plates smeared with the liquid remains of their fallen comrades – they broke into a feral mass of shrieking. They surged towards him in a tumbling, crashing wave, ignited into sudden terror, hatred and bloodlust.

Ingvar thundered into them, his blade whipping around him in wide sweeps. His body arched and swayed as he moved, thrown into a whirl of power and poise. *Dausvjer* ceased to be a weapon and became a part of him, an extension of the killing potential he'd unleashed. It rose and fell, danced and flickered, tearing up rotten flesh and carving through atrophied bones. He crunched, stabbed, crushed and shattered, throwing the tattered remains of the slain away before piling into the wavering throngs that remained.

The gangs of mutants and cultists held firm while their numbers remained, but as he sliced through their ranks their green eyes began to waver. Fear shuddered through them like a wave, and the weakest began to peel away and slink back down the long nave.

'Flee while you can!' cried Ingvar, cutting more down with every two-handed swipe of his rune-sword. '*Death* has come among you!'

The rump of the horde broke then, finally giving up on the prize of the altar and scampering away from the unleashed kill-machine in their midst. Ingvar pursued the greatest of them, a needle-toothed monster with oyster-grey skin and flapping, barbed hands, plunging *dausvjer* into its neck and ripping it out in a grisly flourish. He spun round, primed for more slaying, only to see the rest racing away from him.

He switched weapons, pulling his bolter from its holster and firing one-handed. Shells sprayed across the nave, exploding and splintering against pillars and thudding wetly into the backs of the retreating horrors. Dozens fell under that ear-splitting barrage, adding to the heaps of mouldering bodies already staining the floor.

The barrage only stopped when the last of them had fallen. Ingvar released the trigger and the cathedral slowly fell silent. The results of his epic butchery stretched away from him – rank upon rank of twitching limbs, carpeting the marble in a melange of sagging, clotting meat.

By then he was close to the altar. He strode slowly towards it, scanning the corpses at his feet for any yet living. He saw the bloodied uniforms of Shakeh Guardsmen mingled among the sore-raddled limbs of the damned, locked together in death as they had been in combat. It looked like they had held their positions until their ammunition had run out, resorting at the last to their knives, their lasgun-butts, their fists.

The bodies of five Battle Sisters were slumped amongst the slain, each one lying a little further up the steps of the dais. They had fallen back as far as they could, their empty flamers and bolters discarded on the way. Each of them was surrounded by a knot of corpses. They had killed dozens upon dozens; an honourable tally, one that reflected credit to their order.

Ingvar waded grimly onwards, seeking the one he knew would be there, whose fate it had been to defend her domain to the last. When he saw her at last, half buried under the grey hands of a fly-masked mutant, he thought she was dead. Her helm was gone and her dark skin was a mess of lacerations.

Ingvar crouched down, lifting the weight of her dead assailant from her and pushing it away. It was then that she drew in a faint breath. Her eyes flickered open, bleary at first but then clarifying.

Bajola looked up at him. She smiled.

'Your fate,' she croaked. 'To be here.'

Ingvar nodded, clearing more space around them, assessing the damage. Her breastplate had been punctured in three places. A jagged shard of iron protruded from a gash under her ribcage. Blood still oozed from the wound, pooling on the stone in thick dark slops. She didn't have long.

'As it was yours,' he replied, but his voice was bleak.

Hafloí descended into the bowels of the Halicon, his limbs throbbing. The pain still radiating across his body was an embarrassment, a constant reminder of the dark power that had shut him down so contemptuously. Even after his return to combat he knew he was not yet himself again. The weight of the witch's magick still plagued him, needling away at him like the memory of failure.

As he passed through the long trains of tunnels and twisting corridors, the ceiling-mounted lumens flickering as the big wall guns boomed, he was struck by the almost complete emptiness inside the citadel. The few remaining civilians too old or young to fight huddled inside bunkers dotted around the upper city. Everyone else manned the inner walls or the snaking battlements of the citadel. He'd walked past teenagers tottering under the weight of bolt-round cases, old women working in gangs to carry the bodies of the wounded to the field hospitals set up in chapels.

Once Hafloí might have felt contempt for that effort, but no longer. The mortals were making as much of a fight of it as they could. He'd seen the respect that Olgeir had for them and that had rubbed off on him a little. Perhaps he was growing up at last.

He kept moving, removing his helm as he went. Only then did he notice the damage done to his comms array. It looked burned out, eaten away by some stray gobbet of acid.

Hafloí smiled. Having some time to himself would be no hardship. Given what he intended to do, he might have been tempted to shut down the incoming feed in any case.

He looked down the long passage leading towards the apothecarion where he knew Baldr and Ingvar waited for him. The lumens along there were very dim, as if some localised power drain had taken the area grid down. He listened carefully.

No sounds at all; just the dim, ever-present roar of the battle taking place outside the walls.

He hesitated for a moment, doubting himself right at the last.

It would be easier to do what he'd been ordered to do. He certainly owed it to Baldr, not least for saving his life in the ravines, and Gunnlaugur's orders had been clear enough. The Gyrfalkon's blade was second only to Váltyr's in deadliness – it was needed on the walls.

So he almost did it. Hafloí nearly went on down to the medicae bays to take up his place watching over the stricken Fjolnir. Only at the last moment did he exhale his defiance, shake his head and ruffle his slicked-down hair, restoring its rust-orange spikiness.

He had never been good at following orders. The day would come when that rebelliousness was curbed, but it had not arrived yet. Battle called, and he intended to be a part of it.

Working hard to suppress a mischievous smirk, Hafloí turned on his heel and strode off in the opposite direction.

'So close,' he muttered to himself, disbelieving, now looking forward to more of the action that made his blood burn and his hearts pump. 'Really. I nearly did what they told me to. Blood of Russ, what am I turning *into*?'

Váltyr moved with all the perfection of his long training. His body flowed like water, propelled further by his armour, darting and wheeling with a velocity that belied his ceramite-heavy bulk. *Holdbítr* snaked around him, flashing in the firelight, the blade blurring with speed.

His opponent was not fast. Thorslax moved like his arms were weighed down by lead chains. His body swung around cumbersomely, sloughed in the bloody mud that sucked at his hooves. His twin cleavers were hurled about, seemingly at random, with careless, ill-aimed strokes. The stinking cloud of spores and insects spiralled around him, drifting in the wake of the blades.

For all that, Váltyr's rune-wound blade made little impact on the monster's hide. Thorslax barely tried to evade the strokes. He angled his huge body into the path of them, gurgling with delight whenever Váltyr managed to slant a cut in.

'Well *done*,' he would chortle. 'Very quick. Very nice.'

Váltyr kept his head. He worked methodically, avoiding the trajectories of the cleavers, staying close to his enemy and seeking the vulnerable spot. Despite unbroken hours of combat he felt alert and poised.

His foe's almost cheerful boredom was something he had encountered before. The Death Guard had learned to revel in their degradation. If some small part of them retained a sense of horror at what physical depths their primarch's treachery had forced on them, then it was deeply buried under layers of superficial contentment. They had ceased to suffer under the onslaught of the diseases that ravaged and wasted their sinews; they had *become* those diseases.

That no longer appalled him. It didn't enrage him. Váltyr was not a hot-blood like his brothers; he sought a way to use it, to lever the knowledge against the creature he faced. There would be a weakness; there was always a weakness.

Thorslax took a heavy stride forwards, his whole body shuddering as the hoof landed. His swollen arms flailed as he hurled the bloody cleaver in at Váltyr's shoulder. Váltyr ducked away, leaning out of danger before plunging in again, aiming his blade at Thorslax's gut-spilling stomach. The point punched deep, sliding between nests of polyps, doing no damage that he could see.

Váltyr wrenched it clear just as the pus-dripping cleaver hammered down. He spun out of the encounter, feeling the metal's edge hiss past his shoulder guards. Then he was back in tight, dancing through more heavy blows, probing for some way to do damage.

'So can you hold me here until your brothers arrive?' mused Thorslax, his voice a moist drawl. His single eye glanced up at the distant bridge, then back down. 'And even then, would it help you?'

Váltyr redoubled the flurry of strikes. As fast as he worked, Thorslax's defence responded. Though his individual movements were slow, the Blighted seemed able to anticipate what he was going to do, as if part of his soul somehow existed fractionally ahead of time.

Despite that he almost connected with a blistering sideways swipe, a blow that would have surely sliced Thorslax's chest-cabling away, but the bloody cleaver jammed down, clashing with *holdbítr* in a shower of sparks.

'Fast,' Thorslax observed appreciatively. 'You're really very good. Were I younger I would toy with you for longer.'

Váltyr charged back in, hauling his blade around two-handed, hacking at the creature's implacable defence. His blade bounced from Thorslax's hide, barely scratching the corrupted flesh-plates. The impact rocked him, though; it pushed the creature back down the slope, forcing him to use his weapons in defence.

'But I am not younger,' Thorslax remarked. 'I am *so* old. And you have become boring.'

Suddenly, his movements changed. His fists flew out, far faster than before. Váltyr saw the change and adjusted, bringing his blade into guard. The metal connected with a radial shudder, sending Váltyr rocking backwards. The green light bleeding from Thorslax's eye-socket flared. He seemed to grow even larger, swelling and bursting with grotesque, bulging growths. The swarm of flies reared up over him like a wind-whipped cloak.

Váltyr didn't flinch. He corrected his stance and brought his blade round for the parry, twisting the metal before him in a tight, glittering curve. Thorslax bore down, loosing a torrent of cleaver-strikes in quick succession. Váltyr parried the first few but the rain continued, flying in with deadening force. The impact was incredible – jarring, dense blows that cracked the ground beneath them and sent the rubble skittering.

Thorslax grunted. He sounded surprised.

'Very good,' he murmured, pressing the attack. 'Really very good.'

But then one got through – a cleaver thunked into Váltyr's breastplate, biting through the armour-plate and deep into the flesh beneath. Váltyr twisted away, ignoring the pain and keeping *holdbítr* moving.

The wound unbalanced him, though. His left shoulder fell, opening up a gap. Thorslax pounced, hurling the pus-drenched blade in hard. It connected with Váltyr's neck, cutting deep and severing the shielding under his helm.

Váltyr's vision went black. He pressed forwards, feeling his hands go numb but still seeking the elusive way through. Blood ran down his breastplate, cascading across the runes graven across his chest and sinking into the channels.

Thorslax had stopped talking by then. He was fighting hard, wheezing through his rusty vox-grille, concentrating furiously. His cleavers, now both dripping with Váltyr's own blood, flew up and down, hacking and chopping. Both fighters landed blows, and for the first time Váltyr's strokes seemed to hurt. Each of them piled on the pain, locked together in a brutal close-range dance of hew and counter-hew.

'Enough!' Thorslax cried, raising both fists up and slamming them down on Váltyr's reeling defence.

Váltyr got his sword up just in time, bracing the blade against the impact, but his strength was gone. *Holdbítr* broke asunder with a hard clap like thunder, its rune-strength broken. Thorslax's cleavers plunged down, burying themselves deep into Váltyr's chest and puncturing both hearts. The monster then ripped them out, dragging trails of blood and flesh with them.

Váltyr stayed on his feet for a few moments more, his chest torn open, his arms limp. His vision was gone. The pain had left him, replaced by a cold nimbus that raced up his limbs towards his brain.

Thorslax withdrew without saying another word, already turning to face new enemies. Dimly, as if from a long way off, Váltyr could hear the battle-cries of Gunnlaugur closing in, as familiar to him as his own voice. He'd heard that cry across the war-torn continents of a hundred worlds. He could hear Olgeir's cries as well, and Jorundur's. The pack had arrived.

He collapsed to his knees, watching his lifeblood drain from him. His shattered sword, the weapon he had carried for over a century and whose soul he had come to know better than any living man's, lay before him in the gravel.

None shall wield it but me, he thought with a final, grim satisfaction, seeing how irreparably the sword had been destroyed.

They had died together. That, at least, was fitting.

Then, his consciousness draining away into darkness, Váltyr toppled forwards, crashing atop the shards of his beloved *holdbítr*, and moved no more.

Ingvar held Bajola's broken body carefully. She felt impossibly fragile. He could feel her heart beating, shallow and fluttering like that of a trapped bird.

Her skin was grey. The ebony richness of it had faded and it looked matt and grainy in the gloom.

'They will come back soon,' she warned.

'When they do, I will kill them.'

Bajola nodded wearily. 'That is what you excel at.'

'Of course. Someone has to.'

Bajola's eyes momentarily lost focus and her head lolled. She recovered, but the spirit was draining out of her quickly.

'You said you'd tell me what your name meant,' she said.

'Now?'

Bajola nodded.

'Gunnlaugur gave it to me,' Ingvar said, speaking softly, feeling like he was wasting precious time. 'He called me that on the eve of my departure from the home world. He decreed it would be my pack name, since I had no other.'

Ingvar remembered the way Gunnlaugur had been then: wounded by his decision to leave even though he'd striven to hide it. A strange look had lit up Gunnlaugur's eyes in those last days. Unhappiness, certainly, but something else. Envy, perhaps.

'And by that he wished to bind you to him,' said Bajola.

Ingvar paused, surprised that she knew so much of their ways.

'The gyrfalkon always comes back,' he said. 'It ranges far but always returns. That was what he was telling me: that I had to return.'

Bajola looked at him with an indulgent smile on her dying face.

'Oh, Ingvar,' she said. 'You did return, and it has not given you what you hoped for.' She swallowed painfully. 'But at least you killed with honour here. That is why you were bred. Or do you choose?'

'Choose?'

She swallowed again. Blood collected on her lips.

'To be what you are, or to be mortal.'

It was so long ago. He had been selected when near death, pulled from the ice by the Priest with the wolf-mask. After that, all he remembered was pain, and instruction, and fear.

'I do not think so,' he said.

Bajola's lids looked heavy.

'I chose,' she said. 'I could have been anything. A scholar. A diplomat. I excelled at it all. But I chose the Sisterhood. Why was that? At times I think I wasted myself. Or maybe I didn't choose at all. Maybe it was my... What do you call it? Wyrd.'

Ingvar felt her heartbeat grow weaker as he held her. Time was running out.

'Why did you destroy the archives?' he asked.

By then Bajola was too weak to bother hiding the truth.

'Secrets,' she said.

'Of your Order?'

'No, not this one.' She tried to lift her head. Ingvar lowered his. He could smell the copper of blood on her neck and face. 'Pointless, no? We were always destined to die here. But old habits. They made us thorough. Completeness.'

Her voice got fainter with every breath. Ingvar had to crane his neck to hear the words over the distant crackle of flames.

'Hjortur's name was stored in there. On a list. A kill-list. A list of those to be killed.'

She was beginning to ramble.

'Hjortur was killed by greenskins,' said Ingvar gently.

'No,' said Bajola, smiling again. 'No, he wasn't. He was killed by the Fulcrum.'

'The what?'

Bajola's face creased into a mask of concentration. She was slipping away. Every breath she took added to the trickle of blood that ran down her chin.

'Look up,' she rasped.

Ingvar did so. The golden mask of the Emperor stared back down at him. Its face was cherubic, surrounded by a spiked halo. The expression on the mask was oddly mournful.

'Their mark has been here all along,' said Bajola. Wincing from the pain, she reached down to her weapon belt and withdrew a small golden bauble. She pressed it into Ingvar's hand. When he looked down at it, he saw a miniature facsimile of the golden mask – a thumb-sized cherub-face ringed with spikes.

'Do you really want to know this truth, *Fenryka*?' she asked, teasingly using Juvykka as if born to it. 'You will be honour-sworn to avenge him, will you not?'

Ingvar said nothing. The golden-faced cherub smiled stupidly at him, its metallic surface glinting in the firelight.

'You think you know so much,' she said, as mockingly as her frailty would allow. 'You are the thinker among them, the one who has learned to doubt. You, out of all your brutal brothers, might understand that some wars never show themselves.'

Ingvar felt frustration rise within him. He needed her to speak plainly, but in her delirium she was drifting into incoherence.

'I didn't want you here,' she mumbled. 'I argued against it. The Adulators posed no problem; they were dutiful and unimaginative. But Wolves? On Ras Shakeh?'

Bajola let slip a bitter laugh, and more blood bubbled up between her lips.

'Once that argument failed, I should have destroyed the archive. I don't know why I didn't.'

Ingvar caught the first faint sounds of enemy troops creeping back towards them. It would not be long before they forgot their fear and re-entered the nave.

'I cannot save you, Sister,' he said softly. 'But you can make our meeting on this world worth something. Tell me what you know.'

Bajola looked up at him. Her deep brown eyes moistened. Some resolve returned.

'More of you will die,' she said. 'They are coming for you now, and they will never stop. They will never tire, never forget. You will not even know you are being hunted. Killed by greenskins, lost in the warp, turned to darkness – those are the stories that will find their way back to Fenris. You make too many enemies, Space Wolf.'

An explosion went off within a few hundred metres of their position. The pillars around them shuddered. The dull thud of mutant feet falling echoed out across the nave, still distant but circling closer.

'Tell me,' growled Ingvar, feeling her go limp in his hands, growing impatient with the evasion.

Bajola smiled at him, her eyes losing their focus and growing dim.

'I did tell you,' she croaked loosely. 'The *Fulcrum*, Gyrfalkon. Take the name, take the golden face. Use them.'

She tried to lift her hand and failed. Her breathing slowed to nothing.

'Against my judgement, I liked you,' she said, her voice little more than an expiring sigh. 'I hope you survive.'

Then her body stiffened, going taut. Her spine arched, holding in place for a heartbeat.

She went slack, her mouth falling open.

Ingvar held her for a while longer, staring at her. The rest of the battle became an irrelevance. He felt as if he'd been in the cusp of something, prevented at the last by Bajola's intransigence, or perhaps just frustrated by time slipping away.

He opened the palm of his gauntlet and looked at the tiny golden face resting there. It gazed back at him, smiling benignly. It looked like any pilgrim's trinket; nothing special, nothing rare or valuable.

The Fulcrum.

It meant nothing.

Ingvar heard her last words echoing in his mind.

They are coming for you now, and they will never stop.

Who? Why?

You make too many enemies, Space Wolf.

The noise of boots rang down the nave. They had got close by then, edging forwards, hugging the walls.

Ingvar rose, lowering Bajola's head carefully to the stone. He placed the cherub's head safely in a clasped capsule at his belt. Only then did he turn, thumbing *dausvjer*'s energy field into luminosity. Ahead of him, perhaps twenty metres away, a crowd of cowled faces jostled against one another, their pale eyes shining in the dark. For once they looked scared, torn between a desire to kill and the knowledge of what they faced.

Ingvar started to walk towards them, swinging his blade lazily to free up his arm. His mind was still racing, trying to digest what Bajola had told him. The presence of plague-bearers in the cathedral was an irritation he could have done without.

'A bad time to take me on, filth,' he snarled, lowering his gaze and picking the first one to die. 'A *very* bad time.'

Chapter Twenty-Two

The lower city was gone, lost to the enemy, now little more than a haunt of unrestrained slaughter and madness. The last of the trenches had been breached and the hordes of mutants, cultists and pestilence-ridden foot soldiers tramped up from the depths, their cold eyes fixed on the summit. The Halicon citadel reared up above all of them, still inviolate despite the bruise-purple pall that swirled above it, its flanks lit a dull crimson by the wavering light of a thousand fires. Down from the citadel's extravagant battlements stood the precarious ring of the inner walls, still held by the city's defenders. The battered Ighala Gate endured at the centre of that defensive line, bursting with anti-infantry weaponry that flashed and burned into the spore-heavy night.

If the advance had been quicker the gate might already have fallen. As it was the hosts of plague-damned still moved slowly, trudging up through smouldering ruins with their stumbling, ill-directed gaits. Hundreds of them had drifted into the shadows, distracted by isolated pockets of survivors and the prospect of feasting on fresh flesh. Others had succumbed to the virulent contagion that coursed through their veins, collapsing to the ground as their stomachs burst asunder or their hearts gave out. The gifts of the Plaguefather were capricious things, as likely to curse as they were to bless.

So it was that in answering Váltyr's call, Gunnlaugur was able to outpace the closing circle of invaders and sprint clear of the advancing battlefront. Olgeir, fresh from a hard-fought victory over the third Plague Marine down by the outer perimeter, joined him in the chase. His armour had taken heavy damage during the encounter and he'd discarded his heavy bolter.

'Tough kill?' asked Gunnlaugur, running heavily.

'They always are,' spat Olgeir, working hard to keep up. 'Pox-ridden bastards.'

Jorundur joined up with them as they neared the cleared wasteland before the Ighala crossing.

'So what is this?' the Old Dog demanded, his strained voice betraying a rare tightness. 'Did he say?'

Gunnlaugur said nothing but ran hard, his hearts thumping viciously.

One got past you, Skullhewer.

Váltyr's voice had been almost resigned over the comm; whatever it was that had broken ranks and pushed ahead to the bridge had knocked the kill-relish out of him. That was almost certainly bad.

'I see it!' roared Olgeir, his voice suddenly thick with kill-urge.

The landscape of ruins gave way before them, opening out into the charred and desolate wasteland just within sight of the bridge. Directly ahead of them, out on the trawled mounds of debris, was the object of Váltyr's summons – a vast and engorged champion in a distended mockery of Terminator plate. He must have teleported ahead of the rest of his sluggish minions, aiming to break the defence at the gates before the defenders had time to rally behind them.

An arrogant decision, one that spoke of misplaced confidence.

'*Fenrys Hjolda!*' thundered Gunnlaugur, swinging *skulbrotsjór* wildly around him as he tore up the slope.

Olgeir and Jorundur joined in the chorus, hurling battle-challenges out like berserks of the Old Ice. They could all see Váltyr being hammered backwards, his armour taking heavy damage from repeated cleaver impacts.

For all their speed, for all their blistering rage, they arrived too late. As Gunnlaugur sped into contact, he could only watch as Váltyr's blade was broken and the *sverdhjera*'s chest was ripped open.

An explosion of grief surged up from his breast. Black fury blazed out of him, kindled in the furnace of his pumping hearts and emerging as a strangled roar of revulsion. Gunnlaugur charged towards the monster like a Rhino careering along at full tilt, lost in a maelstrom of horror and loosed ferocity.

Thorslax turned slowly to face him, his body moving with ponderous clumsiness. His single glowing eye stared down at them, spearing through the murk of the seamy night.

'*More* of you,' he murmured.

The three Wolves hit him almost in unison, crashing into combat with the force of a hurricane, limbs tearing, blades flashing. All four warriors clashed under the lightning-laced storm clouds: one enormous and reeking with millennial corruption, three as vital and vivid as sun-dazzled snow. They ripped into a spinning, crashing cacophony of fearsome blows, each strike landing with the power to crush bone, to dent armour, to pulverise flesh.

Gunnlaugur was ahead of the others by a hair's breadth, his hammer scything imperiously. Olgeir was next, his short blade spiralling, clasped tight in both burly hands. Jorundur brought up the rear, adding his axe-head to the driving wall of steel.

Thorslax was hurled backwards in the face of that coordinated mass. His arms pumped like the pistons of a great war engine, parrying the furious rate of incoming strikes and hitting back with punching cleaver-blows of his own.

Though outnumbered and off guard, his huge bulk gave him a telling advantage. His strength, like all of his kind, was virtually infinite. He absorbed a whole barrage of blows, any one of which would have ended a lesser warrior. *Skulbrotsjór* crashed into his leathery armour plates, driving in the warped ceramite but not breaking it. The Wolves' blades bit deep but did not draw blood. Thorslax was pummelled, battered, beaten back – but not wounded.

As the shock of the first assault was absorbed, Thorslax began to reassert himself. His cleavers cycled with greater intent – not just in defence, but into the attack. He towered above his assailants, and began to use his greater heft and reach. Jorundur was the first to be thrown out of the attack, his right shoulder guard gouged open.

'*Fara tíl Hel, svikari!*' bellowed Gunnlaugur, rolling onwards, hauling *skulbrotsjór* in monstrous arcs. The air seemed to ignite in the wake of the blazing hammerhead. His massive body was a blur of wanton movement. He swung heavily before piling in deep, every gesture loaded with lethal intent. He and Olgeir pressed on, each working seamlessly around the other.

Thorslax uttered no words. He laboured hard at the heart of the breaking storm, striving not be overcome by it. Gunnlaugur landed a searing crack on his turning spine, causing him to roar out loud. Olgeir leapt into a rare gap in his defence, chopping down deep into his thigh, finally producing a jet of oil-black blood from the wound. Jorundur regained his feet and staggered back into range, his axe held ready.

For all their skill, though, for all their strength, Váltyr's judgement had been right: Thorslax was a foe beyond them. His body had been ruined and changed by the slow arts of the Eye, fused with his living armour and shot through with the undiluted virulence of the Plaguefather. His hearts beat with the slow, grinding rhythm of millennia and his blood coursed with the slurry of infinite mutation. No mortal weapon, no matter how skillfully wielded, could break through the aegis of foulness that swept around him, knitting together his rotten thews and animating his disease-riddled organs.

He was an avatar of the plague, suffused with all its poisons and its delights, as indomitable as mortality, as invincible as the dragging entropy that wearied all living things.

He was despair. He was fatigue. He was the essence of mortality in all its putrid, failing imperfection.

Thorslax punched out, throwing Olgeir clear, sending the huge warrior grinding into the rubble on his back. Then the cleavers whirled, beating Jorundur a second time. The Old Dog fell to his knees, clutching at his mangled shoulder.

For a little while longer Gunnlaugur and Thorslax fought on alone, hammer and cleaver battering away at one another, splintering armour and denting metal. The Wolf Guard fought with all the bull-hearted resolve of his conditioning, giving no quarter, powering on after his prey with both speed and power. When *skulbrotsjór* made contact, the sharp crack of the energy field discharging was like the snap of lightning forking down from the heavens; when Thorslax's cleavers connected, the dull boom was like Arjac's hammerhead striking the iron anvil. The two of them like gods duelling at the fire-wreathed end of the universe, outstripping all other powers in their extravagant, unrestrained wrath.

As they hacked and hewed at one another, unnoticed by any of them, the city's ruins behind them slowly filled with green points of light. Mutants limped out of the gloom, their gas masks bulging and deflating as they drew in the airborne miasma. They hung back amid the cover of the shattered rockcrete, unwilling to break cover entirely. With every passing second, though, more of them gathered in the shadows. The vanguard of the enemy host had caught up with its standard bearer.

Olgeir scrambled to his knees, cursing. Jorundur rose more slowly, his armour covered in blood. They started to limp back into range, both moving stiffly.

Neither of them was unable to prevent the strike that floored Gunnlaugur. Thorslax lashed round with uncharacteristic speed, catching the

Wolf Guard in the throat with the blunt edge of his blood-cleaver. Gunnlaugur, off balance and moving too late, was hurled clear of the bulbous mutant, sailing through the air in a bloody swathe, his limbs splayed. Thorslax lumbered after him, striding across the scorched earth like a vengeful Titan.

'And so it ends,' he slurred.

The pack had thrown everything it had at him, and had still come up short. Thorslax was barely wounded; all three Wolves were prone, exhausted and bleeding. The champion of Mortarion stalked across to Gunnlaugur for the kill, his throaty voice wheezing from exertion.

He raised his cleavers, holding them both high, but then the guttural noises died in his calloused throat. Ahead of them all, dim at first under the walls of the besieged upper city, something had broken across the tortured landscape, lighting up the earth beneath it with a sick smear of witchlight. A new fire burned brightly in the night, though its flames were lurid rather than vivid.

As Thorslax watched, his interest suddenly piqued, a lone figure swept down from the bridge towards them, his limbs dark against the raging backdrop of illumination.

Thorslax looked dumbstruck. Then, as the strange warrior drew closer, he relaxed, and a moisture-damp laugh finally broke from his cracked lips. The fire-cloaked newcomer slowed down, striding awkwardly across the craters and ruins, swathed in a dirty corona of whipping green flame.

'Welcome, brother,' said Thorslax bowing in greeting. 'I see that our ranks are set to swell again.'

Gunnlaugur twisted round blearily, still reeling from the blow that had felled him. Olgeir and Jorundur did likewise.

Baldr stood before them, panting slurrily. Trails of saliva hung below his sore-mottled chin, trembling as his loose-jawed face stared out sightlessly into the night. Snaking lines of ether-force scurried across his marsh-grey armour. His eyes were pupil-less and blazed with a pale silver light. Swirling skeins of energy obscured his features, though the lesions clustering around his lips and eyes could still be made out. Silver flame spilled from the corners of his mouth, as if he were filled to overspilling with the blinding power of the warp. His clenched fists crackled and twisted with a growling aegis of witchlight.

'Brother!' cried Olgeir, his voice thick with surprise and horror. He staggered towards the flaming outline.

Baldr didn't turn to face him. He extended a fist in Olgeir's direction and a fork of diseased lightning, black-edged like tarnished steel, cracked into the big warrior's chest, throwing him back to the ground again.

Olgeir landed awkwardly, his back arched in pain, flickers of lightning blistering and dancing across his battle-plate.

Thorslax chuckled. 'A corrupted Son of Russ,' he murmured. 'Quite an achievement.'

He walked towards Baldr, stretching out his massive hand.

'My bro–' he began.

He never finished the sentence.

Baldr exploded. His fists swung around and thrust out before him. Blazing arcs of black-edged lightning leapt out, latching on to Thorslax's neck and twisting into it like an electric current. The Traitor froze, locked in place by columns of witchlight. His limbs went stiff; his cleavers dropped to the earth.

Baldr never said a word. The boiling clouds above him broke open and spears of the world's lightning, as green-tinged as the clouds of warp-essence around his eyes, licked and flickered against his slime-crusted armour.

Thorslax tried to retreat, to pull away from the shimmering spikes that impaled him, but Baldr hauled him back, sending shards lancing into his enormous body. Dagger-edged flickers snaked under the Traitor's battle-plate, ripping it up and exposing blubber-pale flesh beneath. Thorslax's limbs jerked, pierced by glimmering lines of plague-green and warp-silver, locked down amid a nimbus of blazing energies, just as Baldr had been in the ravines.

The Traitor champion tried to fight it. As flakes fell from his armour, crisping and burning amid the veil of lightning, he tried to break free. He managed a single step, crying out from the effort as his huge, swollen leg swung through the fizzing electrical storm.

Baldr hardly seemed aware of what he was doing. His blazing, mono-chrome silver eyes glared wildly. His fists stayed extended, feeding on the lashing columns of tainted warp-energy.

Thorslax held on for a moment longer, outstretched fingers trembling. Then, with a sick crack, his helm fell open, briefly exposing a twisted and blood-blotched face locked in a scream of unbearable agony. Pus-filled lesions burst apart, spewing their yellow contents across his blistering armour plates. His skin stripped away, melting and crisping as it was devoured. Cracks shot up his battle-plate, latticing like atrophied bone. Fragments of it burst clear, shattered into dust by the raw ether-matter that coursed across and through it.

The silver fire consumed what was left, burning through raddled skin and metastasised tissue. Organs popped open, shedding greasy gouts of bile and plasma. Thorslax's screams died away into chokes as his throat was eaten away. His chest caved in, his limbs twisted and snapped, his eyeballs liquidised.

When the storm finally died out, all that remained at its centre were a few thick chunks of burned ceramite. Baldr finally let his hands drop, and the last pieces of Thorslax's war-plate toppled over, half buried in a heap of smoking, rotten meat-chunks.

For a few moments, no one moved. Baldr rocked back on his heels, his arms hanging limp, his unseeing eyes staring emptily. Olgeir remained on the ground, still transfixed with pain. The crowds of plague-mutants congregating in the shadows held their positions, seemingly uncertain whether to fall at Baldr's feet or flee from him.

Jorundur moved first, gingerly inching towards Baldr.

'No,' hissed Gunnlaugur, ignoring the blaze of pain under his shattered gorget as he moved. 'Do not approach him.'

Baldr seemed not to see either of them. His breathing was heavy and snagging.

Gunnlaugur kept his distance, taking up his thunder hammer carefully, watching Baldr the whole time. Conflicting intuitions ran through him. Part of him, driven by his warrior instincts, urged him to take on the abomination, to end it before it consumed them all. He knew he should have done it when he'd had the chance.

But it was futile. If Baldr – or whatever had taken over Baldr – were capable of ripping through the Traitor champion with such ease then the idea of *him* taking him down was ludicrous. The raw power coursing through Baldr's diseased limbs was a force beyond anything he'd seen before, save perhaps in a master of the elements like Njal Stormcaller.

So Gunnlaugur stayed where he was, his weapon held tightly, breathing hard, waiting to see what Baldr would do next.

He did not have to wait long. As the last remains of Thorslax smouldered down into embers, Baldr suddenly looked up. His silver-flamed eyes stared out, past Gunnlaugur, past Olgeir and Jorundur, out into the burning mass of ruins beyond.

Baldr threw his head back. He cried out once – a horrifying, shrieking skirl of inhuman pain – and kicked off again into a limping run. He swooped down the slope, arms hanging loose, reeling madly. Flickers of unholy fire streamed behind him. He looked like a deranged spectre of ice-myths, a fragment of old nightmares conjured up into the world of the living.

The mutants scattered before him, letting him plunge unmolested back into the depths of the lower city. Powerless to prevent him, Gunnlaugur watched him go. A few last scraps of silver witchlight glimmered for a while in the dark, before they too faded into nothing.

With Baldr's departure, the scene around them returned to one of empty desolation. Olgeir managed to drag himself back to his feet, though his every movement looked shot through with pain. Jorundur had been mauled.

'What in Hel was that?' grunted Olgeir, his clipped voice giving away his torment.

Gunnlaugur gazed in the direction Baldr had fled. Only then did he feel how hard his hearts were beating.

'I do not know,' he said. 'And answers will have to wait.'

With the departure of Baldr the enemy had started moving again. They crept out from under the eaves of empty hab-shells and up from the shadows of blast craters, edging into the open along a long, ragged line that stretched across the entire battlefront. First dozens, then hundreds, then thousands became visible, all trudging up the slope towards the Ighala Gate with the same mute determination they'd shown since the opening hours of the siege.

In the face of such numbers the Wolves fell back, crossing the strip of cleared wasteland and backing up towards the bridge. For the first time since the battle had started, Gunnlaugur felt weariness lying heavily on his limbs. Olgeir could barely walk and Jorundur was in poor shape too. They had fought for three days with almost no respite and the battle against the Traitor champion had nearly finished them all. Though he still hefted his hammer, it now felt cripplingly heavy in his hands.

'A last stand on the bridge?' suggested Jorundur dryly. 'Worth a saga, perhaps.'

'We can hold them there,' growled Olgeir, optimistic as ever though his heavy breathing gave away his pain. 'I just need... a few moments.'

Gunnlaugur kept moving, watching the enemy spill out of the ruins and trudge up after them. A broad vanguard of mutants coalesced before him, driving out from the lower city and homing in on the walls. They never hurried, never speeded up, just murmured softly as they came, repeating the same inane whispering mantra they had always done. Gunnlaugur forced himself not to listen to it.

It was only then that he realised something about the situation was wrong. As he came under the shadow of the inner walls, falling back towards the bridge itself, he realised what it was – he shouldn't have been able to hear them at all.

'Why are the wall guns silent?' he asked, looking over his shoulder to the towering bastions of the Ighala gatehouse.

As soon as he looked up, the huge doors on the far side of the bridge began to open to the full, grinding heavily along on metal tracks. Out of the gap, marching in close-packed ranks, issued de Chatelaine's army.

They were the surviving regiments the canoness had held back for the final siege. Ranks of Guardsmen strode confidently out across the single span, all of them heavily swathed in chem-suits and hefting las-rifles. Among them marched a whole phalanx of Battle Sisters – heavily armoured Celestians with black cloaks and flamers, followed by the remaining Sororitas garrison. More Guardsmen followed in their wake, emerging in ordered ranks from the heart of the upper city.

Thousands had come – de Chatelaine was emptying the bastion. Battle standards swung up into place above them, displaying the Wounded Heart symbol proudly.

'Blood of Russ,' murmured Olgeir, watching the mortals draw up in assault formation on the near bank. 'They're breaking out.'

Jorundur started to laugh darkly.

'Excellent,' he said, buckling his axe to his belt and drawing his bolter. 'We'll all die together.'

At the sight of the sortie, Gunnlaugur felt his fatigue suddenly ebb. He strode closer to the bridge, seeking out the canoness.

De Chatelaine, her face masked behind her ebony helm and surrounded by her bodyguard, saw him first.

'Enough cowering!' she shouted, marching alongside her sisters. Her voice was tight with determination. 'Now we end this, one way or another.'

Gunnlaugur raised his hammer in salute.

'So be it,' he called. 'Our blades together.'

He turned back, looking across the wastes to where the enemy was advancing. They far outnumbered the defenders but their progress now looked strangely directionless. They were moving across the wasteland by instinct, driven onwards by their urge to attack the living, but no longer held together by a single intelligence.

With the champion gone, their will looked to be fragile. For all that, their sheer volume remained intact. De Chatelaine's gamble was a perilous one.

Gunnlaugur gathered himself to his full height, reactivating *skulbrotsjór*'s disruptor in a sharp fizz of energy.

'Come, brothers!' he snarled, feeling kill-urge kindle in him again. 'One last push.'

Jorundur fell in alongside.

'We'll need to hit them hard,' he said doubtfully.

'Aye,' said Olgeir, brandishing his blade and glowering down the slope. He looked like he was missing *sigrún*. 'We could really use some firepower now.'

As the words left his mouth, a thunderous, grinding roar suddenly broke out from behind them, briefly drowning the rush and crackle of the fires. The earth shook, rocked by the ignition of something massive far above them. Thousands of faces, defender and Traitor, turned in shock, gazing up to see what dreadful new engine of war had been unleashed on the city. Only the Wolves, as familiar with the sound of a Thunderhawk's engines as they were with their own voices, knew what had happened.

The gunship swooped down from the Halicon landing stages and flew low over the upper city, held precariously aloft on a dirty smudge of trailing smoke, its engines coughing sclerotically and its fuselage tilted heavily to one side. It lurched over the dividing gorge, barely clearing the inner walls and shedding huge gouts of flame from its labouring thrusters.

'The little *shit!*' breathed Jorundur, his voice heavy with outrage. 'He's taken *Vuokho!*'

Haflói's voice crackled over the pack-wide comm.

'*Hjá*, flat-feet!' he crowed, laughing in triumph. 'Follow me down!'

Then *Vuokho*'s spine-mounted battle cannon boomed out, hurling a withering barrage of shells deep into the heart of the enemy ranks. As they exploded in a rolling pall of conflagration the gunship's bolters opened up, bursting earth and splintering flesh. The barrage only lasted seconds, but a Thunderhawk could unleash a frightening amount of ordnance in that time. The entire vanguard of the enemy disappeared under a rolling cloudbank of shattering armour and flying shrapnel.

Then something broke open on *Vuokho*'s battered undercarriage. The gunship slewed violently to the left, dropping like a stone.

'He's killing it!' shouted Jorundur, furious now. 'Gods of ice and iron, I'll *murder* him!'

Vuokho dived steeply, its guns still hammering, until it crashed right into the heart of the horde, crushing hundreds of fleeing figures beneath its bulk as it ploughed deep into the earth and skidded messily down the slope. Its engines raged away for a few seconds longer, hurling streamers of blue flame into what remained of the plague-bearer vanguard. Even after being grounded its wing-mounted bolters continued to judder away, cutting bloody swathes through the shell-shocked troops reeling away from it.

Gunnlaugur laughed ferociously, lofting his hammer high and roaring his humour to the heavens. It felt like a long time since his lungs had opened up in mirth.

'The whelp shows the way!' he thundered. 'Now *charge*, faithful of Ras

Shakeh! *Break* them, and do not relent until you consign the last one of them to Hel!'

With a massed cheer the defenders surged down the slope towards the downed Thunderhawk. The mingled army of Guardsmen, Battle Sisters and Wolves swept across the ruinous landscape, on the front foot at last and with the light of vengeance in their eyes. Gunnlaugur and Olgeir burned along at the forefront, their wounds forgotten, their weapons swinging into position again.

For once, though, they were not the fastest. At the head of the army, moving faster than he had done in more than a hundred years of warfare, came Jorundur Kaerlborn, his limbs flailing and his battle-axe whirling around his head.

'He *killed* it!' he roared, his voice as baying and strident as all the unshackled hounds of Morkai. 'Blood of Russ, I'll *flay* him!'

Chapter Twenty-Three

Ingvar sped between burning buildings, pausing only to slay those unwary enough to stray into his path. The air around him was thick, a soup of toxins that lowered visibility to a few metres. Shells of hab-units loomed up out of the murk, their empty innards glowing.

None of the filth that tarried in the remains of the lower city was much of a threat to him – the biggest and most organised contingents of infantry had pushed ahead up the slopes, their eyes fixed on the summit. The scattered warbands that remained behind were sufficient to slow him down, though; they kept his blade busy in a series of bloody encounters. Ingvar had been fighting ever since leaving Bajola in the cathedral – fighting to get out of the despoiled nave, fighting to clear the courtyards, fighting to force a passage through the broken streets and rejoin the pack.

Only now was he making good progress. Something seemed to have rattled the enemy troops – they were scrambling up towards the citadel faster than ever, heedless of anything but the need to get out of the burning terraces of the lower city.

Ingvar ran along in their wake, loping purposively, keeping clear of the bigger detachments. He'd heard Váltyr's summons but after that the comm had died. A series of dull booms from beyond the Ighala Gate lit up the cloud-heavy sky, indicating something big had gone off, but otherwise he had little idea how matters stood at the inner wall.

He cleared the Cathedral district and started powering up the main route to Ighala when he heard the first scream break out. The noise was a grotesque amalgam of human and unhuman, as if mortal throat-cords had been wound around a core of daemonic madness. More than one voice raised in terror; the plague-damned were shrieking in panic along with... something else.

Ingvar hesitated, listening carefully. He recognised some of the strains within them, and that familiarity chilled him.

Ahead of him ran the thoroughfare that led, after many twists and switchbacks, to the upper city. On either side of him sprawled the maze of alleyways that tangled out across the burning urban zone, all of them sunk into shadow even as the flames licked through the shattered rock-crete around them. The screams came from inside that labyrinth of derelict masonry, fractured and echoing like dancing tomb spectres.

After a moment of indecision, he veered off into the darkness. It didn't take him long to discover the origin of the terror. A narrow passageway zigzagged into a warren of smaller paths, all of them narrow and tightly overlooked. Those led in turn to an octagonal courtyard surrounded by many-storeyed hab-blocks.

In the centre of the courtyard rose a slender tower of dark stone, ringed with skull-pattern friezes and ribbed with iron bands. The pillared icon of the Adeptus Ministorum adorned the lintel of the main gate, surrounded by tattered scraps of old battle standards. Twin doors hung from their hinges, shattered and gaping. A glimmer of ghoulish green light spilled out from within. Corpses, all of them tortured by plague, littered the courtyard. Their exposed skin was scorched black.

Ingvar kicked his way through the bodies and plunged inside. He was immediately struck by the foul stench – a noisome cocktail of decay, excreta and stale sweat. More bodies lay across the stone floor, each one stinking of charred flesh.

The tower interior was gloomy, unlit except for slit windows that ran around the circular walls. An old altar lay in the centre covered with broken candle-stands, vestment caskets and censers. A spiral stairway hugged the stone wall, snaking up to the floor above. The glimmer came from up there.

Ingvar vaulted up the stairs, keeping *dausvjer* unsheathed and activated. Its electric-blue light burned brightly in the dark.

Four levels up, past a series of rooms streaked with bloodstains and thick with corpses, a final chamber opened up in front of him. It had once been the private sanctum of the Ministorum adepts and was strewn with their paraphernalia: robes, scrolls, thuribles, ceremonial staves, polished skull-pendants.

Ingvar barely noticed any of that. His eyes were drawn to the stricken figure cowering against the far wall, hunched over as if dry-retching. Flickers of corpse-gas rippled across dull grey armour plates, flickering eerily in the obscurity.

He froze. For a moment, his mind would not let him believe what he was seeing. Only slowly did he reconcile the data given him by his senses with what must have been the case.

It was Baldr. Or rather, it was the thing that had once been Baldr.

His armour had darkened, as if a shadow had been draped across it and had somehow fixed to the ceramite. Glints of pale light, insubstantial and wavering, leaked out of every joint and opening. Liquid dribbles of it ran across the curved plate like globules of mercury, slowly fading to black and withering away. The illumination was piercing but somehow unhealthy, as poisonous as gall.

Ingvar stayed still. He kept his blade in position; its dull hum was the only sound aside from Baldr's desperate gasping.

Baldr never looked up. His flaming eyes remained fixed on the floor in front of him. His sore-edged mouth looked twisted in pain.

When Ingvar finally spoke, as softly as he could, it felt like he was breaking some kind of sanctity.

'Brother,' he said, taking a single step towards him. 'Fjolnir.'

Baldr's head snapped up. His empty eyes stared directly at Ingvar. For a split second his face betrayed a childlike confusion, the innocent agony of a soul adrift and in pain.

Then it twisted into fury. Baldr's fists clenched and silver-black lightning kindled quickly on the gauntlets.

Ingvar interposed his blade, backing away.

'Do not do this, brother,' he warned. 'You are not yourself.'

Then Baldr *screamed*. At close range, the sound was even more horrifying than it had been before – a keening, pining, unearthly screech of fused souls grappling within a single body.

Baldr raised his fist and clenched it tight. Forks of vivid lightning shot out, slamming into *dausvjer* with the force of a storm-front hitting and sending stark white streaks of light wheeling across the walls.

Ingvar skidded backwards, expending all his strength just to keep his blade in the way. The rune-sword absorbed the inflow of ether-twisted matter, but keeping it in place was crushingly hard. Ingvar felt sweat burst out across his body, his legs bracing, his arms burning.

'Baldr!' he cried, sliding back against the far wall. 'Do you not know me?'

Baldr uncurled himself and straightened up, all the while pouring more fell energy into his lances of dark-edged lightning. The chamber filled with the stench of ozone and the hot crackle of warp-discharge.

Ingvar felt his arms buckle. He set his jaw and pushed back, watching the blade before him shiver under the stress. He was forced down to his knees, his arms locked rigid, his whole body trembling with effort.

Baldr took a shaky step towards him, then another. His eyes spilled silver fire, and the residue ran down his blotchy cheeks like tears. He stared out crazily, drooling from an open mouth.

Ingvar felt his strength begin to fail. His hands struggled for grip on *dausvjer*'s hilt. Baldr staggered up to him, standing barely two metres away, his gauntlets still blazing. Lines of virulent force snapped and licked across the entire chamber, fizzing against the stone and leaving snaking weals.

Ingvar sank down further, his backpack pressed against stone. He could feel *dausvjer*'s grip worming free of his fingers, pushed towards him by the deadening force of the incoming barrage.

'Brother,' he hissed again, his teeth clenched. Baldr's face showed no recognition. It was unrecognisable from the cool, amiable face that he'd been so pleased to see again when he'd returned to Fenris.

We have always been shield-brothers, you and I. We shall be again.

Ingvar suddenly saw the exchange in the *drekkar* chamber, flashing across his mind's eye like a vid-pict.

It has a wyrd on it. It has protected me, and a part of me lives in it.

He took one hand from the sword hilt and grabbed at the soul-ward. Just as he lost control of the blade, he wrenched the totem out in front of him, thrusting the crow's skull in front of Baldr's tortured face.

The effect was immediate. The stream of warp-lightning suddenly snuffed out, plunging the room back into darkness. The stink of ozone subsided. Ingvar's blade fell from his hand, clattering emptily against the stone, blackened and burned out.

Ingvar held the *sálskjoldur* aloft, dangling it before Baldr's eyes. Baldr watched it spin, his face locked in something like recognition.

'This, at least, you know,' said Ingvar, breathing heavily.

A soul-ward, a fragment, a remnant, something to cling on to against the coming of Morkai.

'It *was* a part of you,' he said. 'It protected you, warding you against *maleficarum*. Your soul cleaves to it.'

The rune *sforja*, cut deep into the bone totem, flickered in the dim light. Its empty eye sockets rotated, catching the dull red glow of the fires raging outside the tower.

Baldr watched, transfixed. His arms slumped to his sides. His head hung lower. The silver flames on his body died out, guttering and flickering across his pockmarked skin.

What remained was grotesque. His skin, once tight and glare-tanned, had sagged. Deep bags hung under his red-rimmed eyes. Clusters of lesions and open boils nestled in every fold of flesh. His breath, which came in shallow gusts, was foul.

He tried to say something. His rheumy eyes flickered up to meet Ingvar's, then back down to the soul-ward. The blind fury was replaced by something else: confusion, recollection, pain.

'Bad... dreams,' he rasped, his voice dry.

Then he teetered, losing balance, toppling to his knees. Ingvar caught him and held him up.

Baldr looked up at him, his expression pathetically grateful. His face, criss-crossed with lines of blood, pus and drool, bore little resemblance to the clean visage of the past. It was still his, but only just.

'I had terrible dreams,' he slurred again.

Then his eyes fluttered closed and his body went limp. Ingvar, supporting his weight, lowered him onto his back, watching him carefully all the while. Then he pulled clear and retrieved his sword. *Dausvjer*'s blade was coated in a layer of sooty carbon, obscuring the protective runes engraved along the flat.

He sagged back against the wall, utterly drained. As he looked down on his brother's ravaged face he felt sick. He lifted his sword again, holding it in position. A quick down-stroke would do it – between chin and gorget, cutting the jugular and biting down into the spinal column beneath.

He held it there for a long time, his mind working hard. He was exhausted, weary of the slaughter, weary of not knowing what to do.

Eventually he put the blade down again. Baldr lay unconscious before him, his sallow cheeks hanging loose as he breathed.

'Not dreams, brother,' he breathed, taking the soul-ward and fixing it around Baldr's neck. As the crow's head clinked against Baldr's armour, a faint smile flickered across his diseased face. 'I wish they had been.'

Ingvar stood up again. He felt nauseous, and went over to one of the narrow windows. The glass in it had long since been shattered. He leaned against the frame, letting his head rest against the stone.

He could see across a broad sweep of the lower city. Fires still burned in all directions, but the sounds of battle sounded closer than they had been. As he watched, he saw plague-bearers and mutants running down the streets below him. They were no longer advancing; they were fleeing.

He narrowed his eyes, peering up towards the Ighala Gate. Even his senses failed to make much headway through the rolling clouds of muck.

He could hear enough, though. He could hear the roar of flamers and the battle-cries of the Celestians. He could hear the shouts of Guardsmen trying to keep their spirits in the face of the horrors around them. Loudest of all, cutting through the shifting walls of sound, he could hear the curses of his brothers. He heard Olgeir's deep-chested bellows, Haflói's whooping, Jorundur's strident fury, Gunnlaugur's ferocious war-cries. Only Váltyr's voice was absent, but then he was always quiet in combat.

Hearing the sounds of the pack back on the hunt triggered mixed emotions in him. On the one hand, it meant that the enemy was falling back – a fine achievement for Gunnlaugur's command. On the other, he had played little part in that victory, forced into the margins by his *vaerangi* and distracted by hunts of a different kind.

Worst of all, the reckoning for Baldr would come quickly now. His condition could no longer remain hidden. Death surely awaited him; perhaps worse.

Ingvar glanced over at his motionless body. Baldr's breathing was regular again, deeper than it had been before. The green tinge around his eyes and mouth had lessened. Whatever force had possessed him had been banished, at least for the present.

'I should never have left you,' said Ingvar, speaking softly, just as he had done in the apothecarion. 'I achieved nothing and learned little.'

The noises of fighting grew louder and closer. He felt the familiar nagging urge to participate, to race down the winding stairs and throw himself into the heart of it.

He resisted. If he had remained with Baldr in the Halicon as ordered, perhaps the madness would never have reached such terrifying depths.

Ingvar moved away from the window and crouched down beside his battle-brother. Baldr was locked in the Red Dream. The coma seemed somehow healthier than it had done before: deeper, and with none of the stench of corruption about it. His skin looked to be healing even as Ingvar watched it, its genhanced mechanisms slowly combating the toxins lodged beneath.

Or perhaps that was wish-fulfilment. Some corruptions were impossible to expunge.

'I will remain,' he said. 'I owe you that much.'

As he watched and waited, though, his thoughts turned to Gunnlaugur.

And what will Skullhewer do when he hears of this? he thought. *What will he decide?*

* * *

There was no rout, no disorderly scramble, no massacre. The enemy, bereft of its champions and having taken heavy losses at the Ighala Gate, pulled back steadily, retaining its cohesion. De Chatelaine's spearhead pursued them down from the inner walls and back into the smouldering morass of the lower city.

The fighting remained furious and bloody. Clouds of toxins still hung low over the rooftops, blotting the sky like water-spiralled ink. The bands of mutants still retained their powers of fear and infection, and many units of Guard were lost in sudden counter-attacks or ambushes. After the first push down from the gates the advance soon clogged into resistance again.

For all that, the upper city had been secured. The attacking army had lost its momentum and many of its most dangerous troops. For the time being, the Halicon's survival had been won.

After hewing a bloody passage down towards the warehouse zone, Gunnlaugur caught sight of the canoness and her command squad moving up to join him. He pulled back and waited for them. They met up on a spear of bare rock that jutted out above the lowest terraces of the city. Far below them the outer walls lay in ruins, surrounded by dug-in units of plague-bearers. Straggling formations marred the desert beyond, studded with isolated siege engines and the smoking carcasses of vehicles.

'This is as far as we go,' said de Chatelaine grimly, standing alongside him and looking out across the desolate vista.

Gunnlaugur hoisted his thunder hammer over his shoulder. His arms were weary from swinging it. He knew she was right, but found it hard to admit. In the heat of battle, charging with his brothers amid the rush of flame and blood, he had briefly entertained visions of driving the enemy back out into the dust, of chasing them into the burning sands to shrivel and wither.

Too many still lived for that. They were in disarray but were already recovering. Like the poisonous cells of a recurrent cancer, they were grouping, coalescing, clustering together in the shadows, preparing to hold the ground they had won.

He nodded grudgingly. 'So now what?' he asked.

De Chatelaine holstered her bolt pistol and put her hands on her hips. Her bearing was still regal, despite her exhaustion.

'We have wounded them,' she said, her voice giving away a fierce pride. 'They will not breach the inner defences now, not without rein-forcements. We should consolidate while we can.'

She gazed out to her left, over to where the dark profile of the cathedral still burned. Its triple spires sent twisting cords of inky smoke up into the foul sky.

'Perhaps we should have done so earlier.'

Gunnlaugur grunted. That had always been his counsel.

'What's done is done,' he said. 'Every street was fought for. That satisfies honour.' He looked over his shoulder, up the steep ranks of terraces leading to the upper city. 'But you are right. They will not break the citadel now, not as they are. Give the order to your troops. My brothers and I will guard the retreat.'

De Chatelaine bowed. 'This is your victory, Space Wolf,' she said. 'I should have trusted the hand of providence. You *were* our deliverance.'

Gunnlaugur shook his head. 'You commanded this.' He smiled under his belligerent helm. 'You may yet get the crusade you dreamed of.'

De Chatelaine stood on the outcrop for a little longer, her cloak hanging limply in the thick, unmoving air.

'They will come at us again,' she said. 'This is only one army. We know they have others. Plague Marines may yet live. What have we bought here? A few days?'

'A few days are worth having,' said Gunnlaugur. 'The Imperium will answer your calls in time, and our task is to remain alive until then. We have made a start.'

De Chatelaine inclined her head in apology. 'Forgive me,' she said. 'I learned to suppress my optimism. Perhaps I shall have to unlearn that again.' She laughed. The sound was weary but clear. 'Learning from a savage. That such things are possible.'

Then, ahead of them, out to the south over the wide dust-flats, the low covering of clouds broke open. The rift was fleeting, just a tattered break in the plague-pall that soon covered over again. But for a moment, sunlight shafted down on the battlefield, thick and golden, sweeping across the rusting, burning debris lining the road to Hjec Aleja.

Both Gunnlaugur and de Chatelaine watched it. Even after it had passed and the scene had resumed its preternatural gloom they said nothing.

It would not be the last such break, though. The clouds were thinning.

'I had not realised dawn had come,' de Chatelaine said.

'Nor I,' said Gunnlaugur. 'But it has, and we are alive to see it.'

He looked across the devastation, thinking of Váltyr and Baldr, reflecting on what had been sacrificed.

'Give the order to fall back,' he said gruffly, avoiding such thoughts. Much work remained. 'Let's finish this.'

* * *

As Ras Shakeh's natural daylight began to wane, the last of the toxin clouds thinned and drifted clear of the Halicon. In the deepening twilight, underlit by residual fires still growling away amid the wreckage of the lower city, the battlefield could at last be seen to its full extent. The outer walls had been half demolished, their smooth curve cracked open. The buildings closest to the perimeter had been hit hardest – huge areas had been reduced to black swathes of ash, gently smoking as the flesh, metal and stone all cooled.

The enemy withdrew beyond the walls, drawing up in sombre ranks out on the dust. Their numbers had been depleted by the assault but still remained formidable. The whispering stopped. They moved slowly, sullenly, like a vast beast withdrawing to lick its wounds. Their stench remained thick on the air, fuelled by the sweet tang of decaying offal left behind inside the walls.

The defenders pulled back to the inner walls, drawing closed the Ighala Gate doors and repopulating the long ramparts. The wall-gun magazines were reloaded, and materiel salvaged from the ruins of the perimeter defences was stowed, ready for use when needed. During the final withdrawal heavy lifting equipment was hauled down from the upper city to drag the wreckage of *Vuokho* back inside the walls. Hafloi's haphazard flight had destroyed all of Jorundur's repair work and caused fresh damage to the fragile hull, but what remained was judged worth retrieving by de Chatelaine's surviving tech-adepts.

The Wounded Heart standards still hung on either side of the Ighala Gate. Many other battle-flags remained in place, albeit with rents and burns marring the holy icons. The Halicon had escaped largely undamaged, and still reared its baroque profile up against the far horizon. Though marked by missile-fire and stained from airborne filth, much of the upper city was intact, a final island of defiance amid a world of ruins.

Between the defenders' redoubt and the enemy encampment on the plains stretched a wide swathe of no-man's-land – a waste-zone of contagion studded with the remains of empty hab-shells and hazy with smoke. That was the buffer between the two forces over which artillery pieces gazed and troopers watched. Like a huge circular scar, it ran down from the gorge and out to the shattered perimeter wall, slowly greying and festering, devoid of all sounds but the hissing breeze.

Gunnlaugur and Olgeir stood on the Ighala ramparts watching over those wastes, their helms removed and their weapons sheathed.

Olgeir's mood had improved after he'd managed to recover *sigrún* from a retreating warband of mutants. As they'd died under his fists he'd broken into laughing and hadn't stopped until he'd withdrawn back to the bridge. Even now his ugly face was twisted by a half-smile.

Gunnlaugur, on the other hand, had fallen into brooding. The withdrawal from combat always turned his mood dark.

'Any news from Old Dog?' he asked, his eyes fixed on the ruins below.

Olgeir snorted. 'Not since he dragged the whelp back to the hangars to put right what he did. For a while I thought he'd kill him.'

Gunnlaugur smiled. 'Haflói can look after himself.'

'He can.' Olgeir looked satisfied. 'He's a good fighter. You know who he reminds me of?'

'I was never so foolish.'

Olgeir chuckled. 'You were. And as arrogant. When his hair starts to grey he'll be a formidable Hunter.'

'If he lives long enough.'

Olgeir's smile faded. He looked down at his burly hands where they grasped the parapet edge.

'And Ingvar?'

Gunnlaugur's chin slumped against his gorget.

'He lives,' he said quietly. 'He says he found Baldr's body, and will return it.'

Olgeir looked up at Gunnlaugur. His face betrayed his disquiet. 'Fjolnir was destroyed?'

'I do not know. Ingvar would not tell me. He told me he'd explain when he was back.'

'So you two are speaking again.'

'We *will* speak,' said Gunnlaugur, his voice heavy with weariness. 'I cannot feel anger with him, not now.'

'He disobeyed you.'

'He did. But was the order just?' Gunnlaugur turned to Olgeir. 'Have I persecuted him, Heavy-hand?'

Olgeir shrugged. 'I'm no *vaerangi*. But the bad blood between you: it cannot continue.'

Gunnlaugur nodded, then lowered his head again.

'I hoped he would be how he used to be, but I see the change in his eyes. I see that damned Onyx skull around his neck and I know he carries his past with him like a ghost at his back. At times I wonder if something's possessed him.'

Olgeir made the ritual gesture against *maleficarum*.

'Do not jest.'

'Even so.'

Silence fell between them. The first stars appeared above, pricking silver into the veil of dark blue. The smells of cooking fires wafted up from the buildings behind them, the first wholesome aromas that had been detectable since the enemy had arrived. Although battered and surrounded, Hjec Aleja still clung to life.

'Baldr cannot be suffered to endure,' said Olgeir at last, his deep voice sombre. 'You saw what he'd become. He is as much a brother to me as he is to you, but we should have ended him when we had the chance. You know this.'

Gunnlaugur didn't look at him.

'If we had done so, then we would all be dead and the Halicon would now be the throne room for that monster,' he said. 'Perhaps it was his wyrd to be there. Perhaps he can still be saved.'

As he spoke, a figure emerged from the ruins below and moved across the wasteland. It went haltingly, dragging something along. Only slowly could its shape be made out – a warrior in pearl-grey armour hauling another behind it. The two of them stumbled up out of the desolation and towards the bridge.

Gunnlaugur watched their progress bleakly.

'You will let him pass?' asked Olgeir.

Gunnlaugur remained still for a long time. All along the parapets, defence towers locked on to the moving figures, primed to fire on his order.

He remembered Baldr's own words to the canoness, back when the first of the infected had been discovered.

Do you not understand? They allow them to survive. There are carriers among them. You cannot let them in.

His amber eyes held steady in the failing light as he watched Ingvar struggle under the dead weight of his unconscious brother.

Allow none to pass in or out. Everything contaminated must be destroyed.

'He is one of us,' Gunnlaugur murmured. His voice betrayed his doubt, but it brooked no argument. 'The Gyrfalkon would not have brought him back if he thought Baldr had gone beyond redemption.'

Gunnlaugur took in a deep breath. The air was still foul in his nostrils.

'I must learn,' he said. 'I must change. I must find him a place, now that Váltyr is gone.'

He leaned forwards on the parapet, his brows furrowed.

'I must learn to trust his judgement, Heavy-hand,' he said. 'Open the gates.'

Chapter Twenty-Four

Canoness de Chatelaine knelt before the altar and watched the memorial fires burn in their brazier pans. Dozens had been lit, each one marking the soul of a fallen Sister. The smoke, pungent with incense, twisted up into the chapel's vaults.

As the thin columns rose the choir sang a low, cadenced dirge. The music was a blend of traditional Shakeh death-chants and sanctioned Ministorum melodies. The words had been written by Sister Renata of her Celestian bodyguard. Like so many others, Renata was dead now, her body lying somewhere unmarked in the smouldering ruins of the lower city.

De Chatelaine bowed her head. The rites of remembrance gave her a little comfort. So many of those she had lived with for years were gone, their lives ended in cruel and ignominious ways, but as long as the rites endured some measure of dignity could be restored to their legacies.

As each brazier was lit, a chime sounded and a priest declaimed the name of the fallen. As the list neared its end, ordered by rank in the Imperial way, only a single brass pan remained empty.

An iron-masked acolyte walked up the remaining station with a flame cradled in his metal-gloved hands. As he reached up to the pan and the coals kindled, the chime sounded a final time.

'Sister Palatine Uwe Bajola, of the world Memnon Primus, of the Orders Famulous, afterwards of the Order of the Wounded Heart. Confirmed slain in the conduct of righteous duty. Gathered into the bosom of the Emperor of Mankind. Blessed are the martyrs. Their souls remain inviolate.'

The canoness listened sadly. Bajola had always been a mystery to her. De Chatelaine had never understood why someone with the Palatine's gifts had wanted to take up a station in such a remote world. The pleasures and rewards of ministering to a devoted populace were not something Bajola had ever seemed to feel deeply. De Chatelaine had always felt that her restless spirit would have been better employed elsewhere; perhaps in one of the bigger Orders, or perhaps in the Famulous chambers where she had come from, with all the glamorous system-spanning work that entailed.

She remembered how Bajola had been on the day she'd arrived on Ras Shakeh. De Chatelaine had admired the younger woman's poise, her calm manner, her quiet application. Only later had she been troubled by the amount of time Bajola had spent in the bowels of the cathedral, how disconnected she had been with the work of the other Sisters. When Bajola had so vociferously opposed the decision to seek protection from the Wolves of Fenris, for reasons de Chatelaine had never fully understood, a rift had threatened to open between them.

That had never happened. Now, after so much bloodshed, it seemed pointless to even think of such things. She was gone, and any secrets she had were gone too.

It would have been good to talk before the end. If the Palatine had not been so obsessed with that damn cathedral, perhaps they would have done. But that was in the past now. Perhaps one day it would be rebuilt and a shrine dedicated to her heroic defence of it. It was always comforting to think of the future.

With the last of the pans lit, de Chatelaine got to her feet, bowed a final time towards the altar, and turned back down the chapel's central aisle. As she walked towards the doorway she heard the scurrying footsteps of aides. They kept to the shadows of the aisles, cloaked and hooded. Some were flesh and blood like her; others were at least part mechanical.

As she pushed the heavy gahlwood doors open and stepped into the cool of the night, one of them came up to her, bowing and genuflecting.

When he raised his bald head, displaying an age-lined face and blank white eyes, de Chatelaine recognised her Master of Astropaths, Ermili Repoda.

'Could it not wait, master?' she asked.

Repoda bowed again in apology. 'You commanded me to inform you if the Choir received anything.'

Despite herself, de Chatelaine felt a twinge in the pit of her stomach. It was dangerous to hope.

'And?'

Repoda swallowed drily.

'I do not wish to give you grounds for false optimism,' he said. 'But since that… thing was killed, we have been getting intermittent scraps. Nothing as solid as I would like, and mostly from the acolytes who are not yet trained to interpret soundly.'

De Chatelaine drew in an impatient breath.

'I think we were heard,' he said, his face oscillating between doubt and expectation. 'I do not have a reliable name, nor a time, but someone has been trying to reach us.'

'No more detail?'

Repoda looked uncertain. 'Perhaps. A title, maybe. The Wolves may be able to tell you more. My people interpreted it differently: one of them came up with gibberish, another the title *Storm-caller*. I do not know what to make of it.'

De Chatelaine pursed her lips thoughtfully.

'*Storm-caller*,' she said slowly. 'I will speak to Gunnlaugur of this. It sounds like something he would recognise.'

Repoda bowed again. His hands twitched nervously. He looked on edge. Everyone around her was on edge, driven into a state of fragility by what they had seen and lived through.

De Chatelaine gave him a kind look, not that he would have seen it.

'Do not despair, master,' she said. 'I had almost given up, and then our prayers were answered. The Wolves will not leave their own kind: more will come, and when they do our survival here will count for something. They will find this city still defended, ready to receive their warriors for the crusade we hoped for.'

Repoda tried to smile, but his old face produced little more than a grimace. 'I hope you are right, canoness,' he said.

De Chatelaine drew in a deep breath. The airs around the Halicon were purer than they had been.

'If I had learned to doubt, master,' she said, 'then I have unlearned it again. The Master of Mankind does not desert souls who remain true to Him. That is what we need to remember, is it not? To *believe*.'

She smiled at him again, more for her own benefit than for his.

'After what we have seen,' she said, 'surely even the most lost of us has remembered that.'

In a forgotten corner of the upper city, cloistered away from the overcrowded chapels, converted hab-units and medicae stations, shaded by spear-leaved trees and open to the deep night air, a fire burned.

It was larger than most, a heaped pile of wooden slats stuffed with torn fabric and doused in oils. Váltyr's body lay amid the roaring flames, lying on his back with his open eyes gazing up into the sea of stars. About the pyre were set his warrior's artefacts: his armour pieces, what remained of his pelts and trophies. Set at his feet, hanging from an iron frame and sheathed, was *holdbítr*. The blade looked mournful. It would no longer draw; the pieces had been retrieved but only a smith with the skill of Arjac would be able to reforge the blade.

Gunnlaugur watched the flames consume the corpse of his battle-brother and friend. He knew what Váltyr would have wanted: the sword to be destroyed with him, to perish completely so that none but he would ever wield it.

That would happen in time, but the pyre would not be sufficient to harm it. A greater furnace would be needed to melt the imperishable metal and break the wards of the runes along the blade.

His eyes moved away from the flames and scanned across the pyre's watchers. Four others had gathered before it, each standing silently, each lost in their own thoughts.

Olgeir was closest. He stood proudly, his huge shoulders pushed back, his snub nose and gnarled beard silhouetted against the pyre's glow. His deep-set eyes stared into the heart of the fire. He had not been close to Váltyr, but Gunnlaugur knew they had respected one another. Baldr's affliction had hit him harder. Though Olgeir had argued for giving Fjolnir the Emperor's Mercy, he had done so with pain in his eyes. Since Baldr's entry into the pack they had fought together like kin-brothers, their bolters ringing in unison. If Baldr died, Olgeir would mourn long. If he lived but did not recover, he would mourn longer.

Beside him stood Jorundur. The Old Dog, if anything, looked slightly less hunched than he had done on past campaigns. His fury towards Hafloí had abated; even he could see how *Vuokho*'s last flight had turned the shape of the battle. Gunnlaugur suspected his wrath had never been full-hearted in any case. An odd relationship had developed between those two, as if Jorundur saw something in Hafloí worth protecting or encouraging. If that were so, then it gladdened his heart. Jorundur, for all his bitterness, was a priceless asset to the pack, a repository of knowledge and experience that outstripped even his. It would be good to see him fighting again with his old assurance.

Next was the whelp. Hafloí watched the dancing flames with only perfunctory interest. Death to him was like life: ephemeral, fleeting, of little importance when set beside the raw pleasures of the hunt and the kill. He had not had time to develop a deep connection to either Váltyr or

Baldr and did not pretend to mourn more than he ought. His ruddy face was thrust out belligerently, as if chafing at the necessity to mark the passing. Gunnlaugur smiled with bleak foreknowledge. Hafloí would learn to mourn, should he live long enough. He would learn what it was to lose a soul-brother, one whose life had been shared amid blood and fire. For now, though, he was just as he should be: fearless, alive with boundless energy, uncaring of anything but the feat of arms.

Finally, set apart from his brothers, stood Ingvar. The shadows hung heavily on him, part-masking his stone-grey features. His expression was hard to read. Gunnlaugur knew that Váltyr and he had always chafed at one another, vying for the mantle of the pack's deadliest blade. If Váltyr had become the more lethal swordsman, Ingvar, to his mind, had become the more complete warrior. Now, though, such contests were irrelevant, and Ingvar's face betrayed nothing but grief. If he had stayed in the Halicon as ordered, he might have arrived in time to save him. Or perhaps he too would have died. Gunnlaugur could see the doubts preying on him even as the lambent red light played across his battered armour. Those doubts would not leave him quickly, adding more layers to his already conflicted soul.

Gunnlaugur's eyes turned back to the pyre. Váltyr's body was almost gone, slowly reduced to whitening ashes. The wounds he had taken had been burned away. Gunnlaugur hoped that, at the last, the blademaster had found some measure of peace in what had been a restless, doubting life. He would have deserved that.

Moving slowly, he raised the heavy shaft of *skulbrotsjór*, lifting the weapon in salute against the glow of the dying pyre.

As silently as he, the others did the same – Olgeir raising his sword, Jorundur and Hafloí their axes, Ingvar his rune-blade.

No words were spoken. The four of them held vigil as the last of Váltyr's mortal remains were consumed. Only when the flames had died and the embers were cooling did they lower their weapons again.

'The thread is cut,' said Gunnlaugur softly.

Olgeir was the first to leave, nodding to Gunnlaugur as he stalked off, his face tight with emotion. Jorundur and Hafloí were next, both heading back to the hangars to work on *Vuokho*. Hafloí looked eager to be away; Jorundur pensive.

That left Ingvar and Gunnlaugur alone again, separated only by the smoking ashes. Ingvar made no move. For a while nothing passed between them but the low crackle and spit of oil-soaked wood.

'How is Fjolnir?' asked Gunnlaugur eventually. He tried to keep judgement out of his voice.

Ingvar stepped into the circle of fading light. Gunnlaugur noticed
that the soul-ward pendant he'd worn since leaving Fenris no longer
hung around his neck, though the Onyx skull still did.

'The Red Dream has him,' Ingvar replied. His voice was wary. 'I
believe him to be recovering.'

Gunnlaugur nodded. Baldr had been restrained, clapped in adamantium shackles and buried deep within the Halicon's dungeons. Doors
a metre thick locked him in. Even if he woke to madness again, there
would be no escape from the citadel.

'I hope you're right,' said Gunnlaugur. 'I took a risk, accepting you
both back. The gates had been sealed.'

Ingvar bowed. 'I know,' he said. He needed to say nothing more; the
gratitude was evident.

Gunnlaugur hoisted his thunder hammer, locking it across his back.

'I still don't know if I was right,' he said. 'Even if he recovers he will
be tainted. You saw what he did.'

Ingvar sheathed his blade.

'I share your doubts. I nearly killed him myself.'

'What stopped you?'

Ingvar hesitated. 'Callimachus would have killed him without a
thought. Jocelyn would have done it, as would the others. But we have
never been a Chapter for rules, have we? We have always acted as our
souls warned us.'

Gunnlaugur didn't recognise those names, but he could guess well
enough what Ingvar meant.

Ingvar looked directly at him. Weariness scarred his grey visage.

'For better or worse, I am *Fenryka*. I doubted it for a time, but a wolf
does not shed its pelt. I would give him a chance.' He lowered his eyes.
'If you permitted it.'

Gunnlaugur considered the words. As ever, something about Ingvar's
tone unsettled him. Perhaps he would just have to get used to that.

'Váltyr never argued for your exclusion,' he said. 'You should know
that. It was me. And you were right: that was for pride. I am shamed
by it.'

Ingvar looked surprised. For a moment, he didn't reply.

'Thank you,' he said, his eyes flickering briefly towards the pyre. 'I
had assumed–'

'Váltyr was not jealous. He warred with himself. It was never about
you.'

Ingvar nodded slowly, taking that in. At length his grey eyes rose
again.

'So what now, *vaerangi*?' he asked. 'We have survived. We have been blooded. What comes next?'

Gunnlaugur rolled his shoulders, feeling the deep-set fatigue in the muscles.

'The canoness received word of reinforcements,' he said. 'If she's right, then Njal is on his way.'

'Stormcaller?' Ingvar looked impressed. 'Our hides are worth that much?'

'Not ours,' he said. 'But this is more than one lost world. Hundreds are ablaze. This is a new war, one that has only just begun.'

'At least not garrison work,' Ingvar said wryly, working to raise a smile. The effort was weak, but Gunnlaugur did his best.

'No, at least not that.'

Ingvar looked thoughtful then.

'I have much to tell you,' he said. 'I learned things from the Palatine before she died. It may have been for those alone that fate brought us here. There are things about Hjortur we were never told.'

'We shall speak of them,' said Gunnlaugur. 'Truly, we shall. But not now, not while the ashes of our brother are still cooling.'

He looked down at his hands.

'I was wrong, brother,' he said. 'Your presence wore at my pride, and I let it govern me. Now Váltyr is gone I have need of counsel like never before.' He looked back up. 'Can the river flow cleanly between us again?'

Ingvar came towards him, grasping him by the arm.

'We were both at fault,' he said fervently. 'I forgot myself. Never again, brother. I swear it.'

His eyes held steady – two orbs of flecked grey, like the plumage of the raptor that had given him his name.

'I told the Palatine we were both of the blood of Asaheim,' he said. 'I am not sure I meant it then. Now I do.'

Gunnlaugur took Ingvar's hand and gripped it in his own gauntlet. The two of them stood before the glimmering light of the pyre, alone at the summit of Hjec Aleja.

'I am glad,' he said.

For the first time in a long while he looked at Ingvar's face and saw no challenge there, real or imagined. A future presented itself: their twin animal spirits, as lethal as any in the galaxy, working in tandem, no bitterness dividing them.

'For Fenris, brother,' he said proudly. 'Our blades together.'

Ingvar closed his eyes then, as if some terrible, crushing weight had been lifted from his shoulders. For a moment, he made no reply. When he spoke again, his voice was thick with emotion.

'For Fenris,' he said quietly, his head bowed.

Epilogue

The chamber was carved from a dark, glossy stone that reflected the light strangely. It wasn't even clear where the light came from; it seemed to spin out of the air between ebony pillars, each one rough-cut and many-faceted, just like the walls and floor. The place looked like it had been carved from the heart of an asteroid.

Which it had: the room was a single node within Clandestine Station U-6743, operating under the auspices of the sub-adjutant proximal command group Theta-Lode-Frier, one of several thousand outposts placed at the disposal of Deathwatch kill-teams and scattered throughout the galaxy.

Seven Space Marines stood in the centre of that eerie, echoing space. Callimachus of the Ultramarines, Leonides of the Blood Angels, Jocelyn of the Dark Angels, Prion of the Angels Puissant, Xatasch of the Iron Shades and Vhorr of the Executioners had already received their skull pendant, the mark of their service during the incident in the Dalakkar Belt in which forty-six billion souls had died. They remained silent, their unmoving armour-shells as black as the stone that enclosed them. The atmosphere was one of resigned stoicism. None of them had enjoyed seeing the results of their last mission, not even Xatasch, whose humours were dark.

Only Ingvar remained. He stood among his brothers, his left shoulder guard as grey as dirty snow and bearing the insignia of Berek Thunder-fist's Great Company.

Callimachus, helm-less like the rest of them, approached him. The Ultramarine tried to smile reassuringly. It was hard for any of them to smile after Dalakkar, but he did so for the sake of form. His Chapter placed much store by the manners of occasion.

'Last of all, the Son of Russ,' said Callimachus, holding the pendant before Ingvar.

When he had joined Onyx, a mortal lifetime ago, Ingvar would have resisted bowing his head to anyone, let alone a Space Marine of another Chapter. Now such inhibitions had melted away. The long years, each one filled with strange horror-breeds and murderous missions in the dark, had changed him. He had studied the *Codex* with Callimachus. He had learned the beauty of sword-craft from Leonides. He had learned advanced void-war tactics from Jocelyn, the use of battle-shield variants from Prion, ancient methods of infiltration from Xatasch and close-range bolter techniques from Vhorr.

Like all of them he had become an amalgam, a lethal mix of different martial orders. At times that made him feel stronger than he had ever felt; at times it felt like he had lost his soul.

So he bowed before the Ultramarine, ready to receive the mark of his duty, and, as he saw it in his darkest moments, his shame.

Callimachus placed the pendant around his neck.

'You have had the longest journey,' he said.

Ingvar felt the iron chain settle on his flesh. Once he had been used to bearing all manner of totems and charms on his battle-plate, such as the soul-ward he had given to Baldr as a token of their unbreakable friend-ship. Now, like so much else, adorning his sable armour seemed strange, like rehearsing the moves of a half-forgotten dream.

'We have all travelled,' he replied. Little difference existed between his voice and that of Callimachus; even their spoken Gothic, once thickly differentiated by accent and idiom, had merged into similarity.

'And now we must travel again, but apart,' said Callimachus. 'I grieve to lose your friendship. When we first met I thought you nothing better than a barbarian. Now I know you have a warrior's heart and a schol-ar's mind. I learned a lesson from you, Ingvar, one I will take back to Macragge.'

Ingvar bowed. 'Our paths may cross again.'

Callimachus smiled. 'If they did, we would be honour-bound to say nothing. I would look on you with haughty eyes, and you would snarl at me with contempt, and our brothers would approve.'

'Because they are ignorant.'

'Because they are pure.'

Callimachus looked solemn and regretful. He always looked solemn and regretful, like a statue carved from pure-grain nobility.

'We have become mongrels, forever destined to bestride two worlds. It will be hard to return. It will be hard to become what we once were.'

'But we will.'

Callimachus gave him a hard look. 'Will you, Ingvar? Will you forget what you have learned when you tread once more on the cold plains of Fenris?'

Ingvar held his gaze. 'I intend to forget nothing.'

'Do not expect to find your home world as you left it. Do not expect your battle-brothers to be the same as they were. You may never tread in the same river twice.'

'So you said to me before,' Ingvar said. 'But you forget, brother, I am still a Son of Russ. We are the arrogant ones, the boastful scions of a boastful primarch, and we do not respond well to being told what we may or may not do.'

Ingvar smiled then too. It was a warped smile, one that reflected the infinite horrors he had witnessed, one that still betrayed a certain guilty pride.

The onyx skull hung against his breastplate, dark against the sable ceramite. Already it felt like a repository of secrets.

'With us,' he said, 'anything is possible.'

ABOUT THE AUTHOR

Chris Wraight is the author of the Space Wolves novel *Battle of the Fang*. He has also written *Schwarzhelm & Helborg: Swords of the Emperor* and *Luthor Huss* in the Warhammer Fantasy universe. He doesn't own a cat, dog, or augmented hamster (which technically disqualifies him from writing for Black Library), but would quite like to own a tortoise one day. He's based in a leafy bit of south-west England, and when not struggling to meet deadlines enjoys running through scenic parts of it.

WARHAMMER
40,000

DEATHWATCH

STEVE PARKER

An *extract from* Deathwatch
by Steve Parker

On sale April 2013

The black bulk of the Stormraven assault-transport hovered ten metres over the
kill-block roof on tongues of blue fire. Cables dropped from side and rear hatches.
There was a sharp shout from inside.

'Kill-team, go!'

Three slab-muscled figures in black fatigues dropped at speed, controlling their
descent with gloved hands only. Slung across their backs were boltguns, slightly
smaller and more compact than those they were used to. Cinched around waist
and chest, they wore combat webbing stocked with grenades and other tactical
equipment. Boots hit the rooftop with a subdued, tread-muffled thump. Immediately, the three spread out, securing east, west and north edges of the building,
leaning out, visually sweeping the windows and balconies below for sign of
enemy sentries.

Two others dropped a second later. Onboard winches whipped the drop-lines
back up, and the Stormraven lifted away, tilting as it left the infiltration point.

The last two figures to drop darted to the north edge of the roof. As soon as they
were in place, all five operators pulled a small pistol-like device from a holster in
their webbing, pressed the muzzle to the permacrete lip at the edge of the roof,
and pulled the trigger. There was a crumping sound and five little coughs of dust.
Each pulled on the pistol and a length of black polyfibre cable started to unspool
from inside the grip. With a brief tug to check each line was secure, the five figures
stepped onto the permacrete lip, turned, and dropped backwards from the edges
of the roof.

Karras pushed off with his legs, flying out a little way from the surface of the
wall, and released the trigger on the pistol. He dropped about three metres, then
pulled the trigger again, arresting his descent. He swung back in and braced his

legs on the wall, then bunched his muscles, ready for another push off. To his right, Ignacio Solarion, the Ultramarine, did the same. When Karras had paired them up, he had said nothing, but the look on his face had hardly been one of joy.

Below, a broad semicircular balcony extended out from the wall. From that balcony, a wide set of double doors offered access to the kill-block's rooms and corridors.

Together, Karras and Solarion dropped to the balcony and abandoned their ziplines. They took position on either side of the double doors, backs pressed to the wall. Solarion looked over at Karras, his pale blue eyes cold and hard. Karras nodded for him to proceed. From his webbing, Solarion took a small canister with a long, tubular nozzle, then stuck his head out to check there were no hostiles on the other side of the panes of transparent armourglass. Seeing none, he stepped to the centre, lifted his canister, and began to spray a large, irregular outline – bigger than himself – directly onto the surface. Corrosive black foam began to bubble as it ate away at the windows' molecular bonds.

With the outline finished, Solarion returned the canister to its pouch and gripped the doors' outer handles.

Karras was counting in his head. At sixteen, he gave the go.

Solarion tugged the handles and two large pieces of frame and armourglass came away in his hands – no shattering, only the slightest sound of breakage.

The Ultramarine turned and laid the pieces carefully down. Karras moved inside in a half-crouch, bolter raised, stock pressed to shoulder. He heard quiet footfalls behind him as Solarion followed.

SpACE, thought Karras, sweeping the room.

The watch sergeants had drummed it into them since the beginning of day two.

Spacing, Angles, Corners, Exits.

This room was clear, but it might not have been. Kulle kept changing enemy dispersal every time he sent them in. He kept changing the sentry patrol patterns, too.

Beyond the door in the far side lay the north hallway from which he and Solarion would proceed to the objective room. Moving fast, Karras placed himself on the right of the door. Solarion took his place on the left. Each signaled readiness to the other. So far, so good.

Karras reached out a gloved hand and pressed the access rune. The door slid sideways into its housing. Before it had finished, Karras was already out in the corridor, muzzle covering the left.

'Contact!'

A ghostly eldar sentry spun and, on seeing Karras, raised the fluted muzzle of its alien pistol.

Karras's bolter coughed quietly and the tall, slender alien crumpled, then flickered with greenish static, blurred into lower resolution and disappeared altogether. In the wall behind where it had stood, a small black crater bled thin wisps of smoke. A hololithic projector in the ceiling above buzzed briefly, its indicator light changing from green to red. Karras turned.

Behind him, Solarion had taken out a similar target.

'Let's move,' said Karras, indicating southwards. Together, Karras hugging the left wall and Solarion the right, they stalked off down the now-unguarded corridor. As they proceeded closer to the central chamber at the far end, they kept their muzzles level, covering the metal apertures on either side and the corridor junction ahead where the path split east and west. There was no time to clear each side chamber in this high-speed secure-for-extraction exercise.

The scenario was simple: three high-value Imperial Navy personnel had been taken alive by so-called dark eldar during a xenos assault on an Imperial outpost. The Navy personnel each held critical strategic information, none of which overlapped, meaning all three needed to be recovered alive before they could be broken by cruel xenos torture or mind-manipulation. They were designated *Apollon*-level assets; the loss of even one during the operation meant a mission failure.

Kill-block Ophidion didn't look like any spaceport Karras had ever seen, of course, but that hardly mattered. A little imagination was often called for during training.

A metal door on the right slid upwards and a spidery figure emerged, black hair pinned up with small white bones, pointed ears on either side of a long, narrow, olive-skinned face.

Solarion dropped the target before its shoulders had even cleared the doorway. The image of the dark eldar spun, flickered and rezzed out, giving its simulated cohorts in the room behind it ample warning that they were under attack. Bone-like muzzles suddenly bristled from the doorway. Enemy fire blazed into the hallway. The holo-projected shots whined and buzzed through the air above Karras's head, given worrying realism by the kill-block's advanced audio system.

'Blood and blazes!' he hissed.

Solarion dropped to a full crouch and fired back, bolts smacking into the doorframe behind which the hostiles hid. These rounds didn't detonate as bolter rounds usually did. They were practice bolts, nick-named *clippers* – low-velocity non-explosive slugs of the type used in kill-block training as standard. Sparks leapt from each harmless impact.

Multiple roused targets in hard cover, thought Karras bitterly. *The run is practically scuppered already. That idiot knows better. Kulle was right about him trying to undermine me.*

Over the link, he heard the others report that they were in position around the target room. Karras couldn't let them storm that room without either himself or Solarion coming in from the north side. He wouldn't send them in to be cut down knowing that Kulle always kept the hostages heavily guarded. There would be too many foes inside for three operatives to handle without a casualty or two, Space Marines or not.

Gritting his teeth, he made his decision. He marked the distance to the door from which all the fire was coming, then pulled a smoke grenade from his webbing. Arming it, he tossed it just in front of the enemy. With a hiss, thick grey smoke billowed out, quickly filling the confines of the corridor and much of the side chamber. Visibility dropped to nothing, but Karras had everything he needed in his head. He tugged a frag grenade free and burst into a low run. The aliens were blind-firing now. He did his best to cut a safe path through their simulated barrage. Behind him, Solarion was still firing at the shrouded door, though he could no more see it now than Karras. At least his fire offered some suppression. Maybe Karras wouldn't be cut to pieces.

Or maybe I will, but he has left me no choice.

Between the smoke and the covering fire, it was enough. As Karras passed the door, he didn't slow, but he tossed the primed frag grenade inside and kept running straight through the choking cloud and beyond it. Ahead of him, where the corridors formed a T-junction, the north entrance to the objective room loomed large. He put on a burst of speed. Over the link, he growled, 'Space Marines, breach in three…'

His feet pounded the floor. Six metres to go.

'Two…'

Closer.

'One…'

Closer.

'Go,' he barked.

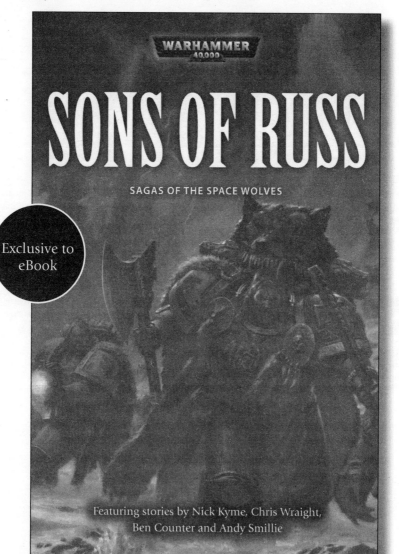